MOTHERS VOL. 1

BEN BURGESS JR.

Mothers Vol. 1 By Ben Burgess Jr.

Copyright © 2023 Ben Burgess Jr.

ALL RIGHTS RESERVED

First Printing – April 2023

Paperback ISBN: 979-8-9875648-0-6
eBook ISBN: 979-89875648-1-3

Library of Congress Control Number: 2023905557

Edited by: Alanna Boutin

Cover Design by: George Reeder and Leah Frieday

Printed in the U.S.A.

Dedicated to my mother, Dianne Burgess, and all the mothers who step up and do whatever is necessary to care for their children. You are appreciated, and I wrote this book to honor all of you.

ACKNOWLEDGEMENTS

I'd like to thank everyone who encouraged, inspired, and supported me with writing this book.

As for my family, I don't want to leave anyone out, so I'll just say thank you to my family that has supported me.

*To all my friends: If I left anyone out, it doesn't mean I don't appreciate you. I could only add a few names here, but if I missed you, I'll add yours in the next one.

A big thanks and appreciation goes to my friends: I wouldn't have fulfilled this goal if it weren't for you guys.

Lauren Burgess	Charlene Bullard	Nina Gagnon-Wade
Tamara Teeger	Dianne Bylo	Lynn Donadio
Terry Small	Tamar Carlins	Constance Arguinzoni
Alvin Cameron II	Kim Fermaints	Christina Cutolo
Joanna Ozuna	Cindy Jimenez	Jennifer McNamara Ray
Michelle Fecker	Candice Chester	Nybia Cooper
Marieta Shi	Judy Mattone	Kerry Olivar
Kelly Melanson	Kristen Adams	Susan Kaylor-Phillips
Vickie Weber	Sharon Meade	Betty Blau
Jen Lindsey	Fern Rankin	Latoya Burton
Nordia Barrett	Leah Frieday	Rachel Alfredson
Jessica Cooke	Lucinda Mitchell	Monique Garcia
Liz Schreyer	Maria Valdez	Chiara Atoyebi
Stacy Campbell	Suk Too	Laura D'Mello
Sequeoia Acacia	Tammy Cymerys	Patricia Morris
Charline Folkes	Heather Blackmon	Cyrus Johnson
Philip Banks III	Jennifer Bumford	Stacy Lawrence
Lisa Muhammad	LaTesha Wagstaff	Marilyn Morton

MOTHERS VOL.1
BEN BURGESS JR.
A-SIDE
TIRED OF BEING TIRED!

CHAPTER 1

I'M GOIN' DOWN

YEAR: 1995

I'm sitting in Jamaica Hospital in Queens, fidgeting uncomfortably in a tan leather chair beside my son, Jerami. Once again, he overexerted himself playing basketball with my oldest, Jalen, and now he's hospitalized with a fever. I don't want to deny him a normal childhood or treat him like he has to live in a bubble. His cancer does that enough, but I don't like seeing him in a hospital bed hooked up to machines, writhing in pain, either.

I used my fingers to smooth out his furrowed brows when I saw lines of distress on his forehead. His brown eyes slowly fluttered open. Disoriented, he groaned and rubbed his chest. He smiled when he saw me and said, "Hi, Mommy."

It warmed my heart seeing him smile. "Hey, sleepyhead," I said, rubbing his hand.

"I'm tired."

"I know. Rest up. I'm right here next to you."

As if our talk drained him, he nodded and quickly fell asleep.

My lower back was killing me, sitting in this uncomfortable hospital chair. I stood up to stretch and saw my reflection in the small hospital mirror. Taking care of my two sons alone was taking a toll on me. I looked tired, worn, and weary. My tired chestnut eyes showed a lack of sleep and tons of stress. No amount of makeup could hide the dark circles under them. My untamed coffee-brown hair was desperately in need of a perm. Chain-smoking cigarettes and being broke and malnourished showed by how my loose-fitting clothes hung on my slender frame.

While there were those subtle physical signs, my reflection didn't show the mental anguish and chaos my life has been through these past three years.

I have a lot of anger inside of me. I'm angry that drug dealers decided to have a shootout in front of the grocery store, killing my husband in the crossfire. I'm angry that my husband's murderer will never be brought to justice and sentenced for his crime. I'm angry because I feel like I have no control over anything in my life.

I sat back down and twisted the wedding rings on my finger. It's been three years since my husband, Maurice, passed, and I still couldn't bear to take off my rings. There isn't a day that has gone by when I haven't missed him.

Some days are etched in your soul forever. For me, that date was Sunday, October 18th. My anger brought me back to that fateful day. Alone with my thoughts, I relived the horrific memory that has been a critical turning point in my children's and my lives... the day my husband was murdered.

I was cooking dinner while my husband watched the football game in the living room.

"Mo . . ." I yelled from the kitchen.

He didn't answer.

"Mo . . ."

He still didn't answer.

"Maurice," I yelled again.

I walked out and heard Mo cheering when the Giants scored another touchdown.

"Do you hear me talking to you?" I asked.

"Uh-huh."

He was trying to pay attention to both the game and me, but the game had the advantage.

I walked into the living room and stood in front of the TV, wiping my hands on my apron.

"What's up, babe? I'm watching the game."

"I need you to go to the store and pick up some pasta."

Mo tried to look at the TV around me, but I purposely stepped in the way to stop him and make sure he was only paying attention to me.

"You want me to go to the store again? Can I do it after the game, baby?"

"No, I need it now. We wouldn't be having this conversation if you had taken the list I made earlier instead of buying groceries from memory. Now, hurry up."

"The lines in Associated are crazy at this time on Sundays," he said.

"If you want to eat dinner any time soon, you'll grin and bear it. I don't need much, only eggs and two boxes of pasta for this mac and cheese."

He sighed and slipped on his shoes. "I'll be right back," he said, kissing me on the forehead and playfully slapping me on the ass.

"Oooh! That'll be for dessert," I said, winking at him.

Jerami and Jalen walked out of their room.

"Where you going, Dad?" Jalen asked.

"Back to the store. Your mom is bullying me into picking up some more things."

"Important things for what I'm cooking, and don't tell the kids I'm bullying you," I said, playfully elbowing him in his side.

"You see this?" Mo said.

The kids laughed.

"Bye, Daddy," Jerami said.

"Can I come, Dad?" Jalen asked.

"Nah, take care of your mom for me."

Mo kissed me goodbye and walked out the door.

Fifteen minutes passed. Out of nowhere, a shiver ran down my spine. I had an unsettling feeling that something was wrong. I tried to shake it off as just nerves, but Mo not being home yet didn't help. I ignored the feeling and kept cooking.

I heard apartment doors opening and closing and people running down the stairs. I jumped when I heard someone pounding frantically on my door like they had lost their damn mind. I knew it wasn't Mo because he would've used his key. I dried my hands on my apron, anxiously rushed to the front door, and looked through the peephole.

It surprised me to see Tracy, a woman who lived one flight up from me on the sixth floor, standing in front of my door with a concerned look on her face, her hands fidgety. We were cordial when I saw her with her twins around the block, but we weren't friendly to where we hung out at each other's apartments, so I knew something was wrong.

I quickly undid the locks and opened the door. Our nosy neighbors peeked out their heads and stood in their doorways to see what the commotion was about.

Tracy's voice was shaky when she said, "You need to go across the street to the food store . . . Your husband was shot."

I heard the urgency in her voice. My pulse sped up. My nervousness took over, but I tried to stay calm.

"What did she say, Ma?" Jalen asked, overhearing what Tracy said from the couch.

I couldn't panic. I needed to find out what happened without scaring the kids.

"Stay with your brother," I said.

"But, Ma—"

"Did you hear what I said? I need you to listen to me and stay with your brother until I find out what's happening."

He nodded, tears glistening in his eyes.

Tracy and I rushed out of our building. Unmarked police cars were used to block off the street. I pushed my way through hordes of onlookers. The cops were cordoning off the scene. My hand shot over my mouth as I gasped in horror, trying to stop myself from screaming. Behind the yellow crime scene tape was Mo, slumped over against the graffiti-covered grocery store gate. His glassy eyes stared at me; blood leaked profusely from his chest. Two paramedics rushed past us with a stretcher. I stepped under the crime scene tape and ran to my husband, but one of the paramedics held me.

"Ma'am, I'm sorry. You can't be in this area," the medic said.

I jerked away from him. "Get your fucking hands off me. That's my husband... I need to see my husband."

"I'm sorry, ma'am, you can't. We're doing the best we can for him."

"I want to see him," I said, tears streaming down my face.

The onlookers shook their heads. Most of their faces showed empathy, but no one was surprised that a shootout happened in broad daylight in this neighborhood. It was common for innocent people to be caught in the crossfire and hit by stray bullets.

The code of the street was no snitching, but I needed answers. I stopped fighting with the EMS workers and turned to the spectators.

"Who did this? Who killed my husband? I know somebody saw something. I know one of you knows who shot him," I cried.

Everyone stayed tight-lipped and averted their eyes.

One dark-skinned brotha who looked about sixteen said, "It's fucked up what happened to your man, but you know how it is. Bullets don't got no names on them."

I heard that stupid justification too many times from so many knuckleheads. To them, Mo was just a casualty in the never-ending war in the street.

I felt faint. My knees gave way, and I fell to the street in a daze. One of the EMS workers walked up to me.

"Are you OK, ma'am?" he asked, waving his hands and snapping his fingers in front of my face.

I felt myself being lifted off the ground. The EMS worker's lips were moving, but I could barely hear what he was saying. I finally made out the last part, but I wished I hadn't.

"I'm sorry, ma'am. His injuries were too severe. He didn't make it."

I wept uncontrollably as the EMS workers placed Mo's body on a gurney, covered it with a white sheet, and put him in the ambulance. The crowd slowly thinned out, and everyone went on as usual, as if nothing had happened. Then I felt a hand on my shoulder. I looked up and saw Tracy. She pulled me close into a tight embrace and rocked me in her arms as I cried on her shoulder.

My husband didn't hang out in the streets. He didn't do or sell drugs. He was a good, hardworking man whose life was taken from our kids and me because he was in the wrong place at the wrong time. I felt guilty. I felt responsible. I couldn't fathom how I'd be able to tell my sons that their father was killed.

"This is my fault. He'd still be here if I had just made something else for dinner instead of making him go back to that damn store."

Tracy hugged me tighter. "It's not your fault. You had no way of knowing this would happened. The only person at fault is the man who killed him."

Tracy never left my side. She rode inside the ambulance with me to the hospital, where I sat for hours answering every question the police asked me. Nobody in the neighborhood said shit to the cops, and the police had no leads or suspects. In their eyes, I was just another poor, pitiful widow whose husband was gunned down because of stupid hood drama.

After talking to numerous police officers, detectives, and a hospital grief counselor, the cops drove Tracy and me back to Queensbridge.

Tracy and I sat on the wooden benches in front of our building, and she helped me get myself together while I tried to mentally rehearse how I would break it to my sons that their father was dead. With my voice hoarse from crying and screaming, I said, "I appreciate you being here, but don't spend all your time with me. You have your own kids to take care of."

Tracy had twins, Akeem and Ebony, who were Jalen's age.

"Juanita, you need a friend right now. Whenever you're ready, I'll head up with you when you go to tell your kids. I'm here for you, and I won't let you do that alone," she said.

There was no way to break such life-altering news to my sons gently, and I already knew it was going to be the hardest thing I had to do . . . explaining to them that their father was never coming home again.

Tracy and I talked for a good forty-five minutes until I was composed enough to face my kids. I have to admit; I was glad she was there with me.

We went inside our building, and I woefully walked to my floor. My hands shook so badly that it took me several tries to put the key into the lock to open the door.

Tracy patted my back. I took a deep breath, turned my key, and stepped inside. Jalen and Jerami's eyes were red-rimmed and teary. They jumped up from the couch and rushed toward me.

I held Jerami; he was crying in my arms.

"What happened? Where's Dad?" Jalen asked, his lips trembling.

My words were stuck in my throat. Tracy placed her hand on my back for support.

"Is he OK?" Jalen asked.

It was so hard to think of the right words to make things better, but there was no way to sugarcoat it. Jalen and Jerami stared at me and waited intently for my reply.

I let out a long, stressful breath, steadying my voice for my next words. "I'm so sorry, babies. Some men were shooting in front of the food store, and one of their bullets hit him . . . and Daddy didn't make it. He passed away."

I saw the innocence die in Jalen at that moment. His eyes widened as my words sank in, and his expression quickly turned to anger.

". . . This is your fault. You made him go to the fucking store," Jalen screamed.

"Jalen, please—"

"I hate you," he yelled, storming to his room and slamming his door. Jerami shook out of my arms and followed his brother.

"He doesn't mean that. He's running high off emotions right now and lashing out at you. He'll come around," Tracy said.

I spent the rest of the night rocking my youngest son to sleep as he cried for his daddy, wanting to know why God had taken his father from him. Those cries hurt my heart, and I had no answers for him. I wondered the same thing.

That week and even a few days after the funeral, my sons cried every day for their father. I comforted them the best I could and told them everything would be OK, but I had difficulty convincing myself of that.

Tracy was a nurse's aide at Jamaica Hospital, where I am currently in the emergency room. We bonded because, like me, she was raising two kids of her own, her twins, Akeem and Ebony, and we both had to provide for our two children with no support. Her kids' drug-dealing daddy split and moved to Philly after he decided being a father wasn't for him.

Tracy helped me through my lowest moments. She was there when I truly needed her, and she immediately became my best friend, someone I could talk to about everything and anything, and she never judged me.

She was so real and down to earth and had an air and strength about her that I wished I had. She saw the best in me and uplifted me when I didn't see shit about myself worth praising. I honestly don't think I could've coped with the loss of my husband without her. When it came time to make arrangements for Mo, I didn't know where to begin with planning for a funeral. Luckily for me, Tracy coordinated everything.

Maurice didn't have a life insurance policy. His parents were dead, and he didn't have much family. The little family he did have was in North Carolina, and none of them had money to send to help with the funeral expenses or even the funds to come down to attend it.

Our church didn't help. Everyone told me how sorry they were for the boys and me, but no one, not even the church itself, gave a dime to help bury my husband. That financial responsibility for Mo's burial fell solely on me.

I maxed out my credit cards, used up the few dollars in our savings, sold some furniture and some of my jewelry, and when that still wasn't enough money to give Mo a decent burial, I sold the '89 Ford Taurus that Mo and I bought to get around.

I couldn't afford to pay for car insurance, tolls, maintenance, or gas anyway, so going without a car for a while made sense. Until I could get back on my feet financially, I was stuck taking public transportation to get around.

The day of Mo's funeral was rainy and dreary. There was a small turn-out. Barely anyone from the neighborhood or our church came. A few of my friends and a handful of his coworkers from the auto body shop paid their respects.

My so-called friends deserted me once Mo died. I was too overwhelmed with work and bills to hang out like I used to, and the few times they visited, they told me I depressed them too much. Now, every time I see them in the street, they avoid me, so I've written them off and moved on.

Getting used to sleeping alone at night was hard, but I had to accept that waking up to an empty bed every day was my new normal. While that was hard, things only got harder. With Mo gone, all the responsibilities of raising our two boys were solely on me. The huge cost of burying him and going from two incomes to being the solitary breadwinner forced me to learn quickly how to budget better for groceries and other bills.

Living in the projects, I didn't have to pay utilities, which helped some-what, but my credit cards, student loans, and other personal loans Mo and I took out during our marriage were kicking my ass. Our house phone was disconnected, and I didn't have enough money to reinstate the service. Cable was an expense I couldn't afford, but I tried to keep it on so the kids could have at least one luxury. It felt like the boys were growing out of their clothes faster than I could buy them.

I learned how to stretch things out, like adding water to laundry deter-gent, juice, and mouthwash to make them last longer. I bought no-frills brands for everything regularly and got clothes for the boys from the thrift store on Steinway Street. I had to be frugal and creative in how I spent my money, and sometimes, we just had to go without and make do with whatever I could afford.

Eventually, I swallowed my pride and applied for food stamps, which helped to buy things like juice, milk, eggs, and peanut butter. It wasn't a lot, but it was still a significant help and made it, so I didn't have to water down everything anymore.

Tears rolled down my face at the memory of my late husband. I lowered my head in my hands and raised it when I felt a touch on my shoulder, breaking me out of my thoughts.

Tracy had come in on her break to check on Jerami and me in the oncology wing. I shivered and pulled myself together as the memory faded.

"You all right, Queen? I see something is heavy on your mind," she said.

Tracy and I called each other "queen" to uplift each other.

"I'm OK. You know how it is—the usual bullshit. Just wishing this nightmare with Jerami's cancer was over, and I'm missing Maurice."

"I know how that last part feels. I haven't had a man touch me in a long time, either. I miss it too," she joked.

"You're so nasty."

We laughed. I needed that.

Tracy held Jerami's frail arm and checked the monitors he was connected to. Then she stepped out of the room, and my mind returned to the stress in my life.

I lost faith in God. How could God take my husband from me and allow my son to be diagnosed with cancer two years later? I watched Jerami slowly wasting away daily and questioned why God would let it happen. He already took my husband from me; I didn't know if I could handle another devastating loss.

My head was barely above water, and things were financially more burdensome with Mo gone, but we were making it for the most part. Two years later, just when I thought I had gotten somewhat of a routine down, all that shit went out the window when Jerami got sick.

"Ma, I'm not feeling well," Jerami said.

I pressed my palm against his forehead. He felt warm. He hadn't been feeling well for a couple of months and complained that he was always tired.

"Boy, you're fine. Wake up and start getting ready because you're going to school today."

He didn't have much of an appetite anymore and was losing weight. Truth be told, I felt it coming. I had a sense of uneasiness that something wasn't right. A mother knows when there's something wrong with her child, but I convinced myself it wasn't anything serious. Maybe just a lingering cold or at least nothing big enough to miss work over, but when it didn't go away, I took off work and had him checked out by his pediatrician, Dr. Cruz.

Initially, Dr. Cruz thought it was the mumps or a recurring strep throat. He prescribed antibiotics, but Jerami wasn't getting better, and he started looking bloated in a matter of days.

"As you're aware, Mrs. Wilson, I ordered Jerami a complete blood count test or CBC finger stick count," Dr. Cruz said.

His face looked grim and serious.

I nodded and asked, "What did the test show?"

"Jerami has an enlarged spleen and liver. I recommend you go to the ER immediately."

"Oh my God, is my son going to be OK?"

"If we handle this swiftly, he has a good chance of being so. You need to take him to the Emergency Room right away."

I rushed Jerami to Jamaica Hospital. The doctors returned to say Jerami had to be admitted for more tests. After the tests were conducted, the dark cloud over my life got darker. Jerami was diagnosed with lymphoma. I heard stories of mothers who had kids with cancer, but I never imagined a reality where it would happen to me . . . that it would happen to my son.

I didn't break down and cry or ask God for strength. I felt guilty and responsible because I knew something was wrong and didn't have him checked out sooner. I put work before my son, and after that shitty day, I promised myself I'd do whatever it took to help my son get through this.

The staff took him to the oncology wing at Jamaica Hospital for more specialized care. They introduced me to Dr. Maier, who was assigned to be Jerami's oncologist. Jerami had a spinal tap, bone marrow biopsy, and an aspiration procedure to narrow down the type and severity of lymphoma he had.

I watched helplessly as Jerami had emergency surgery and started treatment that night. Seeing my baby go under anesthesia for the hour-long procedure pained me. Bone marrow had to be extracted from his hip. A small plastic disc called a "port" was inserted into his chest and used as a catheter to administer the chemo and antibiotics.

Before I had time to digest everything the doctors told me, I was in Jerami's hospital room, holding his hand through another surgery prep. The whole ordeal had me close to tears, but I needed to be strong for him.

Jerami's eyes were so fearful and innocent that when he asked, "Mom, am I going to die?" my heart stopped. I didn't want him to see me break down and lose all hope of beating his sickness. I tried to hide the trembling in my hands and the shakiness in my voice.

"Of course not, silly. You just need to take your medicine, and you'll be fine."

"You promise?" he asked.

"I promise," I said, smiling at him and blinking back tears.

I had to say it with strength and assurance, but it's hard to be strong when your child is poked and prodded in front of you.

Jerami had to stay in the hospital for ten days. It was a hectic, and overwhelming experience filled with loads of information and unfathomable emotions.

"Mrs. Wilson, Jerami needs a blood transfusion. I highly recommend that we act quickly and get this done," Dr. Maier explained.

I nodded. Things needed to be done immediately, and I felt powerless to help my son. There wasn't time to think.

After Jerami's transfusion, I had a lengthy meeting with Dr. Maier. He explained to me the strategy for Jerami's treatment.

"Proper treatment for Jerami will be six weeks of radiation five days a week in addition to fifteen months of chemotherapy," Dr. Maier said.

"Be honest with me. Does my son stand a chance of surviving this? Is his cancer curable?" I asked.

Dr. Maier smiled. "The good thing is, with the right treatment and patience, I believe he has a significant chance of beating this. Have faith."

It was hard to have patience or faith when you've been through the shit I've been through.

"Now for the ugly part. I'll be honest. Most likely, Jerami will start feeling his treatments' side effects about three days after receiving them. Seeing him lose his hair, toenails, and fingernails will be scary, but you can't lose hope. You have to trust this is all part of the process."

My eyes watered, but I bit my bottom lip and fought back my tears.

"Are you OK?" he asked.

I nodded.

"Don't mind me; go on," I said.

"Jerami is going to experience nausea often. I'll give him medication to combat his nausea, but I can't guarantee it'll completely stop it. He'll vomit often, and the long-term effects of everything may cause kidney damage. The thing with chemotherapy is that it kills both cancerous and noncancerous cells, which will lead to Jerami having a low blood count and being susceptible to infections. In other words, he'll have no immune system . . ."

After hearing that, I was a crying mess.

"Mrs. Wilson, I know it's a lot to process—"

"I'm sorry I'm being so emotional."

"It's completely understandable."

"You were saying?"

"Yes, because the entire treatment process is so taxing on the body, some parents choose to have their children remain out of school and pay for homebound instruction."

There was no way I could afford that. The whole ordeal sounded like too much for any child or parent to handle, but I'd do whatever it took to keep my son alive.

"I can't afford to have him homeschooled. Is there any chance he could get treated and still go to school?"

"He can still go to school, but there will be times when he's going to be too weak and will have to miss days. Also, you'll have to be extremely cautious about having him around other children because of his weakened immune system."

After talking with Dr. Maier, I immediately let my job know about Jerami's diagnosis and explained there'd be times when I'd need to take time off to care for my son.

I'm the senior executive assistant and administrative manager at one of the biggest law firms in New York—Wayne, Rothstein, and Lincoln. My boss, Francis Lincoln, one of the partners at the firm I worked at, either did not understand what I had to balance daily or just didn't give a shit.

Francis made it clear that if I wanted to keep my title with the firm, I'd better cut back significantly with taking off. I couldn't find anyone to babysit with my sporadic schedule at the firm, and with Maurice gone, I badly needed help with my sons.

Out of desperation and with no other family or friends to help me, I scraped together my last bit of money to move my unemployed baby sister Carina down from Atlanta to live in my cramped two-bedroom apartment. Living in those crowded conditions has been rough, but I needed Carina.

Our parents passed from diabetes, and we weren't close to any of our uncles or aunts. She and I were the only family we had.

Since she couldn't help me financially, all I asked of her was to help me with Jerami's appointments, keep Jalen in check and out of trouble, and take care of things around the house while I worked to support all of us, but she wasn't very dependable and had become more of a leech than a help lately.

My sister, bluntly put, is a slut. Knowing how she was, I didn't want a bunch of men running in, and out of my house, so I gave her my bedroom to entertain her latest conquests and made her promise to put her hoeish exploits on pause until nighttime when my kids were asleep. I slept on my makeshift bed on the foldout couch in the living room every night.

Tracy walked back into the room with a pillow and blanket, breaking me out of my ugly trip down memory lane. No matter how many pillows and blankets she gave me, nothing made those hospital chairs comfy, but it didn't matter; I needed to go home tonight. I missed Jalen terribly. I hated not giving him as much attention or being there for him as much as I should have. I wanted to get home, hug him, and ask him how his day had gone. I prayed that Jalen had the maturity and patience to understand that his little brother was fighting for his life and needed more of my time and energy.

"Are you staying here tonight, Queen?" Tracy asked.

"Nah, I'm gonna head home and check on Jalen. I got a bad feeling Carina flaked out again and left him to care for himself."

"I feel you. Take care of your oldest; things are good here. I'll see you in the morning."

Most mornings before I left for work, I'd call her to meet in front of our building after she came home from her shift. We'd smoke our daily cigarettes together. Hers was to destress from work, and mine was to prepare me mentally for it.

I nodded, said my goodbyes, and kissed Jerami on the forehead.

In situations like this, where Jerami was admitted after having a fever, Carina usually spent the day with him while I went to work. Once I got off and made my way to the hospital, she was supposed to go home to keep an eye on Jalen, but that rarely happened. She usually left Jalen home alone while she fucked around, hoping one of these losers she slept with would take care of her and put her up in an apartment rent-free.

With my hectic work schedule, taking care of Jerami, and depending on Carina to watch Jalen, it was a constant struggle to stop my oldest from hanging out in the streets and being influenced and consumed by them.

I took the F train to the Twenty-First Street Queensbridge Station. I was home. My boys, sister, and I lived in Queensbridge, a run-down housing project in Long Island City north of the Queensboro Bridge.

I walked up the broken escalator to the street. I ignored the usual losers that stood around the street corner, maneuvering through the pack of men and rejecting them as they spat corny pickup lines at me along my way to walking to my building.

"Psst . . . Come here, baby. Let me holla at you," one man said.

"Hey, pretty lady, I got a stiff nine inches for you right here," another said, grabbing his crotch.

I rolled my eyes and tuned them out as I headed to my apartment building.

The strong, lingering, rank odors of weed and piss hit my nostrils as soon as I opened the door and stepped into my building lobby. The elevator hadn't worked in months, so I trudged up the musty, narrow staircase, climbing five flights up to my apartment.

I opened my door, kicked Jalen's sneakers out of my way, and sorted through the mail. I threw the bills on my kitchen counter and tossed the rest of the junk in the trash. I sighed at seeing the growing stack of bills on the counter. Between all types of lab and imaging tests, radiation treatments, surgeries, clinic visits, and medications, all those things have drained my finances, which have me barely making it check to check. Paying bills became a weekly debate about what could be put off to pay later and what was necessary.

Dirty dishes were piled up in the sink, and I'm sure Carina's lazy ass was waiting for me to give in and wash them. I sighed, quickly washed them, and placed them on the draining rack. A bag of dirty laundry sat in the corner, still waiting to be cleaned. I'd have to tackle that another day. This was my life.

I walked down the narrow hallway to my son's room and looked in on Jalen. He was asleep, tightly tucked under his covers. I stepped around, all the action figures scattered across the floor, and looked down at him as he slept. I knew I shouldn't wake him, but he needed to know I loved and cared for him just as much as his brother. I made it my duty to wake him up and ask him about his day on nights when he went to bed before I got home.

I sat on the edge of his bed and gently tugged on his toes until he woke up.

"Hey."

"Hi," he said, rubbing his eyes and yawning.

"How was your day?"

"Fine . . ."

"Are you excited for your first day of school tomorrow?"

He let out an annoyed breath. "Yeah. Ma. I guess."

"Where's your aunt?"

He shrugged and yawned again. "I don't know."

"All right, go back to sleep. I love you, Sonshine."

"I hate it when you call me that."

I smiled to myself. He might not be fond of the nickname, but it was special to me. I kissed him on the forehead.

"Good night. Get some sleep," I said.

I closed his door and dragged my tired body to the bathroom. I ran the water, getting it as hot as I could stand, stripped out of my clothes, slipped in slowly, and soaked in the tub, grateful that my day was over.

Daily, I tried to create a sense of normalcy with my kids. I tried to keep up the façade that everything was OK and under control so my children could function as normally as possible, but the reality is . . . It's all bullshit. Things are far from OK, and nothing about our lives is fucking normal.

I slipped deeper into depression, realizing that after Maurice died and Jerami was diagnosed, I felt like the veil of faith had been pulled back from my eyes. There was no rhyme or reason to the universe or how it worked. We're all just lost souls that coexist with one another. We try to make sense of the fucked-up things that happen in the world, so we have a somewhat false sense of understanding and learn to live with them, but Maurice's death left me with a pessimistic view that the universe is chaotic and there are no happy endings.

I finished bathing, dried my body, and put on some shea butter while slipping on my nightgown. I laid my clothes out for the morning and stretched out on my makeshift foldout sofa bed. I buried my head in my pillow and silently cried until I dozed off, wondering how this nightmare became my reality and praying my life and luck would improve.

I stirred from my sleep when I heard Carina unlock the front door and creep in. I cleared my throat to make sure the heifer knew I was awake.

"Where were you?" I asked.

She jumped and swayed. "Wwwhat? Huh?"

She was clearly either drunk or high because she was stumbling around and slurring her words.

"I said, where were you?"

"Wwwhat are you? My fffucking mom?" she slurred and giggled.

"You left Jalen here alone when your sole purpose for staying here is to watch him while I'm at the hospital . . . Are you even listening to me?"

Carina wobbled into the kitchen, opened the fridge, and drank the last of the orange juice straight from the carton. Then she put the empty carton on the counter.

I stood up, grabbed the carton, and threw it in the garbage can. I felt my frustration boiling over and coming out in my words.

"I spent my last dime moving you into my fucking apartment when you were damn near homeless. I pay for everything around here for you and the kids, and all I ask of you is to help out, clean, cook occasionally, and watch after the boys. Half of the time, you're out somewhere fucking with some bum-ass sucka, and you leave my boys to fend for themselves. You hearin' me?"

"Ugh, you're using way too many words right now and messing up my buzz," she complained.

"Fuck you and your buzz. If you're not going to do what I need you to do, you can mooch off one of your drug-dealing fuck buddies and move out. It'll be one less mouth to feed, and it'll give me my damn bedroom back."

"All right. Damn, I'm sorry. It won't happen again."

I wish that were true, but I knew it *would* happen again.

CHAPTER 2

WHAT'S THE 411?

At 5:00 a.m., I was already up, showered, and dressed for work. Now was the hard part . . . getting Jalen up.

"Sonshine, wake up and get ready for school," I yelled from the kitchen, pushing the eggs from the frying pan onto a plate for him.

Next, I walked into his room. He groaned and mumbled something under his breath, but I paid him no mind. I stood over him while he lay in his bed. He wasn't responding to my light nudges, so I shook him firmly by his shoulder.

This was my typical daily routine; me waking up early, fighting with the kids to get ready for school while scrambling to get myself ready for work, and making it in on time. Meanwhile, my lazy-ass sister, Carina, was usually rolling over, sleeping peacefully while I struggled to do those tasks.

Jalen was old enough to walk to school, so all I had to do was wake him up, but the hard part was ensuring he stayed awake and went to class. If I didn't constantly stay on top of him, he wouldn't go to school at all.

When Jerami is home, my routine is more difficult. On most days, I need to wake up both boys at the crack of dawn and leave the house two hours before my shift starts. Jalen walked to school. Rather than hear him complain about his brother being too sick to keep up, cramping his style, or not wanting to drop him off, I dragged Jerami early and half-asleep every morning to his chemotherapy session before taking him to his elementary school, PS 111. I dropped him off at the "before care" myself because Carina was never in any shape to take him on time. Fortunately for me, since Jerami stayed overnight at the hospital, I only had to deal with Jalen today.

"Boy, wake up," I yelled, flicking on his bedroom light.

Jalen grabbed his blanket, covered his face, and rolled over. I walked over to him and yanked off his blanket. He curled up tighter, squeezed his eyes shut, and tried to go back to sleep.

"Get up. It's the first day of school, and I don't want you to be late."

"I'm up, Ma," he groaned. Jalen squinted, attempting to adjust his eyes to the brightness.

"C'mon, do I have to go to school today?" he groaned.

"Yes, you have to."

"But I don't feel good."

I put my hand on his forehead to gauge his temperature. "Boy, you're fine. Stop making excuses. Hurry up and get ready. There are scrambled eggs on the table for you."

He rolled his eyes.

"Hey, Ma?"

"Yeah?"

"Can you get me the new Jordans?"

"Boy, I barely have two pennies to rub together right now."

"The sneakers I have are tight on me. It's bad enough I gotta start school with the same old worn-out kicks I had last year, and now you're saying I can't even get new ones?"

I sighed. "You know we're going through a rough patch. I can't throw away money on buying you expensive sneakers."

He sucked his teeth. "Why is buying something for me throwing money away? All the kids around here are getting them. I never get anything. I fucking hate this."

"Whoa, watch your mouth in my house, little boy."

Jalen shook his head. "It's not fair. If it was something for Jerami, you'd get it for him in a heartbeat."

"That's not true, and you know it. With your father gone, I'm trying my hardest to make up for him not being here, but my funds are limited, and I can't spare money like that for sneakers. It would be nice for once to get a little damn appreciation."

"You know why I hate going to school?"

"Enlighten me."

"Because every day I gotta deal with all the kids at school making fun of my clothes and sneakers. At least if I had a pair of Jordans, they'd stop a little."

"Sonshine, trust me, I get it. But right now, I can't afford it. Maybe next month—"

"I already know by now that when you say 'maybe,' it's really a slow 'no. Just forget it.'"

I sighed.

"Save your allowance—"

"What allowance? I haven't gotten any money from you in months."

It was true, but it pissed me off that he was quick to remember everything I didn't do for him but caught amnesia on the things I did, for example, making sure he had school supplies.

"All right, calm down. Recycle soda bottles, help bag groceries at the food store, and ask Joe if you can help sweep up hair at the barbershop to make some extra money. Maybe he'll give you a haircut for free for helping out too."

"I don't want his charity."

I rolled my eyes and shook my head. "You're so stubborn. You need to put your pride aside, stop fighting me, and listen. Save that money from doing all those things, and if you have half of what you need, I'll add the rest and help you buy your Jordans."

"OK," he said dryly.

I didn't know if I'd have the money to do that, but at least this bought me some time and put this conversation on pause.

I dug into my purse, opened my wallet, and handed him some singles.

"Here. Get yourself a snack or something after school."

He quickly took the money.

"Have a good day, Sonshine. Hurry up, and don't be late for school on your first day."

He waved me off.

After separating the money I needed to travel back and forth to work for the week, I had little left. I realized I couldn't afford to buy lunch from my job's cafeteria by giving him that money. I'd have to make myself a peanut butter and jelly sandwich for lunch, but it was the least I could do to raise Jalen's spirits before he went to school.

I stepped outside, about to call Tracy, but she was already waiting for me in front of the building for our daily morning cigarette routine.

"Good morning, Queen," she said.

"Good morning. Can I bum a cigarette?"

Tracy nodded and handed me one as we leaned against the fence and watched what looked like a white woman and her son unloading a U-Haul truck.

"Who's moving out?" I asked.

"Nobody's moving out. We got white folks moving in."

"You're lying. There are no white people in this neighborhood."

"There are now, and they're moving into our building."

A white woman around our age, mid-thirties, was struggling to lift a box out of the back of the moving truck with her son, who looked around Jalen's age.

"How many of them?" I asked.

"So far, I've only seen her and her son. It looks like it's just the two of them."

"Well, that shit won't last. Once she realizes there aren't any of their kind around here, they'll move out with the quickness."

"I hear that!" Tracy laughed.

She took a long drag of her cigarette and said, "I'm about to crash. My shift at the hospital was brutal last night. Catch up with you same time tomorrow morning?"

"God willing. Later, Queen."

"Later."

I put some pep in my step, and power walked to the train station. Once I got off the train and back to the street level, I headed to Starbucks to get Francis's coffee before he came in. Luckily, I didn't have to front the money because Francis was such a frequent customer that the manager allowed him to have a weekly tab.

I walked to the firm and balanced his coffee and my purse against my hip as I pressed the button on the elevator. The firm occupied the fortieth through the forty-fifth floors, but the main floor was the forty-fifth. That's where the reception area and the partners' offices were.

The elevator doors opened, and I prepared myself for what I already figured would be a long, stressful day.

"Ay, Dios mio! Girls, brace yourself. Mr. Lincoln just got off the elevator, and he looks like he's in one of his foul early-morning moods," Francisco said, fanning himself.

"Uh, I don't know if I'm mentally ready to put up with his racist ass yet," Julissa said.

Francisco and Julissa were two of my receptionists. Francisco was openly gay and very flamboyant, but he toned it down drastically or "butched up," as he called it, whenever the partners were around. The partners never openly said anything about his sexual orientation, but it was apparent they weren't comfortable whenever Francisco acted too feminine in their eyes.

Francisco was thin and short, around five foot four. He's a feisty Puerto Rican who entertained me by making me laugh and informing me of the latest gossip in and out of the office. He keeps himself well-groomed, and his hair, eyebrows, and manicure put mine to shame.

Julissa is a beautiful Dominican woman that could easily pass for a sista. She has long, wavy, jet-black hair that hangs to her waist and a dark chocolate-colored flawless complexion. Her calming demeanor helps balance Francisco out when his tongue gets loose.

Even though I didn't understand a word they said whenever they bickered in Spanish, I always found their tiffs and exchanges hilarious because Francisco was so animated and dramatic. They kept me entertained and sane and made my workdays bearable when work at the firm became overwhelming.

"He should be somewhat decent once I give him his caffeine fix. Shh, here he comes." I said.

Francisco swayed his hips like he was on the catwalk until he saw Francis. Once he saw him, he pulled his shoulders back, straightened his posture, mimicking how he figured a straight man would walk, and hurried behind the front desk. He and Julissa pretended to be busy.

As Francis exited the elevator, I stood in front of the reception desk with a plastered fake smile and greeted the dickhead with a chipper voice, his custom Starbucks mocha latte, and the files he requested the night before.

"Good morning, Francis," I said.

Francis snatched his files and coffee without acknowledging my staff or me and continued toward his office. He walked inside and placed his coffee and files on his desk. He took off his suit jacket, hung it on the rack in the corner next to his office bathroom, and then sat behind his desk.

Out of all the partners, I hated Francis the most. Mr. Rothstein, or Tim, was, by far, the nicest of the three partners. He was always polite and talked to me like I was a human being.

Mr. Wayne, or Richard, was cordial, but he made sure we knew he was the head man in charge, and he treated my staff and me as if we were nothing more than "the help."

On the other hand, Francis acted like my staff, and I were nothing. He never looked at me when I handed him files or asked him to sign forms. Instead, he looked right through me as if I didn't exist.

Despite his snub of not returning my good morning, I kept the fake smile I greeted him with on my face.

Francis Lincoln insisted I call him by his first name because, for some weird reason, he didn't like how I said "Mr. Lincoln." When I started at the firm, he said, "I hate the way you call me 'Mr. Lincoln.'"

"I'm sorry, sir. I'm just trying to be professional."

"Yeah, well, from now on, just call me Francis, understood?"

"Yes . . . Francis."

"Ugh, I don't know which way I hate more."

I smiled and made a mental note to call him "Mr. Lincoln" periodically as my subtle way to piss him off.

I laughed at the memory and let Francis settle before I attempted to step into his office and inform him of his daily schedule.

Despite me placing his daily planner open on his desk with his important events and meetings for the week circled in red and highlighted, the asshole still needed me to tell him verbally everything that was going on.

Tim got off the elevator.

"Good morning, Mr. Rothstein," I said.

"Good morning, Juanita. If you don't mind, can you stop by my office and take notes for one of my high-profile cases later?"

"Of course! It's no problem at all, Mr. Rothstein."

"Could you please review everything on my agenda for me today?"

I reminded him of his appointments. He looked at the files for his cases that I made sure were neatly outlined, alphabetized, detailed, and in priority order.

"I also placed Post-it Notes on your computer monitor to remind you of important dates and phone numbers for your most important clients," I said.

"Juanita, you're a godsend. I expect nothing less from you. Thank you for this."

"You're welcome, sir."

Francisco slid his chair next to me and leaned in close. "Hey, boss lady, have you heard the partners are hiring another receptionist?"

"Nope, that's news to me. If they were adding someone new to my staff, I wish they'd tell me about it." I faced Julissa.

"Have you heard anything about this?"

"Yup. Rumor has it that the partners want you to focus more on contracts, closings, gathering files, and stuff for them. They want you to leave the tedious tasks and grunt work to us."

I nodded as they filled me in on more rumors and wondered if this new receptionist would be a blessing or a curse.

Francis stood over the reception desk, thumbing through the files I neatly organized for him and the other partners.

"You!" Francis said, pointing at Francisco. "Where are the files for the McCann merger?"

"Aren't they in that pile, sir?" Francisco stammered.

"Would I be asking you if they were?" Francis snapped.

I had each file separated and placed strategically in alphabetical order for each partner. How he kept missing his was beyond me. Before he got nastier with Francisco, I calmly shuffled through the files on the counter and pulled out the one he was looking for. Francis snatched it from my hand without so much as a thank-you and walked back to his office.

At that moment, a tall, thin, white man stepped into the firm.

"Good morning. I'm Stephen Jackson. I have an appointment with Mr. Lincoln."

Julissa smiled. "No problem, sir. Have a seat, and we will let him know you're here."

The phones began to ring. Francisco picked up one of the calls.

I looked at Julissa and said, "Don't worry about him. Handle the calls, and I'll let Francis know his client is here."

She nodded.

I knocked on Francis's office door.

"What?" he yelled.

I opened the door, walked in, and said, "Sir, your ten o'clock is here."

"Did I say to come in? Do I have all the information for his case?"

I ignored his first question and said, "Before I went home last night, I emailed you his updated file to look over."

"Yeah, I didn't read it, but good, send him in. I'll glance over it while he's here so I can hit him for another billable hour. Oh, I need you to pick up my breakfast, and once you bring that back, pick up Richard from LaGuardia Airport."

Every year, Mr. Richard Wayne went on a trip to law schools nationwide to scout and recruit the top law students. All the potential prospects had to be at the top of their classes and have personalities that caught his attention.

Richard was the most established of all the partners and decided which lawyers were hired by the firm. Tim, who hired me, made decisions on hiring all the other staff, but he left those decisions to me most of the time. The other partners felt Francis could use his dickhead personality as an asset and put him in charge of firing anyone who didn't seem fit to work there.

"Here," Francis said, tossing me his car keys.

I barely caught them and glared at him since now he had me playing the role of gofer and limo driver.

Instead of the partners paying for a car service to pick them up from places, they always tasked me with the responsibility. Francis never saw a problem ordering me to do things that weren't in my job description. The fucking cheapskates.

Despite being a paralegal, the firm made me the administration manager and put me in charge of the secretaries on top of everything else they made me do. Contacting clients in person and over the phone, filing motions and other legal documents, researching information for cases, and entering time for billing clients were just a few of the things I was tasked with doing every day.

"Keep your cell on you in case I need you to do some other errands, and bring your laptop so you can work in the car while you wait for Richard at the airport," Francis said.

I don't know if this asshole realizes it, but slavery is over.

I held my tongue, nodded, and walked to my office.

The firm, or should I say, Francis, thought it would be a good idea to give me a company-issued cell phone and laptop. Mr. Wayne and Mr. Rothstein thought they were nice perks, but, in reality, Francis used them as little electronic leashes to keep me at their beck and call whenever he wanted.

I sucked my teeth, grabbed my purse, and headed out to get the asshole's breakfast and do any other tasks he had for me while I was out.

CHAPTER 3

IT AIN'T HARD TO TELL

I fucking hated school. It was my first day of seventh grade at JHS 204 (Junior High School 204), and kids were already giving me shit for not having a fresh haircut and new school clothes and sneakers. Shit like that was part of why I never wanted to go to school and cut all the time.

It was lunchtime, and since all my old friends had ditched me, I spent most days, like today, chilling off to the side, alone in the schoolyard, not wanting to be bothered.

I get it; my old friends didn't wanna get caught up with the negative attention I attracted, so they kept their distance. Not being popular didn't bother me, but what did and what was always on my mind was how shitty things got for me after my dad died.

When Ma first told me he passed, it didn't feel real. One second, he was sitting on the couch, watching the game and talking to me; the next, he was gone and never coming back.

I remember half-listening to Ma weakly explaining how a stray bullet accidentally killed him. Once she said that, I couldn't hear anything else. I was too angry. Angry at God, angry at the world, but mostly, angry at her.

Ma took his death hard. Even to this day, whenever someone mentioned him, I saw how it still hurt her to talk about him. As it should, since it's her fault.

When my dad was alive, he hated seeing her smoke. She'd sneak a cigarette here and there when she was stressed, but now, with him gone, my bro being sick, and her never having any money, she chain-smoked on the regular. Good for her ass. I won't lie. I picked up the habit, too, and snuck loose cigarettes out of her purse whenever she left them on the table.

Before Dad died, me and moms used to be tight. We used to watch movies together, sing our favorite R&B songs around our apartment, and enjoy each other's company, but with Dad gone, things changed. Now, we barely talked, and I'll admit, that was mostly my doing, but lately, I couldn't say a sentence to her without lacing it with an angry, smart-ass comment, and the two of us ended up in a shouting match.

Don't get it twisted; Mom is no slouch. Even if it took her last dime, she always found a way to make sure my bro and I never went to bed hungry. We had just enough food in the fridge for it not to be called bare. She busts her ass to care for Jerami and me and always makes sure we never go without. I still love her, but I can't stop blaming her for Dad's death. If she didn't bug him, he wouldn't have rushed out to the store, and he'd be alive today.

Now that Dad's dead, my aunt Carina lives with us. Moms moved her in when we found out Jerami had cancer. She was supposed to be around to help out, but she hasn't done shit except bring different guys by the apartment to fuck or leave Jerami on me so she could go hang out.

"Ah, c'mon, Auntie," I said.

As usual, I remember Auntie going out with one of her men and leaving me to watch Jerami until Ma came home. She was in the bathroom, standing in front of the mirror, putting on makeup, and fixing her hair while Jerami and I stood in the doorway.

"I'm dead serious. Don't answer the door for anybody and make sure you do your homework. Y'all can watch TV but wash up later and go to bed on time. You hear?"

"Yeah," I said.

"Your momma called to say she's gonna be working late tonight."

"What else is new?" I said, rolling my eyes. "Why do you always leave us here alone to be with your . . . friends?" I asked.

"First off, I don't always leave y'all here by yourselves, and second, your auntie gotta have a life, too," she said as she put on her lipstick.

"I don't wanna be stuck cooped up in this boring apartment with Jerami."

"So, take him outside with you. Maybe some fresh air will do him some good."

"Why don't you want to play with me?" Jerami asked.

"It's not like that, bro. The doctor doesn't want you around many people because their germs can make you sicker," I said.

Auntie adjusted her boobs in her bra, pushing them up to the point where they looked like they were gonna pop out of her shirt.

"I'm in my prime right now, and I'm not gonna waste it babysitting kids. Anyway, don't be telling people I leave y'all at home by yourselves. Everybody doesn't need to know our business."

"What are we gonna eat for dinner?"

"I don't know. If you're hungry, you're gonna have to make do with whatever is in the refrigerator. I think there's still some of that chicken in there that your momma made the other night. There should be enough left for the two of you. Y'all can just reheat that."

She kissed both of us on the forehead and then walked to the front door. "All right, kiddies, bye."

That was a regular occurrence with my aunt and me, especially since Ma rarely came home on time after her shift. She'd either get stuck at work doing overtime or stay late at the hospital with Jerami whenever he had a fever or felt too sick after chemo. Whatever the reasoning was, I barely saw her.

Out of pity and guilt, she'd usually stroll into my room most nights when she got in late. I'd feel the bed sink down from her weight, and she'd attempt to have a shallow five-minute conversation with me to see how my day went, but I know she only did it because she felt she had to. I know it wasn't genuine and didn't come from the heart. She didn't give a shit about me.

It feels like after Dad died and Jerami got sick, the world only revolved around my little brother—my mom's unquestionable favorite—and I didn't exist.

Some nights I'd wake up and see Mom lying in Jerami's bed, rubbing his back and crying for him.

What about me?

Most nights when Mom came home, she'd sit at the kitchen table frustrated, covering her face with one hand while sifting through mounds of paperwork from the hospital and past due bills.

"We're going to have to cut back on a lot of things for a while. With your dad gone and your brother being sick, money is tighter than ever," Mom would say.

All I heard lately was, "Sorry, Sonshine. I had to spend the last of my money buying Jerami a coat. So you're just gonna have to make do and take care of the old ones you got." Or, "I can't buy you those Timberland boots you want. I spent all my money on your brother's medications; I have nothing left. I know it's hard, but we both have to make the best of things until your brother gets better."

If that wasn't bad enough, whenever she sent me to the store for her, I had to put my head down in shame, embarrassed and humiliated, when kids around the neighborhood laughed at me for having to use food stamps.

I love my brother. I want him to get better, but I wish things could go back to where I didn't have to sacrifice and compromise everything, back to when I mattered and everything wasn't about him. Back to a time when my dad was still here, and I didn't miss him every day.

I felt hands on the middle of my back and went stumbling forward. Someone shoved me from behind, which snapped me back to my shitty reality. I caught my balance and turned around to see Draper, a dark-skinned kid with a short temper that matched his short height. He was a loudmouth dickhead that always had to be seen and heard wherever he went.

"Don't touch me again," I said.

"Whatever, nigga. What's up with all them holes in your wack-ass sneakers?" Draper asked, drawing attention from some kids in the schoolyard.

Seeing he had an audience with some of the boys from our classes with him, I guess he figured he had to put on a show. Of course, the boys laughed and heckled me.

After Dad died, my clothes went from semi-decent to hood unacceptable. I had beat-up old Nike sneakers, two pairs of faded jeans, one black pair and one blue, and three shirts I cycled weekly. Since Mom couldn't afford to buy me name-brand clothes, I was a target for getting picked on daily because of my raggedy ones.

"It's the first day of school, and this nigga is already looking bummy as fuck."

"Knock it off," Akeem said.

Akeem stood beside me and whispered, "I got your back; don't worry about him."

Akeem lived one flight up from me on the sixth floor of my apartment building. He was dark-skinned with neatly braided cornrows. His mom and mine became good friends after my dad died. They hung out and talked on the regular, but Akeem and I didn't click on that level. We saw each other in passing in school and played basketball in the same circle of people on the courts by our building, but we weren't friendly. So it surprised me to see him randomly defending me.

Everyone stopped laughing, but Draper wouldn't let it go.

"Homeless people don't even want those wack-ass kicks you got on, and don't get me started on that ugly-ass Afro you're rockin'," Draper laughed.

"I said cut that shit out," Akeem said calmly.

Draper stepped to him. His face was inches away. He jabbed his finger into Akeem's chest.

"Fuck you. Mind your own business. I'm talking to Jalen."

"And I'm talking to you. Lay off him."

"I don't know who you think you're talkin' to, but you're not the boss of me, nigga. You don't run shit here. I'll say whatever I want to Jalen's bitch ass."

Without flinching or hesitation, Akeem gave Draper a jab-cross combo that connected with his jaw and floored him.

Then Akeem stood over him. "Get up so I can knock your ass down again."

The crowd laughed at Draper. Akeem gave him time to get back on his feet. Draper squared up, ready to fight, and threw a wild right hook, but Akeem quickly stepped back and tagged him with a swift jab and an uppercut that knocked him down again.

"Keep talking that tough shit, and I'll keep droppin' your ass all day. So get up," Akeem taunted.

The surrounding crowd got tighter to hide the fight from the teachers. Draper stood up. His eyes were teary, but he put his guards back up. Akeem faked like he was going to punch him in the nose. Draper flinched and raised his arms to protect his face, leaving his stomach wide open. Akeem hit him with two hooks to the body and a four-hit jab-cross combination to the face. Akeem was hitting him at will, to where Draper just looked defenseless.

The crowd's size got so big it finally got the attention of our teacher, Mrs. Foy, who came to see what was happening.

"Why are you two fighting?" she asked.

The crowd quickly broke up and scattered in different directions.

"We were just playing, right, Draper?" Akeem said.

Draper wiped tears from his face quickly with the back of his hand. "Yeah, we were just playing," he said.

Mrs. Foy looked at them skeptically. "Well, we don't play like that in school. So separate from each other now," she ordered.

They gave each other ice-cold stares as if to say this battle wasn't over. I followed Akeem.

"Thanks for having my back," I said.

"Ain't nuttin'. I know what it's like when these bum-ass niggas pick on you. They used to do the same shit to me."

"What made them stop?"

"It stopped when I started putting my hands on them."

I laughed.

"I heard about your old man. I know you used to have nice gear when he was alive. My pops isn't around either, so I know how it feels when you don't have the dough to buy cool shit anymore."

I lowered my head, feeling embarrassed, but I liked that he understood what I was going through.

"Your clothes are dope, though. I guess your mom is doing better than mine," I said.

"Nah, it's not that. I drop packages off for Drastic now and then. I'm not rolling in the dough, but it's enough to get me a few clothes and sneakers occasionally."

Drastic was a drug-dealing living legend in Queensbridge and the guy we all looked up to around the neighborhood. He was only twenty-two, but everyone in the hood respected and feared him at the same time. He had a six-inch-long scar etched down the side of his right cheek. He was always dressed to impress, having the latest sneakers, clothes, and jewelry. He had the hottest chicks, a dope Chevy Suburban, and money.

"What are you getting into after school today?" Akeem asked.

"Nothing, really. What's up?"

"I'm gonna play ball on the courts by our building after school. You can come if you want."

I was game for anything since I had nothing else to do and hated feeling like a broke bum alone at home.

"I'm down, but I gotta ask my aunt first."

After school, Akeem and I talked as we walked the short distance from school back to our building and vibed immediately. Through our conversation, we found out we had a lot in common—our dads weren't in the picture, we both liked basketball and video games, our favorite NBA player was Penny Hardaway, and our two favorite rappers were Nas and the Notorious B.I.G.

We got to our building.

"I just gotta let my aunt know where I'm goin' first and grab my ball. Come with me."

We walked up the steps to my floor.

"Auntie," I said, opening the front door to my apartment. Akeem was behind me in the doorway. I froze in my tracks and tried to block Akeem from seeing what I, unfortunately, walked in on. Aunt Carina was on the couch in the living room, sucking some random guy's dick.

Her head rose from his lap. She wiped her mouth with her hand and said, "Give us a minute. Stay right there."

I already saw way too much. I sucked my teeth as Auntie, and the random guy tried to make themselves decent. The dude moved his hand from her crotch and pulled up his sweatpants. Aunt Carina fixed her panties under her skirt and put a pillow over his dick to hide his hard-on.

"All right, you can come in," Auntie said.

Akeem and I walked into the living room.

"What are you doing home so early?" she asked.

"I'm always home around this time . . ."

"Jalen, this is my friend, Omari."

"Yo, what's up, kiddo?" the man said, reaching to shake my hand.

I reluctantly shook it, rolled my eyes afterward, and wiped my hand on my jeans, grossed out because I knew where his hand had been.

I didn't try to remember the guy's name. My aunt changed guys more often than most people usually changed socks. As fast as she went through dudes, I figured he'd be replaced within a week.

"Shouldn't you be getting ready to pick up Jerami from the hospital?" I asked.

"Since when do you question me? I'm busy right now. I'll call your momma in a few and tell her to do it. What's up? What do you want?"

"Can I play ball with Akeem? He lives one flight up from us."

Akeem waved.

Auntie wasn't paying me no mind. She didn't even acknowledge Akeem's wave. Instead, she eyed Omari up and down and said, "Sure . . . Whatever . . . Go somewhere with your friend and play."

She didn't like me around when she had one of her men over, and the feeling was mutual.

Whenever Mom spent the night at the hospital with Jerami, Auntie would wait until she figured I was asleep and always bring men over. It was embarrassing knowing that my aunt was a known gold-digging ho in the hood.

"I'm not sure if I'm staying here long. I might go to Omari's place where there's more privacy. Leave a note on the table for your momma, so she knows where you are when she comes home."

I nodded. I grabbed my basketball and keys from my room, wrote a quick note for Ma, and left it on the counter.

"A'ight, Auntie, I'm out."

"Cool, bye."

I shut the door and shook my head. "That shit is embarrassing," I said.

"Don't sweat that. Everyone has at least one fucked-up family member. So come on; let's hit up the courts before they get crowded."

"You wanna hang out at my crib for a while?" Akeem asked.

We finished playing ball, and I was in no rush to get home to either an empty apartment or to hear my aunt sexing her latest man in her room, so going to his house was a no-brainer.

"Yeah, I'm up for that."

As we walked to his room, Akeem gave me a tour of his apartment.

The sound of the Notorious B.I.G.'s "Juicy" was booming behind his bedroom door.

Akeem pushed open the door, and his twin sister, Ebony, was dancing with her back to us. She didn't realize we were in the room.

Akeem crept up to her and yelled, "Get out!" in her ear.

She jumped, screamed at the top of her lungs, turned around, and slapped him on his arm.

Akeem laughed and said, "Seriously, though, you need to get out."

"Why?" she whined.

"Because I'm talkin' with Jalen, and I don't want you snitching on me to Ma about the shit we're talkin' about."

"If you weren't talking about bad stuff, I wouldn't have anything to tell her."

"Whatever. Just get outta my room and put some damn clothes on. You see, I got company with me."

Ebony had a deep chocolate complexion that matched her eyes and a long, silky ponytail that ended down the middle of her back. She was wearing tight shorts, and I won't lie. I was staring at her ass and thighs.

"I got clothes on," she said.

"Just listen to your big brother." He laughed.

She slapped his arm again. "Punk, you're only a minute older. So relax with the big brother crap."

"Whatever, but I'm still older. Bye," he said, pushing her out of his room and closing the door in her face.

He had huge posters of Nas and the Notorious B.I.G. on his walls. The desk by his window had a chessboard and a stack of books and magazines. His silver-framed 8 x 10 picture on his dresser caught my attention. In the picture was a muscular guy holding two babies. I figured the man was his father. On the man's left arm, the same one he held Akeem with, was a king chess piece tattoo. In addition, the man wore a huge, thick, gold-diamond-encrusted Cuban link chain around his neck with a medallion of the same piece. Akeem caught me looking at the picture.

"That's my pops. I don't remember much about him, but my mom said he used to be really good at chess."

I nodded, and he continued.

"She said he could've been anything he wanted to be, but he loved the streets. When he rolled out on us, the only thing he left me was his chain."

Akeem went to his dresser and pulled out the chain from his top drawer. He looked at it and handed it to me before he continued talking.

"Even though my mom is dead broke and could really use the money, she can't bring herself to pawn or sell it. So she gave it to me and told me to keep it so I'd always have a piece of him with me. Do you have any of your pop's things?"

"Nah, nothing like that. I got lots of pictures, but I can't look at them without missing him."

His face got serious. "You're lucky. At least your old man was in your life. Do you remember the last thing he said to you?"

"Yeah."

"What'd he say?"

Even though I hated to admit it, my dad's last words were, "Take care of your mom for me."

I reluctantly told Akeem my dad's last words.

"That's deep, man. At least you actually got to do things and have talks with your dad. My pops was a bitch who didn't man up to take care of his kids. He split and left my mom because he said he wasn't built to be a good father to Ebony and me."

We were quiet for a while.

I tried to break the awkward silence by saying, "You never know. Maybe he'll realize he fucked up and come back."

Akeem shook his head. "I can't fill my head with hopes and maybes. He's gone, and he's never coming back. But like I said before, everyone has at least one fucked-up family member."

"You miss him?"

"Nah, you can't miss a stranger you never knew."

I nodded.

"I never told anyone about my pops...don't make me regret it."

"That's my word. I won't tell anyone about your business."

"Good. Look, I keep my circle small and don't trust many people. But talking and playin' ball with you today, you seem like cool people. If you keep it real with me and stay honest, I promise you I'll never do you dirty and do the same."

"No doubt. I wouldn't cross you. I got your back just like you had mine today."

We made a pact that afternoon to always look out for each other. We spent the rest of the afternoon playing video games, listening to our favorite rappers, and becoming better friends.

CHAPTER 4

OPTOWN ANTHEM

After running errands for Francis, which included getting his breakfast, picking up his dry cleaning, and going to the post office, I swiftly maneuvered my way through bumper-to-bumper traffic on the Grand Central Parkway to LaGuardia Airport. I pulled up to terminal nine, hit the emergency flashers, and waited curbside at the Delta baggage claim.

I spotted Richard talking on his cell, towing his carry-on hard-case suitcase behind him. He stopped, stood curbside, and waited. I pulled up and stopped next to him.

Richard was tall, at least six foot two. His salt-and-pepper hair gave him a distinguished look, and he had an authoritative air that exuded strength and commanded attention and respect.

I waited for him to finish his call before I said, "Good afternoon, Mr. Wayne."

"Hey, Juanita. I'm glad Francis and Tim sent you instead of Francisco to get me this time."

I didn't respond to that. I already knew Francisco made Mr. Wayne's homophobic ass uncomfortable whenever he was too flamboyant at the firm.

Mr. Wayne pointed to his luggage, opened the car door, and made another call as he climbed into the back seat. I popped the trunk and hauled his luggage to the back of the car. He rolled down the window and watched me struggle to heave his heavy suitcase inside the trunk.

"Careful with that, Juanita. It's expensive, and I don't want it damaged," Mr. Wayne yelled from the window.

I held my tongue and fought back all the curses I wanted to say to him.

As I drove, I waited for Mr. Wayne to finish his call before asking him about the new hire rumors.

"Mr. Wayne, if you don't mind me asking, word around the firm is Francis hired a new receptionist. Is that true, sir?"

Richard chuckled to himself before answering. "Yup, Francis hand-picked Meghan himself. He met her at a gathering he attended and thought hiring her would be beneficial since the workload for the firm has more than tripled because of all the cases we've won recently."

I nodded.

"According to him, she's very qualified. Francis wanted to finalize the hiring and have you start training her immediately. She should be at the firm by the time we get back. You'd oversee her just like Francisco and Julissa."

"I guess Mr. Lincoln didn't feel having me involved in the hiring process was important, huh?"

"No," Richard said flatly.

I left our conversation at that.

After fighting through traffic, I parked Francis's Mercedes in his spot in the firm's underground garage. We rode the elevator up in silence. Finally, the elevator chimed, the doors slid open, and we stepped off to our separate ways.

I walked up to the reception desk. "Is the new receptionist here yet?" I asked Francisco and Julissa.

"Yup, she's here, all right," Julissa said.

"She's sitting in the waiting area . . . and she's a piece of work," Francisco said.

I looked around and noticed a pretty twenty-something-year-old woman sitting with long-toned legs crossed at the knees. She looked annoyed, waiting impatiently, chewing gum, bouncing her legs, and repeatedly checking her watch.

She had a decent figure for a white girl. She wore a curve-hugging black skirt with black stilettos. Her makeup was flawless. Her fire-red hair was long but pinned up into a tight conservative bun, and her D-cup breasts peeked out from the neckline of her dark emerald-green blouse that matched her eyes.

I smiled as I approached her. "Meghan, is it?" I asked, extending my hand.

She left my hand hanging, eyed me up and down, and frowned at my ill-fitting outfit. "Yeah, I'm not the warm and friendly type. I'm here to meet Mr. Lincoln and Mrs. Wilson," she said.

"Don't you think it would be wise for a new employee such as yourself to be friendly and polite to everyone?"

"Nope! Only to those that matter. I'm not here to make friends."

My first impression . . . The bitch had a serious air of arrogance about her and a superiority complex. I understood what Francisco meant by her being a piece of work. I needed to knock her down a peg if she was going to work for me.

"I beg your pardon?" I asked.

Meghan sighed. "Is Mr. Lincoln or Mrs. Wilson here yet? I'm tired of waiting and wasting my time."

"You're not making a good first impression with me, and before you slip and say something you'll regret and upset me further, let me stop you by introducing myself. *I'm* Mrs. Wilson."

She covered her mouth in embarrassment, then extended her hand to me. I reluctantly shook it.

"I'm so sorry. I'm Meghan Flanagan. It's nice to meet you . . . You just weren't what I was expecting."

"And what exactly *were* you expecting?"

Before I could lay into her further, Francis walked out.

"Juanita, this is Meghan. She's one of your new receptionists. She's a paralegal like you, so she can help you out with looking over paperwork."

"I still need to interview her to see how well we gel together."

"That's not necessary. I have already interviewed her and offered her the job. Everything else can be worked out over time." Then Francis opened a folder.

"Your résumé is impressive," he said.

He licked his lips and scanned her body, almost like he'd bend her over right there if I weren't standing with them.

Meghan smiled and said, "Thank you."

"Train her thoroughly, Juanita. I can tell she will be very helpful around here," Francis said, staring at her huge tits. Then he quickly switched his eyes to her face and smiled.

I watched Meghan pretend not to notice his eyes darting from her cleavage to her face, but her flirty grin gave it away.

I had to catch myself from rolling my eyes.

"I'm happy to be a part of this firm. I look forward to working under you and learning everything I can, Mr. Lincoln."

What an ass-kisser! She wasn't ten minutes in, and this heifer was already brown-nosing.

Francis smiled at her.

"The pleasure is all mine. Juanita will show you around the firm and answer any questions you might have," Francis said. His smile waned when he turned back to me.

"Juanita, make sure you explain what her role is and what will be expected."

"You got it, Mr. Lincoln," I said, purposely as a subtle jab to irritate him.

Tim approached us and said, "Hey Juanita, I still need you to take those notes I told you about earlier. It shouldn't take more than fifteen minutes. Can you meet me in my office in five?"

"No problem, Mr. Rothstein."

Overhearing our conversation, Francis requested me too. "Right after you finish with him, I need you for the same thing."

"Yes, Mr. Lincoln."

Francis shuddered. "Francis, just call me Francis. Every other way you address me makes me cringe."

"Yes, Francis."

He frowned, stopped briefly like he would say something, but shook it off, and walked with Tim to their offices.

I faced Meghan. "Have a seat with Julissa and Francisco. You can put your things down under the desk and get settled in. Pay close attention to how Julissa and Francisco answer calls and the proper way the firm wants you to file folders for cases. The partners have a specific way they want phone calls handled, and each partner has certain ways they want things done for them. They hate mistakes, so take notes to avoid making a lot of them. Once I finish with Mr. Lincoln and Mr. Rothstein, I'll show you around and have you shadow me to understand better what's required of you."

"Cool," Meghan said while cracking her gum, loud and obnoxious.

I started to head to Tim's office but turned around to face Meghan. "One more thing. Don't chew gum at the desk. It doesn't look professional to clients."

Meghan rolled her eyes, spit it into a napkin from her purse, and threw it in the trash.

I didn't care for her attitude. She needed to understand that she'd be taking orders from me.

I knocked on Tim's door and poked my head inside.

"Come on in, Juanita. Have a seat."

I sat on one of the leather chairs in front of his desk.

"I don't have too much for you to write down, but you have a way of outlining my thoughts perfectly, and I want to go into this case ready."

I was familiar with the case; one of his extremely wealthy Wall Street clients was caught in a police raid at a massage parlor screwing the masseuse. When he was brought back to the precinct and searched, he was found with coke in his pockets.

With my pen in my hand, I wrote down everything of importance that Tim dictated to me, making particular bullet points for the high-priority things.

When he finished, I said, "I'll type these out and have a copy of the outline on your desk within the hour."

"I really appreciate it, Juanita."

Francis barged into Mr. Rothstein's office. Tim looked annoyed.

"Are you done? I need her," Francis said.

Tim sighed. "We're finishing up now."

"Good."

Francis faced me. "Be in my office in two minutes."

"Yes, sir."

Francis closed the door.

"He's a great lawyer, but he's a huge asshole. So don't let him stress you out too much."

"I'll try."

We shared a laugh.

I grabbed my purse, stood up, and headed to Francis's office. When I got there, his door was open, and he was closing the blinds to his windows. He had an enormous corner office with a fantastic view of Manhattan. He pointed to a chair already pulled out for me opposite his desk. He sat on the edge of his desk and folded his arms.

"Hurry up and sit down so we can get started," he said.

I shut the door behind me and made myself comfortable as I sat down and put my purse next to my feet.

I grabbed the small notepad and pen I jammed in my purse and had them ready in my hands to jot down everything he dictated. Francis talked, and I scribbled frantically, jotting down everything said.

"Wait, where's the recorder I got you?" he asked.

"It's in my purse, sir, but I don't think—"

"I don't pay you to think; I pay you to do what I tell you to do. Now, use the recorder. I can tell I'm talking way too fast for you, and I hope you didn't miss something already."

"Yes, Francis."

I didn't miss shit, but I kept my comments to myself. I reached into my purse, pulled out my recorder, and placed it on the edge of his desk. I hit record and continued to write down his notes as he spoke.

After typing out the outlines for Tim and Francis, I spent the remainder of my workday with Meghan shadowing me. I gave her a tour of the different floors and showed her the partners' offices, the cafeteria, the file rooms, the conference room, my office, and the front desk. I prayed her hiring would be a blessing, but the vibe I got felt more like it would be a curse.

I was exhausted from working all day, but my day was far from over. Carina called me last minute with some lame excuse to tell me she couldn't pick Jerami up from the hospital. Allegedly, she was looking for jobs all day and was called back for an interview by one of her prospects. I'm sure she was full of shit, and truth be told, I don't even think the lazy heifer has been looking for work at all. But now, I had to go to Jamaica Hospital. I'd call her out on her lie once I picked up my baby and got home.

Most nights, I brought my work home and tinkered with it while I helped the boys with their homework. It helped to keep me from falling behind when I left early for anything Jerami-related.

I took a deep breath and exhaled slowly as I stepped to the nurse's station. I've become too accustomed and tired of the hospital, cancer vernacular, and seeing doctors. I could tell by the irritated expression on Jerami's face that he was too through staying in the hospital and wanted to go home.

"Hi, Ma," he said.

"Hey, baby."

"I thought Aunt Carina was supposed to pick me up earlier."

"She was, but she got caught up trying to get a job and was running late."

"Mommy, I'm bored. I just wanna go home," he said.

Dr. Maier laughed. "He's still a little nauseous, but he should be fine to be discharged. How he feels in the morning should determine if you should let him go to school tomorrow. How are you holding up?" Dr. Maier said.

"I'm surviving. I'll be happy when he finally goes into remission," I said.

"Fingers crossed."

I thanked him for everything, and Jerami and I went home. On the train ride home, I thought about what I could whip up quickly for dinner for the kids and me. Hopefully, Jalen's attitude would be tame and not add to my already stressful day.

CHAPTER 5

C.R.E.A.M.

(CASH RULES EVERYTHING AROUND ME)

Mom walked in the door with Jerami. Her eyes looked tired and bloodshot. She didn't pay me no mind; she was too busy flipping through today's mail on the table. Jerami sluggishly walked up, hugged me, and plopped beside me on the couch.

"What's up, bro?" I asked.

"Nuttin'. I'm sleepy. I'm gonna lie down," he said, heading to our room.

"Hey, Sonshine, don't mind him. He's a little tired and weak after being poked and prodded at the hospital."

Mom tried to kiss me on the cheek, but I moved away.

She sighed and asked, "Did you finish your homework?"

"Nah."

"Then cut off that T.V. and finish it."

"I will when the Knick game is over."

"Boy, I'm not asking you to do it after the game; do it now."

"Ma, chill. I will. Just let me finish the game. Jeez."

"Don't tell me to chill. I'm not one of your little friends. I told you to do something, and you need to do it."

I didn't budge. Ma exhaled, then rubbed her forehead and neck.

"I don't want to hear you complaining about being tired when I wake you up for school because you stayed up late doing what you should've done right after school."

Her voice sounded low and tired, like she had no fight left in her to argue with me.

"Where's your aunt?" she asked.

"I don't know. She might be with this guy Omari I saw her here with earlier."

"You saw her today when you got home? She told me she was out all day looking for jobs."

"I don't know about looking for work, but she was definitely giving a job to the guy on the couch when I walked in here," I said, snickering.

"Sonshine, don't be fresh. I know exactly what you meant. Have some respect, and I hope you're kidding about that. But seriously, was she here when you got home?"

I didn't want to snitch on my aunt, but I couldn't cover it up now.

"Yeah, I saw her before I went to play ball with Ms. Williams's son, Akeem."

"You guys are hanging out now?"

"Yeah."

"Well, that's good."

Mom massaged her temples and said, "Are you hungry? I'll cook something quick for you."

"Nah, I ate at Akeem's place."

Mom nodded.

"I had a long day. I don't want to fight with you. Finish up your homework while you watch your game and get ready for bed, you hear?"

I opened my mouth to say something slick but did as she asked. I thought about being a dick and giving her a hard time, but the only reason why I did what she asked was so I didn't have to hear her bitching and complaining about it in the morning.

When I was done with everything, I lay down in my bed. The light knocking of the heat pipes kept me from falling asleep. I heard Jerami whimpering in his sleep. I got up to check on him. I felt sorry for my little bro, who was always sick and in and out of the hospital. I fixed his pillow and blanket to make him more comfortable. He stirred and smiled at me.

"Better?" I asked.

He nodded.

I went back to bed. Jerami ran up, climbed in, and snuggled up next to me.

"C'mon, bro, my bed is way too small to share with you."

Jerami playfully tweaked my nose. That made me laugh.

"I know, but I don't want to be alone," he said.

I rubbed his bald head. He was still little and didn't realize the world around him sucked yet, so I cut him some slack and let him stay. Sometimes I was jealous that everything revolved around him, but he was my little brother, and I loved him. He didn't ask for any of this shit he was going through.

While Jerami slept and hogged up my bed, I lay with my hands behind my head, staring at the ceiling, reflecting on my day. I was glad I was friends with Akeem now and had a good dude in my corner.

I woke up to what sounded like crying. I stood up, rubbed the sleep from my eyes, and checked on Jerami to see if he was straight. He was sound asleep. I listened closely. The crying sounded like it was coming from the living room. I followed it, stood in the darkness of the hallway, and saw Mom sitting at the kitchen table sobbing with her head down, holding a framed photo of my pops. Even though I blamed her for his death, I know Dad being gone still hurt her. I sighed. I hated being soft, but I gave in and checked on her.

"Are you OK, Ma?"

She jumped, put down the picture, and quickly wiped her face with the back of her hand.

"I'm fine. Go back to bed. You have school in the morning," she said, snapping at me.

It was rare for me to feel a momentary twinge of sympathy for her, but every time she acted tough and pushed me away, it made me go right back to not caring about her stupid-ass feelings. Finally, I shrugged, yawned, and walked back to my room. I went back to bed and let her go back to sobbing quietly.

Since that day Akeem stuck up for me, we'd been hanging out daily, reciting our favorite rap songs, and playing ball together to get ready for our school's basketball team.

Akeem was an interesting cat. When he wasn't playing ball or chess, his face was buried in books about street life by authors like Iceberg Slim or Donald Goines. I didn't read much outside of school besides comic books, but Akeem did because he thought being street and book-smart was good. Being around him a lot, I started looking at him like a cool, wiser brother, and it felt good to have a friend that understood me finally.

On this day, I was walking home alone because I had to stay late after school for detention because I cursed some kids out in my English class for making fun of my clothes and Afro.

As I got closer to my building, I saw a bunch of people rushing to the chess tables near the basketball courts. I pushed through the crowd and saw Akeem getting jumped by three older boys.

"Give up your dough, and we won't have to fuck you up," one of the boys said.

"I ain't giving up shit! If you think I'm gonna let y'all punk me, you're buggin'," Akeem said defiantly.

Even though he was outnumbered, he was holding his own, but he was getting noticeably tired, and the boys were starting to get the best of him.

A chromed-out Chevy Suburban was parked by a fire hydrant. The dark tints made it damn near impossible to see who was inside, but everyone knew it was Drastic. He stepped out and leaned against his truck with his driver, Boogie Brown.

Word on the street was that when Drastic was thirteen, he put in work, sold drugs, and was quick to shoot people to establish himself in the street. It didn't matter if they were male or female, young or old. He'd take out anyone who got in the way of his money.

He quickly rose up to be the man, and as a sign of respect to the old-timers, he kicked money up to them, which got him their additional protection. With the old-timers having his back, hardly anyone tried to cross or test him. He had the streets on lock. Queensbridge had lots of nickel-and-dime hustlers, but none moved major weight like Drastic. Most of the heroin, crack, or weed sold in Queensbridge came from him.

Drastic took out a pack of Newports from his pocket. He pulled a cigarette loose, pointed, and laughed while he and Boogie watched the fight.

No one helped Akeem, but everyone talked shit and enjoyed the show. I saw Draper, but he just smirked and fell back with the crowd to watch the fight with everyone else.

That day Akeem stood up for me, we made a pact always to have each other's back. I couldn't stand there and watch him get jumped. I won't lie. I was scared to get involved, but he looked out for me when I needed it, so it was time to return the favor.

I got off the sidelines, and while one of the random boys was off guard, I sucker-punched him. The boy charged toward me. That was all Akeem needed to get the upper hand on the other two. He threw a wild haymaker that knocked one of the boys on his ass and had him down for the count. Now, we were both fighting one-on-one.

The boy swung a wild left hook at Akeem, but 'Keem sidestepped it, kicked him in the dick, and hit him with a four-punch combination to the face. The kid staggered and fell to the ground.

It was just the boy I was fighting and me. I won't lie. He was whoopin' my ass. He was way bigger than me, and every straight punch he caught me with snapped my head back. I blocked one of his jabs and connected with a straight cross. Akeem punched the boy I was fighting in the back of the head. I hit the boy with an uppercut that floored him, then Akeem and I kicked and stomped the shit out of him.

The two boys Akeem were fighting used the fence next to them to scramble to their feet. I thought they'd help their friend that we were stompin' out, but they ran off. We cursed the last boy out and let him stagger to get up. Blood seeped between his fingers as he covered his nose and mouth and ran off toward his friends.

"Thanks for lookin' out," Akeem said.

"No doubt."

We fist-bumped.

Drastic was leaning against his ride, laughing and clapping.

"Yo, 'Keem, come here," he shouted, pointing at him.

Akeem nodded.

"You too, lil' homie," he said, waving at me.

We walked over.

"Do you know who I am?" Drastic asked me.

"Yeah, everybody knows who you are. You're Drastic."

He looked at his driver and nudged him. "You hear that, Boogie? Everybody knows who I am."

The jacked brotha smirked and shook his head.

Drastic pointed to his driver. "This is my right-hand man, Boogie Brown. You and Akeem reminded me a lot of us when we were coming up."

I heard about Boogie too. He was about six-foot-three, built like a linebacker, and had long dreadlocks that hung down his back. Word on the street was Boogie didn't talk much because he had a bad stuttering problem. Only a very select few teased him and lived to tell about it because Boogie had a rep for beating people half to death with his bare hands whenever they did.

"You two did your thing out there. I like tough little niggas that can scrap."

Akeem and I smiled as he continued.

"Akeem, you've dropped packages off for me in the past, but after seeing you handle your business today, I think I might be able to use you for bigger things real soon. Your boy too. Y'all tryin' to make some money today?" Drastic asked.

We nodded.

"Cool. It's really simple." He pointed at Akeem. "All you gotta do is take a package to 41-08 Vernon Boulevard, knock on apartment 3E, and ask for Naleighna. She's a dark-skin shorty with blond dreads and a phat ass. When she comes to the door, hand her the package. That's it. If you do that for me, I'll give you fifty dollars. You good with that?"

"Hell yeah!" Akeem said.

"What's your name, lil' homie?" Drastic said, pointing at me.

"I'm Jalen."

"Jalen. Cool. I want you to go to 41-13 Tenth Street, knock on 2B, and ask for Erica. She's a dark-skinned Dominican chick with big-ass titties. When she comes to the door, hand her the package, and I'll give you the same amount I'm paying Akeem. How's that sound?"

"I'm in," I said without hesitation. I was down for anything that would put money in my pockets.

Drastic smiled. "That's what I like to hear."

I didn't know what was in that package and didn't care. All I knew was I would get fifty dollars for a few minutes of work.

"Yo, both of y'all hop in my truck," Drastic said.

Akeem and I climbed in the backseat of Drastic's Suburban. Boogie Brown climbed behind the wheel, shifted the truck into gear, and peeled out, driving us between Twenty-First and Vernon Boulevard to a place right underneath the Queensboro Bridge called "Baby Park."

All the debris from the construction on the bridge turned the park into an abandoned area. It was mainly a spot for junkies and rats. The only things there were a grungy handball court and two six-foot broken-down basketball hoops.

Boogie honked the horn, and a Black Honda Civic with deep-tinted windows and shiny rims flashed its lights.

"Y'all go over there. My boys Rasheed and Shyne are gonna give y'all the packages."

Drastic flashed a wad of cash in front of us.

"Once y'all take care of business, come back here, and I'll hit y'all off with the dough."

Akeem and I walked over to the car. Rasheed and Shyne didn't say a word; they just tossed us brown paper bags and watched us put them in our book bags.

This was my shot to prove that I wasn't shook and could handle the task. I couldn't mess this up by being a pussy and getting cold feet. I needed money. If I handled this right, Drastic would probably have 'Keem and I do more drops later on, and I'd finally be able to buy all the shit my mom couldn't get for me.

Akeem and I split up and walked to our separate buildings. Cop cars were driving back and forth around the block. Plainclothes cops were swarming around the building when I walked up to it. A couple of them stopped talking and glared at me but went back to their conversation.

I stepped into the lobby and walked up the two flights of stairs to 2B. I opened my book bag and looked in the brown paper bag. Inside was a plastic Ziploc filled with clear glass vials with red tops that had something inside them that looked like beige pieces of soap. It didn't take a genius to realize this had to be crack.

I lightly knocked on the door and stepped back when a dog angrily barked on the other side. I heard movement and muffled voices inside. I noticed the peephole turn dark, then go back to light again.

"Who is it?" I heard a deep voice yell from the other side of the door.

"Drastic sent me," I said.

I heard the sound of two deadbolts being removed before the door swung open.

"What did you say? Who the fuck are you?" a muscular, dark-skinned Spanish guy asked, staring me down.

There was no way I was telling him my real name. "Drastic sent me . . . Is Erica here?" I asked, my voice cracking.

The man stared me up and down, then looked around to make sure I was alone, and walked away without answering, letting the door slam in my face. I stood there and waited a minute, not knowing if Erica was there or if I should leave. I was about to go back down the steps when the door finally opened again, and a hot Dominican lady with her tits spilling out of her shirt waved to me.

"Don't mind, Buddha. He's an asshole. What's up, handsome? You got something for me?"

I wasn't giving her shit until she confirmed she was Erica.

"Are you Erica?"

"Yup, that's me."

I nodded.

She laughed.

"What's your name?"

"Jalen," I answered.

"What you got for me, Jalen?"

I handed her the bag.

"Hold up. I got something for you to take back to Drastic."

She reached behind her back, and my heart raced. I wasn't sure if she was going to shoot me or what. She giggled, as I flinched when she pulled out another brown paper bag. She handed it to me, and it had some weight to it.

"Tell Drastic business is booming, and we need this shit faster."

I nodded.

"All right, handsome, until we meet again, peace," she said as she waved and closed the door.

In the stairwell heading back down, I looked in the paper bag Erica handed me and saw it was loaded with money. The thought crossed my mind to take some, but I shook off the temptation. I didn't want to risk Drastic killing me if he found out. Instead, I hid the paper bag in my drawers in case anyone tried to rob me on my way back to Drastic.

I rushed back to Drastic's truck. Akeem had already finished his drop and was sitting inside. I took the bag out of my drawers and sat in the backseat.

"Little homie, why you got my shit in your underwear?" Drastic asked, shaking his head.

"There were cops everywhere, and I didn't want to chance them stopping me or getting robbed on the way back here. So it was the safest place I could think of."

"Smart. That was quick thinking."

"Erica said business is booming, and she needs the shit faster," I repeated. I handed him the paper bag she gave me.

He pulled out a thick wad of bills and peeled off a crisp fifty-dollar bill.

"Here you go, little man," he said.

"Thanks!"

Drastic looked at Akeem and me. "Yo, you two aren't doing anything right now, right?"

We both shook our heads.

"Cool. Hang out with Boogie and me for a minute. I want y'all to see what I'd have y'all doing when you're both ready to make serious money."

Drastic faced Boogie and said, "Yo, Boogie B, park the truck. I want to walk around and check on my corner boys."

Then Drastic faced us and said, "When they see my truck, they act correct, but I want to catch them slippin' to see what really goes down when I'm not around."

Boogie nodded and parked.

Akeem, Drastic, Boogie, and I walked to Twelfth Street and headed toward the basketball courts.

A group of boys around Akeem's and my age were laughing and hanging out by the park benches. Drastic crept up and pressed his fingers against one of the boy's backs as if it were a gun and said, "See, this is the shit I'm talking about. Y'all little niggas out here playing games and not paying attention to your surroundings. I could've been some random nigga out here trying to jack y'all or the cops creepin' to bust your asses. Pay attention and make my money."

A frail, smelly brotha came walking toward us. His eyes were bloodshot, and his cheeks were sunken in. It was apparent he was a fiend. He walked up to Drastic and flashed some money.

"Lemme get three," he said.

Drastic snatched the money, counted it quickly, and signaled for one of the boys to come over.

"Don't stand there looking stupid. Get the man his shit," Drastic said.

The kid pulled three vials out of the pouch of his hoodie and handed them to the fiend.

"See how easy that was? Pay attention, stay focused, and most importantly, under no circumstances do you *ever* give a customer product until you have their cash in your hand. Then, when it's time to re-up, hit up Rasheed and Shyne. Y'all understand?" Drastic asked.

The boy nodded and returned to where he was posted.

Drastic pointed to Boogie, Akeem, and me. "All right, let's move on to my other spots."

I noticed a black unmarked police car with two white officers inside it that seemed to be looking at us in my periphery. The unmarked vehicle pulled away from its parking spot, swerved, skidded to a stop, and damn near hit us. The corner boys bolted in different directions.

"TTTThhhhhaaaattt's O'Sullivan," Boogie Brown stuttered.

"Shit, I got my piece on me," Drastic said.

Through gritted teeth, Drastic said, "Akeem, without being too obvious, stand next to me."

Akeem did as he was told, and Drastic quickly and discreetly tucked his piece into Akeem's book bag.

A jacked cop with a receding hairline and a black, bushy mustache got out of the driver's side of the police car. O'Sullivan was notorious for being a dick that terrorized every Black male he saw. Everyone in the neighborhood saw him as a racist bully with a badge and a gun. The cop with him, whose nameplate read "McIvor," was young, thin, and blond.

"You know what time it is, Jiggaboos. Up against the railing," O'Sullivan said.

Boogie, 'Keem, and I did what he asked, but Drastic stood there defiantly.

"Damn, O'Sullivan. You're not even a housing cop. You're a regular patrol cop. So why aren't you off doing regular cop shit?"

"You might live in these shithole projects, but this entire area is my sector, so I *am* doing regular cop shit."

"The P.S.A. 9 cops don't do shit to us. So why you always fucking with us?"

"Stop selling dope, and I'll stop fucking with you. I make my overtime off shaking down you dirty bastards."

O'Sullivan looked at Akeem and me. "Who are these two nigglets you got with you, Drastic? What, you taking them under your wing to teach them how to be a degenerate drug-dealing piece of shit like you?"

O'Sullivan pushed him against a black iron fence along the sidewalk, turned him around, and frisked him.

"I don't know what you're talking about. I told you I ain't no drug dealer. I'm just a poor Black man trying to give back to my community by mentoring these kids. Besides, you've been frisking me for years and never found shit on me."

O'Sullivan continued to go down the line, spreading our legs apart and patting us down while he bickered with Drastic. My heart was beating hard because I was scared they would find the gun in Akeem's book bag. But lucky for us, the officers were too distracted arguing with Drastic to check.

"You gotta be shittin' me. You're no choir boy. You've just gotten better at hiding your dirt. Did you forget who used to bust your ass when you were their age?" O'Sullivan said, pointing at us. He continued, "Eventually, you'll slip up. Your kind always does, and don't feed me that 'woe is me, I'm poor' shit. For someone unemployed, your jewelry costs more than what I make a year in salary, and don't get me started on your truck. Welfare and food stamps don't buy shit like that. There's only one way a punk like you is getting money like that, and it's by pumping that poison in the street."

"Don't hate me because you got a shitty-paying job."

O'Sullivan smiled, walked up to him, and kneed him in the balls. Drastic fell to the ground as O'Sullivan knelt and leaned over him. "I'm sorry. I don't think I heard you right. Say it again."

Drastic shook his head and kept quiet.

O'Sullivan smiled.

"In reality, I should thank you. With you selling all these drugs in the neighborhood, it gives me more niggers to arrest for overtime. You make me look like a superstar to my bosses for cleaning up the streets." Finally, O'Sullivan stood up.

"All right, jungle bunnies, I'll be watching as always, so be good." He and his partner slid into their unmarked and drove off.

Boogie Brown helped Drastic to his feet.

"I fucking hate that pig," Drastic yelled.

Akeem handed his book bag to Drastic. Drastic put his gun back in his waistband and said, "All right, y'all, that's it for today. I got other business to take care of, so I'll see y'all later."

"When can we do more work?" I asked.

"I like that! You're an eager little nigga that's tryin' to get his money up. Shorty, I know where you and 'Keem be at. I'll find you when I need you. In the meantime, I'll catch y'all later and keep your mouths shut about everything that happened today."

"We don't snitch," Akeem said.

"Make sure it stays that way. Peace!"

Drastic and Boogie Brown walked off.

The money I just got was already burning a hole in my pocket. I couldn't wait to spend it.

"Yo, you want to take the F train to Steinway Street and check out some stores?" I asked.

"I'm down for that, but first things first. You need to use some of that money for a haircut. You need one bad," Akeem said.

"Yeah, let's do that first."

I had money in my pocket for a change and was happy with how easily I made it. Usually, it took me weeks sweeping hair at the barbershop and bagging groceries at the food store to make what I got in a couple of minutes delivering a package for Drastic. I hoped I could make more easy money doing jobs for him soon.

CHAPTER 6

SHOOK ONES PART II

"Straight up, sh-t is real, and any day could be your last in the jungle. Get murdered on the humble, guns'll blast, niggas tumble." Akeem and I sang Nas's "Represent" in unison.

"So, you hanging out with me this afternoon or what? I know you hate being home with your aunt and little brother when your mom works late," Akeem said.

He was right; I never wanted to be home. Being home reminded me that I was poor, my dad was dead, and my brother was sick. Hanging out with Akeem helped me escape all the personal shit.

"Hell yeah," I said.

We were coming home from school and going to hit up the courts when we saw Drastic on the block standing outside his truck, talking with a group of high-level dealers and street soldiers. He spotted 'Keem and me.

"Yo, y'all come here," he said, waving us over.

We walked over. Boogie Brown was standing next to him. Rasheed and Shyne were there with a lady and two guys I didn't know. I noticed that guy, Buddha, and the girl Erica from my drop were talking amongst themselves. Erica smiled at me.

"Hey, handsome," she said.

I smiled shyly and waved.

"What's up, Naleighna? What's up, Joakim?" Akeem said.

The dark-skinned woman with blond dreads waved, and the light-skinned brother with the big gold rope chain beside her gave Akeem a nod. I figured 'Keem knew them from his drops.

Drastic pointed to us and said, "These two are gonna be our new run-ners. They're fresh faces, so we can move more weight without the cops constantly seeing our regulars."

The guy I didn't know sucked his teeth and mumbled something.

"You got something to say, Taevaughn?" Drastic asked.

"These young cats don't look like they're built for this," Taevaughn answered.

Drastic walked up and stood face-to-face with him. "So, you're making executive decisions now, big man?"

Taevaughn looked nervous and stammered when he said, "Nnnah, they just look soft, like they'd drop a dime if they got knocked, is all I'm saying."

"You're out-of-pocket right now. That's not something you need to worry about. Me and Boogie approved it, and that's what it is. So know your place, and don't come out of your face again," Drastic said.

Taevaughn nodded and glared at Akeem and me.

"Akeem, J, if the cops catch you and ask where y'all got this shit from, what are y'all gonna tell them?"

"We found it," we said in unison.

"See how quick they were with that shit? My little soldiers are ready."

We couldn't stop smiling.

Akeem and I started dropping off packages for Drastic on the regular. Since we were young, the cops never suspected us. We walked right past them with lots of weight and guns.

What Drastic was having us doing was smart and made sense. If he or another dealer got caught with those things, they'd go to prison for a long time, but in the eyes of the law, 'Keem and I were still kids, and if we were caught, we'd get nothing more than a slap on the wrist.

The two of us made a name for ourselves in the streets. Drastic was happy with us and let us sell weed for him on top of dropping off pack-ages. He wanted us to sell mainly to high school kids.

The old-timers liked how we operated and spread the word that we weren't to be messed with. People we knew from all over the neighborhood gave us respect, so we walked around like royalty. Older kids didn't think about robbing or beating us up out of fear of what Drastic, Boogie or the old-timers would do to them once word got back to them. Boys our age and even older wanted to be down and put on with working for Drastic, so they did anything Akeem asked so he'd vouch for them. Surprisingly, one of those boys was Draper.

Even though they had bad blood between them, Akeem let Draper hang with us. I knew Draper didn't care much for Akeem, and vice versa. Personality-wise, they clashed. Draper was loud and obnoxious, while Akeem was calculated and calm. I saw Draper as a grimy-ass snake that would fuck us over whenever he saw the chance to strike, and I didn't get how, as strategic as Akeem was, he could underestimate Draper's ability to cross him. I guess they both lived by the old saying: keep your friends close and your enemies closer.

'Keem and I were so focused on making our paper that school got put on the back burner, and we skipped it a lot. The school would call, and Mom would bitch about not wanting me running the streets with Akeem, but it went in one ear and out the other.

One day, Mom entered the living room while I was sitting on the couch reading *Word Up!* Magazine and listening to my Walkman. She snatched my headphones off me and yelled, "There's no reason why I'm getting calls at work every other day that you're not going to school."

I rolled my eyes at her chewing me out and ignored her.

"What are you doing when you're not going to school?" she asked.

I didn't answer. I just sat there with my arms folded, sighing.

"Little boy, you better cut out this rudeness and answer me."

"Nothing. We just play video games at our friend's apartment and hang out."

"Who is this friend? And why is he not going to school either?"

"He's our friend, Draper. I don't know. School is boring."

"Boring? Child, there was a time when little Black boys like you couldn't even *go* to school. You're lucky times have changed. Where are his parents?"

I shrugged. Mom sighed and rubbed her hand down her face. I knew she was mad and trying not to flip out, but she was losing her patience.

"I miss a lot of work as it is with your brother's sickness. I can't miss more of it, going back and forth with making sure you're going to school.

If I get one more call from that school saying you're absent or late again, I will spank your little ass. Do you understand me?"

"Yeah, yeah," I said, standing up and heading toward my room.

Mom could be mad all she wanted, but she was too busy working and caring for my little bro to stop me. As far as things with Auntie went, as long as I wasn't in her way, she didn't give a shit about where I was or what I did.

Akeem and I started dressing better. Instead of my fucked-up Afro, I rocked a high-top fade. I didn't have only two pairs of jeans anymore; I had fifteen pairs now with shirts to match. My old sneakers with the holes in them went straight into the trash. I rocked Air Jordans now.

One day when my mom got home after work, Akeem and I were sitting in his living room watching music videos when our mothers walked into the apartment.

"Sonshine, those sneakers look new and expensive," Mom said.

"Yours too, Akeem," Mrs. Tracy added.

"Where are you boys getting all this money from? I hope you two aren't doing anything stupid or illegal," Mom said.

"Nah, Ma, it ain't even like that. We've been going hard, cashing bottles, sweeping hair at the barbershop, and bagging groceries," I lied.

"Tips have been good, and we've been saving our money, so we don't have to bug y'all to buy these things. We know money is tight," Akeem added to make it seem more truthful.

Our mothers smiled and nodded.

"It's good to see you boys working hard, but make sure you're putting the same effort into your schoolwork," Mrs. Tracy said.

We "yessed" them to death, but school was the furthest thing on our minds. Since we weren't bugging them for money anymore, they hardly questioned us about it and left us alone.

"Now, class, I want you all to welcome our newest student, William O'Neil," our teacher, Mrs. Foy, said.

We were in our morning homeroom. I sat in the back of the classroom next to Akeem, eyeing the new kid. Bill was a skinny white boy with blue eyes and brown hair.

Some of the class greeted him with head nods and waves, while others laughed and whispered how out of place he was.

"Um, Mrs. Foy, can you call me Billy or Bill?" the new kid said.

I made my voice nasally and mimicked him, "Can you call me Billy or Bill?"

The class roared with laughter.

"Unless you want me to call your mother at work and explain that you're bullying a student on his first day, I suggest you knock it off, Jalen."

That shut me up.

The class laughed and teased me for getting yelled at.

"Hey, Mrs., is he your son or something? There ain't no white kids around this neighborhood," Draper said.

"No, Draper. Billy and I are not related. However, I wish you were as inquisitive about your schoolwork as you are with me and another white person being related."

"Mrs. Foy got jokes," Akeem said.

The class laughed again.

Our class was full, so we knew the chump would have to sit in our row.

Mrs. Foy faced him and said, "You can take the empty desk next to Ebony in the third row, OK?"

Bill nodded and kept his head down while walking to the empty desk beside Ebony. A big smile grew on Bill's goofy face when he sat next to her, and it was obvious he thought she was pretty.

"Hi," he said.

"Hey," Ebony said, smiling back at him.

Akeem crossed his arms and slumped in his seat. I could tell from him watching the interaction between Bill and Ebony that he was gonna flip out.

"Stay away from my twin, white boy," Akeem said.

"Huh?" Bill stammered.

"I saw you eyeing my sister. Don't try frontin' like you weren't."

"Chill out, Akeem. He's just being nice," Ebony fired back.

Bill smiled slightly at her after she said that.

Akeem jumped up from his chair. He never took his gaze off Bill. Everyone in class turned to watch them.

"You heard what I said. Keep gawking at her, and I'm gonna fuck you up."

Mrs. Foy quickly stood up from her desk and rushed to break them up. "Akeem, I'm not going to have you threatening students and using that type of language in my classroom. Go to the principal's office now!" she yelled.

Akeem kept staring down Bill and shoved Bill's forehead so hard his head snapped back. "This ain't over, chump," Akeem said.

I knew the beef had just gotten started with them.

"Stop running like a bitch, white boy!" Akeem yelled.

Bill ran full speed down Tenth Street. Akeem, Draper, some of the other neighborhood boys who were trying to be down with Akeem and me, chased Bill from school all the way to our apartment building.

We fucked with him at school and chased him, beating his ass and running him into the house in tears daily.

Draper tackled Bill from behind and held his arms down. Eight of us circled Bill in total.

"Fuck him up," Akeem ordered.

I sucker-punched Bill while Draper yanked him to the ground. Bill was in the fetal position on the concrete, trying his best to protect his face and head as we all stomped and kicked the shit out of him.

The loud sound of a police siren stopped us in our tracks. A cop car with flashing lights screeched to a stop near us.

"Shit, that's O'Sullivan. Let's bounce," Akeem said.

I gave Bill one last kick to the gut before we all ran off in different directions. I looked over my shoulder and saw Bill groaning and grimacing in pain as he tried to sit up.

"Run. Scatter like fucking roaches, you bunch of savages," O'Sullivan said, sprinting out of his cruiser and swinging his nightstick.

We hauled ass down the street, laughing about the beating we put on Bill.

"Auntie, you going somewhere?"

She was standing in front of the mirror, combing her hair and putting on her makeup. "Yup. I'm about to step out to see one of my . . . friends, so I'm gonna need you to look after your brother until your momma gets home."

"Can you meet up with your friend another time? I was trying to sweep hair at the barbershop to make money," I lied.

"Nope. Your mama is working a double shift, so she's not gonna be home for a while, and I got shit to do, so you're gonna have to watch your brother."

I sucked my teeth. I wanted to play ball and see if I could sell more weed.

"Stay out of trouble, and I'll see y'all later. Bye."

She was out the door before I could even say anything back.

Minutes later, someone was throwing pebbles at the living room window.

Whap! Whap! Whap!

I looked outside and saw it was Akeem and Draper, so I opened the window.

"Yo, J, come outside. We're tryna hoop. Are you down or what?" Draper asked.

"My aunt went out, so I'm stuck watching my brother. It's cold as hell out there and raining, anyway."

"Stop being a pussy. It's only drizzling," Draper said.

"C'mon, J, just bring him with you," Akeem added.

I knew I shouldn't. The last time I brought Jerami out with me, he got sick. I knew his immune system was weak, but I figured if I dressed him warmer this time, I wouldn't have to stay in the house all afternoon and night playing board games with him.

"Gimme a minute, and I'll meet y'all on the courts."

I walked into my room. Jerami was playing with his action figures on the floor.

"C'mon, we're going outside," I said.

"I can't go out there; I'll get sick again."

"You'll be all right. We just gotta make sure you're dressed warmly."

"But Ma said—"

"Don't worry about what Ma said. She doesn't know everything. As long as you're covered up, you'll be fine."

I grabbed his coat, gloves, and scarf while Jerami fought with me.

"Stop fussin' and put on your coat," I said.

I zipped up his coat and put his beanie on his head, followed by his hat. Then I put one of the masks Ma got from the hospital on his face and wrapped his scarf around that. I put his gloves on last. Then I gave him a once-over. He looked warm enough to me.

We went outside, and Akeem and Draper were waiting for me on the courts.

"Took y'all long enough," Draper said.

"I'm cold," Jerami said through chattering teeth.

"Don't be a baby. Cover your mouth with your mask and scarf. You'll warm up as soon as you start playing."

He was shivering, but he nodded and did what I said.

Draper, Akeem, and I played ball while Jerami played on the playground by the courts. The rain made the weather feel colder. We rubbed our hands together and blew hot air into them to keep them warm so we could shoot.

We played some games and let Jerami shoot around with us afterward. When we finished playing, Akeem and I hung around the courts selling weed bags to make a little money before heading home. I kept Jerami in sight and didn't plan on staying out too much longer, but he didn't mind. He made friends with some other kids and played with them. He didn't look sick, so I figured everything was good.

When we got back to our apartment, Ma still wasn't home from work yet, which was good for me because I didn't need to explain why we were outside.

"Did you have fun?" I asked Jerami.

"Yeah!"

"Good. You gotta promise me you won't say anything to Ma about what we did."

"But why? We were careful."

"Nah, Ma won't go for that. You're not supposed to be outside, and if she found out, she'd punish us both. You don't wanna get in trouble, do you?"

Jerami shook his head.

"Then you can't say anything, or we won't be able to do anything fun like this again. You understand?"

"Yeah."

"You can't say anything about me selling stuff, either."

"I wasn't gonna—"

"Good, now, promise me you won't tell Ma about anything we did."

He looked like he wasn't sure he should.

"Promise me, or next time I'll leave you here by yourself."

"OK, OK, I promise."

"Good."

Ma didn't need to hear about anything. What she didn't know wouldn't hurt her.

CHAPTER 7

IT'S NOT RIGHT, BUT IT'S OKAY

Tracy and I were leaning against the fence, smoking our morning cigarettes and laughing, when a petite white woman approached us.

"Excuse me, but are you two Jalen and Akeem's moms?"

She was in her early thirties, about five foot two, with long blond hair and blue eyes. I'd seen her around the building, but I didn't know what her deal was. I pushed away from the fence, stepped on the butt of my cigarette with the toe of my shoe, and asked, "Depends on who's asking. Who wants to know?"

"Hi, I'm Debbie O'Neil, Billy's mom," she said, smiling and extending her hand.

Tracy folded her arms and said, "State your business."

Debbie pulled back her hand. "Right . . . I don't mean to ruin you twos good time, but my son, Billy, and I just moved to the neighborhood, and he's having a hard time adjusting to being here and making friends—"

"And your point is?" I asked.

"My point is every day after school, your sons have been beating on Billy, and I wanted to talk to you ladies, woman to woman, mother to mother, and ask if you could please talk to them. I'm sure if they got to know Billy, they'd all be friends . . . I'd like to be friends with the two of you also."

"I'll talk to Jalen. I'm not raising any bullies," I said.

"I'll speak to Akeem about it, too," Tracy added.

"We can't force our kids to like each other, but at least they'll stop messing with him after school," I said.

"Thank you. I appreciate that." Debbie smiled.

"As far as us being friends, my life is pretty busy, and I don't have time for new friends, so don't get your hopes up," I said.

"Same here," Tracy said.

Debbie's smile waned, and her shoulders slumped. She walked back inside our building, her head lowered in defeat. I knew I was wrong. I knew I was being a bitch to her for no reason, but I was taking my frustration out on her because of the shitty way some of the white people at work treated me. It wasn't right, but in a way, I felt justified.

"All right, girl. On that note, I'm going to bed," Tracy said.

"Akeem and Jalen are hanging out at my apartment before they leave for school. I'll tell them to lay off this woman's son, so we don't have to hear her mouth again."

"Yup, the last thing we need is for them to keep beating on him and her going to the police and pressing charges. I don't want our boys anywhere near these cops."

"I hear that. Let me hurry up and talk to them so I can take my broke ass to work."

Tracy laughed. "I feel you on that. Later, girl."

"Later."

I walked up to my apartment, and Jalen and Akeem were watching cartoons in the living room.

"What's this I'm hearing about you and Akeem beating up on this white boy, Billy?" I asked.

"It's not like that, Ma. He's got a smart mouth, and he's always trying to flirt with Ebony," Jalen said.

"Yeah, Mrs. Juanita. That white boy ain't no saint either," Akeem added.

"I don't care. Stop beating on him," I said as I glared at them. "I don't need that white boy's mother coming up to me and Tracy because you two are kicking his ass every day."

I faced Akeem. "I already talked to your mother, and she feels the same way. Now, both of you lay off him. Do y'all understand?"

"Yes," they said in unison.

"Good, I gotta go. Don't be late for school."

I ignored Jalen and Akeem's moans and groans and prepared myself for another shitty day at work.

"Boss lady, your sister is on line four. She said it's an emergency, and the way she was talking all fast, it sounds important," Julissa said over the intercom.

"Thanks, I'm on it."

I was sitting in my office. I snatched up the receiver and punched the blinking light on the phone with my finger.

"What's going on?"

"Jerami is burning up, and I can't break his fever." Carina's voice was filled with panic.

"What's his temperature?"

"102.6. I just retook it two minutes ago."

"Tell him Mommy is on her way. I'll meet you in the emergency room," I said.

I took a deep breath, exhaled as I ended the call, and walked to Francis's office. I knocked and waited for his confirmation before walking in.

"Come in."

Francis was on the phone and signaled to give him a minute. He swiveled his chair from facing me and continued to talk. With his back turned, I gave him the finger. He ended his call and faced me.

"Sir, my son is in the emergency room. I have to go—"

"No, you have to be here. You have closings to do this afternoon; you can't leave." he said.

Clearly, he wasn't moved by my dilemma.

"My son is being taken to the emergency room. His fever isn't breaking, and in his condition, something like that can be fatal."

Francis waved me off. "As I said, you have closings this afternoon. So from now on, before you leave every day, I want you to type and print out an in-depth breakdown of everything you've done for the day."

"You see me working nonstop from when I walk in the door until I leave. So why now would you question my work? Did you ask Meghan to do this assignment you're asking me to do?"

"No, I don't need to. Meghan is competent and doesn't need as much supervision as you do."

The way he'd been acting lately, I should've known he'd give me some bullshit, tedious, time-consuming task that he'd never ask her to do. He knows I have a life outside of work and children to get home to, but he pulled shit like this just to mess with me.

"When have I ever needed your supervision? For thirteen years, I've always completed my work on time."

"Just get back to work without giving me a speech, thank you, and close my door on your way out."

I stood firm.

"I'm going to the hospital to be with my son."

"You've got some nerve. Your little excuse is getting played out and will reflect on your performance review."

I couldn't worry about that. I needed to get to my little boy. "Meghan can fill in for me. According to you, she's the competent one, right? She shouldn't have any trouble handling everything without me . . . I'm wasting time right now; I have to go. Right now, my son needs me."

"You're not going. This isn't up for discussion."

"Watch me."

"OK, I'll continue to play this game with you . . . for now, but we seriously need to reevaluate your position with this firm."

I didn't respond. I slammed his damn door on my way out, walked to my office, and grabbed my belongings off my desk. I told Francisco and Julissa I'd be out for the rest of the day and to call me on my cell phone if they needed me. Then I rushed to the hospital.

My feet hit the ground running for the train station. I talked tough to Francis, but I had to be kidding myself if I thought he wouldn't hold this against me. I called Mr. Rothstein and explained everything to him. He was more sympathetic to my dilemma and promised to smooth things over with Francis.

Now that my work situation was taken care of, my focus was entirely on Jerami. I tried my best not to panic as I took the E train and walked the rest of the way to the hospital. My nerves were on edge.

My shoes click-clacked on the white-checkered linoleum floor as I double-timed it to the waiting room. My heart pounded with every breath

I took. I've been through this many times before, but it never got easier. I hated the familiar sterile smell of the hospital because it made me think about sickness and death. I didn't need to think of those things right now. I needed to stay positive and keep my spirits up for my son.

I pushed through the doors and saw Carina sitting in the waiting room.

"Does he have a room yet?" I asked.

"Not yet. They're getting one ready. You got it from here, right? I can go home?" she asked.

I sighed. "I got this. Go home and check on Jalen."

"Jalen likes to hang out with his little friends; he'll be fine. Stop trying to stick me with babysitting all the time."

"Just watch my son, please; you always want to do everything except what I need you to do."

She sighed and waved me off. "I'm sick of being cooped up in that apartment daily."

"I don't care. I don't want Jalen to come home to an empty apartment, understand?"

She walked out of the hospital without acknowledging me.

I stopped at the nurse's station, and she told me that Jerami had a room. I rushed to it.

Jerami was lying in a hospital bed. He looked so frail and thin, attached to all those wires and tubes. Hearing and seeing all the machines he was plugged up to didn't help calm me. His eyes bulged, and his hacking cough caused his body to jerk violently. Then his eyes fluttered as the coughing spell ended. Jerami squished my cheeks together and played with my face. That made me smile a little.

"Hi, Mom," he said, sounding breathless and raspy.

"Hey, baby. Did you run around and overheat yourself again?"

Jerami looked down at his hands and said, "Yeah."

I didn't want to lecture him. While I hated returning here, he was still a kid. It wasn't his fault that his sickness limited his ability to do things and detracted from his childhood.

Doctor Maier walked in. "Back so soon? How is my favorite patient doing?" he asked, looking at Jerami's chart. "Oh, I see Jerami has another fever."

Doctor Maier leaned in and asked, "Were you playing basketball again, young man?"

Jerami nodded. Doctor Maier smiled.

"I know you want to make it to the NBA, but you must get better first, understand?"

"Yeah," Jerami said.

Doctor Maier faced me. "We'll keep him overnight for observation and to bring his fever down. Most likely, he should be released tomorrow evening."

"Thank you. I'll let my sister know so she can be here to take him home."

He nodded.

After Jerami got more medication, we watched some TV, and afterward, I sat next to him in his hospital bed, held his hand, and read him a bedtime story until he nodded off. His fever wasn't breaking fast enough. I listened to the monitors he was connected to and prayed for everything to improve.

I nodded off for ten minutes in a chair next to his hospital bed, with a blanket on me that I'm sure Tracy must've put on me at some point.

My eyes burned from being tired and fretting all night. My head hurt, and my stomach growled from being too broke to buy something to eat in the hospital.

Tracy walked in, and as if she had read my mind, she handed me a hospital tray of food.

"Girl, I love you," I said.

Tracy laughed. "I know."

I devoured the food, eating it like I hadn't had a meal in years. After I finished stuffing my face, Tracy said, "Queen, he's out for the night; you should go home. Hug Jalen and get some real sleep. If anything changes with Jerami, I'll call you."

I nodded.

I watched my son sleep and kissed him on his forehead. I know he was exhausted from being tested all day. Physically, my body was tired from work. Mentally and emotionally, my energy was sapped from being with him at the hospital all night.

When I got home, I removed my shoes and walked to Jalen's room. My feet were killing me. I gently nudged him until he woke up. He sucked his teeth.

"What?" he asked, snapping at me.

"I just wanted to see how your day was."

"It was fine. I didn't do anything, OK? I'm tired. Let me sleep."

I sighed and let him be. Outside of his room, I bent down to pick up the shoes I had taken off. I walked to the living room, pushed the coffee table out of the way, and pulled my folding bed out of the couch. I plopped my exhausted body down on the mattress and crashed. I closed my eyes, welcoming sleep, and just wanted this hellish day to end.

I attempted to lift my sleep-deprived body off the mattress, but to no avail. I hit snooze on my alarm clock and pulled my covers tight. I tried to fight off my nodding but lost that battle and slept through my alarm. I didn't even remember falling back asleep. I rolled over on my side and opened my eyes, squinting to see Carina making herself a bowl of cereal at the table. I sprang up and grabbed my alarm clock.

"Shit! What time is it?" I yelled. I looked at the time. It was 7:45 a.m. There was no way I was making it to the firm by eight o'clock.

"Why didn't you wake me up?" I yelled.

She shrugged. "When I saw you still lying there, I thought you called in sick."

"You know I don't call in sick, and I don't take days off. I can't be late; you should've woken me up."

"Well, yelling at me isn't gonna change anything. So get ready and get out of here."

"Did Jalen wake up yet?" I asked.

"Nope."

"Well, get him up and make sure he goes to school. I don't want him missing days for no reason."

Carina gave me a weak salute and said, "Sure thing, boss."

I ignored her sarcasm and hurried to the bathroom. I hopped in the shower, scrambled to throw an outfit together, dressed as fast as possible, and rushed out the door.

After leaving work early yesterday, I knew Francis would have a con-niption if I strolled in there a minute after 8:15. I already felt this would be a rough day.

After a long day, I walked home to my building. Luckily, I got out of work on time for a change, and Carina picked up Jerami from the hospital, so the only things on my mind were taking a warm bath and going to bed at a decent hour.

As I approached my building, I saw Tracy smoking a cigarette in front. Usually, she was at work around this time. She had a sad, faraway look in her eyes.

"You look stressed. Don't you have work tonight?" I asked.

"I took off. I just found out that my kid's father, Cedrick, was killed. His sister called not too long ago and told me the news. Apparently, he was selling drugs on another dealer's corner and was shot point-blank in the head."

Tracy looked away when she spoke, like it bothered her to talk about it. I know the feeling. I always felt awkward whenever I spoke to people about Mo's passing.

I hugged her. "Damn . . . I'm sorry. You OK?"

"I will be."

"How are you going to break it to your kids?"

"I'm just gonna give it to them straight. I doubt Ebony will care, but Akeem, even though he's mad that Cedrick wasn't in his life, I know my son. He's gonna feel it."

Tracy took another drag of her cigarette and blew her smoke up in the sky before continuing.

"I never bashed his daddy in front of him, and I often told Akeem that he had all of his daddy's good qualities. Of course, he'll act tough and never admit it to me, but I know it will bother him that he never met his father."

I nodded. "How are you taking it?"

"I'm not gonna lie. It hurts."

Tracy shook her head and chuckled before going on. "I don't know why I'm wired this way, but I like the thug types. Cedrick was the only man I ever loved. He was a bad boy, exciting, tough, street, and book smart. He had everything I was attracted to, but even though I loved him, his actions showed me that it wasn't mutual. I always attract the broken ones."

"Don't say that, Queen. I'm sure you'll find a nice doctor or something at work."

Tracy sighed and said, "I doubt it. I don't date anymore. I've been celibate for years now. I'm too drawn to the wrong kind of men. I attract the bad boys, and those types bring nothing but drama and stress. So I'll stick with my vibrator and fingers. They don't cheat. I can't get in trouble, catch a disease, or get pregnant with those."

"Girl, you're crazy."

We shared a laugh, and I continued to comfort my friend.

CHAPTER 8

INCARCERATED SCARFACES

Akeem and I headed home after playing some intense one-on-ones on the courts by our building. Our moms were out front smoking together.

"Akeem, we need to talk," Mrs. Tracy said.

"Later, Ma."

"Boy, don't tell me later. This is important."

"Come on, Ma, what is it?"

"I'd rather talk in private."

"I ain't worried about it. You can say whatever it is in front of J."

"Well, I don't know if you care, but your daddy died today. Your aunt Roxanne called me earlier to break the news."

Akeem kept quiet, and I couldn't read him.

"Is that it?" he asked.

"Yeah. You OK?"

"Yup, I'm fine. That deadbeat didn't mean nothin' to me. It's not like he ever called or came to see me. So, how'd he die, anyway?"

"He was gunned down in the street selling dope on another dealer's block.

Akeem nodded. "If that's all you got to tell me, do you mind if me and J hang out a little longer?"

Mrs. Tracy took a drag of her cigarette and said, "Ask his momma."

Akeem faced my mom. "Juanita, do you mind—"

"Boy, I raised you better than that. Does she look like one of your little friends? Show some respect and come correct when you ask her."

"Sorry, Ma, you're right. Mrs. Juanita, do you mind if me and J hang out a little longer?"

Mom smiled and said, "Not a problem."

After we left our moms, Akeem only spoke to say he wanted to go to Queensbridge Park. We walked there in silence, and he looked like he had a lot on his mind. We sat on the benches by the water. The spot had a cool view of Manhattan's skyline.

Fifteen minutes passed, and 'Keem still didn't say anything. He just sat in a daze and stared off into the distance. He didn't look focused on anything in particular but blinked away whatever he was thinking about and said, "This is my favorite spot in the world. I come here when I need to think."

"Why?" I asked.

"It's peaceful, but more than that, the view here shows me that the world is bigger than our block, you know? Seeing all the lights, buildings, businesses, and shit shows me that there's a whole big world out there, and I'm stuck here. I know I'll never fit in that world, but maybe if I make enough dough doin' hood shit, I can visit now and then."

I didn't know what to say, so I stayed quiet and nodded. Part of me felt the same way; I think he knew that and knew I'd understand his reasoning for coming here.

"You're the only other person I've ever taken here besides Ebony."

Akeem went back to staring at the water in front of him. He turned his head away and touched the corner of his eye. I saw a tear roll down the side of his face. He quickly wiped it away and returned to looking off into the distance.

"You all right?" I asked.

"Yeah, just thinking about shit," Akeem said, staring at the water.

I saw him quickly wipe away another tear.

"Sometimes, I sit here and wonder what my life would be like if my pops never left me and Ebony."

Akeem shook his head and continued. "I don't know why I care that he's dead. I guess a part of me always thought he'd eventually realize he fucked up, come around, and actually try to be a good father, but that was me thinking like a kid."

I felt terrible for him, but hearing him talk about his pops made me think about and miss my father.

We chilled for a while before walking back to our building. When we got to the door, Akeem said, "I'm sorry, man."

I was confused. "Sorry about what?" I asked.

"I'm sorry I was weak in front of you today. It'll never happen again."

CHAPTER 9

T.R.O.Y.

(THEY REMINISCE OVER YOU)

"Nooo," I screamed.

I jolted awake from my nightmare, gasping, sobbing, and covered in sweat. I shuddered and held myself as the image of my husband's bloody body flashed vividly in my mind. Today was the anniversary of Mo's death, and even in my sleep, I couldn't escape feeling guilty and responsible for it. That day played on repeat in my head often. There were times when I could drown myself with work or things with the boys and push memories of that day to the side, but there wasn't a day that went by when I didn't think about my husband. I missed our intimacy, physically and emotionally. I missed his humor, our conversations . . . I missed *him*. If I could go back to that day, I would've never sent him to that damn store.

After that dream, I tossed and turned, trying my best to fall back asleep, but there was no point. I knew I'd just lie there staring at the clock because I had to go to work in a few hours anyway, and if I fell back asleep, I'd risk oversleeping, and I didn't want to chance being late.

This day always made me emotional, and I usually spent most anniversaries mourning, looking at our old wedding album, and reminiscing about our good times. But instead of wallowing around depressed all day like I usually did when the anniversary came around, I decided to get out of bed, shower, and get ready for my day.

Usually, I wouldn't smoke in the house because of Jerami's cancer, but that dream had my nerves on edge, and my body ached for a cigarette. I tapped the filter of my unlit cigarette on the coffee table. I had the lighter in my hand, and my cigarette was dangling from my lips, but I couldn't do it. I felt like a piece of shit, wondering if my smoking in the house before Jerami was diagnosed caused his cancer. I shook off that thought and got ready for work.

After getting dressed, I began the dreadful process of waking my sons up for school. I started with Jerami.

"You gotta wake up and get ready for school, baby."

Jerami did what I asked without a fuss. Jalen, on the other hand, was his usual defiant self.

"Let's go, Sonshine. You're gonna be late." However, asking him nicely evolved into me yelling at him, flicking the lights on, and yanking the covers off him. After all of that, he still fought with me. Finally, Jalen pulled his pillow from under his head and covered his face. I snatched it off.

"Boy, it's too early for this crap. I shouldn't have to fight with you every morning to get ready."

"Whatever," he said as he went to the bathroom.

I walked to the kitchen and started cooking breakfast for my children. "Boys, come on and eat," I yelled.

The boys sat at the table, and I loaded their plates.

"Eggs again?" Jalen groaned.

I slammed the spatula down on the stovetop. "Yes. Eggs again. I spent the few dollars I had buying something for you boys to have for breakfast. I'm here slaving over this stove for you, and the least you can do is show some damn appreciation."

"I don't want eggs . . . Do you even remember what today is?"

I sighed, calmed down, and rubbed my face. "Of course, I know what today is, Sonshine, and if your father were still with us, he'd tell you to stop giving me a hard time and eat your breakfast."

Jalen frowned at me, stood up, and went to his room.

I didn't have the energy to chase and yell at him. I needed my damn morning cigarette.

"I'll eat his, Mommy," Jerami said.

"OK. Eat and finish getting ready. I'll be back. I'm going to see Mrs. Tracy outside."

"OK, Mommy."

After dealing with my kids, I *really* needed that cigarette. I called Tracy for our usual daily cigarette ritual, but the call went straight to voicemail. I went outside and leaned against the railing in front of my building. With my lit cigarette in my left hand, I checked my watch on my right. Tracy wasn't here. I wasn't mad. Knowing her, she probably worked late last night.

I walked back upstairs, zipped up Jerami's jacket, and put his hat on his bald head. Then I walked to the boys' room and saw Jalen putting on his shoes.

"We're leaving now, Sonshine. This day is hard for all of us, but try to have a good day, and don't be late for school."

"Yeah, yeah, bye," he said.

Jerami and I walked past the grocery store where Mo was killed, and I couldn't stop the flood of memories and emotions that hit me every time I saw the spot where his body was. It was painful to pass every day, and it never got easier. Being the anniversary of Mo's death and the nightmare, I had only magnified my sadness. Financially, I'm far from being in a position to move anytime soon, so, unfortunately, I had to pass by this reminder often and grin and bear it.

"Mommy," Jerami said.

"Yes, baby?"

"Can you tell me more about Dad?"

I sighed.

Passing the grocery store already had me emotional. Jerami asking me to tell him more about his father would put me over the edge, and I hadn't even made it to work yet.

"You've heard these stories a million times. I've told you everything there is to know about him."

"I know, but hearing them helps me remember him, and I feel like he's still here."

That broke my heart. I couldn't say no after that, and I felt like an asshole for not wanting to talk about Mo when Jerami asked.

"Sure, baby."

I took a deep breath before saying, "Your dad was my everything. He was my best friend, my protector. He treated me like a queen and loved me, flaws and all, and he loved you and your brother so much."

"Am I like Dad?"

"Of course, baby."

"How?"

"The way you're so brave with handling your cancer and the way you go to school after getting your treatment, even if you're not feeling well, that's exactly how your dad was. He was always brave and made sure we were safe. He never panicked whenever there was a problem. Even when he didn't feel well, he always went to work to provide for us."

Jerami smiled.

Everything I said was true. Reminiscing about Mo made me miss him and reminded me of how my life has been on a downward spiral since he passed. When Mo died, a big part of me died with him. I felt lonely and like I'd never be whole again. I was at a point where I hated seeing happy couples with their kids in public because I knew I'd never have that again.

After Jerami's treatment, we walked to his elementary school, P.S.111. I signed him up for the before and after-school care programs during the summer. This allowed me to drop him off in the mornings before work. I knew Carina's lazy ass wouldn't wake up early to bring him on time, and the after-school care was late enough that if Carina flaked out and didn't pick him up like she did all of last year, I could leave work and get him myself.

The best part of bringing Jerami to school early was the free breakfast the school provided. Times when I'm running late, it's a godsend, plus between hospital deductibles, co-pays, and transportation costs going to and from the hospital for Jerami and me, those expenses cost a grip. At this point in my life, I appreciated anything that could save me a few bucks.

"Bye, baby. Have a good day," I said.

"Bye, Mom."

After dropping Jerami off at school, I put some pep in my step and went to the train station on Twenty-First Street. I made it onto the train right before the doors closed. I was making good time and figured I'd be at least forty-five minutes early, but the conductor announced that a man jumped in front of a train ahead of us, so we were being held in the tunnel. Fucking great!

Instead of getting to work early, I ended up getting to the firm fifteen minutes late. I slid in, hoping to go unnoticed, when Meghan immediately blew up my spot. Smacking on her gum, she lowered the phone, put her hand over the receiver, and shouted, "It's nice of you to join us, Mrs. Wilson." She laughed and went back to her phone call.

The phones for the firm were ringing off the hook. Julissa and Francisco were handling the phones while Meghan was busy laughing and gossiping on a personal phone call.

"Is that a firm-related phone call?" I asked.

She rolled her eyes and said, "Personal."

"You need to keep your personal calls to a minimum. As a matter of fact, tell whoever you're talking to that you have to go; you're at work. The phones here are ringing off the hook, and everyone else is working *but* you."

Meghan cut her eyes at me and said, "That's funny coming from our 'boss' who's late."

Francisco and Julissa exchanged shocked glances.

"You're still new here, so I'm going to let you slide this one time, but let's get one thing straight. I don't report to you; *you* report to *me*. You're still on probation, so I suggest you do what I tell you to, and don't piss me off."

She mumbled something under her breath.

"Do you have something to say?" I asked.

"No."

"Good."

Incoming calls were coming nonstop. But instead of helping, Meghan took out nail polish from her purse and started painting her nails.

"Are you kidding me? Stop doing your nails and pick up a phone."

She slammed the nail polish down, blew on her nails, and carefully answered the phone. Then she covered the receiver and asked, "Happy . . . boss?"

"You're late, Juanita," Francis said. The bass in his voice made me jump where I stood.

Fuck! Just when I thought my morning couldn't get any worse, this asshole popped up.

Francis flicked his wrist and glanced at his gold Rolex.

Francisco and Julissa busied themselves with the stack of paper-work on the reception desk. Meghan had a shit-eating grin on her face as Francis scolded me.

"You're always late, Juanita," he said, tapping his watch.

My head was spinning, trying to come up with a decent response to calm him down.

"I'm sorry for this morning, but I'm not always late, sir. The trains were messed up and—"

"I don't want to hear excuses. I want you here on time. I don't care if you have to leave your house three hours early. I don't care if you have to sleep in your office. Get here on time, or you can start looking for other employment. Do we understand each other?"

"Yes, sir," I said.

I didn't bother to say anything else. I knew he wouldn't hesitate to write me up to impress Meghan if I said anything he deemed disrespectful.

"Good, get to work," he stated.

I nodded, avoiding eye contact with him.

He walked back to his office while Meghan sat at the reception desk, smirking. I already knew I was in for a shitty day.

"Make yourself familiar with these clients and their accounts. You'll be dealing with them often. They're the most important clients to the firm, so none of their cases are handled by junior associates. Instead, the partners handle these clients directly," I said to Meghan.

Since it was slow and Julissa and Francisco were on their lunch break, I figured I'd continue training Meghan, but she seemed to be half-listening and was more concerned with her manicure than learning what was necessary for her job.

"Juanita," Meghan said.

"Yes?"

"I know you've worked at this firm for a while now, and you're far more experienced than me, but did you even go to college?"

Is this heifer trying to be cute?

The look on my face must've shown that I didn't appreciate her question because she smirked when she said, "I know few Blacks do, and a lot has changed in our profession over the years ..."

I felt insulted by her statement about us "Blacks" and didn't appreciate what she was insinuating. I leaned back in my chair, trying my best to compose myself and not lose my temper.

"Is there something you want to ask me specifically?" I asked.

"I'm just wondering if I'm more qualified to have your position as an administrative manager than you. Do you have an education that qualifies you besides having experience?"

"Not that it's your place to question how I earned my position, but I have both an associate's and bachelor's degree in paralegal studies on top of my years of experience here. I read your résumé, and you only have an associate's degree. Last time I checked, my bachelor's degree trumps your associate's. Contrary to popular belief, there are *lots* of African Americans who have degrees."

She didn't look the least bit impressed by my response.

My late husband, Maurice and I knew to be taken seriously in my profession, I needed a college degree for validation. So, when Mo was alive, he watched the boys while I went to class at night. He didn't worry about buying things he wanted for himself. Instead, he busted his ass during the day, working overtime and working odd jobs around our neighborhood on weekends to help put me through school. Hunter College was expensive, and despite all he did, my student loan debt was still a lot, but Mo's hard work stopped my school debt from being astronomically high. That was Mo, though. He always put the kids and me ahead of himself.

"I wasn't trying to imply anything," Meghan said.

"How else was I supposed to interpret that?"

"How's she doing, Juanita?" Francis asked.

I jumped out of my damn skin. This was the second time today Francis crept up on me and saved her ass from hearing the full extent of my mouth.

"She's coming along," I said nonchalantly.

"Is Juanita explaining everything to you clearly?" he asked Meghan.

"Yes, she's a good teacher. I can't wait until my training's over so I can *really* help with things around here."

"In due time. Right now, just take things slow and soak in all the knowledge you can from Juanita."

"I will."

I wanted to fucking gag. Francis put up a front like he was only checking on her constantly to ensure she was adjusting to the firm smoothly, but by the way he looked at her, I knew he wanted to fuck her.

CHAPTER 10

BRING THE PAIN

"Where do you think you're running off to, pussy?" Akeem asked Bill.

We were walking past 40-15 Tenth Street after school. I was already in a lousy mood because today was my dad's death anniversary. Akeem, Draper, and I circled Bill. Draper had been asking Akeem nonstop to put him on with Drastic, so he was eager to show out to get on 'Keem's good side.

I ran in front of Bill. He tried to walk past me, but I blocked his path.

"C'mon, man, I just wanna go home. I don't want any trouble," Bill said, backpedaling. He gripped his backpack straps and looked like a cornered animal, swinging his bag to fight us off. I shoved him, and he stumbled backward. Then Draper pushed him back toward me, and I punched Bill as hard as I could. The blow landed square on his jaw and dropped him. Bill staggered to get up, but I dragged him back down to the pavement.

Akeem stood and watched while I mounted Bill, grabbed him by his straight, brown hair, and slammed his head onto the concrete.

Draper wanted to jump in, but Akeem waved him off. "Nah, fall back. Let J handle him," Akeem said.

Dazed, Bill squirmed, kicked, and fought to push me off with all his strength, but I pinned his arms to his side with my knees. Bill was helpless on his back, and I pummeled him, raining down blows, busting his nose, and splitting his lips until his blood covered my knuckles.

All the negative shit in my life that I had pent up inside me, my dad's death, my brother's cancer, my anger toward my moms, I let it all out on Bill. I didn't hate him, but I was so mad at the world that I wanted to hurt someone . . . anyone to let that anger out. Unfortunately, Bill was weak, so I preyed on him, and he felt my wrath.

"Stop!" Bill begged.

"Shut the fuck up," I said, ignoring his pleas, grabbing him by his hair, and banging his head on the pavement.

A housing authority worker came, grabbed me from behind, and snatched me up from the ground with my arms pinned to my side and my feet kicking. The name stitched on his uniform said, "Miles."

I was still squirming and cursing. Finally, I managed to give Bill one last kick to the rib cage while he groaned on the ground in pain.

"Calm down, young brotha. You're gonna kill him," Miles said.

"So? Fuck him and fuck you! Get the fuck off me."

"You don't need to ruin your life over something stupid. Leave that boy alone."

Bill crawled away, staggering as he pulled himself to his feet, and ran off, limping up the block and into our building.

Miles put me down, and I pulled away from him. Then Draper, Akeem, and I ran off. I didn't care if I hurt Bill. It felt good to get my anger out.

After kicking Bill's ass, we headed to the bodega and saw Drastic's Suburban parked on the corner of Forty-First Avenue and Tenth Street.

"Yo, there Drastic goes right there. Can you put me on?" Draper asked.

"Soon, man," Akeem said.

"Ain't no time like the present. All I need is the plug."

Akeem rolled his eyes and said, "All right, come on. I got you."

I didn't like Draper hanging around us. We were doing all right, selling weed and making drop-offs for Drastic by ourselves. I knew putting Draper on would ruin it, but 'Keem kept saying, "He's harmless. Don't worry about him."

Drastic had his window rolled down. We walked over, and Akeem introduced Draper to Drastic and Boogie. Draper was his usual stupid self, being cocky and touching all over Drastic's truck. He was acting way too familiar and asking dumb-ass questions.

Leaning into Drastic's open passenger window, he asked, "Yo, how much this shit cost you? You're rich, so why aren't you rocking a BMW around this bitch?"

"Look, I know you're 'Keem's boy and all, but I don't know you like that for you to be all up in my shit. So, little nigga, take a walk. 'Keem, J, both of y'all come here," Drastic ordered.

Draper's face fell, and he walked off while we stepped to Drastic's passenger-side window.

"Yo, 'Keem, what's up with your man? Who is this punk you bringing me?"

"That's Draper. He's cocky, but he's all right."

"I don't know about that cat. He just met me, and he's already too comfortable, like we've been boys for years and shit. I ain't about to have some kid come up in my ride, disrespecting me."

"I'll talk to him. He's stupid sometimes, but he's a decent enough dude, and he'd be loyal to you. Just think about letting him do a couple of drop-offs. That's all I'm askin'."

"If I put him on, it'd only be as a favor to you because you vouched for him." Then he faced Boogie Brown and asked, "What do you think, Boogs?"

"HHHHeee got a bbbbigg mouth, but he's a fresh face. The ccccops nnnnever seen him before, so it mmmmight work."

"That's true. A'ight, tell your boy to come here."

At first, things were working out. Draper was delivering packages and holding guns for Drastic, but as usual, Draper couldn't keep his fucking mouth shut and kept bragging about all the things he was doing. All this time, the cops hadn't caught on that dealers were using kids to carry the bulk of their shit, but word went around the projects quickly that Draper was blabbing all over the place on how drops were done. The cops started searching kids' book bags. A couple of the kids did time in juvie, and a bunch of corner boys got locked up and did bids in Rikers. The hood was hot, and Drastic automatically blamed Draper.

"I told y'all I didn't like that nigga. Shorty couldn't keep his fuckin' mouth shut, and a bunch of my soldiers got locked up because of him. Now, I can't make moves without O'Sullivan and the rest of these pigs being all over my people. I got to be incognito for a minute, so I can't have y'all doin' shit for me until this shit cools down. Y'all can thank your boy Draper for that and tell him he ain't ever doin' work for me again."

I wanted to kick Draper's ass for affecting my money, but Akeem calmed me down and kept the peace. I just hoped we weren't cut off for too long. I liked having money in my pocket and didn't want to return to how things were without it.

CHAPTER 11

SO MANY TEARS

I woke up feeling queasy and immediately dashed to the bathroom and stumbled in front of the toilet to puke my brains out. I was hunched over the toilet, and my head was spinning. I staggered back to my bed and quickly rushed back to the bathroom to throw up again.

Shit! I couldn't keep running myself ragged the way I was doing. My body was giving out on me. I couldn't afford to be sick, and there was no way I could take a sick day, I thought. On top of everything, it was my time of the month, so that only made matters worse.

I knocked on Carina's door, but there was no answer. I knocked again, and when I got tired of waiting, I walked inside. The room was pitch black. Carina had all the shades pulled down. She was resting peacefully while I felt like hell. I flicked on the light.

"Girl, wake up. I know you heard me knocking," I said.

Carina sucked her teeth. "What? Turn off that damn light," she groaned.

"I need your help with the boys this morning. I'm not feeling well."

"Sounds like a personal problem. Neither am I."

Carina snuggled under her sheets and said, "I'm still tipsy and tired from last night. I got in late this morning. I'm not in any condition or mood to babysit."

I yanked the covers off her.

"Come on!" Carina whined.

"You're always fucking tipsy. I need your help, and you're blowing me off because your do-nothing ass came home late from hoeing around."

Carina reached for the sheets and pulled them back onto her. "Now, I'm *definitely* not doing shit."

"I'm telling you I'm sick, and you're just gonna lay up in bed all day?"

"Yup."

"I'm getting real tired of your shit, Carina."

"Yeah, yeah. Turn off that light and close my door."

I couldn't afford to waste more time and risk being late for work. I stormed out of the room without doing either. I heard her huff and puff and slammed the door behind me. I didn't wake up early enough to drop Jerami off for the free breakfast at school, so I walked to the kitchen and worked on making breakfast for the boys and me.

"Boys, come eat," I yelled.

They ran to the table.

I didn't feel like hearing Jalen's mouth or dealing with his attitude, so I made eggs for Jerami and dropped a bowl of cornflakes in front of him. I was too nauseous to eat. I rubbed my temples. When I looked up, of course, Jalen made a face.

"What is it now, Sonshine?" I asked.

"Why did you give me cold cereal?"

"I'm tired of you complaining about me making you eggs, so you can eat cereal instead. Is there a problem with that now, too?"

Jalen sighed. "Nah."

Once the kids were set up with their food, I grabbed my purse to go outside.

"I'm going to get some fresh air. You and your brother finish getting ready."

They nodded.

As I walked down the staircase, the rank smell of piss made me gag and amplified my queasiness. I walked out, leaned against the building, took a deep breath, and tapped the filter of my cigarette on the fence. I called Tracy.

"Morning, Queen. I'll be there in two minutes."

"All right, cool."

I ended the call and saw Tracy heading toward our building. I took out my pack of cigarettes and offered her one. She stood next to me, nodded, and quickly took one.

"Long night in the ER?" I asked.

"Yup. It was the night from hell. You all right?"

"Nope. I'm sick, and on top of everything, I'm on my period."

"Uh, that sucks. You going to work today?"

"I can't miss time from work when I can help it, so I'm going to have to suck it up and deal with it as always."

"I hear that. You got a light? I left my damn lighter at work," Tracy said.

"I think I have one in my purse. Let me check."

Digging in my purse, I couldn't find my damn lighter. Then finally, our building door opened, and the white woman, Debbie, who had interrupted our morning ritual once before, walked out. All I wanted was to enjoy my morning cigarette with Tracy, but this chick had to stand next to me and ruin that.

"Good morning," she said, smiling at us.

I ignored her and kept looking for my lighter.

"Do you need a light? Hold on. I got you," Debbie said.

She reached into her pocket and handed me a small BIC lighter.

Tracy and I lit our cigarettes and tossed it back to her.

I took a long, slow drag on my cigarette and exhaled a thick cloud of smoke in her face. She coughed and fanned away the vapor.

I laughed. "I don't get you, white girl. You don't even smoke. Why are you so fixated on talking to us?" I asked.

"I see the closeness you two have, and I want to be a part of that. I watch you two go to work daily without help, and I respect and can relate to that."

I had to give her credit. She got cool points from me for playing on our vanity.

"I don't feel like having small talk with you, so what do you want, white girl?" I asked.

"My name is Debbie . . . I know you can't be around your kids 24/7, but can you please try to convince them to stop beating on my son?"

I sighed. "Uh, is that still going on?" I asked.

Tracy shook her head. "I can't speak for Juanita, but I'll see what I can do."

"I'll talk to Jalen again. I heard the boys talking, and Akeem thinks Bill has a crush on Ebony. He's very protective of his sister."

"Being protective of his sister is understandable, but every day, Billy comes home bloody and bruised from being viciously beaten by Akeem and Jalen, and it's becoming a big problem."

"I *said* I'll see what I can do," Tracy snapped.

"I'm not trying to come off as a pest or a bitch, but put yourselves in my position. I'm only trying to protect my son."

I gave Debbie the side-eye. "What's your story, white girl? What are you doing living here in Queensbridge?" I asked.

"What do you mean?"

"As you can clearly see, there aren't any whites around here. Everybody in this neighborhood is a person of color going through some shit. Personally, my husband was killed, my son has cancer, and I'm struggling to take care of my two kids. Not to put my girl's business in the street, but Tracy is going through a similar struggle to mine. What's *your* story? You must have some drama if it has you living around here."

"Ummm . . ." she stammered.

"Is it drugs? Wait! Your last name is O'Neil, right? You're Irish, right? I'll bet money on it. It's alcohol. You drink a lot, right?" Tracy asked.

Tracy and I chuckled.

"Nope, I'm not a drinker. I'm just a single mom trying to survive, keep my head above water, and raise my son to be a decent man, just like the two of you. My husband left when I was pregnant with my son, Billy, and I have no help from him at all. I got diagnosed with multiple sclerosis, which caused me to always be in and out of the hospital, so it's hard for me to keep a job. Lately, my MS has been OK, but with my limited funds, Queensbridge was the only available area I could afford."

I saw the pain behind her eyes, and while I hated to admit it, Debbie had more in common with me than I initially thought. Her story mirrored many of the single mothers in this community. She was just a poor woman, struggling to make ends meet like me, Tracy, and many other single mothers, but what made me feel for her was she was sick. Being a broke, sick, single mother had to be hard. I couldn't imagine doing everything I had to and being sick on top of it all. I decided I'd cut her some slack from then on.

Based on Meghan's slick comments and most of my interactions with her, my defenses were up. I suspected she was looking to steal my position from under me. I realized I was right when I walked to Francis's office to take notes.

My stomach was churning, and I had to will myself not to puke with every step I took when I approached his door. As I got closer, I heard Meghan say my name from inside his office. The door was cracked, and I stopped and listened. When I realized she was talking shit about me, I pushed the door open a little more and stood in the doorway unnoticed with my hand on my hip.

Meghan made her way around Francis's desk and sat on the corner with her legs open and her cleavage spilling out in front of his face. I listened as she continued. I couldn't believe the nerve of this heifer.

"Can I be blunt with you, Mr. Lincoln?" Meghan asked, staring seductively into his eyes.

"Of course. You can say anything you want to me."

"I don't mean to overstep."

"Don't worry about that; speak your mind."

"I'm not trying to come across as a bitch, but Juanita's clothes are a little ratty and outdated."

Francis chuckled as she smiled and continued.

"I mean, come on, you have to admit, she's an eyesore when you first step in here. Seriously, image is everything when it comes to our clients, and I'm not sure having Juanita wearing her raggedy clothes as the first person the clients see is a good representation of this firm. I get it. She's been here a long time, she's very knowledgeable, and she works hard, but if you don't mind me saying so—"

"I don't mind," Francis said, eyeing her up and down.

Meghan smiled. "I think I'm a good example of what the clients should see when they first walk through those firm doors."

I looked down at my clothes. They weren't brand-name, made by famous designers, or fashionable, but they were clean, pressed, and acceptable business attire that I kept in decent condition for the most part. Unfortunately, they were all I had in my closet, and with my limited funds, I couldn't afford to buy anything new.

I stared at this heifer, bad-mouthing me. I thought we at least had some sort of mutual respect, but she was out to replace me. I pushed the half-cracked door open and dropped my tape recorder on the floor, purposely to make my presence known.

They jumped and quickly corrected themselves.

"You told me to stop by at this time, sir. I'm here to take notes for you."

"Oh . . . yes . . . That's right."

Meghan walked past me with a smirk on her face, as if she didn't give a shit that I heard her.

"Bitch!" I mumbled under my breath, not caring if she heard me.

Francis looked me over and shook his head.

I took the notes for him, then walked back to the front desk.

"Where's Meghan?" I asked.

"She's on her fifteen-minute break, which is now going on forty-five minutes," Francisco said.

Julissa shook her head.

"So, what I've always suspected was confirmed today. Meghan has it out for me."

"What happened?" Julissa asked.

I told them everything that went down in Francis's office.

"What are you going to do?" Julissa said.

"Right now, I just have to keep my eyes open. I've seen firsthand that she's worked on Francis. If she got to him, I know she's also working on the other partners and influencing them. Her being a pretty white woman, I already know they'll side with her before listening to me."

"We're in your corner, boss lady," Francisco said.

"Yeah, we got your back," Julissa added.

I thanked them and tried to figure out what my next move was.

"Boss lady, you have a call on line three," Francisco said over the intercom.

I was in my office finishing up my work for today.

"Wayne, Rothstein, and Lincoln. This is Juanita Wilson speaking. How can I help you?"

"Good afternoon, Mrs. Wilson. This is Mrs. Green from P.S. 111."

"Hey . . . Let me guess, Carina didn't pick up Jerami."

"Yup, that's it. Will you be able to be here within the hour?"

"I'll be there."

"Thank you. See you soon."

I was too through with my fucking sister. I know she pulled this stunt out of spite because of our spat in the morning. As soon as I saw her, I was going to curse her ass out. I finished my work for the day, logged out of my computer, and picked Jerami up from school.

My head was pounding. I felt achy and lightheaded as I held his hand and ran with him toward the Q66 bus to Steinway Street.

"Mom, where are we going?" Jerami asked.

"I have to get a couple of things for my job."

He sighed. "But, Mom, I'm tired."

"We won't be long."

All the traveling back and forth to hospitals, work, and unexpected trips was killing my pockets, but I had to at least attempt to resist the partners from demoting me and handing Meghan my job. I thought about possibly wearing some of my sister's outfits, but her clothes were too skanky and were nowhere near respectable or business appropriate. I couldn't afford to go to a regular department store and buy designer clothes, so I went to Steinway Thrift Shop.

For the umpteenth time, I half-listened to Jerami talking my ear off, going on and on about action figures and other toys he wanted for Christmas, which would be here before I knew it, while I sorted through the racks of blouses and skirts. I tried my best to piece together decent outfits that still had the tags on them and were never worn, or at least were in better condition than the ones I currently wore. Unfortunately, I didn't have the money to buy these clothes, but I used my already extremely maxed-out credit cards to buy them.

Then I cooked dinner, helped the boys with their homework, and made sure they went to bed on time so I didn't have to fight with them to wake up for school in the morning. After that, I waited for Carina to come home, so I could curse her ass out for not picking up Jerami this afternoon, but it was getting late, and she still wasn't home.

I spent most of the night tossing and turning. Instead, I lay awake staring up at the ceiling, stressed that I now had to watch my back at work since Meghan was after my job and upset that buying those clothes today put me further in debt.

Soon, I heard the low murmur of voices behind my front door. Finally, the latches unlocked, and the front door slowly opened.

I kept my eyes closed and pretended to be asleep. Then I squinted and saw Carina creeping inside the house with some random man. Carina wore a skanky black, low-cut dress that barely covered her ass. She and her late-night visitor were giggling and staggering, clearly drunk from their activities.

"Yo, who's that?" the man asked.

"Keep your voice down; that's my sister."

"Does she want to get down with us?"

"Don't play yourself. I'm not having a three-way with my sister... But bring another girl, and it's on."

They snickered, went inside her bedroom, and locked the door.

I heard the bed squeaking, followed by Carina moaning loudly.

God, I hope they don't wake my kids.

I covered my head with my pillow, trying my hardest to drown out the moans, but it was useless. I closed my eyes and tried to force myself to sleep. I'd have to tell her off another time.

I walked into the firm, put my purse down at the front desk, and entered Francis's office. I placed his coffee on his desk and jumped when he and Meghan walked into his office, laughing.

"What are you doing here?" he asked.

"I brought you your morning coffee, sir."

"Oh . . . yeah. I came in early to . . . work on some things, and Meghan and I already got some. So, you can have it."

". . . Thanks."

I grabbed his coffee and left his office. He continued his conversation with Meghan and closed the door behind me. I dropped the bastard's coffee in the trash.

Francis and Meghan tried to be slick, but the subtle way she brushed against him when they were in elevators, the lustful way she looked at him and licked her lips when she passed him in the halls, and just their body language whenever they saw each other, I knew they were fucking. When they thought I wasn't looking, I'd see them out of the corner of my eyes being all touchy-feely and smiling in each other's faces. I could already see that a big problem was brewing.

A direct page went straight to the phone Meghan was sitting at. She picked it up and smiled.

"I'll be right there, Mr. Lincoln!"

She immediately grabbed a legal pad and a pen, I'm sure just for appearance, sprang up from her chair, and slipped into his office.

Ten minutes passed. Francis specifically told me earlier to be in his office at 1:00 p.m. and not even think about being a second later to take notes for him. So I went to his office, pushed open his door, and saw him holding Meghan's ass and sucking on her neck.

I cleared my throat, and they jumped.

"You really need to knock, Juanita. I was just whispering something to Meghan," Francis said.

"Sir, you told me this morning to be here at this time and not a second later."

"Uh, it's OK. I'm grooming Meghan to take over that responsibility from you."

Meghan sat down in the chair across from Francis. She crossed her legs. Her boobs were spilling out from her half-unbuttoned sheer blouse. She looked up at him and seductively licked her lips as she held her notepad and pen, ready to scribble notes.

"I'm ready, Mr. Lincoln," she said.

Francis smiled at her like he was about to fuck her as soon as I stepped out of his office.

"All right, Juanita, you can go. I have a lot more that I need to tell Meghan. Hold my calls for at least half an hour."

I headed to my office, and Julissa stopped me as I passed the reception desk.

"Where's Meghan?" she asked.

"She's in Mr. Lincoln's office taking notes."

"I thought that's what he wanted you to do."

"She's in there now, and apparently, he's grooming her to handle that responsibility. I'm sure she's taking all of his dick-tation," I joked.

We laughed.

The phone rang, and Julissa picked it up.

"Please hold."

She paged Francis. "Excuse me, Mr. Lincoln, you have a call on line two," she said.

Francis stuck his head out of his office and said, "Juanita, I just told you to hold all my calls. Take a message. Tell whoever it is I'm busy, and I'll call them back."

"It's your wife, sir," Julissa said.

He sighed. "Give me two minutes, then send her through."

"You got it, sir."

Meghan scurried out of his office, slid back behind the reception desk, and wiped her mouth as she sat down. Julissa, Francisco, and I couldn't stop laughing.

Finally, Meghan's training was finished, and I was cautious about what I said and did around her. I didn't want her to have ammunition to use against me to steal my job.

On top of being a total bitch, Meghan was a terrible paralegal and secretary. On most days, I had to work through my lunch break and stay later for overtime correcting or doing the shit that incompetent bitch forgot to do.

Whenever I'd tell the partners about her mistakes, they'd shake their heads and tell me I had to handle that with Francis.

When I talked to him about her, he was no help, and somehow this heifer convinced him that it was *my* fault she wasn't getting her work done.

I busted my ass at this firm for thirteen solid years, working hard, getting two degrees to master my craft, and move up in the ranks to earn my position. This bitch comes in shaking her tits in Francis's face, and everything I've done seemed to be forgotten and overlooked. I felt over-worked and unappreciated.

There was definitely preferential treatment for Meghan over me, and I started noticing that lately, Francis was only having me work late. But at the same time, he let Meghan leave early every damn night. It didn't matter that before my son was diagnosed, I never took a sick day or came in late. Francis must've forgotten that Meghan was under me, and I was her supervisor. Of course, I had more education and experience than she did, but the truth was she had the complexion for his protection, and when it came to me, none of the shit I did mattered.

CHAPTER 12

GIMME THE LOOT

It had been three weeks since me and Akeem put in work for Drastic, and we both needed money badly. We spent most of our free time playing basketball outside when the weather wasn't shitty and playing video games and board games with Jerami when it was, since his treatments had been draining his energy lately.

With Mom always working and Auntie always out and about with her boyfriends, I was always stuck watching him.

I lucked out on this particular day since Auntie decided to stay home with Jerami, so I could hit up the courts with Akeem. We were quiet while we shot around. Akeem looked lost in his own thoughts. My mind was on my dad and how we shot on these hoops when he was alive.

Drastic and Boogie Brown pulled up and walked to us.

"Yo, let me holla at y'all real quick," Drastic said.

"You got any work for us?" Akeem asked.

Drastic smiled. "Why? Y'all tryin' to get on?"

"Hell yeah," I said.

"A'ight. Cool. Shit with the cops died down somewhat, so I'll put y'all on. I still want y'all selling weed for me, but now, I want y'all to boost shit for me too. I mostly want wallets, credit cards, jewelry, and shit like that, but hit up stores, too. Take clothes, video games, and if you find anything that looks worth something and you think I can have niggas hustling it on the street, I want that too. Y'all can keep some of the cash you get, but kick half of it up to me. Y'all down with that?"

I knew what he asked could get us in serious trouble, but I was down for damn near anything if it meant having money in my pockets again.

Akeem and I looked at each other and nodded. "Yeah, we can do that," Akeem said.

"Good. I'll meet up with y'all on the courts every other day. Have my shit and break me off with my cut of the cash y'all bring in. The cops are still watching everything, so remember this, if y'all get knocked, that's on y'all. Keep my name out of your mouths because if the cops come around here looking to charge me for some shit y'all did, that's both of your asses. Y'all understand?"

"Yeah," we said in unison.

I smiled, happy that we were back on again.

"Stop those boys!" a woman yelled.

Akeem and I bolted down Steinway Street while the two women whose purses we snatched chased after us. We dodged through people and traffic and lost them at the train station on Thirty-Fourth Avenue. Finally, we caught our breaths and looked through the purses, dumping whatever we deemed junk in the trash can on the sidewalk.

The whole week, we skipped school and spent all day and afternoons ripping and running. First, Drastic had Rasheed and Shyne teach Akeem and me how to pick pockets and lift purses. Then, when women were busy chatting it up with their friends, not paying attention, we snatched their bracelets, chains, and purses.

We boosted radios from cars whose owners were dumb enough to leave them inside when they parked and lots of clothes from stores. We were becoming notorious around Steinway Street, but even with an increased police presence, that didn't stop us.

Even with our kickbacks to Drastic, we were bringing in decent money. Akeem used his to buy clothes and sneakers for himself, but he made sure to give cash to Ebony for clothes, shoes, and extra to get her hair and nails done.

When his mom was asleep after work, he'd sneak into her room and put money into her wallet. I didn't do shit for my mom, but I bought candy and action figures for my bro to cheer him up, since he was always cooped up inside the apartment.

We slowed down and thought we were in the clear . . . until a cop car swerved in front of us. I saw the women chasing us in his car's backseat, pointing.

"Shit! Let's get the fuck outta here," Akeem said.

Two white cops jumped out and chased us. They were both tall, in decent shape, and were closing in on our asses.

Akeem was faster than me. He was further down the block and didn't see me when I tripped on a divot on a street grate. I stumbled getting up, and those few seconds it took me to get my balance allowed the cops to catch up to me. One of them grabbed my arm. I tried to shake out of his grip, but he was too strong.

Akeem turned around, saw I got caught, and ran back toward me. The cop's partner cuffed him. Then they opened the door, letting the women we stole from out, and stuffed us into the back of their patrol car.

I shook my head. "Yo 'Keem, you were in the clear, man. That cop couldn't catch you. Why'd you come back?" I asked.

"We went into this together. I wasn't gonna let you take the fall by yourself. If you go down, *we* go down together."

Akeem was a true friend. I didn't know anyone else that would've done that for me.

The cops dragged us into the precinct and brought us in front of the desk sergeant. He was a middle-aged white man whose nameplate under his shield read Sergeant Hansen.

"Rembert. Washington. Whatcha got there?" Sergeant Hansen asked the cop holding me.

Rembert, the one holding me, said, "We were driving around our sector when two women flagged us down. We did a canvass, and the women identified these two as the perps that snatched their purses on Steinway Street."

"All right, search them and toss them in the juvenile room," the sergeant said.

Washington patted us down and found twenty dime bags of weed on us.

"Looky what we got here. Not only are these punks snatching purses, but we got ourselves a couple of baby dealers," he said.

Akeem and I rolled our eyes and sucked our teeth once we spotted O'Sullivan walking past the desk. He stopped when he saw us, smiled, looked at the sergeant, and said, "Boss, if you don't mind, I'll take these two arrests off Rembert and Washington's hands. These punks are from the Queensbridge Projects. I see them around that drug dealer, Drastic, all the time. Since that's my sector, this'll give me a chance to talk to their parents and try to pry some information out of them about Drastic."

The officers holding us looked at Sergeant Hansen with pleading eyes, as if they wanted no part in dealing with us all afternoon.

"All right, but don't question them until their guardians are present," Sergeant Hansen said.

"Roger that," O'Sullivan replied.

Rembert and Washington looked relieved to be handing us off to O'Sullivan.

O'Sullivan faced us. "Come with me, mutts," he said. He grabbed us and shoved us onto a bench in the juvenile room. Then he opened one cuff for each of us and attached the ends to a metal pole behind the bench.

Afterward, he sat at a desk beside the bench and turned on a computer. He looked at Akeem and asked, "So, did Drastic put you two up to this?"

We stayed quiet.

O'Sullivan smacked the top of the desk hard. "Fucking speak when spoken to."

"I thought your boss said not to ask us any questions until our parents were here," Akeem replied.

"All right, smart-ass. Guess whose mother I'm calling last?" He laughed to himself.

"You know you two aren't the only nigglets he suckers into stealing for him, right? He uses lots of you little gullible idiots to do his dirty work."

Akeem and I continued to keep our mouths shut.

"I just told both of you an important fact to help you make smarter life decisions and nothing, huh?" O'Sullivan shook his head at us like we were lost causes.

"This is why prisons are filled with people that look just like you two. Your kind will never smarten up and know how to save yourselves."

O'Sullivan started doing our arrest paperwork. First, he asked for basic information like our names and birthdays and the numbers to reach our mothers.

"What's your phone number, Jalen?" O'Sullivan asked.

I told him the number, knowing damn well my house phone had been cut off for months. O'Sullivan called it and quickly hung up.

"Why would you give me that number if you knew it was disconnected?"

"You just asked for the number. You didn't ask if it worked."

"If both of you keep playing stupid, I won't release you to your mothers. Instead, I'll send your dumbasses to Spofford, where you can spend the night fighting with the rest of the little savages."

Spofford Juvenile Detention Center was on Hunts Point in the Bronx and was a youth jail for kids caught up with the law. I heard horror stories from kids around the neighborhood who'd been there. It had a reputation for kids being beaten up and robbed when left there for a while.

I unwillingly gave him my mother's name and work number. He called and put the phone on speaker.

"Wayne, Rothstein, and Lincoln. This is Francisco. How may I assist your call?"

"This is Officer O'Sullivan from the 114th Precinct. Can I speak to Mrs. Juanita Wilson? I'm calling regarding her son."

"Oh, please hold. I'll forward your call immediately."

I knew she'd come to the precinct and try to play the concerned parent routine, but I didn't want to hear her bullshit lecturing, especially in front of this cop. It was gonna be a long night.

CHAPTER 13

RAINY DAYZ

I didn't want to fall behind, so I stayed in my office and worked straight through lunch. I couldn't tell if my headache came from hunger or all the tension and stress I'd been going through. I took bites of my peanut butter and jelly sandwich in between calls. Francisco paged me on the intercom and said, "Boss lady, you have a call on line two from the police . . . It's about your oldest son. It sounds serious."

I sighed. "Thanks. I'll take it in here."

I closed my door and picked up the call.

"Wayne, Rothstein, and Lincoln. This is Juanita speaking. How can I help you?"

"Good afternoon, ma'am. This is Officer O'Sullivan from the 114th Precinct. I'm sorry to contact you like this, but your son, Jalen, was arrested."

"Oh my God. Is everything all right?"

"Well, yes and no . . . He's not hurt or anything like that."

My shoulders relaxed when Officer O'Sullivan told me Jalen was OK, but tensed up again as he went on.

"I've been trying to reach you, but your home phone was disconnected, and your son, Jalen, didn't want to give up your work number."

I was irritated that Jalen didn't give him my cell number to save me the embarrassment of having this cop call my job and even more embarrassed that the officer needed to mention that my house phone was disconnected.

"I'm sorry to rush you, but why was my son arrested?"

"Jalen was picked up for grand larceny," O'Sullivan said.

"Grand larceny?"

"Purse snatching, ma'am. Jalen and his friend, Akeem, were caught near Steinway Street with the victims' belongings and were identified by the two women at the scene. When they were searched, they both had numerous bags of marijuana on them. It's more than what would be seen as recreational use, so I suspect he and his friend are selling it."

"That's your assumption, but my son isn't a drug dealer."

"I get it. All parents want to believe their kids can do no wrong, but that isn't the case here. Those are his charges, and I have Jalen in custody. I need you to come down to the precinct so I can release him to you. If you can't come down, I'll have to lodge him at the Spofford Juvenile Detention Center in the Bronx."

Hell no! Spofford was like a mini-Rikers Island jail for kids. There was no way I'd want Jalen to go there.

"Can you put my son on the phone, please?"

"It's on speakerphone, ma'am. He can hear you."

"Do you mind taking it off speakerphone so I can talk to him privately?"

"He's in custody. When you come here to pick him up, you can talk to him privately at home."

I wasn't going to fight with this asshole.

"Put my son on, please."

I heard Jalen suck his teeth before he spoke. "Yeah, Ma."

"What the hell is wrong with you? I miss enough work taking care of your brother. I don't need to miss more work for your nonsense."

"I'm so sorry that you actually have to do something for me for a change."

"Don't start with that shit. You know I love you just as much as your brother. I'll see you when I get there. Let's hope I don't get in trouble with my job because of this."

I told Francis I had an emergency with my oldest son; as expected, he wasn't happy about it. He wouldn't let me go until I defined what the emergency was. I didn't want my son to sound like a stereotypical hoodlum, but he knew I wouldn't rush out for something simple. I couldn't go with the "He's sick" excuse because I would've said that from the jump if that was the case, and I know he was tired of hearing that because I used it all the time with Jerami. I just told him that there was a fight at school, and the principal wanted to see the parents of the kids.

After yelling at me for almost fifteen minutes and telling me how much better Meghan was than me, he allowed me to go.

I called Tracy and woke her up. "Hello . . ." she said groggily.

"You're not going to believe this. We have to go to 114th Precinct. Jalen and Akeem were arrested."

"Queen, are you serious right now?"

"I wouldn't joke about that."

"You sure Akeem was with Jalen? I didn't get any calls from any cops."

"I spoke with their arresting officer and everything. He specifically said Akeem was arrested with Jalen and told me they would lodge him at Spofford if I didn't come down to pick him up."

"I don't know what game these cops are trying to pull, but I'll meet you there."

Tracy was already inside the precinct when I got there, screaming at Officer O'Sullivan and letting him know she didn't appreciate her best friend having to tell her that her son was arrested before the cops did.

"Ma'am, I'm sorry about that. Unfortunately, I'm still processing Akeem's arrest, so you'll have to wait," O'Sullivan said.

Jalen was already processed and ready to be released.

"Don't wait up for me, Juanita. Deal with yours because I know for damn sure I'm gonna deal with mine," Tracy said.

"I hear you on that. I'll see you in the morning."

"Yup. I already need that cigarette."

"Later, Queen."

"Later."

O'Sullivan explained that Jalen had a court date scheduled for the next day. I had to be there for that, which meant I would be late for work.

Jalen and I walked out of the precinct, down Astoria Boulevard, to the subway to catch the N-train. Once we were a few blocks away from the precinct, I let him have it.

"Why the hell are you stealing purses off women, and why the hell did you have weed on you?" I asked.

"I needed money to buy things for myself. You never have any."

"I never have any because I'm too busy making sure you have a roof over your head and food in your damn stomach every day, but not once do I hear a thank-you."

"Ma, chill. It's not that serious."

"Not that serious? You're kidding me, right? I had to leave my job to get your unappreciative ass from the precinct. I'm already getting flak from my bosses that I leave work too much as it is, and you have the damn balls to tell me it's not that serious? I don't need this shit. Your father and I raised you to have enough decency and common sense not to steal from people. What's the matter with you?"

"Nothing's the matter with me. If you bought me stuff like you bought Jerami, I wouldn't have to steal."

"Oh, so now this is *my* fault? It's *my* fault that I pay all the bills and your brother is sick? I do what I can, Jalen. Explain why you had all those damn bags of weed on you."

"You want the truth or a lie?"

"Don't insult my intelligence, Sonshine. I better not hear that you're selling it. In fact, I don't want to know if you were. I just know that after today, you better not be doing it anymore."

Carina was supposed to make sure that Jalen wasn't hanging in the streets, yet here I was, picking him up from a police station. I just prayed the judge would have mercy on my hardheaded son.

CHAPTER 14

DROP A GEM ON 'EM

"You two, hurry up and finish sweeping that hair up. Then when y'all are done with that, take the garbage out and straighten up those haircare products on the shelves," Joe said.

Akeem and I groaned but did as he asked.

Two weeks passed since we got bagged by the cops. We had to go to the Queens County Family Court for our juvenile delinquency case. Mom tried to get sympathy from the Assistant Corporation Council by telling him that this was my first time being arrested and that I had decent grades at school. She poured it on thick to the council, telling them I didn't resist when arrested and that I was a good kid who missed his father and was acting out.

We lucked out. The Assistant Corporation Council agreed to probation for Akeem and me if we agreed to do ten hours of community service for the 114th Precinct. We had to clean up graffiti around the neighborhood and help out at the monthly community council meeting by putting out chairs and cleaning up when the meeting was over. We did what we had to do to get the courts off our backs but planned to return to doing the same shit we'd been doing.

Since we both told our moms that we only took the purses because we needed money, they arranged for us to help out Joe at the barbershop every day after school.

Joe was around six foot three and pretty jacked for an older man. He was respected around the hood and had street-cred because he was a big-time hustler back in the day. He got knocked by the cops and did a fifteen-year bid in prison. Once he got out, he decided to retire from the streets and become a legit businessman.

The barbershop was small, and Joe only had one other barber working there with him, Phil, but a lot of the old-timers around the neighborhood came there to get their cuts.

"This fucking sucks," I said under my breath, but unfortunately, Joe heard me.

He paused cutting the guy in his chair's hair, and said, "I know I don't hear you two complaining."

I sighed and opened the trash bag wider while Akeem dumped the dirt from the dustpan into it.

Joe pointed at me to Phil and said, "That one's momma said Drastic got these two knuckleheads snatching purses for him."

Phil shook his head and said, "And you're letting them help out here? You're a better man than me. I'd say fuck them."

Akeem and I both scowled at Phil.

Joe looked at us. "Does that make y'all feel tough? Robbing helpless women for their purses? How would y'all feel if someone did that to *your* mommas?"

Akeem and I stayed quiet.

"Oh, you were so chatty a minute ago. What happened now? I hit y'all with some real shit, and it got y'all thinking, huh?"

Akeem and I kept our mouths shut and kept sweeping.

"I spit knowledge for these youngsters, but they don't hear me, though. They don't get that I say this shit from experience. The actors might change, but what goes on in these streets is all the same, tired, rerun script to me."

I sucked my teeth and rolled my eyes. Joe stomped up to me and snatched the broom and dustpan from my hands.

"I gave up fifteen years of my life to these crackers, working for a nigga just like Drastic. When I was upstate, *nobody* gave a fuck about me. I was on my own. When I came home, I smartened up. I used a skill I learned on the inside to make something of myself, so I could break the cycle and not go back to selling dope and get myself locked up again. I'm trying to give y'all an opportunity to earn honest money."

"More like pennies," I said under my breath.

Joe got in my face and said, "By all means, youngster, if you don't appreciate what I'm giving you, you can take your ass out in the street,

hustle, and get locked up again. It ain't no sweat off my sack. I'm only looking out for you ungrateful bastards because both your mommas are good
women, but that's my word . . . Disrespect me in my business again, and
that nice shit'll go out the window, y'all understand?"

"Yes, sir," we said in unison.

Joe went back to cutting the guy's hair.

"You two are so dense that you don't even see when you're being
hustled. Do you ever see this cat, Drastic, on the corners, selling? Do you
see him snatching purses or doing any of the other dumb shit he has you
and all these other little niggas around here doing? No. Back in the day,
he used to be the idiot getting suckered into doing the shit he has y'all
doing. After doing a few stints in Spofford and getting his ass whooped,
he wised up and realized that if he keeps his hands clean and uses y'all
to do his dirt, he can make his money without getting locked up. As soon
as one of y'all gets arrested, he can always find more dumbasses like y'all
because you're expendable."

Joe finished cutting the guy's hair. The man paid him, gave him dap,
and said, "I know they're hardheaded, but keep schooling them. You'll get
through, eventually."

"I'll try. You know, though, you can lead a horse to water, but you can't
make it drink."

"I hear that."

They said their goodbyes, and the man left. Joe faced us, saying, "Your
savior, Drastic, isn't tough. He's just smart enough to figure out how to
play the game. You boys better smarten up quick."

After what felt like forever working at the shop, we went to 'Keem's apartment to chill out. I needed a haircut. Even Akeem's braids were frizzy at the
roots, but since Joe thought we were sassing him earlier, he wouldn't do
anything with our hair for free. Akeem saw me looking at his hair.

"Does my hair look that bad?" he asked.

"Not as bad as mine."

"No disrespect, J, but if it looks *half* as bad as yours, that's a problem."

We both laughed.

Akeem took out his braids while we watched TV and talked about our next move. Then Ebony walked in and said, "Ew, what's up with your hair?"

"I'm broke, and I don't have money to pay the lady that usually does it," Akeem said.

"Well, I can't do all the fancy styles she does, but at least let me braid your hair, so you look somewhat decent. I can't have my twin going outside looking tore up, rocking that played-out Afro."

Akeem nodded and sat on the floor between Ebony's legs as she greased his scalp, combed it, and braided his hair.

One thing was for sure . . . We needed to make fast money again and knew what we needed to do to get it.

"So, the bishop moves up and down on a diagonal," Akeem said.

We sat at the tables near the basketball courts by our building after school, and Akeem was teaching me how to play chess. When he wasn't playing ball or putting in work in the street, he was always reading something or playing chess. He showed me how all the different pieces moved, and the game made more sense to me the more we kept playing.

"Why do you like chess so much?" I asked.

"It keeps my mind sharp, and on top of that, it reminds me of life on the streets. In chess and on the street, you always gotta strategize and be a couple of moves ahead of the next man. You can't be a pussy, but you can't be too aggressive, either. You gotta think before you act because one bad move can be game over for you."

"That's exactly why I play this shit," Drastic said.

Neither Akeem nor I heard or saw Drastic and Boogie creep up on us.

"Y'all need to be more conscious of your surroundings. Getting caught slippin' can cost you your life or freedom," Drastic stated.

"Yeah, we know. What's up? You play?" Akeem asked.

"Now and then. I don't got that much time for the shit nowadays, but set 'em up. I'll play a game."

I got up so Drastic could sit and stood next to Boogie Brown.

"So, what's up with y'all? I heard y'all got pinched by the cops for lifting wallets."

"Yeah, we did, but we didn't say shit," I said.

"Oh, I know. O'Sullivan came by to fuck with Boogie and me and said y'all were like little soldiers. He was pissed that he couldn't get y'all to crack. I like that shit."

The way he looked at us with a nod and smile, I knew we had his respect.

"If you still got that work, we're ready to get back out there and get this money," Akeem said.

Drastic nodded. "That's what I like to hear."

Drastic's two lieutenants, Rasheed and Shyne, walked up to the tables and gave us all fist bumps. Rasheed was tall, skinny, and had neatly braided hair. He had a reputation for being a cool dude but had a slick mouth and was always snapping on somebody. Shyne was short but stocky and baldheaded. He had a reputation for being a cool dude too, but he was kinda dumb. Drastic always talked shit about him being stupid and making mistakes when it came to business in the street. Whenever we needed to re-up for weed, though, we got it from them.

"You play chess now?" Rasheed asked Drastic.

"This shit ain't nothin' new. I've always played. I like to keep niggas on their toes and leave them guessin' when it comes to what I know and do."

Akeem and Drastic played an intense game, but eventually, Drastic won.

"You're pretty good, shorty. Of course, you ain't on my level yet, but I know none of these young cats around here is touching you if you're challenging me like that," Drastic said.

"Yo, I got next," Rasheed said.

"Set 'em up, but this is my last one. I don't got time to be playing all day."

Rasheed set up the pieces. They were two minutes into their game, and Rasheed was already getting beaten badly. He was irritated and started talking shit to Boogie out of frustration.

"Yo, why you smiling, Boogie? Does your stuttering ass even know how to play?" Rasheed asked.

"Yyyyou dddon't wwwant nnnone of this. I'll bbbbeeeat yyyyou wwworse than Drastic is now."

"I don't know about that shit. But if you play like you talk, it'll be a long-ass game," Rasheed teased.

Everyone chuckled except Boogie.

"I'm gonna warn you now. Stop fuckin' with him. He don't like that shit. Keep fuckin' around; you're gonna be sorry," Drastic said with a smirk.

"He knows I'm just playin' with him. I got nothing but love for his stuttering ass."

Boogie looked noticeably pissed. "Ssssttop," he shouted.

"Ddddon't bbbbeeee so sensitive," Rasheed laughed.

Before Rasheed moved his next chess piece, Boogie lifted him from the bench he was sitting on, slammed him on the ground, and beat the shit out of him. Drastic didn't break it up. Instead, he sat there calm and collected while Rasheed got wailed on.

Drastic laughed and said, "I guess that's game. I told you not to fuck with him. Next time, come correct, and Boogie won't have to beat your ass."

Shyne, Akeem, and I tried our hardest to pry Boogie off him. When we finally did, Rasheed's face was all bloody, and he was writhing in pain on the ground.

Drastic stood over him.

"Clean yourself up, and when you're done, give my boys some more bud to push. They're ready to get back to work."

Drastic faced Shyne and said, "Don't just stand there, dopey. Help your boy up."

Shyne quickly helped Rasheed get off the ground.

I learned two things that afternoon. One, Akeem and I were back in business, and two, never tease Boogie about his stuttering problem.

"I guess you mutts will never learn," O'Sullivan laughed as he tossed Akeem and me into the back of his patrol car.

We got caught by the fucking security guards at Coconuts Music Store on Steinway Street. We walked around the store nonchalantly, planning on boosting tapes, CDs, and posters. We loaded our book bags with a good haul and were slowly making our way toward the door, not knowing that the store's loss prevention team was on to us. By the time we made it to the door, the security guards were all over us and blocked the doorway before we could run out of the store with the shit we had in our bags.

"This must be my lucky day. I was looking for overtime, and it looks like I just found it," O'Sullivan said to his partner, Officer McIvor.

"Last time we got bagged, you said this wasn't your sector. So why are you even here?" Akeem asked O'Sullivan.

"Officers Rembert and Washington are on vacation this week, so you're stuck with me."

Again, we were brought to the precinct, and again, O'Sullivan called our moms to come get us. This getting arrested shit was getting old.

CHAPTER 15

DOO-WOP

I was looking over files at my desk when Francisco paged my office phone. I picked it up.

"Boss lady," Francisco said.

"What's up?"

"You have a call on line one . . . It's the cops again."

"You gotta be fucking kidding me."

"I wish I was."

I sighed. "I'll take it in here. Thanks."

I blew out a heavy gust of air from my nostrils. I needed a moment to mentally prepare myself for the shit storm that was about to come.

Finally, I picked up the phone.

"Wayne, Rothstein, and Lincoln. This is Juanita speaking."

"Good afternoon, ma'am. This is Officer O'Sullivan from the 114th Precinct. I'm sorry to contact you like this again, but your son, Jalen, was arrested . . . again."

"What did he do this time, officer?"

"Well, on the bright side, he isn't snatching purses off women. No, this time, he was shoplifting from a record store."

He chuckled. I didn't find shit funny. He corrected himself and said, "I'm gonna need you to come down to the station again."

"I'll be there as soon as I can."

"Jalen was caught with his friend, Akeem, also. Oh, remember the last time your son and Akeem were picked up when you said that it was just my 'assumption' that they were drug dealers? Well, this time around, they had even more marijuana on them. I know you don't want to hear or believe it, but those boys are selling that weed, not just smoking it. Finding it on them today wasn't a coincidence or an assumption. This proves it's a fact."

"You're right about one thing."

"Oh, what's that?"

"I don't want to hear or believe your assumption. As I said before, my son isn't a drug dealer. I'll be there as soon as I can."

"Good. Before you come, can you contact Akeem's mother? I couldn't reach her and let her know her son is locked up again with yours. That would be a big help."

"Uh-huh."

"One more thing. Did you know that excessive truancy is against the law, and you, as a parent, can get fined and possibly arrested for educational neglect?"

"I wasn't aware of that."

"Yeah, I'm sure you weren't. Try keeping your non-drug-dealing son in school so he doesn't get you locked up with him."

I wanted to curse his ass out, but I didn't want him to take his anger out on Jalen. "I'm on my way."

I hung up, and once again, I had to ask Francis to leave early, and again, he gave me shit about it.

"Are you *kidding* me? You're either making an excuse for being late because there's a delay with the trains after dropping your youngest to school, or you leave early because your sister forgot to pick him up. Then, when it's not one of those excuses, I hear the excuse of taking your youngest to a doctor's appointment or having to take him to the hospital. Now, on top of all of that, your oldest is affecting your work?"

"Mr. Lincoln, I—"

Francis held up his hand like he had heard it all before.

"Save it. I don't want to hear excuses. We have a firm to run, and we can't do that with our administrative manager taking off every other minute for nonsense. If your life is too chaotic and you can't keep up with your responsibilities, apply for FMLA (Family Medical Leave Act) and take time off. Then I can put someone more competent in your position that'll be here when needed," Francis said.

"My family can't make it without my salary. I'm barely surviving on what I make as it is now. I need to work, but I can't control emergencies with my children, and when you say someone more competent, do you mean Meghan? You might not notice it, but all I do is pick up her slack."

"When you're here, you do work. I'll give you that, but with all the time you miss, you're like a part-time employee. So say what you want about Meghan, but at least she's here."

I couldn't fight with him. The only thing I could do was take the scolding and yes him to death, so he'd let me go to get my son. One thing was for sure . . . I couldn't keep missing work for Jalen's bullshit.

I met up with Tracy a block away from the precinct.

"Hey, Queen. I can't believe we're right back here at this damn precinct," I said.

"I know. I talked to this boy about this shit too many times. He knows I don't want him getting in trouble with the damn police. On top of that, he knows I have to work a double shift, and I need to get some type of sleep to function tonight. I don't need to be wasting my time on this nonsense."

We walked into the precinct and stood before the front desk.

"I see you fine ladies are back. Let me guess . . . Your sons got arrested again," Sgt. Hansen said.

Tracy and I rolled our eyes.

"No, we're here for our health. What do *you* think? We need to see Officer O'Sullivan," Tracy replied.

He smirked and pointed to an officer by the desk. "Harrison, escort these ladies to the juvenile room."

"10-4," Officer Harrison said.

As soon as we walked in, Tracy smacked Akeem on sight.

"Boy, you are your father's son. I told you about doing this hoodlum shit, and here we are again," she said.

Akeem stayed silent.

I walked up to Jalen and hugged him. Jalen squirmed at my touch and shrugged me off as if my showing him affection was a sin.

"Boy, I'm here worried about you, and *that's* how you're acting?"

Jalen shrugged and looked away.

"This is the second time I'm down at this damn police station because you got yourself arrested. I can't take this. It's bad enough I have to worry about your brother—"

"That's all you ever worry about. I'm surprised you even came down here at all," Jalen said.

"You need to cut out this jealous shit. I love you both equally. Your brother is sick. I give him more attention because of that, but it doesn't mean I don't love you just as much as I love him."

"You got a funny way of showing it."

"I'm here, aren't I?"

"Don't explain shit to him, Juanita," Tracy said.

I looked at her as she continued.

"Obviously, these two need to learn a lesson. We keep coming here and taking them home after they mess up, and *we're* the stupid ones. They keep testing how far they can push us without repercussions. Maybe it's time they spent a few nights at Spofford to give them a wake-up call."

I was hesitant about that. She was right, but I didn't know if I had the guts to follow through with that threat.

"Is that what you want?" I asked Jalen.

He shrugged. "You don't do anything for me, anyway. So how would this be any different?"

I winced at his words. I loved this boy with every breath in my body, but what he said shook me to my core. I felt like I was stabbed in the heart. I busted my ass at work every day to make sure he and his brother were fed, clothed, and sheltered, and *this* was the thanks I got? I swallowed the hurt.

"Oh, hell no, you're not gonna talk to your momma like that. Both you and Akeem need to learn that there are consequences for your actions," Tracy stated.

She faced me and said, "Let's go, Juanita."

"Mom, c'mon, you can't be serious right now," Akeem said.

"Ma'am, it's Friday. If you two leave, they're spending the weekend in Spofford," Officer O'Sullivan said.

"Good. They need a wake-up call. Maybe a weekend there will make them act right," Tracy answered.

I was still angry and hurt by Jalen's words. "You're right. They need to see what it feels like being locked up," I agreed.

"Come on, Ma, stop playing," Jalen said.

"Oh, I'm not playing. You said I don't do shit for you anyway, right? So maybe being there will teach you to appreciate me."

"Ma . . . Ma, come on, Ma."

I ignored Jalen calling for me and walked toward the door. I'd be lying if I said I didn't feel guilty for leaving him at the precinct and letting him spend the weekend in Spofford, but I knew it was for his own good.

"Are you sure this is what the two of you want?" Officer O'Sullivan asked.

"Absolutely," Tracy said.

"All right. I'll tell the desk officer, and you can meet your sons at family court Monday morning."

We nodded.

Officer O'Sullivan instructed us on what we needed to do for Monday.

"Ma, stop playing," Jalen said, sounding distressed.

Tracy turned to me and said, "You wanna order takeout and hang at your place tonight?"

"Ma!" Jalen yelled.

I ignored him and answered, "Sure, if you're buying, I have no problem hosting."

She laughed. "Cool. Let's go."

"Ma! Come on! Stop playing," Jalen shouted.

I left the precinct with him calling my name.

CHAPTER 16

SURVIVAL OF THE FITTEST

The shackles that chained Akeem's and my wrists and ankles to each other rattled with every bump on the Department of Corrections bus headed to the Spofford Juvenile Detention Center in the Bronx.

I acted like I wasn't scared of anything, but the truth was I was shitting bricks. I gradually looked around at all the other boys on the bus. It was filled with nothing but black and brown faces, and I wondered what they were going in for. I didn't want anybody to think I was a pussy and try to punk me, so I kept a mean mug on my face.

Akeem was staring out the window, looking like he had a lot on his mind. I know how that felt because all I wanted was to be home, watching my own TV, and not locked up with these guys in Spofford. I missed my little bro, and even though I'd never tell her to her face, I missed Ma, too.

"Do you think Drastic will still want his cut when we get out?" I asked.

"We don't need to worry about that right now. I know he ain't worried about us. Here, we're on our own, J. We all we got. We just gotta focus on making it through this weekend."

"Hey, hey. Shut up back there. I don't want to hear a peep from any of you little shits," one of the guards warned.

We rode the rest of the way in silence. Then, finally, the bus screeched to a stop. The double doors opened, and more guards came on and barked orders at us.

"All right, mutts, we're here. All y'all fall out now," one of the guards yelled.

We got off the bus in rows of two. The guards brought us to the main compound, where we were brought into the receiving corridor in a single file and processed for intake. Boys of different ages were pressed against the windows, watching our every move and sizing us up. I was scared, but I couldn't let it show. I kept quiet and made sure not to make eye contact with anyone, but I heard their chattering and tried to ignore it.

"Yo, look at those two chumps wearing Jordans," a stocky, dark-skinned kid said.

"I know I'm takin' those kicks off at least one of them." one short Hispanic kid affirmed.

"The kid with the braids looks like he's wearing my size, too. Dibs on his shit," another tall boy said.

"Once these guards are out of sight, it's a wrap for those two," a tall, muscular kid stated.

I knew this weekend was going to be far from fun.

Finally, it was dinnertime. Akeem and I kept to ourselves and found an empty table off to the side in the back corner of the crowded cafeteria, hoping we'd be left alone. Instead, a tall, brown-skinned dude with braids sat at our table. We didn't know if he was a friend or foe after hearing the other boys talking shit about robbing us, so we avoided eye contact with him and acted like he wasn't there.

"This y'all first time here, huh? What'd y'all do that got y'all in here?" the boy asked.

We didn't answer.

"That's good. Keep niggas guessin', but listen, I'm not trying to fuck with y'all, so y'all don't have to worry about that."

We still kept quiet. Neither of us trusted him, but he just kept talking.

"Most of the niggas in here have been here before, so we're used to certain faces, but nobody has ever seen y'all around. I'm Cory."

Akeem and I nodded and told our names.

"Akeem."

"Jalen."

"Lemme give y'all some advice. Most of these niggas are gonna test y'all tonight, so as soon as somebody steps up to you, knock their fuckin' head off. I'm gonna be honest wit' y'all. Everybody can tell y'all aren't built to be locked up in here. But, as I said before, we know all the usual faces, and people are going to question where y'all fit on the food chain," Cory said.

I quickly scanned the cafeteria and noticed all eyes were on us. Akeem noticed too, and said, "We're nobody's herbs, so you can put out the word that nobody is punkin' us."

Cory laughed. He stood up, and as he walked off, he said, "That's what's up! Keep that energy. Y'all gonna need that shit in here. Everybody is fiending over y'all sneakers. Just remember what I said to do when someone tries you in here. Lata!"

Cory wasn't kidding. Once we left the cafeteria, every second a guard wasn't looking, a different group of boys stepped up to us and attacked us. Akeem and I already knew, we had each other's back and didn't plan on losing any of our shit. Unfortunately, the other boys weren't so lucky. Some of them got chumped out of their kicks and even their food. Our first time seeing this was when we went to the dayroom.

When we walked in, we saw some kids sitting around watching TV, but a bunch of kids our age were standing around, chilling too. We found an empty spot on one of the walls and stayed to ourselves.

One of the new boys who arrived at Spofford with us was leaning against the wall alone. He was skinny, and just from his body language, being all fidgety and looking nervous, anyone could tell he was a pussy who would be an easy mark and wouldn't last here.

A six-foot-tall fat kid strolled into the room with three of his flunkies following behind him like a pack of hungry wolves. The fat kid pointed. Then he and his crew stepped to the skinny boy.

"Yo, take off your sneakers," the fat kid said.

"Come on, man. I don't want any trouble," the skinny boy said, trembling. The skinny boy dug into his jeans pockets, searching for something to give the fat kid instead. The fat kid laughed and sucker-punched him. While the boy lay on the floor dazed, the fat kid and his wolves riffled through his pockets and took off his sneakers, then their eyes scanned the room, looking for more easy targets. Finally, one of the wolves pointed at me and said, "Check out his kicks."

The fat kid's eyes narrowed in on me. He walked up, looking as if he was sizing me up. He pointed to my sneakers. "Yo! Run your kicks . . . Oh yes, and they're my size too! Yup! Come up out of those," he ordered.

I waved him off, looked away, and said, "I ain't got nothing for you. Go on with that bullshit and try that shit with someone else. You ain't punking me."

Akeem got off the wall and stood next to me. Then, out of the corner of my eye, I saw the fat kid grin and turn to his crew.

"Tough guy here thinks I'm asking," he said.

Then the fat kid stepped in front of me, grabbed me by the shirt, and pulled me close.

"I'm not asking you. I'm *telling* you, and I'm not gonna say it again. Give me all your shit before I *take* all your shit."

I shoved him off me and looked for the guards, but they were nowhere to be found. The fat kid noticed.

"Yeah, nobody is gonna help you here—"

"I'm not giving you shit," I said, interrupting him.

A crowd gathered around us to see what was going on. The fat kid poked me in my chest.

"This is the last time I'm gonna tell you. Come up out of them kicks and run your pockets."

Akeem's fist blew past me like a blur as he punched the fat kid in the nose. After that, it was a complete melee. Eventually, the guards broke up the fight, but that was only the first of many for us that weekend.

I don't know if the guards were oblivious or just didn't give a shit, but we took our cuts, bruises, and lumps fighting off the wolves. The entire weekend, we didn't sleep. It wasn't worth the risk of getting caught slippin' and having guys get the drop on us.

After being in that hellhole, Akeem and I decided that neither of us wanted to ever be in Spofford again. We were going to dead that stealing-for-Drastic shit. I worried about what the Assistant Corporation Council would say in court now that this was our second time getting bagged.

CHAPTER 17

LIFESTYLE OF THE RICH AND SHAMELESS

That night, Jerami, Tracy, and I lounged around in my living room. Tracy did me a solid, washed and permed my hair, and then treated us to pizza. We stuffed our faces while we watched TV. Carina was out on a date and had already told me not to wait up for her. Jerami was lying on the floor, drawing superheroes. Tracy was laughing at an episode of *Family Matters* that was on, but my mind was on Jalen. I didn't want to look soft in front of her, but I was having second thoughts about having him spend the weekend at Spofford.

Lately, Jalen has been nothing but disrespectful and a royal pain in my ass, but I felt that maybe I let his rudeness today make me too emotional, and I acted too hastily. I love him; he's my firstborn. He definitely needed the reality check, but I couldn't stop worrying about him. Was he eating? Was somebody hurting him? Could he die in there? I couldn't shake those questions out of my head, so I tried to distract myself by looking over case files on my laptop.

"Mom, what are you doing?" Jerami asked.

"Just some things for work."

"I thought you were off now."

"I am, but I had to bring some of my paperwork home since I had to leave work early because your brother got in trouble."

"Aww, man," Jerami pouted.

"What's wrong?" I asked.

He sighed. "I wanted you to draw something with me, but you're always busy working on stuff."

My eyes misted up. I know his comment was based on innocent observations of what's been going on, but it made me feel like a shitty mother. My oldest son felt like I didn't care about him enough and was acting out and getting in trouble with the law lately.

My youngest felt I was always working and didn't have time for him. Money was always tight, and I felt like I wasn't doing anything right in their eyes, like nothing I did was good enough.

I sighed, pushed my emotions aside, put down my laptop, and devoted my full attention to giving Jerami the quality time he deserved.

It was Saturday. I left Jerami with Carina while Tracy and I spent most of our morning sweeping every floor of our building. We were finishing up in the front, sweeping up the shards of broken glass from 40-ounce bottles, little drug baggies, guts from blunts, and crack vials on the ground. It bothered us that these things were out in the open as soon as our kids walked out the door. We fought with the other tenants to help us keep our building clean, but they didn't seem to give a shit if it looked dirty, dilapidated, and tagged up with graffiti. Despite that, Tracy and I picked up the slack. We lived in the projects, but that didn't mean we couldn't take pride in our neighborhood. We didn't want our building to be another stereotypical eyesore.

Kisha and Joyce, two of our building's bench dwellers, had to throw their negative two cents at us.

"These uppity bitches are always acting like they're better than everybody, cleaning up and shit like they're too good to be around this shit," Kisha said.

"I know that's right," Joyce added.

"Y'all uppity bitches live in the same ghetto as the rest of us, but think you're better than us," Kisha added.

"I ain't gonna be too many more bitches today. Keep calling me out my name, and both of y'all are gonna have a problem," Tracy warned.

I patted Tracy on the shoulder to calm her down while Kisha and Joyce rolled their eyes and sucked their teeth.

Those two were in their early thirties. Kisha was light-skinned, short, and frumpy. Her hair was always in curlers. Her crony, Joyce, was dark-skinned with a tall, thin, string bean-like figure. They spent most of their days sitting on the bench, talking shit about everyone who went to work daily. In their eyes, anybody who went to work daily was a "sucker, kissing the ass of the white man," as they often told Tracy and me.

Tracy and I kept sweeping while Kisha continued to talk shit.

"Look at them. They're always turning up their damn noses at everybody in this building just because they got themselves some decent-paying jobs. Both of their boujie asses need to realize that they live in the projects just like the rest of us, and they ain't better than nobody," Kisha threw in.

"Yup, they sweep up and think that shit makes a difference when it comes to keeping the riffraff out, but these snooty bitches can't see that their sons are the main culprits," Joyce smirked.

"Enough. Y'all are always running y'all fucking mouths, but do nothing but sit there on that bench. Instead of talking shit, why don't both of you get off your fat asses and find a fucking job?" I said.

"True. I guess I could sell weed or rob people like y'all's sons do, right? Nah, being in handcuffs isn't a good look for me," Kisha smirked.

That caught me off guard. If she knew about the boys getting arrested, that meant the whole neighborhood knew because they stayed talking shit.

"I don't know what you think you know, but our sons don't rob people, and they for damn sure aren't fucking drug dealers," Tracy said, stepping up to Kisha.

"Yeah, yeah, keep tellin' yourself that bullshit, but while y'all workin' y'all little jobs and think your delinquent bastards are saints, they be selling drugs, beatin' up kids, and robbin' people. Y'all can try to act oblivious to the shit, but the truth is, both of y'all sons are fuckin' hoodlums," Joyce said.

"Facts!" Kisha said, slapping her five.

"You don't get that you can fix another queen's crown without telling the world it's crooked. So even if our kids were doing the shit you're accusing them of, you don't have to be a bitch about it," I said.

Tracy and I had heard enough. We stopped cleaning and went inside my apartment. I spent the rest of the day questioning whether my little angel was a demon.

CHAPTER 18

QUIET STORM

On Monday, Officer O'Sullivan and ACS (Administration of Children's Services) brought 'Keem and me into the courtroom. Our moms jumped up the second they saw us. Ma saw my black eye and the fresh cuts and bruises all over my face, covered her mouth with her hand, turned to Mrs. Tracy, and asked, "What happened to them in there?"

Mrs. Tracy shrugged and shook her head.

Cuffed, Akeem and I quickly stopped in front of our moms. Mom opened her arms to hug me, but I stood there, stiff and emotionless, not giving in and hugging her back.

One of the white court officers saw me, shook his head, and said, "Hug your mother, you little monster. I see a lot of punks like you come and go through here every day, and most of those boys aren't lucky to have a mother that cares and shows up for them. Show some type of decency and respect. It's probably killing her to see you in cuffs like this."

I rolled my eyes, reluctantly stepped forward, and hugged her halfheartedly. At first, it felt good being comforted by her, but I pushed back the feeling and pulled away.

My mom asked, "Oh my God. Did they hurt you two in there?"

"We're all right, Ma, relax," I said.

I walked up to Jerami and hugged him.

"Are you going to be in jail for a long time?" he asked.

"Nah, I'll be outta here soon," I said, smiling at him.

I was annoyed that Ma brought him here, but knowing her, she was probably using it as a scare tactic so he wouldn't get locked up in the future. Ebony was here too for 'Keem, but she was older than Jerami and understood things.

The Assistant Corporation Council agreed to probation for us again, but this time, we had to agree to do *fifty* hours of community service for the 114th Precinct, go to school regularly, and pass every class for the semester. We were warned that this was our second strike, and if we messed up again, we'd stay in Spofford for longer than a weekend.

On the way home from Queens County Family Court, Mom kept lecturing me while we walked to the train station.

"Boy, if your father could see you now," she said, shaking her head.

I glared at her. She knew how I got whenever she brought up my dad.

"We raised you better than that . . . I was so worried about you," she said.

"You couldn't have been that worried. You left me in there."

"I left you in there because your ass needed a reality check. You don't appreciate me, and the way you're talking, it looks like you still haven't learned your lesson." A look of concern was on her face.

"You're all bruised up. Was all this bullshit you've been doing worth it? I don't want to go to any more precincts for you, you hear?"

"I hear you, Ma."

"I don't know when you decided that getting in trouble was a good idea, but that shit needs to stop."

I kept walking and didn't say another word.

I knew she probably thought Akeem was a bad influence on me, but she wouldn't say shit because Mrs. Tracy was her best friend, and she didn't want to make things weird or risk messing up their friendship. She didn't have to worry, though. I was going to be on the straight and narrow . . . for a while. I wasn't trying to go back to Spofford again.

It was crazy warm for a Sunday afternoon in winter. Bored and loaded with eggs and shaving cream cans, Draper sat with Akeem and me on the wooden benches in front of his building, 40-02 Tenth Street, joking and laughing about the poor suckers he planned on using them on.

O'Sullivan and McIvor were cruising slowly in their patrol car. They stopped and stared us down from the street. Draper threw his hands up in the air.

"What the fuck you lookin' at, pigs?" he yelled.

Akeem shook his head. "You're so fucking stupid," he said.

"What?"

"You play too much. Now, because of your big-ass mouth, if they come over here to fuck with us, it's on you for instigating the shit," he said.

"Man, fuck them. They ain't gonna do shit," Draper said. Then he opened one of the egg cartons and took out two eggs.

"What did I just say? Don't be stupid," Akeem warned.

O'Sullivan started to drive off slowly.

Draper laughed. "Yo, watch this," he said, tossing the eggs rapidly at O'Sullivan's car.

"What the hell is the matter with you?" Akeem yelled.

The patrol car screeched to a stop. O'Sullivan's face was firetruck red.

We all jumped off the bench and ran. Draper snickered and bailed on us, running inside his building. The door automatically locked behind him, leaving Akeem and me to fend for ourselves. O'Sullivan started to get out of his car but got back inside and sped after us once he saw us running down the block.

Akeem and I ran into the street, darting in and out of traffic, and bent down between some parked cars. In a matter of seconds, the block was flooded with cop cars speeding down the block, blaring their sirens.

Our heads were on a swivel, trying to see where the sirens were coming from. O'Sullivan spoke to the other officers as they drove up to his car.

"These fucking savages couldn't have made it too far. Check everywhere," O'Sullivan said. Then he grabbed the mic for his patrol car's PA system.

"You punks are going to pay for egging my car," he said over the car's loudspeaker.

We were hunched over with our hands on our knees, gasping for air, when Akeem said, "We gotta split up. If we run in different directions, it'll throw him off."

"Nah, I'm not leaving you. That's a bad idea—"

"Look, it's not up for debate. I'll run down Tenth Street. You run down Forty-First Avenue. He wants me. He's not worried about you. We'll meet up at our building once we shake him."

We fist-bumped and ran off in different directions. As soon as we moved from behind the parked cars, the sirens blared from O'Sullivan's patrol car, and just like Akeem said, O'Sullivan sped after him, ignoring me. I ran, looked over my shoulder, and saw Akeem bolt toward our building.

"Go!" he yelled, rushing inside. O'Sullivan parked his car on the sidewalk and ran into the building behind him. I kept running in the opposite direction, praying that O'Sullivan didn't catch him.

"Yo, remember what I said? We ain't gonna beat on the white boy no more," Akeem said.

Akeem, Draper, and I were playing ball on the courts near our building with two other boys who were trying to kiss up to Akeem.

"I still don't get why," Draper complained.

"Because Bill ain't no snitch. After all the shit we've done to him, he still didn't rat me out to O'Sullivan, that's why. He could've got the cops involved when we were fucking with him too, but he didn't. If that were anyone else, they would've snitched on us in a heartbeat. I respect that." Then Akeem turned to me.

"Plus, it'll get our moms off our backs. I already gave the word to everyone else to leave him alone. So now I'm tellin' y'all again."

I spotted Bill heading toward us. The ball bounced out of bounds. He picked it up, passed it back, walked up to the sidelines, and asked, "Can I get next? Can I play?"

"Hell no!" Draper, the other boys on the court, and I yelled.

Even after everything Akeem said, I still didn't want him hanging around us.

"White boys can't play no ball," I shouted.

We all cursed and tried to convince Akeem to kick him off the court, but he wasn't having it.

"Yo, he's got next," Akeem said.

"C'mon, man. You know he's gonna suck," I murmured.

"Chill, J. It's better this way. Now we can play three-on-three."

We started a new game. Draper, me, and one of the new guys, Danny, versus Bill, Akeem, and the other new guy, Cliff.

"You better be ready to play some defense, chump," I said, checking the ball into Bill's chest, knocking the air out of him.

Surprisingly, Bill was good at basketball. His ball handling was sick! He made some nice passes and, defensively, shut down everyone he guarded, including me.

After winning all the games they played, Akeem was impressed. I hated that we lost, and I didn't like that Akeem acted like he wanted Bill to be down with us.

"I didn't know you had game like that. You busted my boys' asses," Akeem said.

"Thanks," Bill smiled.

"Good looking out for not giving me up to O'Sullivan."

"It's cool."

"Nah, that's a big deal to me. I already gave the word for everyone around here to stop beating on you."

"Thanks!"

"You should play ball with us from now on. We play almost every day after school. Me, J, and Draper are getting ready to try out for the school team now. You should too."

"Nah, I want to, but I can't. I gotta be home. My mom has multiple sclerosis, so I help care for her most of the time after school."

"Where's your pops at? He can take care of her, right?"

"I've seen pictures of my dad but never met him. He left when I was younger. It's just my mom and me."

"I didn't know your pops wasn't around. I thought all white people had both parents in their lives."

"Not in my family."

Akeem laughed. "Between you being good at ball and your pops not being around, I swear, Bill, I'm starting to think you're secretly Black."

Bill laughed. I didn't find shit funny. Akeem kept talking.

"My pops took off when me and my sister were babies. The coward left us to fend for ourselves. It's all right, though. I didn't need him then, and I damn sure don't need him now. One day, I'm gonna be paid, and my mom and Ebony will never have to worry about money again."

"I'm right there with you, man. I want to do the same thing for my mom and me."

"Cool."

Akeem turned to me. "Yo, J. Bring it in."

Draper started walking over to Akeem, too.

"I didn't call you. You can stay over there," Akeem said as I walked over. Draper looked mad that Akeem had dissed him in front of us.

"What about me? What did I do?" Draper said.

"You dipped on me and J and left us behind when it was your fault that O'Sullivan was running after us in the first place. On top of that, you made me look like an asshole to Drastic because I vouched for you, so I don't want you and money in the same sentence when I'm talking."

Akeem pointed at me and told Bill, "J's my right hand. Now that you're down with us, the three of us will get this money together."

The three of us fist-bumped, and I wondered if this was the start of Bill replacing me as Akeem's best friend.

Akeem was true to his word and kept all the corner boys and wannabe followers off Bill's ass. Now that Bill played ball with us all the time, he got respect and developed a reputation for being nice in ball. Akeem gave him the nickname "Ill Bill" since his skills were "sick" on the court.

Once Bill started hanging out with Akeem, Draper, and me, it was easy to see he and Ebony were feeling each other. They were always smiling and teaming up together for school projects. We busted Bill's balls and gave him shit over him crushing over Ebony all the time.

Most of the boys around our neighborhood wouldn't talk to or even approach Ebony out of fear of pissing Akeem off and having to deal with the wrath of Drastic and Boogie, so I got why Bill tried to keep his feelings a secret.

After school one day at Akeem's apartment, we caught Bill and Ebony kissing. Akeem and I had just come back from shooting around on the courts. Bill said he couldn't go with us because he had a school project to do with Ebony. When we walked into the apartment, Ebony and Bill jumped out of each other's arms and collected themselves. Akeem glanced back and forth between the two of them. Then he and I shot each other looks.

"I thought you and Bill were supposed to be studying, twin," Akeem said.

"We are studying. Mind your own business," Ebony shot back.

"I guess y'all studying anatomy, huh?" he laughed.

Ebony rolled her eyes.

Akeem hooked his elbow around her neck and tweaked her nose.

Ebony broke out of his embrace and shoved him off.

"Twin . . . just make sure you don't get yourself knocked up. Too many kids our age are having babies, and I don't want you to be a statistic. You're the smart one, remember? You got goals to accomplish."

"I know, and I won't be a statistic. I can take care of myself."

I thought Akeem would've kicked Bill's ass, but he shook his head and laughed it off.

Akeem was letting Bill slide on a lot of shit, and I didn't get why until Akeem took Bill to Queensbridge Park one day.

"This is where I come to think. It's my favorite place—"

"*Our* favorite place," Ebony said, correcting Akeem.

Akeem rolled his eyes. "Our favorite place."

Akeem, Bill, Ebony, and I were hanging out and talking at the park. I hated that Akeem brought him here.

"Me and Billy are gonna walk around. We'll be back," Ebony said, smiling at Bill.

Akeem nodded and stared at the city skyline.

Having Bill hang out with us all the time and seeing Akeem all chummy with him had me in my feelings.

"Yo, what's up with you and Bill? One minute you wanna kill him, and the next, you're all buddy-buddy and shit with him? What's up with that?" I asked.

"Relax, J. He's not replacing you."

I was taken aback that he read my mind, and I guess my expression showed it.

"Bill makes me think about how my life could be if I was on the straight and narrow. Living around here, Bill kinda understands 'the struggle,' but he'll never have to go through it like you and me. For us, unless we get a scholarship playing ball, rap, or hustle like we've been doing, our asses are stuck in the hood. We both suck at rappin', and there are plenty of cats out here that can ball. You and me see the world the same, and that's why our bond is different and stronger than the one I have with Bill."

I slowly nodded while Akeem continued.

"Bill sees the world through rose-colored glasses. Personally, I could never live like that, but I don't mind it for Ebony. She's lived in the hood her whole life and seen a lot of foul shit, but she still has faith in the world and in people. I don't want her to lose that. I don't want her to be like me."

"Why? Your way is the truth; hers ain't realistic. Thinking positively like that is bullshit. Don't you want her to be able to handle herself in the street?"

"Of course I do. I've toughened her up over the years, so I know if it comes down to it, Ebony can hold her own, but me and her have enough negative shit going on in our lives, and I want more for her. Bill is a good dude. I know they're feeling each other. At first, I hated it, but after thinking about it, I know he'd treat her right and give her a better life than any of these niggas around here."

Akeem paused and looked at the skyline again. I wasn't sure what exactly he was looking at, but he continued to stare off in the distance and said, "Did you know my great-grandmother, grandmother, and mother all grew up and lived here in Queensbridge?"

"Nah, I didn't know that."

"Yeah, Ebony is going to break that chain. That shit is gonna end with her. She got the brains to be more than our block. Look at you and me. The furthest we've been from Queensbridge is probably going to Green Acres Mall in Valley Stream. There's an entire world outside of Queensbridge. I already know my future is pretty much set, and I'm gonna be working in these streets like my pops did, but I want more for Ebony. She can be something special, and I don't want her to end up with a guy like me. Bill's a good dude. He and Ebony are both smart, but because he's white, I know he'll eventually leave the hood, so I'm cool with them being together because he'll help her get out, too."

I nodded.

"What about you, though?" I asked.

"I'd be frontin' if I said I didn't want that for myself one day, but let's be real. That might not be in the cards for me. But if I'm lucky, I can stack up my money from hustling and get out before I get caught up."

I finally understood how Akeem thought about Bill, and after that day, I stopped looking at Bill as a threat and started accepting him as a friend.

"Me and Ill Bill are gonna start spotting you guys' points to at least make our games challenging," Akeem joked.

"You're just lucky you had a white boy who could shoot. I was stuck with this brick-laying scrub," I said, pointing at Draper.

"Whatever, punk. At least my man wasn't scoring on me at will," Draper shot back.

We had just finished playing ball on the courts by our building. Ebony was there too and used the excuse that she was waiting for Bill to finish playing so they could work on some school project together, but we all knew she was full of shit.

We were leaning against the fence, doing our usual routine of joking around, talking shit, and snapping on each other. Across the court from us, some girls from our school were smiling, pointing, and giggling at us. Akeem was staring at one girl, particularly, Nia Evans. Nia was talking to her fraternal twin, Rita, and some other girl named Ladi from around the neighborhood. The way Nia was staring at Akeem, it looked like the feelings were mutual when it came to them both feeling each other.

Nia was pretty, about five foot two, had a smooth, deep chocolate complexion, big brown eyes with long eyelashes, and a China doll hairstyle that looked good on her. She was definitely one of the baddest chicks in our hood. All the boys our age wanted her. She never went anywhere without her sister, Rita, and like 'Keem, she always had a book in her hand.

Rita was hot, too. She was about five-five with a caramel complexion and rocked box braids. She was a little thinner than Nia, but I thought her body was on point.

Draper was next to Akeem, running his mouth as usual, when he realized what Akeem was focused on. Draper shoulder-bumped him and said, "Don't be a pussy. Man up and go talk to her."

'Keem frowned at him. I nudged him with my elbow and added, "Y'all are obviously feeling each other. You should stop being a fan and just go up to her."

"Yeah, before I go over there, show her my dick and ruin any chance you got of getting her," Draper joked.

"Yeah, right. Go over there and show her your little quarter-inch killer. Once she sees your junk, she'll come running to me."

Ebony laughed. Draper looked embarrassed.

"Whatever, nigga," Draper said, pissed off.

'Keem faced me.

"He's right, though. I need to man up and talk to her," Akeem said.

He faced Bill, Draper, and me. "Guys, come with me. I think Rita is feeling you too, J. I've been seeing her eyeing you. Bill, Draper, you two can fight over who's gonna kick it to their friend."

Bill was looking directly at Ebony when he said, "I'm not interested in any of the girls over there."

Ebony tried to hide a smile. Akeem noticed, smirked, and said, "Yeah, I'm sure you and Ebony gotta rush home and do that 'project' for school anyway, so why don't y'all do that so my twin doesn't cock block me."

"Nobody cares about you, but that sounds like a good idea. Let's go, Billy," Ebony said.

"You know the streetlights are coming on. You better get home before your momma gives you a whoopin'," Draper joked.

"Ha-ha," Bill said sarcastically.

"I'm just playin'. You know I gotta mess with you, B," Draper said.

Bill nodded while Ebony pulled him away from us so they could walk home.

Bill's mom was overprotective. He was her only child, and she didn't want him hanging outside late since our neighborhood had so many shootouts.

"You ready, J? Watch your boy work!" Akeem said.

Before I could get a word out, he was already walking in their direction. Nia smiled when Akeem came across the court and nudged her sister, Rita. Rita caught me looking at her and winked at me.

"I saw you checking me out, so I decided to come over here so you can get a better look," Akeem said.

"Is that right?" Nia said.

"Nah, I'm kidding, but on the real, I'm feeling you, and I want to see if we could talk and get to know each other better."

Nia smiled. "I'm cool with that," she said.

"Why don't you and Jalen walk me and my sister home?" Nia looked atme, then faced Akeem. "I know she's feeling him, too."

"Nia!" Rita said.

Nia waved her off. "Oh, shut up. Both of you are shy. If I didn't say anything, neither of you were gonna say or do shit, so I told him the truth to get things moving."

Rita and I laughed shyly.

Nia and Rita said goodbye to their friend, Ladi, who seemed to be hitting it off with Draper. When Ladi wasn't looking, Draper gyrated like he was humping her. Akeem and I laughed, but I turned my attention back to Rita. I grabbed her hand, and we walked together while Akeem and Nia strolled behind us. We got to know them as we walked them to their building.

"So, word around the block is you and Akeem work for Drastic. Is that true?" Rita asked.

"Something like that. Why? You don't like guys that hustle?" I asked.

"Are you kidding? I love tough guys like you that run the streets. My daddy was a hustler. He and my momma used to run shit together until they got caught. Now, they're both doing time upstate in prison."

After hearing that, I knew she was feeling me.

"Damn, I'm sorry about that, shorty."

I didn't know what else to say, but I liked that we were talking, so I wanted to keep the conversation going.

"Who are y'all staying with now?" I asked.

"We live with our grandma and my auntie Kiera a few blocks from here at 40-15 Tenth Street."

"Cool, cool."

We pulled up to Nia and Rita's crib, and they invited us in. For the most part, their apartment was pretty clean. Their grandmother was sitting in the living room in a wheelchair, staring out the window.

"Hey, Grandma!" Nia said.

Their grandma nodded, and Nia and Rita both gave her kisses on the cheek.

"Do you want some water, Grandma?" Rita asked.

She nodded again.

Their grandma looked like she was in bad shape. Her hands were trembling, she had a nasty cough, and she looked like she was having difficulty breathing. Then a woman came out of the bathroom and walked into the living room.

"I'm about to go to the store . . . Who are these two young brothas you got up in here?" Kiera asked.

"These are our . . . friends, Akeem and Jalen," Nia said.

Akeem and I immediately recognized their aunt. She was one of Rasheed and Shyne's regular customers. As she got closer to us, she recognized us, too. Word around the neighborhood was late at night, she was out sucking dick on the corner of Fortieth Avenue and Twenty-First Street to support her habit.

"Yeah, I've seen y'all around," Kiera said.

When Rita and Nia turned their heads, Kiera pressed a finger to her lips for 'Keem and me to be quiet. We both smirked and nodded.

"Well, I'm out. Y'all can chill in your room if you want. Make sure Grandma takes her meds. I'll be in later tonight," Kiera said.

As soon as she stepped out of the apartment, Nia and Rita dragged 'Keem and me to their aunt's room instead, because they said she had the best weed stashed there. We all sat on Kiera's king-size bed, joking and laughing about shit that goes on in the neighborhood. Then Rita stood up and dug in her aunt's dresser drawer.

"Jackpot! I found Auntie's stash," she said, dancing excitedly.

Rita faced 'Keem. "Do y'all smoke bud?" she asked.

"Hell yeah, we smoke," Akeem said, answering for both of us.

In reality, we sold the shit but never actually smoked it. The hardest thing we ever smoked was cigarettes, but I guess, like me, he didn't wanna look like a pussy in front of the girls, so we played along like we did it on the regular.

Rita pulled out a dime bag and a white owl cigar. She gutted the cigar, rolled the blunt, winked, and flickered her tongue at me when she licked it to seal it. Seeing her work her tongue like that got me hot, but I tried to stay cool.

Nia rolled her eyes at Rita. Rita didn't give a shit. She was puffing out smoke rings in the air and blowing smoke out her nose like a pro.

"We were having a good time already without it. We don't need it," Nia said.

Rita nudged her and said, "Now, we'll have an even better time. If you don't like it, don't smoke it. Plus, Ms. Goody Two-shoes, don't act like you don't do this shit too," Rita said, lighting and taking a big toke of the blunt.

Rita passed it to Nia, and she took a pull.

"I only do it to keep you company. It's peer pressure," Nia laughed, passing it to me.

I took a big pull. The weed filled my lungs, and my throat felt like it was closing. I coughed violently.

"Amateur!" Rita laughed.

We all laughed, and I passed it off to 'Keem. We completed the cipher, and I learned a lot from talking to them. Nia was into school and didn't want to end up like her parents, while Rita idolized them and wanted to follow in their footsteps. Akeem told Nia that he did what he did to care for his mom and sister, but he didn't plan on doing it forever. He didn't know what he'd do in the future, but he just wanted to stack enough loot to make sure that he and his family never had to want for nothing.

Rita didn't care about school and seemed to only really be into me whenever I talked about hustling. I thought she was gorgeous, so I kept talking about it to keep her turned on. Eventually, Akeem and Nia wanted more privacy, so they went to her room while Rita and I stayed in her aunt's room. I kept her entertained with stories of us boosting clothes and snatching purses, and in return, Rita gave me head for the first time.

It wasn't long before we all started dating. Now that Akeem and I had steady girlfriends, we spent every free moment trying to get some. Nia got along great with Ebony because they were into nerdy school shit. Jerami loved Rita because she would rub his bald head and tell him he was handsome.

One afternoon, my mom and Mrs. Tracy were outside smoking, and we introduced them to Nia and Rita.

"Ma, this is my girl, Rita. Rita, this is my mom," I said.

"What's up, Jalen's moms? How you?" Rita said, slapping Ma five instead of shaking her hand.

"I'm good. It's nice to meet you," Ma said, looking at her skeptically.

I could tell by Ma's face that she wasn't feeling Rita. Introducing Nia to Mrs. Williams was much smoother and nicer than Rita meeting my mom.

"Good afternoon, Mrs. Williams. Akeem speaks so highly of you. I'm glad we're finally meeting," Nia said, hugging Mrs. Williams.

"Oh, thank you. It's nice to meet you too. You must be special because Akeem never stops talking about you."

"Ma!" Akeem said.

Mrs. Williams waved him off. Nia laughed and nudged him.

"He better. I plan on marrying him someday, so I want to be close with you," Nia said.

Rita had a smirk on her face.

"Wow, OK . . . I'm sure we'll talk," Mrs. Williams said.

My mom and Rita looked like they were sizing each other up more than bonding, so I figured that was our cue to leave.

"All right, Ma. We're gonna hang out at their house," I said.

"Girls, it was nice meeting you. We have to talk to our sons privately for a minute, though. The boys will catch up with you in a minute," my mom said.

Rita looked like she would say something, but Nia interrupted and said, "No problem. It was nice meeting you two, also. See you around!"

Nia grabbed Rita's hand, and they walked down the block toward their place.

I looked at my mom. "Ma, what was that?"

"That girl looks fast, and I don't trust her ass. You better not get that little hussy pregnant. Lord knows we don't have room for any more people in our apartment, and I'm not gonna be a grandmother anytime soon, understand?"

I rolled my eyes.

"That goes for you too, Akeem. Yours seems nice and respectful but keep it in your pants."

"I know, Ma," he said.

We left our moms and caught up with our girls. 'Keem and I didn't want kids any time soon, but that didn't mean we wouldn't try to get some every chance we could.

Plenty of girls threw themselves at us. I messed around with a few on the low, but Akeem was faithful to Nia.

"With all the girls offering you pussy, how come you don't take them up on it?" I asked.

"They only look at me now because I'm known in the streets. Nia doesn't care about any of that shit. She likes me for me, so I know what we have is real. I could fuck around, and she'd probably still stick by me, but why risk losing her if she does everything I ask for, doesn't ask me for nothing, and our relationship works?"

I nodded.

What he said was true, but I didn't think Rita looked at me the same way Nia looked at him. If I wasn't talking about street shit, I felt Rita quickly got bored with me. On the other hand, she was too hot to lose to another hood dude, and I liked having steady sex with her, so if I had to act extra "street" to keep her around, so be it.

Swish!

Akeem, Bill, and I made our school's basketball team, and our season was here! Bill did a nasty crossover on the boy guarding him and passed it to Akeem. Akeem drove to the basket and quickly got double-teamed but dished it out to me, and I drained an open corner three to put us in the lead by one point with two minutes left against IS 126-Ravenswood.

Rita, Jerami, and Aunt Carina were cheering hard while Mom was in the stands, barely paying attention. I saw Mrs. Tracy and Nia pointing at the court, telling her I scored. Moms shifted the paperwork on her lap and tried to clap with a highlighter in her hand when Ravenswood called time out.

We were four games into the season but lost only one game so far. There was one undefeated team, IS 141-Astoria, and we had them next. Mom rarely made it to my games, but when she did, I won't lie, I was happy to see her in the stands, even if she brought her work to the game.

A month passed, and after our stint in Spofford, we stopped boosting for Drastic. He was tight about it but understood we needed to fall back with everything for a while.

Draper made the team too, but he mostly rode the bench. He still hung around us because he wanted Akeem to put him back on again with Drastic since we were staying clean, but this time around, Akeem wasn't hearing it.

"All right, boys, we need one stop on defense, and we got this game won. Bring it in," Coach Clark said.

We all put our hands on top of one another.

"On three, win. One, two, three—Win!" Coach Clark said.

The whole team nodded and shouted, "Win!"

We played tight defense and shut Ravenswood down to get the win. My mom, Mrs. Tracy, Rita, Nia, Jerami, and Aunt Carina came down from the bleachers while Akeem and I celebrated with the team.

"You did great, Sonshine!" Mom said.

"That's funny. I didn't think you saw any of the game. Every time I looked in the stands, your head was buried in one of your files."

Mom sighed and ignored my attitude. "I'm proud of you, Jalen."

She wrapped her arms around me. I tensed up at first, but then relaxed. As much as I didn't want it to, hearing her say she was proud of me made me happy, and I wanted her there when Akeem and I took down Astoria next Friday.

"Ma, you're sure you'll be out of work in time to make it to my game, right?" I asked.

"Yes, Sonshine. I'm going in early, so I can handle everything and not be forced to stay late."

"Today is important, Ma."

"Yes, Sonshine. I know. I'll be there."

She didn't even have the decency to look at me. It was six in the morning, and she was already distracted, reading over and running a highlighter on some files on the countertop while she cooked eggs for Jerami and me on the stove AGAIN.

Mom didn't acknowledge the day at all. I gave her the benefit of the doubt. I knew she couldn't have forgotten what made this specific day important. It was more than just because of the game. Today was my *birthday*.

"Astoria is undefeated, and me and Akeem want to be the first to hand them a loss."

"I'm sure you will. But look, I have to leave now so I can be there tonight. I love you, Sonshine. I'll see you tonight."

I hoped she'd stay true to her word for once.

CHAPTER 19

KEEP YOUR HEAD UP

A few stragglers and a couple of junior associates were finishing up last-minute work in their offices. Meghan had already left for the day. Julissa was out the door when her shift was over to pick up her son, and Francisco was gathering his stuff to go home.

I finished all of Meghan's and my legal briefs, paperwork, and torts for the day when Francis barked on the intercom for me to come to his office. I gathered my things, put on my coat, grabbed my purse, and went to his office, praying that he would see I was on my way out and wouldn't force me to stay later tonight than I already had. I was shaking as I knocked on his door and stood in his doorway.

Francis was on the phone. I hoped that would be the distraction I needed to get out of there.

"Do you need anything else from me before I go home, sir?"

Francis waved his hand, signaling for me to come inside. He lowered the phone, placed a hand over the receiver, leaned back in his chair, and said, "I need you to stay late tonight. Meghan had to leave early, and there's a lot of things that need to be done."

I stood in his office and waited for him to finish his call. Once he was done, I said, "Francis, I can't stay late today. I promised my oldest—"

He rose to his feet, came around his desk, stood directly before me, and got in my face. He crossed his arms, narrowed his eyes, and asked, "What are the names on the wall behind the reception desk?"

"Mr. Lincoln—"

"What are they?" he yelled.

"Wayne, Rothstein, and Lincoln."

"That's right, and the last time I checked, you were this firm's administration manager. Get this through your head. You work for the firm; the firm doesn't work around you."

"Mr. Lincoln, any other day, I wouldn't even question staying but—"

"Do you want to be able to feed your family?"

I was taken aback by his question.

"Don't just stand there looking at me. Answer me."

I swallowed the lump in my throat and slowly nodded in agreement, afraid to speak.

"You want benefits to take care of your sick son, right?"

I opened my mouth to answer, but Francis cut me off.

"Rhetorical question. I know you do, so shut your mouth, get behind that desk in your office or wherever the hell else you want to sit, and do whatever I tell you to."

My hands were trembling. I held back tears and curled my bottom lip to stop myself from saying something I'd regret. He knew I needed this job, and he was purposely doing this to fuck with me.

"Close the door on your way out," he ordered.

Tears streamed down my face. I turned around, slammed his door, walked back to my office, and tossed my purse on the floor beside my desk. I flopped down in my chair and looked at the endless pile of paperwork on it. I sat forward and rested my head in the palm of my hands.

There was a knock on my door that made me jump. I quickly looked up and wiped my eyes with my hand. Francisco wrapped his brown leather satchel around his shoulders and asked. "You staying late again, boss lady?"

"Yeah . . . As usual, Francis has me doing some last-minute bullshit work."

"If you need help, I'll stay with you."

"As much as I'd love that, the partners would have my head if I gave you overtime without getting their approval first. Unfortunately, I have to handle this on my own. I appreciate the offer, though. Thanks."

"No problem, boss lady. I'll see you tomorrow."

"See you tomorrow."

I logged on to my computer and prepared for a long night.

Every day, I'm reminded that things here at work will never change, and the more I look at my reality, the more the truth hits me that I'm trapped at this job, and I'm powerless to do anything to make things in my life better.

CHAPTER 20

GET DEALT WITH

"Yo, I'm not tryin' to lose to these Astoria pussies tonight, especially not on your birthday. So get open, and me and Bill are gonna feed you for jumpers all night. Let's get this win!" Akeem said, giving me a shove to amp me up.

We fist-bumped.

"Word! Let's get it!" I said.

I didn't want to disappoint him, but I'd be lying if I said I wasn't nervous. As mad as I was at my mom, seeing her in the stands during games calmed me down, and I played better when she was there. I already knew Auntie and Jerami wouldn't make it to the game because after my little bro came home from his chemo session, he was sick as a dog.

People started filing into our school's bleachers, but there was no sign of my mom. The buzzer before the opening tip went off, and everyone settled in their seats. The stands were packed. Akeem waved at his mom, Ebony, and Nia. I scanned the bleachers for the seats next to Mrs. Tracy, but my mom wasn't there. Rita blew me a kiss that lifted my spirits somewhat. I winked at her and huddled up with my team.

Drastic and Boogie walked into the gym. Out of fear and respect, two guys sitting in the first row moved and gave up their seats so they could sit down. Drastic and Boogie nodded at me and 'Keem. Then they glanced over to Neville Bailey, another well-known, old-time drug dealer and Drastic's rival, who was at the game.

Neville had corners in Ravenswood, but mainly stayed on his side in Astoria. There were many small-time dealers in the hood, but Neville was the only one with enough notoriety in the street to rival Drastic. As a result, no drugs moved in Ravenswood or Astoria unless they came through him.

Neville sat behind the IS 141-Astoria team, hyping them up. He looked over at Drastic and made hand signals to let Drastic know he wanted to bet on the game. Drastic nodded and shouted at us, "Y'all better win. I got money on y'all."

The Queensbridge Projects and Astoria Projects always had a history of bad blood between them, so I wasn't surprised to see that there'd be money bet on even our junior high basketball game.

I started off hot, burying a three-pointer off a bounce pass from Bill. Then I made two back-to-back steals on defense and drove in for easy layups. Akeem set a pick for me, and I hit another baseline jumper to put us up by eight. IS 141 called a time-out, and our team headed to the bench.

In the huddle, Coach Clark said, "You're playing a hell of a game tonight, Jalen. Keep it up! We need your offense tonight if we're going to beat this team."

Coach Clark was drawing up a play, but I wasn't listening. I was too busy looking at the doorway and doing quick checks of the stands, wondering when my mom would show up. I never had much faith in her, but she knew how important this game was to me, and I figured she wouldn't let me down on my birthday.

Fuck that! I needed to forget about my mom, block out everything stressing me, and put all my anger and energy into the game.

We in-bounded the ball, and the kid guarding me was on me tight. The kid bit on my jab step, and I blew right by him, but he fouled me on a layup, causing me to miss. I headed to the stripe for two free throws and knocked both down.

If a defender played me too close, I drove past him. If a defender gave me too much space, I punished him with my jump shot. I was having the game of my life, hitting shot after shot, and I stupidly kept looking in the stands to see if my mom showed up, but she never did.

When the final buzzer sounded, the crowd gave me a big standing ovation. They hooted and stomped for me, having fifty-seven points in our twenty-two-point blowout win. Astoria's players hung their heads when we shook hands with them and filed off the court, cursing and arguing with each other.

Akeem, Bill, and I were so happy we took it to those chumps, but the win was bittersweet for me. I was happy we won, but pissed that Mom broke her promise.

Neville sucked his teeth and slapped a wad of money into Boogie Brown's hand while Drastic laughed and talked shit.

Mrs. Tracy, Ebony, Nia, and Rita walked up to us. Mrs. Tracy kissed us both on the cheek and said, "Congratulations, boys! I gotta rush out of here. I'm already late for work, but I'm proud of you two. Oh, and Happy Birthday, Jalen."

"Thanks, Mrs. Tracy," I said.

She waved and quickly headed out. Ebony punched Akeem in the arm.

"Good job, punk. Thank God, you didn't embarrass us," she said.

"You know your big brother got it," he replied.

She rolled her eyes. "We're twins, asshole."

Akeem pinched her nose, and she batted his hand away. Nia, Rita, and I laughed at their sibling squabbling.

"As long as you understand I'm the older one, we're good," he smirked.

Nia kissed 'Keem on the cheek and said, "We gotta go. Our grandma is sick, and we gotta rush back to give her some meds."

"No doubt. Handle your business," he said.

"Bye, guys. Happy Birthday, Jalen!" Nia added.

Rita wrapped her arms around my neck. "Good game, handsome. Happy Birthday! I'll give you your present next time you stop by my house," she said, kissing me.

I smiled at that.

We all said our goodbyes, and then the girls left. We laughed and celebrated with our team when Drastic and Boogie headed our way. Ebony nudged Akeem, lowered her voice, and said, "Didn't Ma say to stay away from that guy?"

"Be cool and don't say shit like that in front of him."

Drastic and Boogie approached us and gave 'Keem and me fist bumps.

"Good game, y'all," Drastic said.

He pointed to Ebony and said, "Yo, is this your sister, 'Keem?"

Ebony rolled her eyes and folded her arms. Akeem lightly smacked her arms and said, "Yeah, this is my twin, Ebony."

Drastic laughed at her attitude.

Seeing Drastic around us and trying to be down, Draper walked up.

"What's up, Drastic? How you doin', Boogie?" he asked.

Drastic still didn't want shit to do with him. He didn't even look in his direction when he asked sharply, "Did I ask you to come over here? Did I say you could even speak to me? Get the fuck from around me."

Drastic looked at Boogie and said, "Get this little nigga out of my sight before I hurt him."

Boogie stood chest to chest with Draper, staring him down to let him know he wasn't playing with him.

"Tttttake a walk," Boogie said.

Draper hung his head, hunched his shoulders, and walked off. Neville saw the whole thing and smiled at the drama. Then Neville wrapped his arm around Draper's shoulders.

"Come here, kid. If he doesn't want you around him, you can hang out with me," he said.

"Go ahead and be friendly to that bum-ass nigga. Don't worry. When he gets you knocked by the cops because he can't keep his big-ass mouth shut, I'll take over your corners while you're doing your bid upstate."

Neville gave Drastic the finger and walked off the court with his arm around Draper's shoulders, whispering something in his ear.

Drastic faced me and said, "Yo, J, you played your ass off today."

Boogie Brown nodded.

"When are you gonna come on the court? I heard back in the day you used to be nice," Akeem said.

"Yup, I was. I had white dudes offering me scholarships and the whole nine, but I gave up on that school shit years ago. School is for suckers. I tore my ACL in the ninth grade, and once I got hurt, none of those cats from those colleges gave a fuck about me. So I started putting in work in the streets, stopped the school bullshit, and focused on getting paid. It was the best decision I ever made. Playing ball is cool when you're a kid, but when you become a man, that school shit and playin' ball is just dumb. I'm not about gettin' all sweaty and messin' up my clothes. I'm about gettin' this paper."

Drastic reached into his pocket, pulled out a big wad of cash, counted off ten crisp twenty-dollar bills, and handed half to me, and Akeem like it was nothing to him.

"That's for representing the neighborhood, little homies. I gotta handle some shit, but I'll check y'all later."

Drastic pointed to Boogie. "Yo, we're out." Then he faced us and said, "Good game, y'all. Oh, and, J, Happy Birthday."

"Thanks!"

He nodded, and they left.

Even Drastic remembered my birthday, but my mom didn't.

"Why are you taking money from that guy? Mama told you to stay away from him," Ebony said.

"Mind your own business," Akeem yelled.

Ebony slapped him upside his head.

We walked home together while Akeem and Ebony bickered over him dealing with Drastic and Ebony threatening to tell their mom.

I got home after the game, and as soon as I walked through the door, Auntie jumped off the couch.

"Tag, you're it! I'm goin' out. Jerami is asleep on my bed if your mama asks," Auntie said.

She grabbed her purse, put on lipstick, and walked toward the door.

"Where are you going?" I asked.

"Out with one of my men. Tell your mama not to wait up for me. Oh yeah, Happy Birthday, nephew. Later."

Yeah, I was heated that Auntie left Jerami on me again, but at least she had the decency to wish me a happy birthday. Where was my mom?

I bet as soon as she came home, she'd blame her job for forcing her to stay late, missing the game, and forgetting my birthday. She's been using the same line since Jerami got sick, and the shit was getting old. I didn't want to hear the same lame sorry-ass excuse or empty apology. This was just another event that Mom missed that was important to me.

CHAPTER 21

PAIN

I made my way up the musty, narrow, urine-scented staircase to my apartment. Jalen usually gave me shit about everything I said or did, so I knew I was in for war when I stepped through the door after missing his game.

I walked into my apartment and hung up my purse by the door. Jalen was in the living room, slumped on the couch, holding the TV remote and scowling at me.

After my long, chaotic day, I had no energy to fight or deal with his bullshit.

"Nice of you to finally come home," he said.

I sighed. "I really don't need your shitty attitude tonight. Where's your aunt?"

"I don't know. I'm not her keeper."

I gave him a death stare.

He sucked his teeth and answered me. "She went out with some guy," he said, with an attitude.

"Boy, have you lost your mind? You better bring that bass down a notch in your voice when you're talking to me. I had a long, stressful day, and when I come home, all I want is some damn peace."

Jalen looked at me with so much anger in his eyes. *I knew I should've smoked before I came home.* I needed one to calm my nerves.

I massaged my temples to collect myself. "I know you're upset. I'm sorry I missed your game. I wanted to be there, but I got stuck at work, and my boss wouldn't let me leave."

"You always use that excuse. I'm used to you disappointing me, but you don't even get why I'm so mad."

I closed my eyes momentarily and let out a long, irritated breath. The way I saw it, Jalen was mad at me for every problem in the world.

"I'll be at your next one, I promise," I said.

"Your promises don't mean shit."

I rushed over and slapped him. "As long as you live under my roof, you'll watch your mouth and show me some damn respect. I'm not one of your little friends. I'm your damn mother."

He rubbed the side of his face and scowled at me. "Today was more than just my game. This day should've been special for you too, but as usual, you only care about your stupid job and Jerami."

I searched my exhausted mind for the right words. I knew he was jealous of all the attention and time I gave his brother. I had to do better at being there for him more.

"That's not—"

"Today's my birthday, but as usual, everything else was more important than me."

I gasped and covered my mouth. "Baby, I'm so sorry—"

Jalen stood up. "You're always sorry."

"Sonshine—"

"Oh, don't act like you care now."

His eyes were glassy. It broke my heart that he believed I valued everything else over him.

He stood up and walked toward his bedroom. I followed him down the hall, calling his name.

"Jalen, I'm—"

He stopped but didn't turn around to face me.

"Just go and check on Jerami. He's sleeping on Auntie's bed. I'm sure that's the only thing on your mind anyway."

He slammed the door with more aggression than I cared for, but I didn't chase after him. I was too tired and didn't have it in me to fight anymore today. Nothing I said was going to make him understand.

"Mommy, I don't feel so good," Jerami said, standing in the hallway. I saw him dry heave. I rushed to the kitchen to grab the garbage can to put in front of him before he vomited all over the floor. Unfortunately, I didn't make it in time. Jerami covered his mouth, but the vomit was seeping through his fingers and went all over the hallway floor.

I sighed, frustrated that I now had to clean that up on top of being tired and caring for him for the rest of the night.

"I'm sorry, Mommy," he said.

"It's OK, baby."

I walked him to the couch in the living room, placed a blanket over him, cleaned up the vomit, and lay with him while I rubbed his back to soothe him and get him back to sleep. Just when I thought it was working, he started throwing up again, and he did this off and on throughout the night. I needed to get some sleep. I gave him some Pedialyte from the refrigerator to calm down his nausea. It seemed to work. He finally slept peacefully, but it was already three in the morning, and I was still waiting on Carina to bring her ass home. I hoped she would get in before I left for work, but I didn't stay up anymore, fretting over it. I was way too tired to continue worrying about her.

I was supposed to be out the door already, but Carina didn't make her way home last night. I waited on her lazy ass for as long as I could, but once seven-thirty passed, I scrambled to get the boys ready. Now, I had no one to watch Jerami, and I couldn't take the day off. I wanted to make it to work as quickly as possible, but I already knew I would be late.

Tracy worked overnight last night, so I couldn't be a bitch and ask her to take care of Jerami when I knew she had to get some sleep before she went back to work in the evening.

Leaving Jerami with Jalen was not an option. I know he loved his brother, but I didn't think he was mature or responsible enough to care for him properly. On top of that, I didn't want him missing any more school.

"I can't miss work. Make sure you go to school. I don't want to find out you cut today, you hear?"

Jalen waved me off.

"I mean it. Go to school."

"Can I stay at home with Jalen?" Jerami asked.

"No, Jalen isn't staying home. He's getting ready to go to school, too. Isn't that right, Sonshine?"

Jalen didn't say a word. Instead, he walked to the bathroom and slammed the door.

I ignored his rudeness, snatched my purse, and grabbed Jerami by the hand.

"Boy, come on," I said, rushing him out the door.

"Mommy, where are we going?" Jerami asked as we walked down the stairs.

"To school."

"But I don't feel good."

"I know, baby . . ."

"Is everything all right?" I heard a voice say.

I stopped in my tracks and looked over my shoulder. Debbie stood in the hallway, tying the ends of a big, black trash bag. She struggled to empty her garbage bag in the incinerator.

I faced her. "I got a lot going on, Debbie. I can't talk right now. I'm late for work."

As soon as those words left my mouth, Jerami threw up on the steps. I rubbed his back, raised my eyes to the ceiling, and prayed for the strength to make it through this already hectic day.

My cell phone vibrated in my purse. I woefully grabbed the phone, placed it to my ear, balanced it on my shoulder, and answered it while I rummaged in my purse for the folded paper towels I kept there.

I wiped Jerami's face while I used my shoulder to hold my cell phone to my ear.

"Yes, Francis."

His voice boomed through the phone the second I answered it.

"Where the hell are you? You're usually here by now."

"I'm sorry, sir. I'm running late. My son is sick from his chemo—"

"That's not my problem. I don't want to hear excuses. I need you here *now*."

His voice roared through the speakers so loudly that I had to move the phone away from my ear. Finally, when he finished yelling and berating me, I asked, "What should I do with my son? I can't take him to school like this. As soon as he throws up, they'll call me to pick him up."

"Again, that's not my problem or a problem for this firm. Make arrangements. I expect you here within the hour. Oh, and I'm writing you up for being late again."

Francis ended the call.

I closed my eyes and let out a deep, frustrated sigh. Of all mornings, Carina flaking out on me and not being around to watch Jerami couldn't have come at a worse time.

"You look like you're having a rough morning," Debbie said, sympathetically staring at me.

I held my index finger up to her, telling her to give me a moment while wiping Jerami's face and clothes. Then I faced her.

"I am. Jerami is sick from his chemo. I can't take him to school like this, and my unreliable sister isn't here to watch him. With him being sick, I've already missed too many days at work. I can't take off . . . I don't know what I'm going to do. I was going to take him to school, and if he felt too sick, I would beg the school nurse to take care of him."

"I can watch him for you," Debbie volunteered.

I didn't know her like that to trust her with my son. Through my interactions with her, she seemed decent, but I knew very little about her. But I was desperate. Carina put me in an uncomfortable spot, and I couldn't risk losing my job. I had no other choice.

"I appreciate it . . . Look, I'm trusting you with my son. My kids are all I have in this world. So please . . . Don't fuck me over."

"I promise you; you can trust me. I wouldn't do anything to harm your son. But to give you more peace of mind, I'll give you my phone number so you can check in on him throughout the day."

The fact that she suggested that made me feel a little more comfortable.

I pulled a couple of dollars out of my purse and handed them to her.

"I...I don't have much money to pay you to watch him. I don't know how much you're looking for, but—"

She pushed my hand away and looked as if offering her money offended her. I insisted, but she wouldn't take it.

"Put your money away. I don't want anything. I'm doing this because I want to, and it's the right thing to do...I know you're late for work, so head on out, and I'll take care of Jerami."

Debbie smiled, bent down, and talked to Jerami. "Do you want to hang out with me today? I'll make us chocolate chip pancakes."

His eyes lit up when he heard that.

"Bye, Mommy," Jerami said, hugging me tightly.

Debbie opened the door.

I watched my son walk inside and prayed that I was making the right decision to let her watch him.

"The TV is on, and the remote is on the couch. So you can put on whatever you want to watch," she told Jerami.

"My sister should be home soon. I'll leave her a note explaining that he's with you for now, and she can pick him up here."

"I can tell you're nervous. It's OK. I promise you; your son is safe with me. Does he have any allergies to food or anything?"

"No, but his medications are in his book bag. The instructions are on the bottles."

She nodded.

"Here's my number," Debbie said, reaching for my cell phone. I handed it to her.

She typed her phone number into my cell phone and returned it to me. I fumbled in my purse for some paper to write on and jotted my job and cell phone number on a napkin.

"Take care of your business. We'll be here all day. I'll call you if there are any problems."

"Debbie, you're seriously a lifesaver. I appreciate this. Thank you."

She smiled. "Don't worry about it."

I rushed to my apartment, left a note for Carina on her bedroom door, then ran out. Tracy was headed inside the building as I was going.

"Damn, Queen. What are you still doing at home? I did overtime on the back end of my shift, so if I'm seeing you, I know you're late right now."

"I am. Carina never brought her ass home last night. I stayed up most of the night waiting for her and woke up late. I had no one to watch Jerami, and I didn't want to ask you because I figured you were either asleep or too tired. That white woman, Debbie, is watching him for me."

"You trust her like that? You barely know her."

"I had no choice at the time, but she seems genuine and decent."

"I'm exhausted, but I'll stop by her place periodically throughout the day to check up on him, too."

"Thanks, I appreciate that."

I looked at my watch. "Shit, I gotta go."

"Are you gonna be able to function on such little sleep like that?"

"I have no choice. It's not like I can take off."

"I hear that. Take care of yourself, Queen."

"Thanks. I'll talk to you soon."

I was sure Francis would make today a living hell for me. I sprinted to the train station, praying it would come on time.

I knew it was the beginning of a tough day when Francisco and Julissa called in sick. I was stuck handling the reception desk with fucking Meghan. It felt like I had just left this place, and here I was, back at it.

My eyes were heavy and burned while I read contracts. I was running on too little sleep to think straight. I felt myself dozing off. I went to the break room for another cup of coffee, but nothing helped. My concentration was shot. I found myself reading the same line of a contract about ten times. I was lost in my thoughts, worrying about Jerami, and couldn't focus on any of the information I was reading. My eyes were heavy, and I could barely keep them open. Before I knew it, I drifted off to sleep.

Francis slammed his hands down on the reception desk and scared the shit out of me. I jumped and abruptly sat up straight in my chair.

"Wake up right now. What the hell do you think you're doing?" he said with his arms folded.

My head was spinning, wondering what I could say to calm him down.

"I'm so sorry, sir. I must've dozed off. I didn't get much sleep. My son had chemo last night, and it made him sick. I spent most of the night taking care of him. I apologize."

"I don't care about what you did last night. This isn't the place to be sleeping. We have clients and potential clients coming in and out of here all day. How does it look if they see our administrative manager sleeping on the job?"

Meghan was on a phone call with a client, smiling to herself while

Francis screamed at me. The bitch could've woken me up and warned me before he caught me, but I know she purposely did nothing.

"You have problems, we all have problems, but we have to deal with them on our own time. When you're here at work, you check them at the door. Do I make myself clear?"

"Yes, Francis."

"Good, now give me the file for the merger I'm handling," he ordered.

My hands shook as he snatched the file. He rolled his eyes and walked away. I called Debbie to check on Jerami. He sounded like he was having a ball, drawing, watching movies, and eating ice cream with her. That put my mind at ease and brightened my shitty day a little, but I still made a mental note to check on him at least once more.

A direct page went to my phone at the desk. I picked up the receiver.

"Yes, Mr. Wayne."

"Juanita, can you bring me a copy of the file from the merger Francis is handling?" Richard asked over the intercom.

"Yes, I'll be right there," I said.

I printed out copies, made a new file, and walked to his office. Mr. Wayne's door was open, but I knocked anyway.

"Yes, come in," he said.

Francis stood in front of Richard's desk when I walked in. He snatched the folder from my hand.

"I'll take that. You can leave now," Francis said.

Francis tossed the file on Richard's desk. He didn't even wait for me to leave before saying, "We need to fire her."

I gave him the stank eye and closed the door behind me but stood close so I could eavesdrop on the rest of the conversation.

Richard laughed. "Juanita is wonderful. She's been with us for years and keeps all the secretaries in check."

"I don't know what illusion she shows you and Tim, but she's terrible. She's always late and—"

"And what? Let's be straight with each other, Francis. You're fucking that pretty redhead you hired, and you want to promote her."

Francis didn't confirm or deny it but responded with, "Meghan is more qualified to be our head assistant, even if she is less educated and experienced than Juanita."

Richard laughed. "I'm sure you've already observed her 'head' skills."

"I'm serious. Juanita is always late, and I caught her sleeping at the front desk. We need to set an example for the other workers. What if our clients saw her nodding off? We've worked too hard to lose clients because a glorified secretary can't keep her home in order."

"Relax. I'll monitor things with Juanita. If her performance slips, we'll let her go and move your redheaded conquest up, OK?"

"Perfect!"

I walked past the reception desk and stared down Meghan. I wanted to curse that bitch out, but I thought about the repercussions. All it would take was one slip-up, and my decision would ruin my kids' lives. I walked into my office, slammed the door shut, and then focused on my work since I was powerless to do anything else.

After my hellish day at work, I walked into my apartment and threw my purse on the table. Jalen was sitting on the couch watching TV.

"Have you seen your aunt?"

Jalen sulked and shrugged.

"What's with the attitude? Why do I have to fight with you every day? Now, answer me. Did you see your damn aunt today or not?"

His face told me that the thought of ignoring me and staying quiet was on his mind, but he saw my pissed-off expression and knew I wasn't in the mood for his shit today.

"Nope, didn't see her," he finally said, unmoved by my temperament.

I left him sitting there with his funky attitude and knocked on Debbie's door to pick up Jerami. She opened the door, and I walked inside her apartment. Jerami was so engaged in his cartoon show in her living room that he didn't even realize I was there to pick him up.

"Thank you so much for watching him today. I really appreciate it." I said.

"It's no problem at all . . . Tracy stopped by a couple of times today to check on him, too."

I smiled and made a mental note to thank Tracy later.

"Yeah, she had to get some sleep before her shift but just wanted to make sure he was OK since I told her how sick he felt when I passed her on my way to work," I said.

"I understand. Is your sister, OK?"

"I haven't heard from her, but I can't keep having her flake out on me like this. It's causing problems at my job, and I can't afford to lose it."

"You can always leave him here. If you need me to watch him regularly, I'd be happy to do it free of charge. I enjoyed his company today. He's so respectful and well-behaved."

"I might have to take you up on your offer, if you don't mind."

"It's no problem at all. We can start tomorrow if you want."

"That would be great . . . I'll give you some type of money for watching him."

"Nope, your friendship is all I want."

"You got it. Tracy and I usually have our morning cigarettes daily in front of the building. I know you don't smoke, but you're welcome to join us from now on."

"Sounds like a plan!"

Debbie turned and faced her living room. "Jerami, your mom's here. Grab your stuff," she said.

His big brown eyes lit up once he realized I was there. He gathered his stuff and ran to hug me.

I scooped him up in my arms. His thin arms wrapped lovingly around my neck, and he held me tight. I put him down and mouthed a thank-you to Debbie, then listened as Jerami excitedly told me about all the crafts they did during the day as we walked upstairs to our apartment.

"So, you had a lot of fun today, huh?" I asked.

"Yeah!"

"Would you like to hang out with Ms. Debbie more often?"

"Yeah, being with Auntie is boring. We never do anything. Ms. Debbie has lots of stuff to do at her house."

I asked the typical "mom" questions to make sure he wasn't being abused in any way, and I was happy that at least one part of my day went well. When I entered my apartment, Jalen saw me, walked to his room, and closed the door. I ignored that for the time being and got Jerami ready for bed. One thing was for sure. I had it with Carina and was finally putting my foot down.

I was sick of her using me, disappointing me, and being a flake when she knew I needed her around for the boys. I went inside her—correction, I mean *my*—bedroom, pulled her clothes off the hangers, and emptied her drawers. I stuffed her clothes into garbage bags, lugged them through the living room, and left them packed at the front door.

Around 11:30 at night, a key jiggled in the lock on the door. Carina tried strolling her drunk ass in the house but was blocked by the safety chain and wrestled with the door. I removed the chain, and she nearly tripped over the bags I had directly by the door.

"What's this shit? You going somewhere?" she asked.

"Nope, but you are. I packed all your shit. You need to get out of my house."

Carina waved me off. "Yeah, all right. You're so overdramatic," she said, rolling her eyes.

"Where the fuck have you been?" I yelled.

"Relax. I was hanging out with Omari."

"Did you forget that the only reason I have your mooching ass living here is to help me? You were supposed to be here for Jerami today. I was late for work again."

"How is that my fault?"

I scrunched my face in confusion. "You're kidding, right? You knew Jerami was sick after his chemo yesterday, and you weren't here to watch him. I know you're not that dense to understand that I need to go to work to take care of this family."

"You could've just taken the day off," she replied with an attitude, not grasping why she was in the wrong.

"There is no 'taking the day off.' I'm already on thin ice at the firm, and if I get fired and lose my job, who will take care of my kids and me? You? Who is going to pay for Jerami's medical expenses, huh? I can't afford to lose my job, and you keep fucking up. You're not responsible or dependable, so since you can't do the small tasks I ask you to do, you need to get the hell out of my house."

"Are you serious?"

"You heard me. I don't ask for much. I have too much to lose. You fuck different men in here all the time. You're always drinking and partying. You don't cook or clean, and you're rarely here to take care of the boys. If you can't do the small responsibilities I brought you here to do, you got to go."

"That's fucked up, sis. Why are you trippin'? Where am I supposed to go?"

"Not my problem. All I know is you can't stay here anymore. Stay with Omari or any of the other random dudes you're fucking."

"You know what? Fuck this. I don't need this shit. I'm tired of you throwing in my face that I don't have a job. Just because you don't have a life doesn't mean you can hate on me for living mine. You don't appreciate the shit I do for you anyway, so I'm out. Take care of your own damn kids. You're doing me a favor."

She struggled to gather her bags, but I didn't care. She was out of my house and someone else's problem.

The next morning, I met Tracy outside our building for our usual daily smoke.

"Good morning, Queen," she said.

"Good morning."

"Cigarette?" Tracy asked, offering me one from her pack.

"Hell yeah," I said, taking one.

I took my lighter out of my purse and lit it.

"How did things go with Carina last night?"

"I kicked her ass out. I'm tired of her shit, and I'm not putting up with it anymore."

"You serious?"

"Yup! Whatever guy she's with, she's his problem now."

I took a drag of my cigarette and said, "You'd think she'd be tired of being used and passed around by every 'baller' she fucks, but she never smartens up. Instead of trying a different approach when looking for a man, she just keeps moving in circles, and I can't have that around my kids or me anymore."

"I feel you, but who will watch Jerami for you?"

"I'm gonna have to rely on Debbie until I can muster up the funds to find another reliable source for childcare."

As soon as the words left my mouth, Debbie stepped out of our building.

"Good morning, everyone," Debbie said.

"Morning, Debbie," I said.

"Morning . . ." Tracy said.

Tracy leaned in and whispered, "Is this chick hanging out with us now?"

"Yeah, she's cool, and she's helping me out with Jerami," I whispered back.

"Say no more. I get it."

The three of us chatted about our lives, laughed, and Tracy and I got to know Debbie better. After our conversation, Debbie came to my apartment to get Jerami.

With Carina gone, Debbie picked up the slack. Over the past couple of days, Debbie watched, fed, and even took Jerami to his chemo sessions for free while I went to work. I felt like I was taking advantage of her kindness after being a total bitch to her early on, but she was the only person I could depend on to watch Jerami for me. She was a blessing and quickly became one of my best friends.

It had been over a week, and Jalen had barely spoken to me since our spat for missing his game and forgetting his birthday. It hurt, but I let him be. He needed to cool down before I could reach him.

Even though I couldn't spare the money, I had no desire or energy to cook, but I thought I'd surprise Jalen with his favorite Chinese food. After work, I headed to Friendly Chinese takeout on Fortieth Avenue. A brotha wearing an NYC Housing Authority uniform waved at me and said, "Excuse me, sista."

I paid him no mind and walked past him. I didn't feel like being bothered, and I had more important shit to do than hear another loser try to pick me up.

I walked inside, and the brotha followed behind me. In my peripheral, I could feel his eyes on me. I quickly glanced in his direction. I was right. He was watching me. I wanted to ask him what the hell he was staring at but opted not to.

I placed my order, speaking loudly so Wong, the Asian man who owned the restaurant, could hear me behind the inch-thick bulletproof glass that separated the customers from the workers.

I turned my head and saw the brotha still smiling at me. I shook my head and slid the money for my food through the slot. Then, clearly realizing I was ignoring him, the brotha left.

Not a second after stepping out of the restaurant, he approached me.

I had to give him credit. He was persistent.

"Excuse me, miss."

I rolled my eyes. "What? Do I know you?" I asked.

"Please, hear me out. Just give me one minute of your time, that's all I ask, and after that, if you want me to step off, I'll leave you be and won't bother you again."

I sighed. "State your business," I replied stiffly.

I gave him a quick, discreet head-to-toe glance-over. My eyes raked over his tall, athletic frame, taking in all of him. He was six-foot-three, well-built, and around his mid-thirties. He had a gorgeous caramel complexion, dark brown eyes, and beautiful white teeth. His jet-black, wavy hair was cut low, and his trimmed beard was perfectly lined up.

I scanned down and landed on his left hand, looking at his ring finger. There was no band or sign that one was taken off. Now that I had a good look at him, I couldn't deny that the brotha was FINE. He didn't have the usual cocky asshole approach that most men that approached me had, so my interest was piqued. I cut him some slack and figured I'd hear him out.

"First, let me introduce myself. My name's Miles."

"I know."

He looked confused about how I knew that.

I giggled and pointed to the embroidered name badge on his uniform. Most of the toads that tried to get my attention were either drug dealers or unemployed. At least this man had a job.

"Your name tag gave you away. I'm Juanita."

He smiled. "I know you probably get approached by a lot of losers around here, but I'm not one of them. I'm not out here doing anything illegal or drinking my life away on the corner. I have my own place and make an honest living, as you can see. I want to get to know you, and I'm asking you to give me a chance."

"I'm not trying to come across as a bitch . . . I'm extremely flattered, and you seem like a decent brotha who has his shit in order, but I'm not interested."

"And why not?"

"I have a lot on my plate, and there are a lot of things I need to focus on. Right now, I'm taking care of my two sons. I don't have time for a personal life, and I don't need any distractions. I'm sure many women around here would jump at the chance of being with a handsome brotha like you who has his shit together, so why are you pressing me?"

"You're right, many women out here would date me, but I'm not interested in them. I'm interested in you."

I gave him a slight grin. "Oh yeah? What makes me so special?" I asked.

"Well, I've seen you around, and I like your style. I'm not going to lie. I think you're beautiful, but what draws me to you is that you carry yourself with class. You're sexy, but you're not conceited. I can tell you're educated just by listening to you speak, but you're not naïve about how things in the streets work, either. I like how you're not impressed with guys who make their money being in the street. You're about something, and that's special to me."

I sighed. "I don't have free time. Most days, I'm working late, slaving away doing overtime, or at the hospital with my youngest son, who's battling cancer. When I'm not doing those things, I'm trying to spend time with my oldest son, who I severely neglect because of the other two things. Now, if you'll excuse me, I'm extremely flattered, and you seem really nice, but I have to bring this Chinese food home so my kids can eat dinner."

I turned to walk away when Miles said, "We can start off as slow as you want. For now, can I call you sometime?"

"I don't have a house phone."

"Oh," he said, looking disappointed.

I sighed. "Look, I really shouldn't be using this for anything that isn't work-related, but you can call my work cell phone after nine p.m."

He perked up and said, "That'll work!"

I dug into my purse and pulled out a pen, tore off a piece of paper from my Chinese food bag, and handed it and the pen to him. He jotted down my cell number and gave me his.

"Thanks for hearing me out. I'll call you tonight, beautiful."

"Uh-huh."

"Do you mind if I walk you to your building?"

"I'll manage. We just met. I'm not comfortable with you knowing where I live yet."

"I get it. I'll call you tonight."

I waved and walked home.

When I entered my apartment, I handed the boys their food. Jalen continued to give me the silent treatment. I put up with it . . . for now.

Truthfully, I didn't expect Miles to call me immediately, or even at all. I figured the challenge of getting my number was over, so he'd leave me alone, but just as I was climbing into my bed that night, *it felt good to have my bedroom and bed back*, he called.

"Hi, Juanita," Miles said.

"Hey."

"You sound tired . . . Were you calling it a night?"

"Yup."

"The night's still young, though."

"Not for me. I have work early in the morning."

"True. I know you just said you need to work early, but do you mind if we talk briefly?"

"We're talking, aren't we?"

"True . . . So, how did the rest of your night go?"

"It was all right. I fed my kids, tidied up around the apartment, and watched TV. The usual. How about you?"

"Nothing much. I just had dinner and watched the Knick game. So, tell me something about you that I don't know."

"We just met. There's a lot about me you don't know."

"Good, then we should have a lot to talk about."

"You're not going to learn everything about me in one night."

"I know. That gives me an excuse to call you every night."

I laughed. "I'm flattered."

"Good! So . . . Tell me about yourself."

"How about this? You ask questions, and if I feel like answering them, I will. I'm not going to volunteer information openly about myself."

He made small talk, and I was deliberately vague, giving him basic information about myself in small doses. I didn't know or trust him enough to tell him significant things about myself yet, but talking to a man for a change was nice. We talked and talked until my eyelids got heavy. I knew I would be exhausted in the morning, but I enjoyed our conversation.

"This has been fun, but I seriously have to go to bed," I said, fighting back a yawn.

"All right, I'll let you go. Get some rest, beautiful. I'll call you tomorrow."

We told each other good night, and I ended the call and slept in a better mood than most nights.

CHAPTER 22

SWEET THANG

I walked into my apartment building in a better mood than usual. Since Jalen was sleeping over at Akeem's apartment, and Debbie agreed to keep Jerami overnight to give me a break, I was looking forward to some much-needed "me time." I had the perfect Friday night planned: I was going to take a warm bubble bath, drink wine, and have a night free of attitudes, cooking dinner and child care.

It had been over a month since I'd seen or heard from Carina. I loved my sister, but I'd have to let her fail doing things her way for her to learn a lesson.

Speaking of the damn devil, as I walked up the steps, there she was, sitting on the staircase leading to my floor. Her elbows were on her knees, her head was hanging down, and her face was buried in her hands. Bags of her clothes and other personal shit were sprawled along the steps and landing. It was apparent her latest man had kicked her out.

Carina looked up. Her eyes were bloodshot and puffy. I shook my head, stepped around her, and walked up the stairwell. I didn't have any-thing to say to her. Carina reached for my arm, but I recoiled and pulled it back.

"C'mon, don't be like that, sis. Please, take me back. I got nowhere else to go," she said.

I turned and faced her. "Good luck trying to get sympathy from me. You don't need me, remember?"

She looked down at the floor, then back up with a broken expression. Her eyes were glassy.

"I said all that shit out of anger. I didn't mean any of it. Don't you think I know I'm a fuckup? You have a degree. You have a career. You have a family. I have nothing. I thought I could get everything easily by being with Omari, but he made it clear that I didn't mean shit to him when he dropped me. He said he had no more need for a used-up ho."

"Sorry to hear that. Not my problem, though."

I reached in my purse for my keys and put them in the door.

"Please, I know I was wrong. I know you're tired of me not making any contributions, but don't leave me to sleep in the street. Please help me. I'll be better, I promise."

"I heard that before."

"Sis, please."

At the end of the day, she was the only family I had left and the only person besides Tracy and Debbie I trusted to watch my sons.

I turned and faced her again.

"If, and that's a strong *if*, I take you back, things will be different."

"How so?"

"Well, first things first, you're not bringing any more men into my house. Second, you're not getting my bedroom again. As long as you're staying here, your ass will be sleeping on the couch from now on. Third, if you're going to live with me, you'll start pulling your weight around here, and by that, I mean you're getting a job. Debbie has been helping me out with Jerami, and things have been going smoothly, so I don't need you for that anymore. But you'll support yourself financially from now on and kick some money back to me to contribute to groceries. Those are my terms if you're going to stay here. Take it or leave it."

"Fine."

"Good."

I opened my door, moved aside, held it open, and said, "C'mon."

"Aren't you going to help me with my bags?"

"Nope."

Tracy had a little pull at a beauty salon on Fortieth Avenue, so she got Carina a job doing nails and cutting hair. It took some adjusting, but she was helping out financially and was holding on to her job. While I was happy for her, I was happier having my bedroom back.

Things with Miles were nice. Our first talk evolved into an every night thing, and before I knew it, we had been talking to each other for over a month. Miles made it a priority to call me daily and ask how my day went. Every night, we talked until my eyelids got heavy, and I couldn't stop myself from yawning.

While I didn't want to admit it, I looked forward to our daily conversations. I didn't feel lonely anymore, and the mental connection we were forming made me feel so much closer to him. Then, one day, Miles decided to take things to the next level.

"So . . . We've been talking for a while now," he said.

"We have."

"I want to take you out."

"You mean a date?"

I was looking for a way to make an excuse not to go.

"Yeah . . . dinner would be on me. The only cost for you would be your time. So give me a chance."

I didn't get out much. The only times I went anywhere were for work or Jerami's treatments. So it's been a while since a decent man asked me on a date.

"OK," I heard myself say, shocking both of us.

"OK?" he repeated.

I figured, what the hell? I'd give him a chance and go on a date to break the monotony of my chaotic life.

"Sure, I'd like that. We can go out to dinner," I said.

"I know you're busy with the kids, so is eight o'clock on Friday alright with you?"

"Eight works."

"Cool."

I finally gave him my address. I could feel him smiling through the phone.

"I hope I don't regret telling you where I live," I said.

"No, no, I promise you can trust me."

"I hope so . . . Well, I need to get to bed. I'm looking forward to our . . . date."

"I am too. See you then, gorgeous."

I'm always worried about my bills, my kids, and whether I will regret every decision I make. So maybe it was time to put on my big girl panties, do something out of the norm, and live a little for a change.

I walked to Carina's closet . . . correction, *my* closet, and tried to put together the sexiest outfit I could assemble. My outfit was casual, but sexy enough to turn a few heads. I wore her form-fitting black jeans, a red blouse with moderate cleavage, black four-inch heels, and a black Chanel clutch purse. I looked myself over in the mirror again, happy with my appearance.

I wanted to look pretty more for me than for Miles. Since Mo passed, I had no one to dress up for, so I missed feeling pretty. Jalen was hanging out with Akeem while Carina agreed to watch Jerami for me.

I looked at myself in the full-length mirror in my bedroom. Being broke made me thinner than usual, but I still had curves in all the right places.

It was a little after seven. I combed my hair and put the finishing touches on my makeup.

Carina walked into my room, sat on the bed, looked me up and down, and smiled.

"Wow! Looking good, sis," she said.

"Thanks."

"Did I say you could wear my clothes?" she joked.

Still staring at myself in the mirror, I asked, "Do you really want to piss me off when I just let you move back in here?"

That shut her up.

She dropped that topic and said, "I can't believe you're actually going on a date."

"Yup."

It felt good to break out of my shell for a change.

Soon, I got a call from Miles.

"Hello."

"Hey, beautiful! I just pulled up in front of your building."

"OK. You don't have to come up. I'm coming out right now."

"See you in a few."

I ended the call, faced Carina, and said, "Don't wait up for me."

I stepped outside and walked up to Miles. He was standing against the passenger side of his Blue 5 Series BMW holding a bouquet of beautiful red roses. He wore a dark blue suit that fit him like he was born to wear it.

Miles's eyes lit up at the sight of me. I thought I looked good too, but the hungry look in his eyes showed that he was *definitely* feeling me.

Miles licked his full lips. "You look great," he said.

"Thanks. You don't look too bad yourself. You clean up nicely. You look very handsome."

"These are for you, beautiful," he said, handing me the roses.

"Thank you."

He smiled. "Oh, let me get that for you," he said.

I moved back, allowing Miles to open the door for me. I held his hand as I got in. It was nice to see that there were still some gentlemen in the world and that chivalry wasn't dead.

"Thank you," I said.

Once I was seated, Miles closed the door and walked over to the driver's side. I opened the driver's side door for him.

"I guess you're one of the great ones!" he said.

"What do you mean by that?"

"In the movie *A Bronx Tale*, one of the characters said if you open the door for a woman you're on a date with and she reciprocates the gesture, it means she's a good quality woman."

I laughed and joked, "They should raise their standards. In reality, I was trying to make sure the door was locked."

Miles laughed. "You can try to deny it, but I know you're a good woman."

We entertained each other with idle chitchat as he drove. He took me to Sylvia's, a nice soul food restaurant on Malcolm X Boulevard in Harlem. We parked. He exited the car and walked around to help me out of my seat. He held the door open for me as we entered the restaurant and were greeted by the hostess.

"Good evening. I have a dinner reservation under 'Miles Hickson.'"

The hostess smiled, looked for him in the reservation book, and pointed to his name. "There you are. Please follow this young lady who will take you to your table, Mr. Hickson."

The waitress escorted us to our candlelit booth and seated us in a quaint, secluded section of the restaurant.

"Here are your menus. I'll be with you in a few to take your drink and food orders," the waitress said.

While we looked at our menus, I gazed around the place. The ambiance of the restaurant was beautiful. It had nice, warm lighting with a soothing décor.

"So, tonight, can you tell me more about you, the person, and not just you, the working woman?" Miles asked.

"Maybe after I get a couple of drinks in me."

"If that's what it'll take for you to talk openly, I'll tell her to leave bottles on the table."

"Be careful what you ask for. I'll hold you to that."

Our waitress came to our table. "How are you guys doing tonight? Would you like something to drink to start off?"

I decided on one of the restaurant's signature drinks. "I'll have a South Carolina Rum Punch," I said.

"I'll have a rum and coke," Miles answered.

"No problem. Are y'all ready to order just yet, or do you need more time?"

I looked at Miles, and he nodded.

"We'll order now," I answered.

Our waitress took our orders and quickly brought back our drinks. We started with the usual mundane first-date questions until Miles asked, "If you could change one thing about your life, what would you change?"

"That's a deep question."

"You seem like a deep woman."

"What makes you think that?"

"Your eyes and the way you talk and carry yourself. Your eyes give off the vibe you've seen and been through a lot. But truthfully, sometimes, you come across as guarded to me."

I nodded.

"I am guarded. I don't like to waste time, and I don't like people to feed me bullshit, so I'm direct, to the point, and expect the same."

"Fair enough."

I let him talk first.

"I know you work for NYC housing, but what do you do there?" I asked.

"I'm a maintenance supervisor. So when your heat isn't working, or when high brothas decide to do target practice and shoot up their walls, me and my crew fix up the apartments."

I sipped my drink and listened to him babble about a typical day at his job.

At some point, I spaced out while toying with the straw in my drink, wondering if I should've spent time with my sons instead of being here on a date. Another thing stressing me was Christmas was around the corner, and I had no money to buy my boys any gifts.

"A penny for your thoughts," Miles said across the table.

I tried to think of what he'd been saying before I zoned out, but I couldn't remember anything for the life of me.

"Oh, I'm sorry."

"You looked like you spaced out for a minute. You seem distracted. Is everything OK? Are you having a good time?"

"Yes, it's not you. It's just . . . I haven't been on a date or hung out without my kids in a long time. I don't have much free time with them since I'm always working, so I won't lie. I feel kind of guilty being out like this."

He looked taken aback and disappointed. "I see . . . If you need to get back to them, I'll understand."

I smiled, feeling my defenses soften a little bit. "Order me another drink, and I'm sure I'll be more comfortable."

He smiled and said, "Not a problem . . . I know I've bored you enough talking about my job. So why don't I ask you questions to keep our conversation interesting?"

I chuckled softly and said, "Go ahead."

The waitress came and placed our meals on the table.

"Another drink for you, ma'am?" she asked.

"Yes, please."

The waitress returned with my drink, and I quickly gulped it down, trying hard to push back my inhibitions.

"If you don't mind me asking, I didn't want to ask during our conversations over the phone, but how did your husband pass?" Miles asked.

"It's a long story."

"If you're OK with telling it, I have nothing but time."

He locked his fingers, looked me in the eyes, and prepared himself to listen intently as I told him the abbreviated details of my husband's murder. Finally, I sighed, feeling misty-eyed, and said, "He was killed. A stray bullet hit him when he was on his way home from the grocery store."

"I'm sorry."

"It's fine. He was just at the wrong place at the wrong time . . . Can we talk about something else?"

"Sure."

Mo's death was still a sensitive topic for me. I didn't want to ruin my night reminiscing about that.

"You told me some things about your work during our phone conversations, but what do you like about your job?" he asked.

"Anything else but that," I laughed.

"I take it there's nothing you really like about your job."

"Nope, I hate it with a passion. I'm underappreciated, overworked, and underpaid, but it's a steady job with weekends off, and the benefits keep my youngest son alive, so I put up with it."

"If you weren't working at the firm, what would you do?"

"I honestly don't know."

"C'mon, what's your passion? What would be your dream job?"

"I don't like to think about what-ifs. Sometimes, events in our lives divert our plans. My dreams were pushed aside once my husband died and Jerami was diagnosed."

"I'm sorry—"

"Don't be; that's life."

There was silence for a minute until Miles asked, "So, what's it like being a single mother?"

"I don't know if I can explain that. There's no way to give you a complete answer."

"I'm sure you have a lot to say about it."

"I do, but I don't want to bore you."

"You wouldn't, trust me."

I hesitated for a minute. I wasn't sure if I should confide in him or if he wanted to hear the long or short version of my drama-filled life. Then, for some reason, I guess you can blame it on the alcohol. I opened up to him.

Miles listened intently as I vented about my pains and struggles as a single mother.

I took a long breath. "Where do I start? It's hard trying to juggle a career and raise kids. In the mornings, I have to fight to wake them up, get them ready for school, and make sure they have something to eat. Then I go to work, and after working all day, most of the time after doing overtime, I come home and can't relax. By the time I check over their homework, cook dinner, and let them stay up to watch a little TV, I'm too exhausted to do anything for myself."

Miles slowly nodded.

"Did I bore you yet?"

"Hardly. Go on; vent. Talk to me."

I sighed. "If that's what you want..." I took a deep breath as I prepared to say my truth.

"My kids are my world. They're the reason I work so hard. They don't deserve the shitty hand that life has dealt them. They're my motivation to wake up daily, and I bust my ass to provide for them. I try to give them the best life I can, and every day, I come home exhausted, wondering if I did enough for them."

Miles nodded as I continued.

"I'm their only nurturer and provider. It's hard for me, and it breaks my heart when I have to console them after telling them they can't do something or that they can't have certain things because I don't have the money for them. When my kids are sick, or there's a snow day or emergency, there's no one for me to call. I have no help. Single moms don't get a day off. I don't get a break when I'm sick, tired, or stressed out. My biggest fear is that my kids will grow up having issues because I wasn't enough on my own after all the drama they've been put through."

"Damn. I take it your sister doesn't help you?"

I let out a slight chuckle. "My sister is a freeloader. Once in a while, she surprises me by not being completely selfish, and lately, she's been helping out, but the truth is, I enable her because I'm scared of being alone, so I put up with her shit."

"Damn, you're a strong woman."

"Thanks. That's just the condensed version."

"I applaud your strength. I gotta give you your props for being so level-headed, despite everything you're facing."

"Thanks."

I sipped my drink and stared at him. "Enough about me. Tell me more about you. What's *your* story?"

"There isn't much to tell—"

"Before we go any further, do you have a woman or any baby mamas that are going to crawl out of the woodwork and attack me for being on this date with you?" I asked, giving a look that dared him to lie.

He laughed. I didn't.

"No. I told you before. I'm single."

"I'm single too, but it doesn't mean I don't have kids. I have enough stress in my life. I'm not looking to add to it with more drama. Is there, or should I say, are there other women in your life that you're romantically attached to?"

"No. I've been a workaholic all my life. Unfortunately, being that way prevented me from having a family, but I'm trying to change that."

I pressed on. "How many women have you taken on dates like this?"

"I don't date much. I know what I like, and I don't come across women like you often."

I smiled at that and eased up a bit.

We conversed for about an hour about everything from our families to our dreams for the future. The way Miles looked at me made me feel warm inside. He made me feel beautiful, appreciated, and sexy, things I haven't felt and missed since Mo died. I forgot that I could smile and laugh so much. It felt good to laugh and have a meaningful conversation for a change. I realized this was precisely why I needed this date night away from my kids.

"I'm having a really good time tonight. I don't want this to end," I said.

"We don't have to call it a night yet. I was planning on taking you to the movies."

"Nah, not tonight. I love movies, but I'd rather talk and get to know you more."

"I know if I asked you to hang out at my apartment, you'd probably think I'm just trying to have sex, so why don't we go to your place? We can watch TV and continue our conversation."

"Sorry, but we're too new, and it's too early to bring you around my kids. I like you, but I don't know you well enough to have you around them like that. Plus, my oldest would probably try to kill you if he felt you were trying to replace his father."

Miles looked disappointed but said, "Fair enough."

"How about this? If you continue to be the gentleman you are now, I'll hang out at your place."

He smiled.

"If you start getting all handsy, I'm out."

"I promise I'll behave."

Miles flagged down the waitress. She collected our empty plates and asked, "Do y'all want anything else tonight?"

I shook my head.

"Just the check, please," he said.

Minutes later, she returned with the check and placed it in the middle of the table. I reached to pay for it.

"No, no, I appreciate the thought, but I got this. You're my date," Miles said.

He took care of the bill. I insisted on leaving a tip, but he wasn't trying to hear that either.

I took his hand, and he helped me out of the booth.

After we left the restaurant, the entire ride to his place, I thought about sex. I knew I shouldn't. I knew it was way too early to be thinking about that. I knew it was destined to be a mistake, but I wanted him.

We walked to his building and took the elevator to his apartment on the fifth floor. He unlocked his door, and we walked inside.

"Here we are," he said.

I stood inside for a moment, taking in the apartment. I was pleasantly surprised and impressed with the setup. It was small but neat and well-organized, and his furniture was beautiful, which made it feel cozy. He had a huge black leather sectional couch, and his bookshelves, end tables, and coffee table were made from mahogany.

We drank Hennessy, sat on his couch, and watched TV. I let him do most of the talking, but at some point, I kissed him. I'm sure all the liquor I drank gave me more courage than usual, but I needed to feel some affection for once.

Miles moved in and pulled me closer. His lips touched mine as he held me. Miles slipped me his tongue. As our kissing intensified, I slid my hands up his chest and wrapped them around his neck. Then I pulled away to end the kiss and stood up. Miles stood up too and rested his forehead on mine. His hands and lips traveled over my shoulders, down to my breasts. They glided down my back, around my hips, and he grabbed two hands full of my ass. My mind told me to stop him, but every part of my body craved to be touched.

A million emotions were going through my head. Desire and guilt were the two most prominent. Sexually, I've only slept with Mo. I questioned if I was having sex too soon after his death and if Miles were worthy of giving myself to.

Miles held my hand and walked me to his bedroom. He pulled the bedspread back, and before I knew it, I was lying on my back on his navy-blue satin sheets with his face buried in my treasure, having a deep-rooted orgasm.

Everything I did in life, I did for my children, but tonight, I wanted to enjoy this one night for myself. Even if our feelings weren't real, even if it meant nothing the next day, I wanted one night where I didn't have to be the backbone of my family—just *one* night where I could escape my responsibilities.

"Are you sure this is what you want?" Miles asked.

I nodded, pulled him to me, and kissed him to shut him up. If he kept asking me if I was sure, I'd probably lose my nerve and change my mind. All I wanted to do was focus on the now.

I sighed in pleasure as he slid his length inside me. He started off slow and gentle before giving me all of him in one hard thrust, knocking my breath out. I moaned his name, exciting him enough to feel him fill me to the brim with his thick cock. His strokes were gentle but deep.

I held my hands on the sides of his face, which was inches from mine, looked him in the eyes, and whispered, "Fuck me." I didn't want this experience to feel like love; I wanted to be fucked. The alcohol had thrown my inhibitions out the window, and my pent-up sexual tension had me wanting it rough. I wanted it to hurt. I wanted my pussy to throb and feel sore the next morning. My brain screamed for me to stop him, but my body needed this release. I needed to remember what it felt like to be wined, dined, and pleased sexually.

Miles transitioned from sliding inside me slow and easy to firm and strong. One of my hands traveled down to my clit, rubbing it furiously as he pushed and pounded into me. Miles touched places inside of me that I thought would never be touched again, and when it was all over, we lay on his bed in exhausted bliss. He spooned his body against mine, kissed my cheek, and stroked my arm. I snuggled close and dozed off, wrapped comfortably in his arms, feeling satisfied!

The following day, the sound of a running shower and the sun peeking through the blinds, shining on my face, woke me out of my sleep. My head was pounding. I was still slightly hungover from drinking the night before. I felt a dull throb between my thighs. I rolled over, tangled in sheets that weren't mine. My eyes snapped open. Reality hit me. I was still at Miles's house, and I never went home. I was coming down off my drunken high, and the vivid reality of what I did from the night before played out in my head.

I reached over for Miles, surprised to see he wasn't there. I sat up and looked around. I blindly felt around the side of the bed for my bra and panties. I had them in my hands when I heard the water stop. Miles walked into the bedroom, and beads of water dripped down his completely naked body. Even though we had been intimate the night before, I pulled the sheets up to my neck to cover my nakedness.

"Good morning, gorgeous. Sorry, but you looked so peaceful; I didn't want to wake you," he said while yawning. His dick bobbed as he stretched. I tried to avert my eyes, but that wasn't happening. When I looked up, Miles was smiling at me. I avoided his gaze.

"Look, last night was a mistake. It shouldn't have happened . . . I'm sorry. I can't deal with this right now. I gotta get out of here. But don't worry; I'll see myself out," I said.

I wrapped the sheets around my naked body, sprang out of bed, scrambled across the bedroom floor to gather the rest of my things, and rushed into his bathroom to freshen up and fix my hair.

"I left a washcloth and some extra towels in there for you . . ." Miles yelled through the door.

"Thanks."

I shook my head at my reflection as I stared at myself in his bathroom mirror. My makeup was mostly rubbed off and smeared, and my hair was a hot mess. If anyone could see me now, they'd know I got fucked last night.

I undressed, stepped into his shower, and washed the smell of sex off my body. After I dried off, I dressed, pulled my hair into a ponytail, and put on my lipstick.

Miles was sitting on the bed when I walked out of the bathroom.

With my purse in hand, I slid my feet into my shoes, determined to get out of there as quickly as possible.

"Juanita, wait . . . Please," he said.

I stopped, slowly closed my eyes, and said, "What?"

I opened my eyes to see Miles standing before me, wearing nothing but a pair of black satin boxers.

"It wasn't a mistake for me. I really like you, Juanita. I want us to build a relationship off last night."

"I don't need or want that right now."

Miles sighed. "Can I drive you home?"

"We live a few blocks apart. I'll manage. Thanks."

"Will I see you again?"

"Queensbridge is a small place. I'm sure you will."

"I meant, can we go on another date?"

"We'll see. You can still call me if you want, and we can go from there."

"Please don't think of our time together as a mistake."

The look on his face seemed genuine.

"We'll see. Right now, I need to get to my kids. I'll see you around."

"I'll call you later today," he said, hugging me.

I kissed him on the cheek and sprinted out of his apartment.

I did the walk of shame home from Miles's building to mine. I wanted a cigarette before I stepped into my apartment and heard Carina's mouth, but I was out. I leaned against the fence outside my building, digging through my purse to see if there was a loose one in it, when Tracy walked out of the building and gave me a knowing smile. She bombarded me with questions.

"Are you just getting home? Oh, Girl, what did y'all do? Did you go to a hotel or his place? Was he big? Does he have a brother or single friends? Girl, tell me all about this date with that Miles guy, and don't leave any of the dirty shit out either," she said.

I giggled. "Oh my God. How do you even know about it?"

"Please, you know your sister can't keep a secret. I knocked on your door after I got off work to see if you wanted to hang out, and she said you were on a date with some guy named Miles."

I sucked my teeth.

"So, what's going on with you two? Did you give up the panties or not?"

I knew she wouldn't stop asking me about Miles until I told her every detail, so I said, "You wanna know about last night? It's gonna cost you."

"What's your price?"

"At least two cigarettes."

Tracy tossed me an open pack. "All right, there you go. Now, no more stalling. Spill it!"

I grabbed two cigarettes from her pack and handed it back to her. I lit one and took a drag. Then I faced her and said, "It's nothing serious."

"Uh-huh, I know something went down. You're glowing. Spill it!"

"You're so nasty!" I giggled.

"Girl, you already know my sex life is nonexistent, so I have to live vicariously through you," Tracy said.

"Seriously, it's nothing. We went out to dinner. . . sex was involved, but it was just two consenting adults having a good time."

"You never know. You might've put it on him so good that he might want to be the new man in your life."

"Oh, please. I don't have time for men. I'm too busy trying to raise two of them. Besides, I have too much shit going on in my life right now to commit to anyone. The last thing I need is a man making my already diffi-cult life more complicated."

"Just take it slow."

"The way he talked last night, I think he's looking for a woman now and not later."

"Remember this: relationships are like cars. Men might be at the steer-ing wheel, but women are the brakes. We can pump those brakes and choose what we'll accept and not accept in a relationship. So let his ass know that if he wants a future with you, he will have to be patient, or he can look elsewhere."

I nodded.

I ran down everything that happened last night. I started with Miles coming to pick me up. I told her about us going to dinner and then all the dirty details about our sex session.

Tracy touched her chest, fanned herself, and said, "Girl, jump on that! Do you know how rare it is to find a single brotha who isn't involved in the street, has a decent job, is a gentleman that actually pays for shit, is hung, can handle his business in the bedroom, and has no kids? Shit, send him *my* way if you don't want him."

We laughed.

"All right, girl, I'm going to head upstairs."

She laughed again. "Still worn out, huh? I know it's been a while; you might have to ice your coochie."

"Girl, bye! You're *so* nasty!"

"And you love it!"

We chuckled.

"Later, Queen," I said.

"Later!"

I walked up the steps to my floor, slid my key into my door, and prayed that my sister and kids were still asleep. I didn't want them to see me creeping into the house at this time of the morning, nor did I feel like answering a million questions about where I was all night.

Of course, Tracy failed to warn me that Akeem, Jalen, Jerami, and some other boy I didn't know were in my living room watching TV.

"You just getting home?" Jalen asked.

I avoided his question and said, "I hope you boys aren't still beating on that boy, Billy." I paused and looked at them.

"Nah, we're not beating on him anymore. We're cool with him now. But where were—"

My eyes narrowed on the kid I didn't know. His feet were kicked up on my coffee table like he paid rent here. Before Jalen could finish asking me where I was, I yelled at the kid, "Boy, what's your name?" I asked.

"Uh, Draper," he stammered.

"Well, Draper, I know your mama raised you better than that. Get your feet off my damn coffee table."

"Sorry, Mrs. Wilson," he said, moving his feet and looking down at the carpet.

"Matter of fact, I'm sorry, but Draper, I need you to leave. I need to talk to Akeem and my son about things."

"I'm outta here. Bye, guys," he said, hurrying out the door.

"Good."

I faced Jalen. "Now, where's your aunt?"

"In her . . . I mean your room . . . with some dude."

"Goddammit."

I guess I wasn't the only one having fun last night.

After getting some on the first night, I figured Miles would look at our night as a Wham-bam-thank you-ma'am, and things would be awkward. I truly believed he'd lose interest and stop calling me, but he stayed true to his word and continued calling me every night.

Miles took me out on more dates and was the true definition of a gentleman. Whenever we were out, his attention was focused on me the entire time, making me feel special. He was interested in what was going on in my life, my thoughts, and my goals, but most importantly, he was interested in understanding me and what it took to make me happy. To top it off, he was hardworking, funny, down-to-earth, intelligent, and damn right fine!

I didn't think about Jerami's cancer, my sister, or my job when I was around Miles. He was the only positive thing in my life now, and I opened up a part of my heart that I sealed off after Mo died.

Being with him had its perks. Although it seemed like a never-ending job, Miles always had his men come and fix the elevator in my building. He made sure that anything that wasn't working in my apartment was fixed immediately, and it felt nice to see progress when usually it took housing an eternity to get things done.

Miles wasn't the answer to all my problems, but he made me laugh and helped as a comfortable distraction from my chaotic life. We had been taking our time and allowing our . . . whatever you call it, I guess friends-with-benefits type relationship . . . to flow naturally, but I wasn't sure if the feelings I had for Miles were genuine or if I was just lonely and horny.

"It's getting late. I have to get home to my kids," I said.

After another great date, we had another sex session at his place. Again, Miles watched me as I gathered my clothes.

"Juanita?"

"Yes."

"I love being around you. I guess what I'm trying to ask is, where do you see 'us' going?"

"I love being around you too, but being in a committed relationship isn't on my priority list right now."

"Oh," he said, looking disappointed. "So, I guess we're just fuck buddies then, huh?" he asked.

I sighed, stepped up to him, looked him in his eyes, and said, "Don't be mad and don't call us that. I'm not looking for a commitment right now, but that doesn't mean I will tolerate being treated like a jump-off. Whatever 'this' is that we have will be on *my* terms, understood?"

"I'm OK with that."

I kissed him. "Just let everything happen naturally and enjoy the process. I'm not seeing anyone else, and with how you've been sexing me, I'm definitely not going anywhere."

"I feel the same way. All right, we can go as fast or as slow as you want."

"Good!"

A major flaw that Miles had was that he wanted me completely. He didn't understand that I couldn't devote all my time to him because I had kids to raise. I came up with a solution that I thought would help. Jalen wasn't getting arrested anymore, but I still heard the gossip from Kisha and Joyce that he was still doing dirt around the neighborhood.

Jalen needed a positive male figure around, someone who could teach him skills that, as a man, he should know. I couldn't let pride blind me. There were just some things I couldn't teach him, and I figured I could kill two birds with one stone by introducing Miles to my sons. I knew things wouldn't be easy. I figured Jalen would be rebellious at first, but I hoped, in time, he'd warm up to Miles, and Miles would understand why my children would always come first. Yup, it was time for them to meet.

CHAPTER 23

GET AWAY

It was Friday night, and for some reason, Mom wasn't letting me hang out with Akeem. Something had to be up. Lately, she'd been so busy hanging out herself that she wasn't on my case as much, but today, she had me vacuuming the living room and shit like she was expecting company.

Aunt Carina was still at work, and Jerami wasn't feeling well. He was lying on the couch watching TV while Mom and I cleaned the apartment.

I was closing the garbage bag to take it to the incinerator when Mom hugged me and playfully squeezed my cheeks. For a second, we laughed, and it was almost like it used to be, but then reality hit. Those brief seconds faded quickly. I moved her hands away and went back to throwing out the trash.

As soon as I came back inside, someone knocked on our door.

"I'll get it," Mom said.

"You expecting company?"

"Yup."

"Why are you so done up?"

Mom waved me off and opened the door. A muscular brotha holding a plastic bag and wearing a housing uniform came inside. I immediately recognized who he was, and the look on his face told me he remembered me, too. His name tag said he was Miles, and he was the same dude that held me back when I was beating Bill's ass not too long ago.

"What are you doing here?" I asked.

Moms glanced from me to him and asked, "Have you two met before?"

Miles quickly said, "No."

He faced me and said, "You must be Jalen. How are you, young man? I'm your mother's . . . friend, Miles. She's always bragging about her son, the ballplayer, so it's nice to meet finally," Miles said, holding out his fist for a pound.

I've seen how guys looked at my moms. Every guy in the hood wanted a piece of her. In my eyes, my dad wasn't even dead that long, yet she had this guy coming around, being all friendly and shit, trying to get in her pants.

I left his hand hanging, faced my moms, and said, "Dad isn't even cold in his grave, and you're out here going on dates with some nigga that I don't even know?"

"Boy, have you lost your damn mind? Who do you think you're talking to?" Mom asked, stepping directly to my face.

Miles patted her shoulder. "It's OK," he said.

"No, it's *not* OK. I don't answer to no fucking child, and he's going to respect me."

Miles faced me and said, "I know it's uncomfortable seeing another man around your mother. She's told me how great of a man your father was. I know I can't fill his shoes, and I'd never try to disrespect his memory like that. You don't trust me yet, but all I ask is that you give me a chance and get to know me."

"I'll pass on that," I said, rolling my eyes and sitting on the couch beside my bro.

I don't want to hear that shit.

Miles shrugged and walked up to Jerami.

He bent down, got eye level with him, and said, "Hey, little man, you must be Jerami."

"Hi," my bro said shyly.

"Your mom told me how brave you are with handling your treatments, so I got you a little something."

Miles pulled an X-Men action figure out of the plastic bag he was holding. Jerami's eyes lit up when Miles handed it to him.

"Thanks!" Jerami said.

That shit wasn't gonna work on me. He wasn't gonna buy my approval or pacify me with bullshit gifts. I immediately hit him up with questions.

"Yo, how long have you been seeing my mom?"

"Not too long; maybe like a month and a half."

"Where did y'all meet?"

"We met at the Chinese restaurant on Fortieth Avenue when she was getting food for you and your brother."

"You tryin' to marry her?"

"Jalen!" Mom yelled.

"Right now, we're still getting to know each other, but maybe later down the road, yes," Miles said.

The expression on Mom's face read that she didn't know about the whole marriage thing, but she kept quiet. I had no idea what Mom saw in this loser, but that was on her.

"Well, there's no better way to get to know someone than breaking bread with them. Y'all ready to eat?" Miles asked.

"Yeah!" Jerami said excitedly, standing up from the couch.

Miles's corny, overly nice ass took us to Pizza Hut on Queens Boulevard. He paid for everything and talked a good game, but I wasn't sold on his smiling face and a wack-cheap dinner. I saw through that bull-shit. He might've had Ma and Jerami fooled with his gifts and his nice-guy approach, but I knew better. He was just another nigga tryin' to fuck my moms.

CHAPTER 24

COUNT ON ME

I shook my head at my family's tiny, pathetic-looking Christmas tree in the living room. Christmas Eve was here, and I needed to do something immediately to fill the emptiness under the tree. But with my credit cards maxed out and my nonexistent funds, I didn't know how to pull off that Christmas miracle. I sighed and walked to my sons' room.

Carina had already left for work. I went through my usual routine of waking my boys and making sure they got ready for school.

I smoked my morning cigarette with Tracy and Debbie, and when I returned to my apartment, Jalen was eating cereal at the kitchen table. I took a couple of dollars out of my purse and handed them to him.

"Here. It isn't much but buy yourself something good for your lunch."

He smiled. "Thanks, Ma."

I didn't have money to spare, but I tried to do what I could.

"You know you're my Sonshine, right?"

He rolled his eyes, smiled, and said, "I know, Ma."

"Good. Now, finish getting ready. I don't want to get a letter from school telling me you were late. Get there on time, you hear?"

"Yeah."

"Good. I'll see you later tonight." I turned to leave his room.

"Mom?"

"Yeah."

"I didn't ask you for anything because I figured you'd probably say no..."

I sighed, wondering where he was going with this. "Go on."

"Me and Jerami didn't get anything last Christmas. There's still nothing under the tree, and it's Christmas Eve. All I want is a PlayStation. Can you at least get one for me today, please?"

Before I could answer, he continued, "I don't care if I don't get other stuff. I don't care if you don't buy me a game with it. I'll play with the demo games that come with it until I save up to buy one. That's the only thing I want. Of course, Jerami wants some toys, but he'd be OK sharing a PlayStation with me."

"I'll see what I can do."

He sucked his teeth. "That means no. Whenever you say that, I never get anything."

"I'm really trying, Jalen. I'm doing the best I can. None of this is easy for me—"

"That lame excuse is getting played out. We wouldn't have to struggle like this if Dad was alive."

My lips trembled. I know he still blamed me for his father's death. Jalen walked back to his room. I finished making sure they got ready for school, and then I headed to work, already feeling like a failure of a mother.

I sat in my office and thought back to last Christmas when I was too broke to buy my kids any gifts.

"Mommy, Santa didn't get me and Jalen nothing?" Jerami asked. Jerami had tears in his eyes, staring at our giftless tree.

"I think he ran out of toys this year, baby," I said, feeling like shit.

"But I don't get it. We've been good all year. I took all my medicine and did everything I was supposed to do."

Jalen folded his arms and sucked his teeth. "That's because there's no such thing as—"

I cut him off and got in his face. "Hey, don't you dare ruin that for him. We have enough negativity going on. Don't take that from him," I said.

"Well, he should know the truth why everyone we know gets gifts, and we get nothing," Jalen said.

"I need you to understand that I do everything I can for both of you."

"What does he mean, Mommy?" Jerami asked.

"Nothing, baby. Jalen is just being grumpy."

A light tap on my office door broke me out of my depressing thoughts.

"Earth to boss lady," Francisco said. I looked up to see him and Julissa in my doorway, staring at me.

"Hey . . . Are you guys excited for Christmas?" I smiled, trying my best to hide my sadness.

"Yeah . . . Francisco and I got you a little something," Julissa said.

Francisco walked up and gave me a three-hundred-dollar gift certificate to JC Penny. I fought back the tears. I knew they were giving me this gift to buy more work clothes. While I loved them for that, I couldn't accept it.

"No, no. That's OK. I know you guys have your own stuff going on and can't afford this. Save your money, guys," I said, trying to hand the gift certificate back to them.

"We bought it for you out of love," Julissa said.

"That's very sweet, and I appreciate it, but I didn't get anything for you guys, and I wouldn't feel right accepting this and not returning the favor."

"You do enough for us. This is for you," Francisco said.

I declined again. Even though I knew their hearts were in the right place, I was too embarrassed to take their charity.

"I appreciate the gesture . . . really, but I can't accept your gift."

"Please don't look at this in a negative way. We see everything you do for your kids and know you're struggling. We just wanted to do this for you to keep you motivated to keep fighting for what's important in your life because you're important to us," Julissa said.

I wiped my eyes with the back of my hand and hugged them. I was lucky to have friends here that were looking out for me.

Since it was Christmas Eve, the partners closed the firm at noon. Everyone filed out of the building, and with everyone going for the day, I sat in my office and looked at my credit cards scattered on the desk in front of me. I knew I couldn't afford to buy my kids anything for Christmas, but there was no way I would let them go without again.

I stared at the lone picture of my sons on my desk. It reminded me that they depended on me. I looked down at the rings I hadn't taken off my finger since my husband put them on me on our wedding day. Being a mother is about sacrifice, and my kids deserved better than the shitty hand they were dealt. I knew what I needed to do.

I took the subway around the Times Square area and maneuvered past the tourists standing on the sidewalk watching the street performers and people handing out flyers to comedy clubs. Then I went to one of the pawnshops on West Forty-Seventh Street.

"How much can I get for this?" I asked the heavy-set Spanish clerk behind the Plexiglas window.

"Whoa, mami, that's a beautiful bridal set. You sure you wanna pawn it?" he asked.

"It's an emergency. Hopefully, my luck improves, and I'll return to get it soon."

He looked as if he felt sorry for me. "Look, the most I can give you is five hundred dollars, and that's me being nice."

My rings were worth way more than that, but I desperately needed the money.

I sighed. "OK."

It was time for me to suck it up and get this over with before I lost my nerve, cried, and came home empty-handed without Christmas gifts.

My eyes teared up as I showed him my driver's license and filled out the required forms. I struggled and trembled while doing so, but I pulled the tight rings off my finger for the first time in nearly twelve years and ruefully handed them to the man.

"Look, it's Christmas... no one comes here to sell something like this when times are good. Usually, if you're not back in a month, we sell your stuff. For you, I'll give you three months to get your money together to get your rings back. Does that sound good?"

Tears streamed down my face as I nodded and thanked him.

I walked around Times Square using my newly acquired money to buy my sons the gifts they deserved.

I rode the subway train back to Queensbridge with the boys' Christmas gifts tucked between my legs and the seat. Of course, I couldn't get them everything, but I got them what I knew they wanted most.

I blankly stared out the window, touching the empty spot where my wedding set used to be. No matter how much time had passed, I still couldn't accept that Mo was gone and wasn't coming back. I sure could've used him today.

Carina was off work and distracted the boys while I went to Tracy's place to wrap the gifts. When the boys were asleep for the night, I got the presents from Tracy's apartment and placed them under our tree.

The next morning, Jerami jumped on my bed, his eyes wide with excitement as he shook my arm.

"Ma, wake up," he yelled.

I rubbed my face. "What is it, baby?" I asked groggily.

I got out of bed, and Jerami excitedly grabbed my hand and pulled me to the living room.

"Ma, look, there are presents under the tree! Santa didn't forget about us!" he said joyfully.

I won't lie. I was a little in my feelings about an imaginary white man saving the day and getting the credit for giving my son toys when I sacrificed to get him those gifts, but a part of me loved that he still had a small piece of innocence left. Unfortunately, the gravity of our situation, his father dying early in his life and being diagnosed with cancer, was causing him to grow up too fast. I wanted to preserve his innocence for as long as possible, so I swallowed my pride and nodded.

Jalen jumped up and down excitedly, hugging the PlayStation box. Then he rushed up to me and whispered in my ear, "Thanks, Ma! I know you didn't have the money, but I'm glad you found a way to do this."

I smiled. "You still have to share it with your brother."

"I know; that's fine."

I kissed his forehead and said, "I love you, Sonshine."

"I love you too, Ma."

I needed to hear that from him more than anything.

Carina got up from her sofa bed and asked, "You didn't get me a gift?"

"This Christmas is all about the kids. Besides, you living here with me is a present all year round. Don't take it for granted. Did you get me a gift?"

She smiled. "I got you next time," she said.

"Yeah, I bet."

Carina laughed and lay back on her bed.

I was sitting on the floor, opening more gifts with the kids, when someone knocked on the door. I stood up, looked through the peephole, and saw Miles holding a bunch of grocery bags.

I undid the locks, opened the door, and stepped aside to let him in.

"Well, this is a surprise. I wasn't expecting company today . . . So what brings you here this morning—unannounced?"

"I know we never discussed getting each other gifts, but I wanted to surprise you and do something nice for you and your boys. I hope you don't mind. I bought groceries and wanted to make y'all breakfast this morning."

I laughed. "Well, none of us will turn down a free meal. Come in."

Miles walked in and Carina immediately walked up to him.

"This is my sister—"

"Carina," she said, shaking his hand. She was damn near drooling when she saw him.

"So, you're the guy occupying all my sister's time," she said.

"That's me," he smiled. "My gift to y'all this morning is me cooking breakfast."

"That's a cheap-ass gift," Jalen mumbled under his breath.

"Jalen!" I yelled.

"What?"

"Don't be rude."

Jalen glared at him. "My daddy used to make us breakfast—"

"Sonshine, this isn't replacing those memories. Don't turn something nice Miles is doing for us into something negative."

Jalen sucked his teeth and continued to stare Miles down.

Miles faced me and said, "I hope you don't mind, but I also got the boys some gift certificates for ToysRUs."

Miles handed them to Jerami and Jalen.

"Thank you!" Jerami said, smiling.

Jalen snatched his gift certificate from Miles and put it in his pajama pants pocket. Then he stood up from the couch and worked on setting up the PlayStation on the TV.

"Sonshine! Less attitude, more gratitude. What do you say when someone gives you a gift?"

He sighed, never turning his head from attaching the system to the TV, and said, "Thanks."

"You're being rude . . ."

Miles held my hand, and we hugged. "Let him be. He'll come around."

"Thank you, but seriously, you didn't have to do anything for us."

"I wanted to. You're a good woman, and you deserve to be happy."

Miles locked his fingers with mine. I followed his eyes to my left hand.

"Where are your rings?" he asked, staring at my hand.

I let go of his hand and touched my bare ring finger. "It's a long story, and I don't want to get into it today."

"All right, I'll respect that. Let me get started with cooking."

"You picked a good friend, sis. A man that can cook is hard to find."

Miles smiled, went to the kitchen, and got to work.

He made French toast, scrambled eggs, bacon, and sausages. He went to set the table when he came across my bill tray.

"What's that?" he asked.

"That's the mountain of never-ending debt I have. Just place the bill tray on the counter in the kitchen for now, so we have more room on the table."

He did what I asked, made plates for all of us, and immediately started cleaning up the kitchen.

"Since you're using the sink to wash the dishes, we'll wash our hands in the bathroom," I said.

He nodded.

Carina and I handled our business and forced my boys to do the same.

"Boys, give your new system a break. Breakfast is ready. Wash your hands before you eat."

They sucked their teeth and complained but did what I asked.

I returned to the kitchen and caught Miles thumbing through my bill tray.

"What are you doing?"

He jumped. "Nothing. I see you weren't kidding when you said you're up against a lot."

"Yeah, I am, but I'll manage . . . You're doing good today. Don't mess it up by being too nosy."

"That's my bad. I apologize for that."

We ate breakfast together, and I spent the rest of my day happy that my sons had a good Christmas.

Monday morning, Tracy and I were smoking outside our building before I headed to work.

"I'm just now realizing this, but where are your rings?" Tracy asked, staring at my bare ring finger.

I sighed. "I had to pawn them so my kids wouldn't have another gift-less Christmas."

Tracy had a strange look on her face.

"What?" I asked.

"Queen, you pawned something sacred. That was one of the most important things Mo gave you. Christmas is special, but your presence is more important than presents. Instead of buying them gifts, you could've just spent time with them, seeing that you're constantly working or at the hospital."

"I hear you, and I get it, but my boys needed those gifts. I rarely ever buy them toys or things that they want. I hate not being able to give them the childhood they deserve. I didn't sell my rings, though. I just pawned them. As soon as I get some money, I'll get them back."

"You're my girl, and I'm not trying to be a bitch or sound cynical, but when will that be? When do you ever have extra money lying around?"

She had a point, but I didn't want to think about that right now, especially before I headed to work.

Sitting at the front desk with Julissa and Francisco, Julissa seemed out of it. Finally, it dawned on me that she was unusually quiet and wincing whenever she reached for a file or the phone. I knew she wouldn't show me, but I think she was hiding bruises. I looked closely at her face. She was wearing more makeup than usual and was obviously using concealer to mask a black eye.

This was nothing new. Julissa had domestic violence issues like this in the past with her boyfriend, Javier, and it looked like he was hitting her again. Her man was an unemployed drunk who got violent and made Julissa his personal punching bag whenever he was depressed about his life, which, unfortunately, was too often. When she first started working here five years ago, she confided in me about his abusive nature, and I told her plenty of times after that to leave his ass, but she wouldn't listen because they had a son together, and she didn't want to break up their family.

I leaned in close to her and whispered, "Julissa."

"Yes?"

"Is Javier hitting you again?"

She looked down at the desk and nodded slightly before looking away.

"We all need a mental health day sometimes. Get yourself right and come back stronger tomorrow. I can see you aren't yourself today by the way you're moving."

She nodded.

I smiled. "I have Francisco here with me, and Meghan is around . . . somewhere. Take the rest of the day off. We'll hold it down here."

She stood up, hugged me, and said, "Thank you."

"It's no problem."

She gathered her things and went home. How's my favorite girl doing?"

I looked up from the reception desk and smiled big. I stood and came around the desk to give Mr. Adam Harper a big hug.

Mr. Harper was one of the wealthiest men in the world. He started out with a successful construction business and quickly grew into a mogul, opening and acquiring various companies.

"Boss lady, do you want me to page Mr. Lincoln and let him know his client is here?" Francisco asked.

"Absolutely," I said.

"I'm in no rush to talk business. How are you doing?" Mr. Harper asked.

"Same old, same old with me. How are you doing?"

"My wife is good, so my life is good. How was your Christmas? How are your boys?"

"Christmas was uneventful for me. It's all about the kids."

"Yes, the life of being a parent. Well, I didn't forget you. I got you a present for the holidays."

Mr. Harper handed me a Christmas card with a hundred-dollar bill in it.

"Aw, thanks, but you didn't have to get me anything. I feel bad now because I didn't get you anything."

"You've done more than enough for me in this lifetime. Enjoy yourself."

"Well, thank you, sir."

I hid my joy, but inside, I couldn't be happier. I desperately needed money.

Francisco paged Francis, and he rushed out to greet Mr. Harper with Meghan right behind him.

"How are you doing today, Mr. Harper? Let's go to my office to discuss all the details for your next business acquisition."

"Are you guys taking care of my friend, Juanita?" Mr. Harper asked.

Francis put on a faux smile and said, "Of course."

Mr. Harper and I developed a close relationship when he came to the firm a couple of years back for representation for a divorce. That day, he was a broken man. I remember it like it was yesterday.

Francisco and Julissa were on their lunch break, and I held down the front desk. Mr. Harper walked up to the reception desk wearing a black pin-striped suit with slumped shoulders. He's a tall, thin man, around six-foot-two, in his mid-forties. He has salt-and-pepper hair, and his blue eyes were red-rimmed that day.

"Good afternoon . . . I'm Adam Harper . . . I know I'm early. I'm sup-posed to meet Francis Lincoln at 2:00 p.m."

He was forty-five minutes early, and Francis couldn't see him then because he was busy with another client.

I smiled. "Good afternoon, Mr. Harper. Mr. Lincoln and the other part-ners are wrapping up meetings right now with their earlier appointments, but if you have a seat, I'll make you some coffee while you wait, and Mr. Lincoln will see you shortly."

"Thank you."

"How do you like your coffee, sir?"

"Just black."

I nodded and directed Mr. Harper to our waiting area. I made him a fresh cup from our gourmet coffee machine that the partners bought explicitly for our high-priority clients. Unfortunately, all the other clients got the same shitty coffee we made for ourselves.

Mr. Harper couldn't rein in his emotions and wept right there in the empty waiting area. I rushed over to him.

"Sir, is everything all right?" I asked.

"No, I'm about to lose my wife and everything I worked so hard for because I can't control my stupid dick."

He explained that he married his junior high school sweetheart, Emilia, very young and how she was with him before he was rich and powerful. They had four children, and Emilia stuck by him, sacrificing her career so that he could pursue his while she took care of their kids.

They had no prenuptial agreement, and after catching him cheating on her a ridiculous number of times, she was finally calling it quits. Emilia wanted half of all his assets, alimony, custody of the children, and child support.

"This is going to ruin me," Mr. Harper said, crying on my shoulder.

I awkwardly patted his back and said, "Uh, I know this is hard to believe right now, but everything will be OK."

"You're a woman. What do you think I should do?" he asked with a look of desperation.

"Well, first, I need to know a couple of things. First, do you love her?"

"Of course. I've loved her since the first day I saw her in seventh grade. But when you're a man in my position, beautiful women always throw themselves at you. It's hard not to fall into temptation."

I nodded. I didn't like his bullshit excuse but I didn't openly judge him.

"OK, so you love her. What do you fear most about getting divorced?"

I was waiting for him to say losing money and half of his assets, but he surprised me.

"No bullshit, I'm scared of losing her and breaking up my family. I'm no saint. I know I fucked up. I'm man enough to admit I have a problem fucking every beautiful woman that offers it up to me, but those skanks don't mean anything to me. They only like me for my money."

I smiled at his answer and listened patiently as he told me more about his relationship with his wife.

"I love doing things as a family with the kids. I don't want this divorce to make me look like a monster and taint my relationship with them. My family is worth more to me than money."

"Would you be willing to stop cheating?"

"If she gives me another chance, absolutely! I swear I'm done fucking around."

"Do you feel there's any way you two can work this out?" I asked.

"She won't talk to me. Her lawyer served me with the divorce papers and explained that Emilia wants to end things quickly . . ." He looked like he was deep in thought and just had an epiphany.

"Maybe you can talk some sense into her."

"Excuse me?"

"Yeah, she won't listen to anything I have to say, but if she hears it from you, another woman, maybe she'll reconsider."

"With all due respect, I don't think that's a good idea. She doesn't know me. Why would she listen to a word I have to say, especially when I'm a stranger to her, and this has to do with her personal life?"

He looked at me with pleading eyes. Finally, I sighed and said, "Listen, I hope you get her back, I really do, but I don't want to be responsible for things getting worse—or blamed if they end up not working out."

"I'm sorry; what's your name again?" Mr. Harper asked.

"Juanita. Juanita Wilson."

"Well, Juanita, if you do me this favor, regardless of whether it works, you have my word that from now on, I'll let this firm handle all of my legal matters. I'll also make sure the partners here know that you're why I'm choosing them."

I tilted my head to the side, shook it, and gave him a "you're out of your damn mind" expression.

"That's a lot of pressure to put on me, sir. I really don't feel comfortable talking to your wife about your marriage."

"It's fine, please. I'm begging you."

"Fine, but please don't hold me responsible if things don't work out."

"I won't. All I ask is that you try."

When Francisco and Julissa returned from lunch, I took Mr. Harper to my office, closed the door, and called his wife. I was taken aback when I realized that Emilia, Mr. Harper's wife, was a sista, but nonetheless, I had a long talk with her and told her that he came to the firm in tears and didn't want his marriage to end. I explained to her that he told me his biggest fear was losing his family but, most importantly, losing her, and he was extremely remorseful.

Naturally, she was pissed that he told a complete stranger about their marital problems. Still, she listened to me and, at the end of our conversation, agreed to call off their divorce if he promised to go to counseling with her to work on their marriage.

Francis was furious when he learned I talked to Adam Harper's wife.

"Why was my client in your office?" he yelled.

Francisco and Julissa pretended to be absorbed in their work and averted their eyes to avoid the tension between Francis and me.

I stammered and said, "Hhhhe was having a problem with his wife—"

"I know that, genius. He's getting a divorce. That's why he's here. You had no business calling his wife."

He turned and faced Mr. Harper, who was trying to get a word in, but Francis kept interrupting him. Finally, Tim and Richard walked out of their offices to see what all the yelling was about.

"I'm so sorry, Mr. Harper. That was so unprofessional of her, and this firm does not tolerate that sort of behavior," Francis explained. He faced me and said, "Juanita, pack up your office. You're—"

"Enough! Don't talk to her like that! I begged her to call my wife, and she single-handedly saved my marriage. She could've ignored me and left me in the waiting room, but she took the time to talk to me, and to be honest, she's the only reason I'm going to have your firm represent me exclusively for all my future legal matters. I was considering using your firm, but to be honest, your firm wasn't high on my list. But after meeting her, she swayed my decision."

Mr. Wayne rushed up and shook Adam's hand. "Hello, sir. I'm Richard Wayne, one of the partners here. I'm glad you decided to use us, and I'm happy that Juanita helped to fix the problem you were having with your spouse. Juanita is such a godsend around here and an important part of our firm."

I looked at him like he was full of shit but kept quiet.

That was a good day, but today, after seeing Meghan standing directly next to Francis, I saw the handwriting on the wall that he was trying to push Meghan on Mr. Harper and phase me out.

"Mr. Harper, let me introduce you to Meghan. From now on, Meghan will handle everything that Juanita used to do for you."

"No. I don't like or want that. I love Juanita. I'm comfortable with her, and we've never had a problem. It's nothing against Meghan, but I don't know her, and I don't want anyone new handling my affairs."

Meghan frowned at me. I grinned at her.

"I totally understand, Mr. Harper, but as you know, Juanita has a sickly son, and there are times when she can't commit to doing certain distinctive projects because, as you know, family comes first."

That motherfucker! He didn't give a fuck about my family or my situation, but he continued to lay his bullshit on thick, like he was doing this shadiness for my benefit.

"Rest assured, Mr. Harper, Meghan was trained thoroughly by Juanita, and she's fully capable of taking over for her seamlessly. The other partners and I are very fond of Juanita and everything she does for this firm. We're trying to lessen her workload by having Meghan take over a few of her responsibilities so she's not overwhelmed and can be there for her family."

"Well, that's a good thing, I guess . . . All right, let's head to your office and get to work."

Mr. Harper had a look of uncertainty on his face and gave me a weak wave that told me he wasn't completely buying Francis's bullshit. I gave him a slight grin and waved back at him as he walked into Francis's office with Meghan.

I had to be careful, or Meghan would phase me out of my job entirely, and I couldn't afford to lose my job when I had my sons to take care of.

CHAPTER 25

A Song For You

It was New Year's Eve, and since Tracy, Carina, Debbie, and I were all broke, we decided to bring in the New Year together in my apartment. Even though I figured Miles would rather be living it up, partying at a bar or club than be bored out of his mind spending New Year's Eve at my place, I invited him over to celebrate it with us. Surprisingly, he gladly accepted.

I heard a knock at my door.

"Who's that?" Jalen asked.

"It's Miles," I said.

"Uh, why did you invite that clown over here?"

I ignored him, stood up from the couch, and walked to the door.

"I don't like this guy spending New Year's Eve with us like he's part of the fam," Jalen said.

"Be nice, Sonshine. He didn't have to get you anything for Christmas, but he was kind enough to do it, so cut him some slack."

"I didn't ask him to. He ain't my daddy."

I waved him off and opened the door for Miles.

"Hi," I said.

"Hey."

We hugged, and he followed me inside.

"I brought some snacks and drinks for everyone," Miles said.

"Thanks."

I took them from him and laid them on the kitchen table.

"Miles, these are my friends, Tracy and Debbie. These are Tracy's kids,

Akeem and Ebony, and this is Debbie's son, Billy. Of course, you already met my sister, Carina, and my boys."

"It's nice to meet all of you."

I made sure he got settled, and Tracy followed me into the kitchen while I started cooking.

"Damn, that man is fine!" she said.

I giggled. "Stop before he hears you."

"You did good, Queen."

"It's nothing serious. He's just a friend."

"He's *not* a friend. *I'm* your friend. That right there is a man—a very *sexy* man—and you need to *jump* on that!"

We laughed.

I cooked spaghetti and meatballs and enjoyed everyone's company. Miles played PlayStation games with the boys. Although Jalen still gave him an attitude, I could see he was starting to soften up to Miles being around.

After they finished playing their video games, I turned the TV to Channel 7, and we watched *Dick Clark's New Year's Rockin' Eve*.

Ten minutes remained until the ball dropped. Akeem, Ebony, and Jalen were busy talking with each other. Jerami was on the couch nodding off on Carina's lap, trying his hardest to stay awake, but it wasn't happening, and Tracy and Carina were sitting next to Miles and me on the couch, laughing at how bad the singers were this year.

Miles rubbed my hand, leaned in close, and whispered, "Hey."

"Hey . . ."

"Do you mind if I talk to you alone in your room before the ball drops? It won't be long. I just need like two minutes."

"Why? That sounds suspect. What's going on? . . . If you think I'm doing anything sexual with you in my room, especially with my kids here, you're highly mistaken."

"It's not like that . . . I have a surprise for you."

"I don't like surprises, and you've done enough for my boys and me. What's this about?"

"Can you just trust me? It's nothing bad."

He stood up and reached for my hand before I could object further. It was nice that he was putting forth a serious effort to make me happy, but it was also a little scary. I felt like he wanted our relationship to be more serious than glorified fuck buddies, and I wasn't sure if I wanted more than that right now.

I sighed and said, "C'mon, so you can tell me whatever it is you couldn't tell me right here."

He nodded.

Tracy smiled at me, and while Miles wasn't looking, she fluttered her tongue at me. I giggled and said, "It's not that type of party. We'll be right back."

"Hey, if you're tryna start your New Year with a bang, we don't judge," Carina said.

Carina and Tracy slapped five while I rolled my eyes and pulled Miles to my room. I closed the door behind us. Miles had a hand behind his back.

"OK, what's up? What's this surprise you were talking about?" I asked.

He pulled his hand from behind him, and I saw a velvet ring box. I looked at him quizzically and asked, "What's that? Look, Miles . . . I like you a lot, but it's way too early to be thinking about marriage. There's no way I'm marrying you . . . at least not right now."

He smirked. "Do you see me on one knee? Just open it."

I slowly opened the ring box . . . and saw my pawned wedding set inside. I covered my mouth with my hands and tried my hardest to stop myself from breaking down and ugly-faced crying.

"How . . .? How did you get this? How did you know—"

"Christmas Day, I realized you didn't have your rings on, and you made it clear that you didn't want to talk about it. When you left the kitchen, I looked through your bills and found the pawn slip. I figured you needed the money badly for your kids, so I got your rings back for you."

I couldn't hold it back anymore. Tears streamed down my face. I felt all kinds of emotions. Happy and shocked that he could do something so wonderful for me when he barely knew me, and a little prideful *and* embarrassed that he did.

"Why? Miles, don't take this the wrong way. I'm extremely grateful, but you barely know me to be spending so much money on me. You shouldn't have done this."

"Juanita, to do something so selfless for your kids says a lot about you. I know enough about you to see that you deserve a win. If me doing this can make you happy and help you open up to me, so what we have can grow, it's worth it."

I kissed him deeply and held his hand as we returned to the living room.

"3,2,1. Happy New Year!" Everyone screamed, hugging and toasting with one another.

I kissed Miles again, and even though I knew Jalen was pissed about it, I didn't care. At this moment, I was extremely happy. Once our kiss ended, I walked over to Carina and said, "I need you to watch the boys for me for the rest of the night. I'm going over to Miles's place."

Carina smiled and made her eyebrows bounce.

"Handle your business, sis. I'll hold it down here."

"Thanks."

Even though I made it a rule to refrain from sleepovers when we started our "friends with benefits" relationship, I was so pleased with Miles's surprise that I planned on breaking that rule, packing an overnight bag, and fucking his brains out to show my appreciation. So I guess I would start this New Year out with a bang, after all!

CHAPTER 26

BREAKDOWN

It was a new year! Work was still shitty, but I just had to stay strong and make it through the next couple of weeks of Jerami's chemo, and soon, everything would gradually get back to normal, and this nightmare I'd been living would be over.

I really thought I was in the clear . . . until I got a call from Jerami's doctor while I was at work.

"Good afternoon, Mrs. Wilson. I've been trying to get in touch with you. Can you please come down to my office? I ran some tests on Jerami, and I'd like to discuss the results with you in person," Dr. Maier said.

My heart sank. We were down to one more week of chemo. The end was in sight.

"Is everything all right?" I asked.

"I'd rather talk to you about everything in person. Can you be at my office at around 3:00 p.m.?"

"Sure."

"Thank you. I'll see you then."

I hung up and immediately went to Francis's office. His door was open, and he was eating lunch with Meghan.

"Francis, I finished my work for the day. Unfortunately, I need to leave two hours early because my son's oncologist found something wrong with one of his tests."

"What else is new?" Meghan said under her breath.

She and Francis laughed. I ignored the bitch and waited for him to acknowledge my comment.

"You can go, but I will tell Richard you're leaving early again."

"It's not like I have a choice."

"We all have choices. You choose not to be here at work handling your responsibilities."

"I put this job before my son before he was diagnosed, and if I hadn't, there's a possibility that I could've caught his cancer earlier. I won't make that same mistake again."

"See, we all have choices, but remember, every choice has a cause and effect."

I didn't have time to go back and forth with him. I needed to find out what was going on with my son.

Carina picked up Jerami from school and met me at the train station near my job. She had work later, and Debbie had her own doctor's appointment to go to.

I sat fretting in the hospital waiting room, praying that Dr. Maier wouldn't tell me news to break my heart. The longer I sat there, the more anxious I got. I impatiently tapped my foot and glanced at my watch as if that would change anything.

"Mrs. Wilson," the nurse said.

"Yes?"

"Dr. Maier will see you now. You can head on back."

Jerami sat next to me as Dr. Maier gave me a grim look. There was no sign of happiness or hope on his face. I pulled Jerami close, took a deep breath, and braced myself for what I imagined would only be more bad news.

Dr. Maier looked over the file in his hands. "All of the MRIs, scans, and tests show that Jerami's cancer has returned, and it's spreading."

My eyes filled with tears. I did the best I could to keep my emotions in check. I closed my eyes while Dr. Maier continued explaining the severity of the situation.

"I know this is difficult to digest—"

"There weren't any signs of cancer on his last MRI a couple of weeks ago . . ." I blinked and felt my tears rolling down my face.

"I know . . . but all hope isn't lost. There's a new treatment called Rituximab that scientists have discovered is very effective against this type of cancer."

"Great . . . I guess we'll do that then. Whatever it takes to get this cancer out of my son."

"Yes . . . The problem is the medication costs fifteen thousand dollars, it isn't covered by insurance, and there's no payment plan for it, so you would have to pay for it in full out of pocket."

"If I can't afford that medicine, what are Jerami's chances of surviving without it? How much time would he have? If Jerami gets this treatment, will it guarantee he'll beat cancer this time?"

The expression on Dr. Maier's face told me he didn't want to verbalize what Jerami's chances of making it would be.

"There's no way to answer that correctly. There are too many variables and factors. Every person and case is different. I can't promise he'll be cured, but if he doesn't get the treatment soon, the chances of him not surviving will rise exponentially."

I tried my best to fight back my tears. I rarely cried in front of Jerami out of fear that the sight would scare him and make him give up on fighting his cancer, but I couldn't help it. It scared the shit out of me that there was a serious possibility that I could lose him.

I felt betrayed by God.

Thoughts of my baby boy dying because I couldn't afford his medication made me weep in the doctor's office. I couldn't sit back and watch my son slowly wither away and die. I felt like I failed him. I could've done more. I *should've* done more. Finally, I looked up at Dr. Maier.

I can't lose Jerami.

"I'll find a way to get the money as soon as possible," I said.

"That's the spirit. Stay positive, and I'm sure everything will work out for the best."

He said those encouraging words for my sake, but I could hear a hint of doubt in his voice.

My nerves were shot as I left the hospital. My head was spinning from all the information I was given. The thought of my son dying because I couldn't provide for him had me petrified. With all the shit going through my mind, I didn't know how to sort out everything and form a plan. Was my son *really* going to die because I had no money? I had nothing left of value to pawn or sell. Where was I going to get fifteen thousand dollars?

I was tired of hearing people tell me they were praying for Jerami to get better. I felt like those prayers were falling on deaf ears because God wasn't listening to anything when it came to me. I was already robbed of my husband. I didn't need cancer to take one of the only two things I had left worth living for.

I was lost in thought, trying my best to hold myself together as I held Jerami's hand and walked to the train station.

"Mommy, I'm hungry."

My stomach was growling, too.

"We'll eat when we get home, OK?"

"OK, Mommy."

I sighed once we reached the turnstiles. I looked in my wallet for the train fare and realized I had no more tokens or enough money for me and Jerami to get home.

"Baby, I need you to crawl under the turnstiles and go to the other side," I said softly.

"But don't you have to pay for us, Mom?"

I rubbed my hand down my face.

"Just do what I'm telling you, Jerami, and don't fuss with me," I said through gritted teeth.

He did as he was told and crawled through. I waited until the station attendant was distracted and hopped over the turnstile quickly. Some people shook their heads, and some laughed, but my pride and what people thought of me was the last thing I was worried about. I just needed to get my son home.

On the slightly crowded subway train heading back home, I looked out the window and saw Jerami's and my reflections. The innocence and happiness I saw in his eyes on Christmas morning were gone.

I lay my head against the window, and Jerami snuggled against my arm.

"I'm going to get better, Mommy."

I snapped out of my thoughts. "I'm sorry. What did you say, baby?"

"I'm going to get better after I get my new medicine."

I fought hard to keep my tears at bay. Inside, I was shaken to the core. I couldn't break down. I made that mistake at the hospital. I couldn't do that again. Jerami needed me. I kissed the top of his head.

"That's right, baby!"

I came home to an empty apartment. Carina left me a note telling me she was out on a date, and Jalen was eating dinner with Akeem and Ebony at Tracy's. Jerami rushed to his room and returned to the living room, holding his piggy bank. He handed it to me.

"Here, Ma," he said.

I looked at him curiously. "What's this?" I asked.

"I heard you tell Dr. Maier you'd find a way to get the money for my medicine. You always say you don't have money, so here, I wanna help."

I was taken aback by that. I exhaled deeply to stop myself from crying, pulled him in for a hug, and kissed his cheek.

"I appreciate it, baby, but save your money for something nice once we beat your cancer, OK? Mama got this."

I tried to distract myself by cooking dinner so I wouldn't think about Jerami's medication, but I wasn't having much luck. Finally, after I fed Jerami, he lay down on the couch and nodded off. I guess our long day drained him. Once he was asleep, I tucked him into his bed.

Miles called for our usual nightly talk. I vaguely explained what was going on, but I wasn't in the mood to have a long-drawn-out conversation, so I cut our usual evening talk short. He offered to give me everything he had in his savings account, which was two thousand dollars. It was incredibly thoughtful of him, and it was better than nothing, but I turned him down . . . for now, anyway. We weren't in a relationship. I didn't want to owe him anything, and it still was nowhere near what I needed to get Jerami's medication. So, for now, I turned him down, but if I somehow found a way to scrounge up thirteen thousand dollars, please believe I would take him up on his offer.

When Jalen and Carina came home, I explained everything that went down today at the doctor's office. The severity on my face probably showed Jalen that I wasn't in the mood for any smart-ass comments. He went to his room, hugged his sleeping brother, and went to bed without insulting or arguing with me.

"You gonna be all right, sis?" Carina asked.

"I don't know. I need to figure out how I'm going to get this money. Right now, I need to think."

"Everything is gonna work out, sis. You'll find a way."

I nodded and got ready to shower. I stepped inside, stood under the showerhead, and let the water beat down on me. That's exactly how I felt . . . beat down by life. I lowered my head and let my tears flow.

CHAPTER 27

THE EVERYDAY STRUGGLE

I should've known my day was destined to be shitty. I barely slept. I had too much on my mind. Tracy wasn't around for our morning smoke, and my damn train was late again, which means I was late to work . . . again.

As soon as I stepped through the firm doors, I saw Meghan fixing her makeup in a small compact mirror. She held up a finger and said, "Richard wants to see you."

She had a smug look on her freckled face. I walked into my office, logged into my computer, and headed to Richard's. I was nervous. I couldn't afford to lose my job right now. I tried my best to calm down.

I tapped on Richard's office door.

He took his eyes off his computer momentarily and motioned for me to come in.

"You wanted to see me, Mr. Wayne?"

"Yes, Juanita, take a seat," he said, gesturing for me to sit in the chair across from him while he continued typing away on his computer.

I shut the door behind me and made my way to one of the black leather armchairs in front of his desk.

Once seated, Richard looked up from his computer. I sat nervously, bracing myself for the worst as I waited for what he would tell me.

He leaned back in his chair. "The partners have brought to my attention that you've been late numerous times. You were late today—"

"Sir, I can explain—"

Richard held up a hand to cut me off. I held my tongue, realizing that I was already on thin ice.

"Don't interrupt me; I don't want to hear excuses. Right now, I need you to listen."

I bit down on my lower lip, trying to calm myself and stop having an emotional outburst. I sat quietly like a scared little girl, intimidated, while Richard stared at me. Finally, he straightened himself in his chair and continued.

"Your coworkers have complained about you sleeping on the job, and Francis caught you sleeping at your desk."

"Did my coworkers say that, or was it just Meghan that said that?"

"You're not in a position to point fingers right now. The other partners and I love having you here. We know you have many personal hardships and have fallen on bad times. We've been understanding when you needed time to mourn your husband's death, and we've been more than fair with giving you time for your sick son, but we have to draw the line somewhere. We all like you here, but we cannot put up with you sleeping at your desk or constantly coming in late. As of today, you're on probation. If you're late again or do anything deemed unacceptable by myself or the other partners, we will have to let you go."

I wanted to stand up and run out of the building as fast as I could without ever looking back, but I just held my tongue. There were so many things I wanted to say, but it wouldn't matter.

"Do we understand each other?" Richard asked.

"Yes, Mr. Wayne."

"Good."

He faced his computer and continued typing away. "I have work to do, and so do you. That'll be all. You're dismissed," he said.

I nodded and stood up. He made it perfectly clear that the discussion was closed, and he didn't want to hear my side of anything. By the time I walked out of Richard's office, I could barely hold myself together. I needed air. I needed to breathe. I need to be anywhere but here. The only place in the building where I could be alone to clear my head and figure out shit without being interrupted was the bathroom stall.

I scurried down the hall and rushed to the bathroom.

My hands trembled as I buried my face in them. I locked myself in a stall. I leaned forward, placed my elbows on my knees, hung my head, and let out long sobs. I had only been at work for ten minutes, and I was an emotional wreck. The little strength I had when I first stepped into the office was depleting by the seconds.

Lately, Francis had been riding me like Secretariat, and after being put on probation, and Jerami's health declining, everything stressing me felt magnified, and it was too overwhelming for me.

Thinking about my kids and realizing that my salary and health benefits were the only things keeping my youngest son alive and my family from being homeless was what I kept reminding myself of to make it through the day. I closed my eyes and took a deep breath to center myself and hold my emotions in check to draw the strength I needed to return to my desk, but I couldn't pull myself together. I'd love to walk right up to Francis and tell him, "You can shove this job up your fucking ass! Go fuck yourself, you racist dickhead!" but life didn't work like that. Any decisions I made affected my sons too, and I couldn't do anything that would cause even more instability in their lives. I knew I had to swallow my pride and endure this bullshit to take care of my family.

Blowing out a long breath, I wiped my eyes and exited the stall. Meghan stood in front of the bathroom mirror, touching up her makeup. I didn't hear her come in. I felt the urge to slap the smug look right off her damn face.

"What?" I asked her.

Meghan laughed at me like I was pathetic and shouldered past me.

I stepped out of the bathroom and felt myself becoming visibly upset after that little exchange with her. I wouldn't give her the satisfaction of seeing that she was getting to me, but it was getting harder for me to hide it.

I walked to my office, shut my door, and busied myself by finishing the backed-up work Meghan caused, hoping that would make the day move quicker.

Time crept at a snail's pace, but I finally made it through the day. I had a complete meltdown after work. I got off the train and power walked from the station to the path to my building. All I wanted to do was go home, smoke a cigarette, and be alone.

Tracy was leaning against the fence outside, smoking a cigarette, while Kisha and Joyce sat on the bench. They all saw me trudging my way to our building with my head hanging low.

"Uh-oh. Looks like there's trouble in paradise. Rough day at the office?" Kisha asked.

"Shut the fuck up, Kisha. I'm not in the fucking mood," I said.

Kisha faced Joyce and asked, "Who is this bitch talkin' to?"

Joyce smirked and shook her head. "She's just salty because working for the white man isn't helping her boujie ass," she said.

I ignored the two of them while they continued to talk shit and stood next to Tracy. The look on my face must've said it all and raised Tracy's suspicions.

"You OK, Queen?" Tracy asked.

"Never better."

Tracy tilted her head to the side. She knew me too well to know I wasn't telling her everything, and I wasn't myself.

"Cut the bullshit, Queen. I know you too well, and I know when you're hiding something, so I'll ask you again. You OK, Queen?"

I sighed. "No!"

"Come. Let's get away from these skanks and talk in my place."

We ignored Kisha and Joyce cursing us out.

"I have to be on time for my shift, so I can't talk long, but I want to put you in better spirits before I go," Tracy said.

"I'll be all right. Don't be late because of my drama."

"Queen, you're not yourself right now. Talk to me and get it off your chest," she said, grabbing me by the arm and pulling me inside our building.

We walked into her apartment, and I plopped down on her couch. I held my face in trembling hands as tears streamed down my cheeks.

Tracy pulled me close, and I wept in her arms, letting out all the pain and frustration I'd been holding inside.

"Let it out, Queen. It's OK," she said.

I tried not to choke over my words as I quieted down and said, "I . . . I don't know how much more I can take. I'm on the brink of losing my job. I'm drowning in bills. I can't afford the medicine that might save my youngest son's life. My oldest hates me. I miss my husband. I can't help but think that I'm failing my kids, and my youngest is going to die, and there's nothing I can do to save him."

"Queen, our minds are powerful. Don't think that shit into existence. What do you mean you can't afford the medicine for Jerami?"

"Long story short, Jerami's cancer is spreading, and he needs a new treatment that costs a grip. Unfortunately, insurance doesn't cover it, and I need fifteen thousand dollars for medicine that still doesn't guarantee he'll make it." I swallowed, shook my head, and continued.

"Every day, I wake up wondering what else can go wrong. What else is God going to take from me? I feel so empty, weak, and helpless."

"Queen, stop it right there. You're too strong to be having a pity party. There's nothing weak about you, and you need to change your perspective. When I look at you, I see a strong Black woman. It means nothing that I see that in you every day. *You* need to see it. Every day I watch you go to a job you hate to provide for your children. You don't call in sick. You don't take days off. You bust your ass all year-round for your kids. Sometimes after working fifteen hours straight, you go to the hospital stressed, tired, and hungry, but you're still there for Jerami. Afterward, you go home and make sure to ask Jalen about his day and make sure he's all right. That's strength. That's love. *That's* what strong single mothers do. That's *you*. I know things look bleak right now, but you'll find a way. Your sons will live to be old, successful men because a strong, successful mother raised them. I'm not trying to sound too preachy, but you gotta have faith that God will help you get through this."

"I don't know if I can do that. I've never been one to have blind faith, and with everything that has happened to me with Mo, with Jerami, and my job, I don't know if I want to."

"Queen, I'm not saying that praying and having faith will make everything perfect, but it can at least give you the strength to endure and make it through things."

"I wish I could be like you. You always seem so together and confident."

She laughed. "Girl, please! Like that old saying goes, 'Just because I carry it well doesn't mean it ain't heavy.' It's all part of the illusion. I'm far from having it all together or always being confident, but I pretend to be those things because it's important that my kids don't see me fearful and panicking. You must be the same way."

Tracy looked at her watch.

"Duty calls. I have to head to work, but call me if you're still upset or afraid and it feels unbearable. Even if you think it's stupid or you think I'm busy, call me. You're my sister from another mister, and I want you to be OK. You don't have to carry the weight of the world by yourself."

I smiled. "Thanks."

"Queen, just take it one day at a time. I'll see you in the morning."

"Later, Queen."

We hugged.

Tracy left for work while I walked to my apartment, struggling to clear my mind and figure out my next move.

Growing up, my family was never religious. To be honest, I wasn't even sure if God existed, but at this point, I was open to trying anything if it meant saving my son.

"God, I know we don't speak often, but please, don't take Jerami away from me," I prayed. Hopefully, God would listen.

The next morning, with my head down, I leaned against the fence in front of my building, nervously chain-smoking Marlboros. My head was in a dark place. Right then, I decided that I'd do whatever it took to make sure I'd have the money for Jerami's treatment. I was prepared to do anything. If I had to work twenty-four hours a day or even sell my pussy to every man in the street, I wouldn't hesitate to do whatever was necessary to save my baby.

Tracy and Debbie walked out of our building and hugged me.

"Hey, Queen, can I bum a cigarette?" Tracy asked.

"Sure."

I reached into my purse and handed her one.

"You look stressed," Debbie said.

"More than you can imagine."

"How are you feeling?" Tracy asked.

"Doing what you said and taking it one day at a time."

I brought them up to speed on my current drama.

Debbie looked deeply concerned.

"Queen, you know I love you like a sister, and if I had the money, I'd help you, right?" Tracy said.

"I know," I replied, giving her a warm smile.

"I might not have the funds, but I'm with you every step of the way, Queen. I'll try to help you any way I can."

"That goes for me, too," Debbie added.

I hugged and thanked them both and continued to smoke while they talked. Unfortunately, I was too caught up in my thoughts about Jerami to pay attention to their conversation.

I took one long, last pull of my cigarette, flicked it, and pushed away from the black metal fence.

"I'll catch up with y'all later. I have to head into work early since I'm on thin ice."

"All right, Queen. Take care of yourself and stay strong," Tracy said.

"Have a good day . . ." Debbie added.

I went to work. One thing's for sure . . . something had to give. I couldn't live with any more bad luck. I couldn't seem to catch a fucking break.

My workday was almost over. I spent most of the day at the firm going through the motions, struggling to maintain my composure by fake smiling and giving off the facade that everything was good, but I didn't have the energy to pretend anymore. Finally, I finished my duties and spent the rest of my shift alone in my office. My stomach was rumbling. I couldn't remember the last time I had eaten anything, but it didn't matter. My stress and thoughts were running too rampant to eat anything. I felt lost. I needed help, but there was no one I could turn to. I wanted to cry, but I was tired of crying. I wanted to run away, but there was no escaping my problems. I wanted to be anywhere but at work, but I couldn't leave.

Meghan walked into my office unannounced and dropped a stack of files on my desk. "I'm leaving early. I didn't finish these, and Francis wants them done by the end of the day."

I looked over the files. "These are all the things you were supposed to do during your shift. What did you do all day?"

"Look, I was busy. Just make sure they get done."

"The last time I checked, *you* reported to *me, not* the other way around. Who are you to give me your work?"

"Take it up with Francis. The way you're headed, I won't be taking orders from you much longer." She laughed and said, "Try to finish everything quickly, so you don't have to stay too late tonight. See ya!"

I gave her the finger as she chuckled and left my office.

I hated my job, but I couldn't afford to lose it. I was tired of feeling weak. I was tired of being a victim. It was time to take matters into my own hands. Shit with work was only getting worse, and while I've never been a vindictive, manipulative, or angry person, Meghan was bringing the nastiness out of me. I wouldn't lie down and lose my job because of that bitch. I held my tongue, but I saw the handwriting on the wall, and I knew eventually, the firm would fire me, but if Meghan thought I was going to go out without putting up a fight, she had another thing coming.

I walked to my building, relieved that my setback at work didn't cause me to stay later. Luckily for me, Meghan's assignments weren't too time-consuming. Apparently, Francis gave me the more challenging tasks and gave her the simple stuff, so I was able to finish her assignments quickly.

While I hated that Meghan was skating by while I had to do her work, I needed the distraction to give me a break from thinking about Jerami's situation. Now that I was home, my mind went right back to my problems. I stopped in front of my building to smoke a cigarette. Debbie was sweeping in front of the building.

"Hey, Juanita," she said.

"Hey. You seen Tracy?"

"Yeah, she went to work early. I'll chat with you for a while, though."

Debbie made small talk. Her lips were moving. I knew words were coming out of her mouth, but my mind wasn't in the conversation. Instead, I was in my own head, flooded with thoughts of what I could've and should've done differently. I was worried about my future at my job and, most importantly, Jerami, and how if I didn't do something, my son could die because I couldn't afford to get him the treatment that could possibly save his life.

"Juanita, did you hear me?" Debbie asked.

I blinked out of my thoughts, realizing she had been talking to me while I was absorbed in my own drama.

"I'm sorry. I don't mean to be rude. I just have a lot of shit going on in my head right now," I said.

"I totally understand. Jerami is taking a nap right now. Billy and Ebony are doing their homework and are there in case he wakes up. Hang out with me in my apartment for a bit. I'll make you some chamomile tea to help calm your nerves," she said.

"Debbie, I appreciate you trying to be there for me, but I think I'll just go home. With everything going on, I'd be poor company. I need to be alone."

"Give me ten minutes. We'll talk, drink some tea, and after that, I promise I'll let you go and give you your space."

"OK."

We walked up to her apartment. Debbie put the teapot on the stove to boil and, with a sympathetic ear, listened intently while I vented my frustrations without interruption.

I looked across the table and saw the concern etched on Debbie's thin, pale face.

She dug into her jeans pocket, reached for my hand, and gently placed hers on top of mine. Debbie turned my hand over, opened it, and placed a check on my palm.

"Debbie, what is this?"

She smiled and said, "All the money you need for Jerami's medication."

I shook my head. My eyes misted up.

"After you told me and Tracy what was going on, I knew what I needed to do. I went straight to the bank and got this check."

"I can't take this from you. How would I look taking money from a woman living off disability checks? You're struggling too. You need money for your own health issues."

"Juanita, I have MS. Unfortunately, my sickness is incurable, so I'm already on borrowed time. I couldn't spend the limited time I have left on this earth knowing I could've helped save a child's life and did nothing."

"I appreciate the gesture, I really do, but you're barely scraping by yourself."

"I'll be fine. Don't worry about me. I had some money saved from my tax returns and some left over from my health insurance. Jerami's life is more important than the money."

Tears streamed down my face. In my mind, I was torn. I desperately needed this money, but I didn't know when—if ever—I'd be able to repay her. On top of that, I didn't want to be Debbie's charity case. I didn't want to feel like the poor Black woman that needed a "white woman" to save the day.

"I really appreciate it, but I can't take this from you. I wouldn't feel right, and I don't know how or if I could ever repay you. I'm not taking it," I said as I handed her back the check.

As if she could read my mind, Debbie said, "It's not about Black and white. It's not about if you can pay me back or not. This is what friends do. Friends help each other without expecting anything in return. So put your pride aside and use this money to save your son. I value your friendship, and if I can do something to lift you up when life is beating you down, I'd do it for you gladly because I know your heart, and you would do the same for me."

There was nothing but sincerity in her eyes. I looked away from her, trying to hide my face as tears cascaded down it.

My lips trembled when I said, "Thank you for this . . . Thank you for everything. After all you've done for me, you're my sister for life. If you ever need anything, I got you."

Debbie waved it off like it wasn't a big deal, but her act meant everything to me.

"You don't owe me anything. I appreciate you being my friend."

I hugged her tightly and thanked her repeatedly. I didn't know what the future held for Jerami after getting this treatment, but now, thanks to Debbie, at least he had a shot.

CHAPTER 28

WHEN YOU BELIEVE

I was in my office typing a report for Mr. Rothstein when Francis opened my door.

"I need you to take notes for an important case I have coming up," he said.

"I thought you gave that responsibility to Meghan now."

"Don't get too high on yourself, but she doesn't quite have your eye for details. You're better at preparing the notes for my trials than she is."

"Is that right?" I said, smiling to myself.

He waved me off dismissively. "Just grab your things and meet me in my office in five minutes."

I did as he asked and reluctantly made my way to his office. I sat in front of his desk, pulled out my pen, opened my notepad, and placed my recorder on his desk.

I finished writing his notes and thought I was free from doing tedious tasks when Richard stepped into the office.

"Juanita, I need you to drive me to Brooklyn to one of my client's businesses. He's having a meltdown and said he couldn't discuss what he did over the phone. Before he does or says anything further that he regrets, I need to get to him ASAP."

"Meghan can drive you—" Francis started to say before he was cut off.

"Meghan is nowhere to be found, and I don't have time to look for her. I need to go *now*," Richard said.

I rushed out with Richard, hoping this didn't turn out to be an all-day and -night affair.

I got back to the firm after driving Richard to his client. Whatever was going on with his client, he spent the entire way there and back, making numerous phone calls to defuse the situation.

When I stepped to the front desk, Julissa was on the phone and handed me a file Francis wanted for one of his cases. Once I got the file, it dawned on me that I had left my notepad and recorder in his office. So, before he had a conniption and yelled at me for not having his notes prepared, I rushed down the corridor and headed straight for his office.

I stood in front of his door and overheard the tail end of a heated debate Francis was having with Tim. I raised my hand to knock but stopped myself when I heard Francis mention my name.

I thought about walking away but decided to stay put. I pressed my ear carefully against the door and focused on deciphering what they were saying.

"Did you really have to go to Richard about Juanita? She does a great job here, and I don't know why you can't see that," Tim said.

"Bullshit. She does mediocre work at best, and I'm tired of this firm bending over backward and coddling her because her husband ran off and left her in the ghetto. Sure, her kid is sick, but so what? Boo-fucking-hoo. We all have problems, but we still come into work," Francis said.

"You're being unreasonable. You can't possibly think your problems even come close to what she's dealing with. Her youngest son is more than just sick—he has cancer. She works extremely hard and is a single mom raising two kids, for God's sake. Cut her some slack. She's just going through a rough patch. She's always respectful and polite, and she was usually prompt before her string of misfortunes. Truth be told, she does far more work than Meghan, and you know that. Put yourself in Juanita's shoes," Tim said.

"I don't have any bastard children I can't care for, so sorry. I can't relate. Besides, if she's anything at home like she is at work, there's no wonder why her husband ran off and left her in the ghetto."

I heard enough. I cleared my throat and knocked on the door.

"How many times do I have to tell you? It doesn't mean you can come in just because you've knocked. Now, what is it?" Francis shouted.

I didn't hide my disgusted expression as I walked into his office.

"I forgot my notepad and recorder here earlier, and I have that file you asked for, Mr. Lincoln."

He rolled his eyes and snatched the file I was handing him. "You know how I feel about that. I told you countless times already to drop the 'Mr. Lincoln.' Just call me 'Francis.'"

"Sorry, Francis," I said as I grabbed a stack of folders from his outgoing bin, picked up my tape recorder from his desk, and placed it in my jacket pocket.

He looked even more annoyed by my response.

"You can leave now," he said, waving me off.

I thought about ignoring his comment and going on with my day, but I needed to clarify things for him. It's so hard for people like Francis, who live a privileged life and are on the outside looking in on my impoverished one, to have empathy or even comprehend what I deal with on an everyday basis. I turned to face him but didn't take my hand off the doorknob.

"Oh, and for the record, Francis, my husband didn't 'run off and leave me in the ghetto.' He was murdered. People like you with a higher socioeconomic standing might watch the news and see movies about how minorities live, but you have no idea what it's like to be in my shoes firsthand."

Francis sucked his teeth, shook his head, and stared coldly at me. "Touching story," he said.

I walked away and closed the door behind me before he could respond further, but kept my ear pressed to the door again.

Francis dove back into his conversation with Tim as if nothing I said mattered.

"Oh, I'm supposed to feel bad because the savages in the projects killed her husband? If you don't want to die in those types of neighborhoods, then don't live there."

"You can be so cold and insensitive sometimes," Tim said.

"I'm neither of the two. I'm a realist. All these people want to do is sit around on their lazy asses milking the system and collecting government assistance while people like you and me bust our asses and pay for it. You always hear minorities complaining about how bad their neighborhoods are when their own people make it that way. All the drugs sold, murders, and other shit that goes on in those communities are committed by their own, but they blame whites for their shitty existences. They bitch about having a lack of opportunity, but most of them don't even go to school when it's free for them. If they spent less time complaining and blaming 'the white man' and more time doing what they should, maybe their lives would be better, and there wouldn't be a slew of people killed in their communities every day."

"People should be responsible for their actions, but people can also become the products of their environment. My brother and I had the same upbringing, yet I'm a successful lawyer, and he's an unemployed alcoholic. What made the two of us lead two different lives? Our environment had different effects on us. Our parents were underachievers who did the bare minimum in life. I wanted to go further than they did. He felt limited because of them. My kids do well in school, and his kids are following in his shitty footsteps. They're becoming products of their environments. The same rules apply to minorities."

"Look at how well you've done for yourself. You pulled yourself up by the bootstraps, so why can't minorities do the same thing? Stop making excuses for them."

"I'm not. Juanita isn't one of the negative ones. But you really need to ease up on her. Before all the drama in her life occurred, her work was flawless."

Hearing Tim say that made me feel somewhat better. It felt good to know that at least one of the partners stuck up for me and saw that I worked hard.

I heard Francis sigh. "You're too soft on minorities. That's what's wrong with this country now."

I heard his footsteps on the marble tile and swiftly sprinted to my office. I shook off Francis's dickhead comments and pulled the recorder from my jacket pocket to compare the recording with the notes I had taken earlier. I realized the recorder was still on. I stopped it, hit the rewind button, and heard an earlier part of the conversation that I was eavesdropping on. I rewound the tape even further and listened to their earlier conversation.

"The only reason why we have our 'rainbow coalition' of a reception staff is because of affirmative action."

Tim sighed. "Francis, you're such a dick."

"I'm serious. It felt good to hire Meghan. I see our staff, and the only thing that goes through my mind is that they're taking the job of a more than qualified white person that actually deserves it," Francis said.

My mouth opened in shock. I fast-forwarded the tape and heard another disturbing statement from Francis.

"If working is too much for her, and she needs to focus on her sick kid, she can quit. Her kind has always been good at collecting welfare checks and milking the system."

I sat in my office, furious at what I had just heard.

An hour passed, and I still couldn't function. I thought about going directly to Human Resources, but I wanted answers for Francis's bigoted statements directly first.

I knocked on his office door and didn't wait for him to answer before entering. Instead, I pushed open the door . . . and froze at the sight of Meghan bent over his desk, getting hammered from behind. Her skirt was hiked up by her waist, her panties were around her ankles, and Francis was pumping away. They jumped when they realized I was standing in the doorway.

Meghan stood up quickly and hid behind Francis's back. She pulled up her panties, tugged on the hem of her skirt, and smoothed out the wrinkles to adjust herself while Francis tucked his hard-on into his pants. Neither of them could look me in the eyes.

"Jesus, why can't you grasp the simple concept of coming into my office when I tell you to, not just because you knocked? Get out of here."

"I need to talk—"

"It can wait. Leave."

I walked out, closing the door behind me. I shivered in disgust, trying to erase away that mental image of Francis's pasty ass pumping on Meghan out of my mind.

Next, I heard Francis and Meghan arguing in his office.

"Goddammit, she saw everything," Francis said.

"Who cares?" Meghan retorted.

"*I* care. That's all I need, for her to blab to everyone around here that we're fucking. I specifically told you to lock the door behind you."

"I thought I did."

"Obviously, you didn't. Now, I will have to do damage control before this spirals out of hand."

I laughed to myself and walked to the reception desk. I was about to tell Julissa and Francisco what I had just witnessed, but Meghan walked out of Francis's office. This whole situation gave me an idea. I reached into my purse and discreetly turned on my tape recorder. I strategically held it on my lap so it could record our conversation clearly and set my plan in motion. I didn't feel like hearing her spew some bullshit lie about not catching them fucking, but I hoped she'd say something incriminating.

Meghan pulled up a chair and sat down next to me. She turned her chair to face me. Julissa and Francisco pretended to be busy gathering paperwork for files.

Meghan cleared her throat, leaned in close, and whispered in my ear, "It's not what you think."

I didn't bother to whisper.

"It looked *exactly* like what I've always known to me."

She gritted her teeth. "You didn't see anything. Nothing happened. It'll be our word against yours, and seeing how you're on thin ice, nobody will believe you anyway."

I could barely contain my smile. "If that were true, why do you seem so worried? Why would you even come out here to say anything? Maybe human resources needs to hear about everything that's been going on in these offices."

"If you say anything to anyone, I'll have Francis fire you on the spot. So keep your fucking mouth shut," she warned, struggling to keep her voice low.

"Don't you dare threaten me. Keep your fucking legs closed. You're in no position to try to intimidate me after what I've seen."

"You know what? Fine! I don't care if you or any of the other losers working here know I'm fucking him. I don't care that you *saw* me fucking him. Soon, you'll be fired, I'll be in your position, and I'll be paid a hell of a lot more to do less than you're responsible for now. Good luck in the welfare line, bitch," Meghan said, standing up and heading back to Francis's office.

I smiled to myself. I could've easily gone to human resources with all the incriminating things I had on Francis, but what Meghan and Francis didn't know yet was that they both just helped give me my salvation.

I walked into the firm the following day fifteen minutes early. I passed by the waiting area where Meghan and Francis were laughing with each other. Their heads snapped in my direction the second they saw me. I kept my gaze firm on Meghan. I didn't have the energy to pretend anymore. I hated that bitch, and I wanted her to know I wasn't afraid of her, and she damn sure didn't intimidate me.

I headed straight into my office and booted up my computer. Francis entered my office and said, "Juanita, the other partners, and I need to talk to you. Meet us in the conference room in five minutes."

I nodded. "No problem," I said.

I took a deep breath, shook off my nerves, and stood tall. I was ready for this! I grabbed my purse and walked out of my office. I could feel the eyes of everyone on me. Francisco waved me over to him, leaned in, and asked, "Are you going to be OK, boss lady?"

"Yup. No need to delay the inevitable. I'm ready for whatever the partners throw at me."

Julissa had a worried expression. "Good luck, boss. I don't think I can keep working here if you aren't around."

"I appreciate that, but don't worry. I'll be fine."

I tapped my purse and walked down the long corridor to the glassed-in conference room.

Kimberly, the head of human resources, was sitting near the door when I entered the room.

Francis pointed and said, "Close the door, Juanita."

I did as he asked.

"Sit down," he said, gesturing to the empty chair directly across from him and the other partners.

I made myself comfortable, folded my hands in my lap, and gave them my undivided attention.

Tim stared down at the conference table. This was the first time since I started working here that he wouldn't make eye contact with me. His body language told me everything I needed to know. I guess his conscience was eating at him because he knew what was going on was wrong, and my livelihood was on the line.

Francis cleared his throat. He laid on the bullshit thick, beginning by praising me and telling me how good of an employee I *used* to be, then it gradually turned into how terrible of an employee I had become. All I thought about while he talked was there was no way they were taking my job from me. It took every ounce of my self-restraint to keep from jumping across the table and punching him in his pompous face. I sat back quietly, saving my response until I was sure he had finished bullshitting me.

"Juanita . . ." he stated, folding his hands, "it pains me to do this, it really does, but we're going to have to let you go. You can sit down with Kimberly from human resources, and she'll discuss your severance package."

Once I was sure he was finished, noticing the hasty smirk of victory on his face, I asked, "So, do you already have someone in mind that would replace me?"

"Not that it concerns you anymore, but Meghan will take over your responsibilities," Francis said.

I put my blood, sweat, and tears into this firm, and I'd be damned if they thought they would dismiss me and promote that bitch to my position.

My hands were folded in front of me, and I looked Francis in his eyes. "Before we go any further, may I talk to you and the partners privately, without human resources present? I think things would be better that way."

"Better for whom?" Francis retorted with his arms folded over his chest defensively.

"Honestly, better for you," I responded.

Francis looked pissed. Tim interjected before Francis could say anything else.

"Juanita has worked for us for a long time. Out of respect, we owe it to her to at least hear her out. Richard, your thoughts?" Tim asked.

"Kimberly, you may leave. When Mrs. Wilson finishes talking to us privately, she'll come to you to discuss her severance package," Richard said.

"No problem, sir," Kimberly said.

She faced me, smiled, and said, "I'll be in my office whenever you're ready."

She walked out of the room and closed the door behind her. I glared at everyone at the conference table but stopped at Francis. "I guess catching you in the act fucking Meghan yesterday forced your hand to finally try to fire me, huh?"

There was a lot of confusion on everyone's faces as they waited for me to elaborate. Francis snapped forward in his chair, yanked his reading glasses off his face, and gave me a perplexed look. "*Excuse* me? What the hell are you talking about?"

"Let me tell you a headline that I'm sure the media would love . . . and this firm would hate. 'Single, struggling Black working mother of two sons, one of whom has cancer, bullied and forced out of her job at a prestigious racist law firm.'"

"Oh, please," Francis said. He turned to the other partners. "You see this? This is precisely why she needs to go immediately. I tried to be cordial with her, but there's no need to be nice now."

He faced me. "Pack your things and get out of here now before I have security toss you out. There's no proof to your claims and false allegations. You'll just be a disgruntled, incompetent employee trying to get back at the firm because you were fired under just causes."

I laughed at that. "Incompetent? Hardly. Bullied by you? All the time." Then I pulled out my tape recorder.

"Does this look familiar? I'm sure it does. You bought it for me to assist with my note-taking. Yesterday afternoon, I forgot I left it in your office, and thank God I did. I wouldn't be able to prove my claim without it."

I played a random part of the tape.

"*The only reason why we have our 'rainbow coalition' of a reception staff is because of affirmative action.*"

"*Francis, you're such a dick.*"

"*I'm serious. It felt good to hire Meghan. I see our staff, and the only thing that goes through my mind is that they're taking the job of a more than qualified white person that actually deserves it.*"

Tim slumped his shoulders and shook his head. Francis cleared his throat, his back stiffened, and he shifted nervously in his seat.

"If that's all you have, you're sadly mistaken if you think that gives you any type of leverage against the firm," Francis said.

"Oh, trust me, I have *a lot more* than this," I said.

I fast-forwarded to another spot.

"*Oh, I'm supposed to feel bad because the savages in the projects killed her husband? If you don't want to die in those types of neighborhoods, then don't live there.*"

Tim and Mr. Wayne scowled at Francis.

Francis's hands went up defensively.

I stopped once more and whirled it to another incriminating portion of the tape where Meghan was talking.

"You know what? Fine! I don't care if you or any of the other losers working here know I'm fucking him. I don't care that you saw me fucking him. Soon, you'll be fired, I'll be in your position, and I'll be paid a hell of a lot more to do less than you're responsible for now. Good luck in the welfare line, bitch."

The partners' mouths damn near hit the floor when they heard every word of the conversation crystal clear.

"All of that means nothing. Neither I nor anyone else in this firm knew they were being recorded when those recordings took place. They would be tossed out of court, and you wouldn't have a leg to stand on. Plus, if you ever released those recordings, we'd sue the shit out of you and take every penny from your already shitty existence," Francis said, gritting his teeth.

"That's true. You could do that, but suing a person who has nothing means nothing. You can't take anything from me that would be more than the irrevocable damage that would be done to your firm's reputation."

Francis looked at Tim and Richard, shook his head, and said, "She's trying to intimidate us, but she's nothing to be afraid of."

"Shut up. Shut your damn mouth. You've done enough to muck up this situation," Richard said.

Then Richard faced me and added, "I'm sure we can come to terms with a substantial settlement to avoid litigation."

"It figures she'd do a scheme like this to make a quick buck," Francis added, seething.

"Just shut up. We're being extorted because you can't be a decent human being and keep your dick in your pants," Tim lashed out.

"None of you get it. I'm *not* extorting you. I don't *want* your hush money. All I want is to be in a nonhostile work environment. I want to do my job and not have Meghan's responsibilities piled on me, too. I want my staff, and I treated with respect, but now that you mention it, my staff and I are severely underpaid, so, yes, I want a raise for . . . I'm sorry, what did you call us, Francis? Oh yes, me and my 'rainbow coalition' of a staff."

Richard and Tim shook their heads at Francis.

"Fine," Richard said. "But if we do this for you, how do we know you won't release the tape, anyway?"

"You don't. You'll have to have faith and trust me when I tell you I'm a woman of my word. I've never given you a reason not to."

Richard nodded and said, "OK, Juanita. We'll entertain your request, but I really hope—"

I stopped him before he said something to piss me off.

"You're not in a position right now to threaten me, and I highly recommend that you don't."

He looked like he wanted to say something but kept quiet.

I stood to my feet and said, "Now, if we're done here, I'm sure my revelation to all of you has made you rescind your decision to fire me, and if that's the case, I need to get back to my office. I have work to do."

Before anyone could respond or stop me, I was out the door. The eavesdroppers around the conference room dispersed and pretended to act busy while I walked to my office with my head held high.

"How'd it go?" Julissa asked.

"It looks like you guys are stuck with me. Finally, the partners realized keeping me around was in their best interests."

I gave Julissa and Francisco a wink, and they smiled and laughed amongst themselves.

The partners stayed in the conference room for a good thirty minutes before walking out and going into their separate offices. They didn't say a word to one another, and unless they had appointments, they stayed in their offices and said very little for the rest of the day.

I was proud of myself. I stood up to Francis and got a raise for my staff and me. But most importantly, I finished the day without security escorting me out of the building, and I damn sure didn't lose my job.

CHAPTER 29

BABY, DON'T CRY

"Jerami is coming around nicely!" Dr. Maier said.

"Is he in remission?" I asked.

"Not yet. We can't consider him 'cured' until he's cancer-free for at least five years, but he's responded very well to the new treatment," Dr. Maier said, smiling and shaking my hand.

A burst of relief and happiness washed over me when I heard that news. A little over a year had passed since we started Jerami's treatment. His immune system was getting stronger by the day, which allowed me to be more lenient with letting him play outside.

Things with Jerami were starting to come together, and it looked like he was finally beating his cancer. I saw him gradually improving, but I was scared to get my hopes up. I'd been down that road before, and my heart couldn't take getting disappointed like that again.

I felt a mixture of emotions. Happiness and fear were the most prevalent, but I felt a glimmer of hope for the first time since Mo died and Jerami was diagnosed. I enjoyed not seeing Jerami poked, prodded, and constantly attached to machines or attending frequent doctor appointments. I especially appreciated not having to do hospital stays, sleeping in uncomfortable hospital chairs, and hearing the annoying sound of beeping machines and buzzing fluorescent lights.

While Jerami's health improved, the same couldn't be said about Debbie's. One morning, she and Tracy met up with me in front of our building for our daily morning chat, and she broke down and told us what was going on with her MS.

Tracy and I were enjoying our cigarettes when Debbie walked out of the building looking depressed. Debbie turned to me and asked, "Can I have one of those?"

I laughed and jokingly asked, "Girl, the only time a woman who doesn't smoke wants a cigarette is either after good sex or when she's going through some shit. So, which one are you?"

Her eyes were watery, like she was seconds away from crying when she said, "I'm going through some shit."

"What's going on?" Tracy asked.

"Lately, I've been feeling tired, light-headed, and dizzy. My doctors told me my MS isn't responding to my treatments anymore, and my symptoms are getting worse . . . My body is breaking down, and there's nothing I can do about it. I'm scared."

Debbie hung her head, and I immediately thought about what she had sacrificed for me and knew what I needed to do.

I rested my hand on her shoulder, and she looked at me." No matter what happens, I got you—"

"Nah, 'we' got you," Tracy corrected me.

"When I couldn't pay for Jerami's last treatment, and I felt like all was lost and I was going to lose my son, you were there for me. I'll never forget that. I'll *always* be there for you," I said.

"When you did that for my sister, you became 'our' sister, so whatever help you need, *WE* got you."

"Thank you! I love you guys," Debbie said, smiling through her tears. We shared a sisterly hug.

Debbie forced a smile, but her eyes told me she was scared. I knew things would be hard for her, but at least she wouldn't have to face them alone.

Things at work were gradually getting better. Julissa, Francisco, and I all got raises. It wasn't life-changing money. I was still struggling to get by, but it definitely helped, and surprisingly, the partners hadn't retaliated against me . . . at least not yet.

Francis was still an asshole, but while I waited for snide comments or degrading remarks, he didn't say those things anymore, well, not to my face, at least. I felt happy and comfortable at work for the first time in a long time.

To make things even sweeter at the firm, the partners finally held Meghan accountable for her work. It's funny; God doesn't like ugly because Meghan finally got what was coming to her when her latest fuckup got her fired from the firm. That day was legendary! Adam Harper walked off the elevator and stormed up to the front desk. He didn't have the friendly demeanor he usually had when he saw me, so I immediately knew something was *seriously* wrong.

"Hey! How are you today, Mr. Harper?" I asked.

"Sorry, Juanita, but I have to skip the pleasantries today. I need to speak to Francis *now*."

"I believe he's in a meeting. Is everything OK?" I asked, concerned.

"No. Everything is *fucked up*. Pardon my outburst, but that redheaded bimbo of his never filed the paperwork needed for my last merger. Now, the company I'm trying to acquire has cold feet and wants to back out of our deal. I told Francis I didn't want anyone new handling this paperwork, and now I'm going to lose hundreds of millions because of Meghan's fuckup."

"I'm so sorry, Mr. Harper. Please have a seat. I'll go to his office right now, explain everything, and get him out here immediately."

"Thank you, Juanita. Talking to you is the only thing stopping me from losing my patience."

"I completely understand. I'm on it."

I instructed Francisco on how to make Mr. Harper's coffee and rushed to Francis's office. I knocked on his door.

"What is it? We have intercoms for a reason," he said.

I ignored him, opened the door, and shut it behind me. Francis and the other partners gave me perplexed looks, wondering why I had just burst into the office and interrupted their meeting. I gave them the rundown of what was going on with Mr. Harper.

Richard threw up his hands. "Jesus Christ!" he exclaimed.

"Why am I *just now* hearing about this?" Francis asked.

"Somebody messed up big. There are no excuses; this is an unforgivable mistake," Tim said.

Adding fuel to the fire, I pointed out the obvious. "Oh, there's no 'somebody.' The only person responsible for that account was Meghan," I added.

All eyes were on Francis since Tim and Richard knew that I usually handled paperwork filings for Mr. Harper until Francis insisted Meghan do it from now on, since she was "more competent." Richard's face was beet red.

"This is unacceptable. We can't afford to lose Harper; he's our biggest client. On top of losing his business, the negative publicity from this clusterfuck could ruin us," Richard fumed.

"I'm sure Meghan has a perfectly logical explanation for this mistake," Francis said.

I didn't hesitate to stoke the fires of tension more. "How many times is she going to drop the ball before you all see that she's hurting the firm?" I asked.

"Juanita's right," Tim said.

"Whatever. Nobody asked her for her opinion. Let's bring Harper in here and try to do as much damage control as possible until we figure out how to fix this permanently," Francis defended.

Francis barked on the intercom to Francisco to bring Mr. Harper to his office. Within seconds, there was a knock on the door, and as soon as Francis opened it, Mr. Harper stormed in.

"I told you I didn't want a newbie handling my affairs, and you swore Meghan could do it. Unfortunately, your girl fucked up, and now my deal might fall through. That *can't* happen. I pay this firm big money to make sure shit like this doesn't happen. I don't care what it takes or what you must do—but fix this *now*," Mr. Harper demanded.

"Mr. Harper, we're taking this matter very seriously, and we're sorry that we put you through it. We will try our very best to make this a smooth transition from here on out. Let us handle everything. Give us some time, and I promise we will rectify this problem," Richard said.

"You better. When this is over, I don't want your firm handling my business anymore. Fix this so we can both move on," Mr. Harper said before walking out and slamming the door behind him.

"Get Meghan in here now," Richard said.

Francis called her cell phone and put it on speaker.

"Hey, sexy," she said.

Tim and Richard looked at each other and shook their heads. I couldn't hold in my smirk seeing Francis squirm when he heard that. He cleared his throat and said, "Uh, Meghan, I need you to come to my office ASAP."

"I'll be there in two minutes. You sound upset. Is everything all right? I'm just getting off the elevator. Do you want me to help you release some of that stress—"

"No . . . dammit. Meghan, this is serious. We have a big problem. Come straight here now."

"OK. Sorry. I'll be there in a sec."

He ended the call.

"*Seriously*, Francis?" Tim asked.

"Oh, shut up!"

Meghan walked into the office. The smile on her face dropped when she saw all the angry faces staring at her. "Hey, why does it look like a funeral in—" Stopping mid-sentence, she slowly looked at me with a nasty glare.

Richard got straight to the point.

"Why wasn't the paperwork filed at the courts for the Harper merger that you were handling?"

Flustered, Meghan hemmed and hawed before finally saying, "I . . . I . . . thought I had plenty of time left to do it."

"Plenty of time? That should've been done *immediately*. How fucking scatterbrained and stupid do you have to be not to check on all your responsibilities? What do you actually *do* all day? Because of your incompetence, we could lose our most important client," Richard said.

Typical Meghan. When she felt the heat coming on her, she tried to deflect and blame everything on me.

"I'm sorry. There were a lot of things I didn't know, and Juanita wasn't the easiest person to ask for help. I put it off and lost track of time because I didn't know how—"

"Bullshit. Don't try to pin this on Juanita. She trained you thoroughly, and for you, who's constantly and openly saying that you're so much better equipped to do her job, you should've already known how to do this," Richard said.

I was glad he defended me and wasn't manipulated by Meghan's bullshit. He continued.

"You can't fathom the damage you've done to this firm's reputation, and I can't leave this problem in your incompetent hands to try to fix. Now, I need to go and see if I can patch this up to save this firm."

Richard pointed to Tim. "Come with me. I want to get the ball moving on this. Let's try to save this deal for Harper and convince him not to drop us."

Tim nodded, and he and Richard headed toward the door. Richard stopped in the doorway, pointed to Meghan, and said, "Francis, take care of this problem here. This is unacceptable, and it will *not* happen again." Then Richard slammed the door behind him.

Francis sighed and said, "Meghan, pack your things. You're out of here."

Meghan's face was as red as her hair. "What? You're fucking *firing* me? You can't be serious," she said.

"Do I *look* like I'm kidding? You've embarrassed me in front of the other partners. You're gone, Meghan. Goodbye," Francis said.

"You're not going to discard me like I'm just some piece of shit. This firm needs me."

"Oh, please, get over yourself. To tell the truth, you're useless."

"I wasn't useless when you bent me over your desk and fucked me every chance you got."

"I don't know what you're talking about. Get out of my office, pack your shit, and get out of here!"

"Juanita knows what I mean. Remind him, please."

I gave her the side-eye. "Oh no, don't bring me into this. I know you're not dumb enough to think I'm gonna stick up for you when a second ago you just tried to throw me under the bus. Plus, after all the other shit you've said and put me through, you're horribly mistaken if you think I'd back anything you said. Girl, bye!"

Meghan sucked her teeth, huffed, and folded her arms.

"I'm not going anywhere. You're not going to get rid of me that easily," she stated defiantly.

Francis pressed the intercom.

"You don't have the balls to call security on me," Meghan said.

"Is that right? We'll see about that."

Francis pressed the intercom again and said, "Francisco, have security come up to my office to have Ms. Flanagan escorted out immediately."

"Yes, sir, Mr. Lincoln," Francisco said.

"You motherfucker!" Meghan yelled.

Two security guards walked in.

"See her out, and if she gives you a hard time, throw her ass off the premises," Francis said.

"Fuck you," Meghan yelled, rushing toward Francis.

"All right, ma'am, it's time to go," the taller guard said.

Meghan reached to slap Francis, but the taller guard grabbed her arm just before she could put her hands on him.

"Don't fucking touch me," she yelled.

"Make this easy on yourself. Come peacefully, and we'll treat you like a civilized adult, but if you keep acting like a brat, you'll be tased, and we'll toss you out on the street. Do you want it the easy way or the hard way?" the shorter, muscular guard asked.

Meghan spat in his face.

That guard grabbed her from behind and picked her up. Meghan threw her head back, head-butting him in the nose, and used her heel to kick him in the dick. The guard dropped her and fell to his knees in pain, but the taller guard tased and handcuffed her. She continued to scream and curse as they dragged her out of Francis's office.

Call me petty, but I stood by the window and smiled when I saw Meghan tossed out of the building. She was sprawled out, crying on the sidewalk, while pedestrians walked around and ignored her. Meghan found out the hard way that she was just a piece of ass to Francis. She thought she was better than me, but I outlasted her.

Richard and Tim got lucky and convinced the company Mr. Harper was trying to acquire to continue with the deal. Harper was happy about that, but still wanted to drop our firm because of how things were handled. Desperate, the partners turned to me to convince him to stick with the firm.

"Juanita, please. You have a great rapport with Harper, and he'll listen to you. Can you try to convince him to stay with our firm? Please let him know that you'll continue to handle all his paperwork, and a mistake like this will never happen again."

Francis went to open his mouth, but one look from Richard shut him up.

"If I talk to Mr. Harper, and that's an *if*, this firm will owe me one, and that favor has no expiration date. Is that clear?"

"Absolutely," Tim said.

Richard nodded.

"I also don't want any of you holding me responsible if I can't change his mind," I added.

"Francis, Tim, and I already know that we dropped the ball on this disaster, and nobody will blame you if you can't fix this for us. So all we ask is that you at least try," Richard said.

"OK, I'll try."

I called Mr. Harper, and the next day, he treated me to lunch at Patsy's Italian Restaurant on West Fifty-Sixth Street in Manhattan.

"Thank you so much for lunch, Mr. Harper."

"It's my pleasure, but Juanita, I know your firm sent you here to get me to reconsider. However, you're not going to talk me out of it. I'm not sticking with them. Also, I don't particularly appreciate that they're using our friendship to try to convince me to stay. Why would you let them use you like that?"

I poured out my heart to him and gave him the lowdown of what went down with my son, the firm, and Meghan.

"Damn, I didn't know you were going through so much hell. I have to give you credit, though. You did well setting them up to keep your job, but how would my continuing to do business with them benefit you? Why would you even *want* me to keep doing business with them?"

"If you let the partners at the firm know that the only reason you're sticking with them is because of me and that if they were ever to let me go, you'd drop them, so it gives me more assurance that they won't renege on their promise of not firing me."

Mr. Harper smiled. "You're in the wrong profession, Juanita. You're crafty enough to be a lawyer. How did you get so good?"

I laughed. "Being a single mother taught me how to survive."

"I can't argue with that, but you don't have to continue working there if you don't want to. If things go wrong, and they try to fire you, or you just want a change of scenery, you can always work for me."

"Thank you, sir. If this fails, it's nice to know I have you in my corner."

While his offer was tempting, I didn't know if Mr. Harper had a little chocolate fetish. I knew his wife was Black, and I didn't want to risk becoming a "Meghan" working for him. I knew where I stood at my firm, and with this assurance, things should be better.

Mr. Harper met with the partners and told them everything I told him to say. He let them know that if I ever left the firm, that would be the day he stopped using their services. So, between the dirt I had on Francis and keeping Mr. Harper as a client, I didn't have to feel like I was walking on eggshells at work any longer, and I had further assurance that my job was secure.

While things were great with my staff and me, the firm didn't hear the last from Meghan.

A month after being fired, Meghan rushed past the reception desk and headed straight for Francis's office. I chased behind her as she stormed into his office without knocking. Richard and Tim were talking while Francis was on the phone.

"Let me call you back," Francis said hastily, ending his call. Then he looked at Meghan.

"Have you lost your mind? Why the hell are you barging into my office? Do you want security to escort you out again?"

"You're not going to do a damn thing but pay me. I'm pregnant, and guess who the father is?"

Francis looked flustered. "You're lying," he said.

She tossed papers at him, and Francis skimmed them. Finally, he looked up from the paperwork with a stunned expression.

Meghan had a sly grin and said, "Oh yes, it's real, and if you don't think I'll go public with this—try me! Unless you want me to have this baby, tell your wife everything, and tell the media how Francis Lincoln, one of the partners at this prestigious law firm, took advantage of his lowly secretary, you'll give me whatever the fuck I want."

"Here we go again," Richard muttered.

"Every time your dick runs amok, you end up fucking over Richard and me, too," Tim voiced.

Meghan looked at Richard and said, "It's really simple. While nothing would please me more than to bleed you dry from child support and the money I'd make from telling the media my side of the story, I don't want a daily reminder of this asshole for the rest of my life, but he's not getting off the hook that easy. My lawyer will be in touch with *my* terms, and once they're met, I'll have an abortion. If you try to fight this, I'll have the baby and tell everyone how Francis threatened my job if I didn't sleep with him, and once I told him he knocked me up, he promptly fired me."

"There's no way your lawyer could legally make a settlement for an abortion," Francis said.

"Oh, you're highly mistaken. The deal isn't for that. It's to shut me up," Meghan said.

"How do I know you'll go through with the abortion and not tell the media?"

"Once I get my money, there's no way I'd want to have anything connected to you."

Meghan was smart. She forced his hand, and the partners had to pay a shitload of hush money to save the firm's reputation. When it was all said and done, Meghan had the abortion, signed a confidentiality agreement, and was now a wealthy bachelorette. The partners made every employee sign a very strict good conduct undertaking and instituted a firmwide policy banning employee relationships, and Francis swore never to touch another employee again.

MOTHERS VOL.1
BEN BURGESS JR.
B-SIDE
CROSSROADS

CHAPTER 30

HALFTIME

'Keem, Draper, Bill, and I were hanging out on the wooden bench in front of our building. We were happy that school was over and summer was finally here. Since Bill's mom's sickness returned and worsened, she couldn't watch Jerami as much. Ma didn't know I heard Auntie tell one of her men on the phone that her hours had been cut.

Now, Auntie acted like she went to work every day, but when she wasn't working, she was back hanging out with her men, and I had to either stay home and watch Jerami or drag him out in the streets with me.

I'd often leave him home alone to watch TV and play video games. Of course, I made him promise to keep it a secret between us, but luckily, today, Auntie was off and said she was staying home, so I wasn't stuck watching him.

My boys and I were joking around, snapping on each other, when we heard the deep bass from Drastic's sound system blasting Nas's song "Halftime." His chromed-out Suburban pulled up to the curb and parked by the hydrant. We didn't know it then, but our lives, as we knew them, were about to change forever.

The passenger-side window rolled down.

"Yo, Akeem, lemme holla at'cha real quick," Drastic said.

Akeem walked over.

"Who's that?" Bill asked.

"That's Drastic and his right-hand man, Boogie Brown. Sometimes he pays us good money if we drop off packages in certain buildings for him," Draper said.

"I want those new Jordans. I hope he asks me to do a drop. I already know my mom won't get them for me," I said.

Bill and I stepped closer to hear Drastic and Akeem's conversation.

"Yo, you and your boy, J, wanna work for me again?" Drastic asked.

"If the cops picked us up again, they'd keep us locked up in Spofford for real this time, plus our moms would kill us."

"Don't worry about that. It won't be like last time. I don't want y'all boosting shit for me anymore. Don't worry about your moms either. Mine used to be on that same bullshit when I was coming up. All you gotta do is hit her off with some dough now and then, and she'll chill out."

Akeem looked like he was deep in thought while Drastic impatiently tapped his fingers on his truck door like he didn't have time to wait or chitchat.

"Look, I'm a busy man. I ain't got time for this shit. I need an answer now. You're my first choice, but I'll move on if you can't handle it."

"Nah, I can handle it. All right, bet. I'm in!" Akeem said.

"Call your boy over here. Let's see if he wants to make some consistent money, too."

Akeem turned to face us.

"Yo, J, Draper, Ill Bill, come here," Akeem said.

"Chill. Draper and the white boy can't be down; they're bad for business," Drastic said.

Akeem waved us off. I stood by with Bill and Draper.

"I've been talking to Draper, and he's cool now. My boy B is good people, too. Bill wouldn't snitch or nothing. I can vouch for that," Akeem said.

"Nah, Draper got a big fucking mouth," Drastic said. "Last time he did a drop for me, the block was hot for weeks. Putting Draper and the white boy on would draw too much attention. I can't have that kind of heat on me. Remember this, if you stand in the light, people are gonna see you. If you wanna make money with this, bringing notice to yourself can fuck you up. You wanna stay under the radar, understand?"

Akeem nodded and called for me. "Yo, J, come here."

"Y'all ready to make some *real* money?" Drastic asked. "I'm trying to have y'all selling for me on the block. Nothing too heavy at first. You still gotta crawl before you walk, but you'll be handling more than the little kiddie shit I had y'all doing before. Both of you can make some serious money. Your boy, Akeem, said he's down. What about you? You in?"

I thought about how my mom never had money and how easy and fast I could rake in the dough selling for Drastic consistently. I wasn't trying to be broke again. I made my decision then and there.

"Fuck, yeah, I'm down," I said.

"That's what I like to hear. Drop these two, and I'll show y'all what I want y'all doing to start off. Hop in."

"Yo, Bill, Draper, me, and J gotta do something with Drastic. We'll catch up with y'all later," Akeem said.

Draper scowled at us as we climbed into Drastic's backseat. He looked angry and jealous when we left him and Bill on the block. It wouldn't be long before Draper started showing his true colors. We didn't know it then, but we made an enemy out of him that day.

"Good morning, everyone. I'm Mr. Sealy," the dark-skinned man that looked too fit to be an English teacher said as he closed the classroom door. His arms were bigger than my legs.

He started writing his name on the chalkboard and said, "My goal is to get everyone in this class to love reading."

"Good luck with that!" I joked. The class laughed at me.

I could tell by his frown that he wasn't feeling my joke.

As usual, Akeem and I sat beside each other in the back of the class. We barely went to school, but since it was the first day of ninth grade and Akeem liked reading, we went to this class.

Draper walked in.

"You're late; what's your name?" Mr. Sealy asked him.

"Draper."

"Well, Draper, in the future, please see that you make it to my class on time."

Draper sucked his teeth and walked to the back of the class but didn't sit next to Akeem or me. Instead, he just walked past, giving us a nod and a "Wassup?"

"What's up with him?" I asked Akeem.

"I don't know. Fuck him. Since Drastic put us on, he's been acting shady and jealous. On top of all that, he's hanging out with Neville and them Ravenswood niggas. If he's gonna be like that, he can stay the fuck away from us."

I nodded. "I told you that cat was grimy from the jump," I said.

"Yeah, but at least by having him around us, we could keep an eye on him. Now, who knows what he's plotting with Neville and his crew."

We put our conversation on pause and listened to Mr. Sealy introduce himself to the class.

"All right, everyone, I'll tell you a little about myself. I was born and raised in Queensbridge and went to Long Island City High School, just like you guys are now. Back then, I was a knucklehead, and after barely making it out of high school, I didn't know what I wanted to do with my life."

Akeem and I laughed at that. Mr. Sealy smirked and continued.

"Instead of staying around with my friends who weren't doing anything but hanging on the corner, I decided to go into the Marine Corps. Being in the marines made a man out of me, but when I was done with that part of my life, I knew I wanted to come back and help young kids who were like me and didn't have direction. Growing up, I always loved reading, so I went to college and majored in English and education. I figured being a teacher would help me give back to my old community."

Akeem nodded. I could tell he respected Mr. Sealy for saying that.

Mr. Sealy loosened his tie and picked up a crate full of books. "I believe the reason why many people don't enjoy reading books is that they can't relate to the characters, so in this class, we're going to read a lot of books with characters that are people of color. Starting with this book, which teaches the lesson that one bad choice can affect you for the rest of your life."

Mr. Sealy put a copy of Richard Wright's *Native Son* on our desks. Draper tossed the book to the front of the classroom and asked, "What's this bullshit?"

"First, pick up that book now. Second, you're not going to use that language in my class, and third, read it and find out."

"Nigga, first, I ain't picking up a damn thing. Second, I'll say whatever the fuck I want, and third, I ain't reading shit."

The class quietly watched the back-and-forth between them. Finally, Mr. Sealy picked up the book and walked up to Draper's desk.

"You came to class to learn, right? Well, give the book a try. You might see that you have a lot in common with the main character, Bigger."

"Nah, I doubt that."

"If that's your attitude, just sit there for attendance and let the rest of the class enjoy it."

"Nobody wants to read no book on the first day. Uncle Tom niggas like you are always trying to push reading stupid, corny shit like this."

"If you're not here to learn, get out of my class," Mr. Sealy said.

Draper rolled his eyes, stood up, and said, "You tripping. I ain't going nowhere."

Mr. Sealy walked up to Draper. "I'm not asking you. I'm telling you. You need to go," he said.

"You gonna make me?" Draper asked, folding his arms and raising his chin defiantly.

Mr. Sealy looked Draper dead in the eyes. "Try me. I'm not one of these security guards at the school, and I'm not one of these kids. I promise you; you're not built to battle with me."

Everyone in the class was watching to see what Draper would do next.

"Now again, I'll ask you nicely; if you're not going to read and partici-pate in this class, can you please leave?"

There were a lot of reasons why Draper would give in and do what Mr. Sealy said. First, Mr. Sealy wasn't backing down and wasn't a punk like most teachers. Draper's bark has always been bigger than his bite, but if he did somehow manage to beat up Mr. Sealy, and looking at how jacked Mr. Sealy was, that wasn't happening, but *if* it did, there'd be no doubt the school would call the cops and have him arrested. I'm sure Draper was scared that if he got locked up, he'd go to Spofford and get exposed for being a loud-mouthed pussy. Second, Draper probably didn't want to get an ass-whoopin' on top of getting kicked out of class. Whatever the reason was, Draper sucked his teeth, stood up, and walked out of the classroom.

"Wise choice. You'll be missed," Mr. Sealy said sarcastically.

Mr. Sealy looked at Akeem and me and asked, "Does anyone else want to follow Draper out on his magical journey of standing around doing nothing?"

Nobody answered.

"Good. Let's begin."

"Yo, Othello was a sucka, Mr. Sealy," I said.

"Yeah, he ain't even see that this cat, Iago, was playing him the whole time," Akeem added.

"I wouldn't say he was a sucker. Othello trusted Iago, so it's easy to be blinded by what's going on when you think a person is your friend, but this is another lesson this story teaches. Everyone that smiles in your face and says they're your friend isn't always your friend. Always keep your eyes open and question everything, but make sure you're asking the right questions."

Mr. Sealy was a cool dude. He read books to the class and changed his voice for all the characters. It made us laugh and kept us interested in the story. He always gave us examples of how we could apply the books to our lives and asked the class a lot of questions to keep us thinking and participating.

"If you guys like this book, you should read Shakespeare's other tragedies like *Macbeth*," Mr. Sealy said.

The bell rang, ending class.

"All right, everyone, that's all for today. Remember to write a two-page essay on our class discussion for homework tonight. Akeem, Jalen, let me talk to you real quick."

We walked over.

"I'm proud of you two. You're participating in class, doing your work, and acing all your tests. You boys are smart, and while I'm flattered that out of all your classes, you've been coming to mine, you need to apply that same mindset to the rest of your classes."

"I hear you, Mr. Sealy, but we got money to make. As long as we know how to read and count, the other classes are pointless. You make your class interesting and fun, and that's a nice distraction, but once we get back to reality, we're still here in Queensbridge and have real-life problems," I said.

Akeem nodded.

"I've been in your shoes before. Making easy money is nice, but the two of you have brains. Most of the guys on the corners are dummies. You two have the potential to be something. If the two of you put your minds to something, you can make any legal career feel like easy money. I want y'all to think about that."

"No doubt, Mr. Sealy. We'll think about it, but right now, we gotta do what we gotta do," Akeem said.

It was cool that Mr. Sealy thought we could be something in life, but I couldn't see us being more than corner boys.

CHAPTER 31

TEN CRACK COMMANDMENTS

Akeem and I didn't have to do drop-offs in buildings anymore. Instead, we graduated to standing on rooftops with walkie-talkies and binoculars, looking out for the dealers and alerting them when Five-O was nearby. On our first day, Drastic gave us a pep talk on the roof of one of his stash house buildings.

"My boy, Daunte, is gonna show y'all the ropes," Drastic said.

Akeem and I gave Daunte dap and introduced ourselves. We didn't know him personally, but we heard about him and saw him around the neighborhood. He was two years older than us and quit school when he was around our age to work for Drastic full-time. Daunte had brown skin, sported a low Caesar fade, and stood about six foot one. Word on the street was Daunte was Shyne's cousin.

"Y'all got an important job. You're my soldiers' extra eyes and ears. If y'all slip, it can cost them their lives or their freedom. So don't let them or me down. Watch their backs!" Drastic said.

Akeem and I nodded. We were happy to be given more responsibilities. Daunte was a cool-ass dude. Talking with him about hip-hop, girls, hoops, and street shit every day made our boring assignment bearable and fun. Daunte quickly became one of our boys. I never said anything to Akeem, but I was glad Bill couldn't be down with working for Drastic. I already felt like I came second to my brother at home. I didn't want to be second fiddle when it came to business in the street.

After a short stint of being lookouts, 'Keem, Daunte, and I leveled up and started working different corners, helping Rasheed and Shyne hand out product to fiends on the sly once we got the signal. It wasn't long before we got our own corner and made our base of operations the corner of the Twelfth Street deli. The owner of the deli, Hector, was cool. He sold us loosies and liquor, even though he knew we were minors, and he didn't care that we were doing our dirt at the side of his store or that we hung out in front of it because he felt we actually brought in more business for him.

Drastic was happy and liked having Akeem and me around. He took us under his wing and saw a lot of himself in Akeem, treating him more like a protégé and eventual heir to his operation than just a corner boy. 'Keem wanted to know every detail of Drastic's operation. He hung on to Drastic's every word and tried to soak up all the knowledge he could about street life. Me, I was happy just to be making money, hanging with my boys, and being around for the ride.

Money was pouring in for Akeem, Daunte, and me. We bought ourselves cell phones, clothes, and all types of jewelry. Now that our money was consistent, Akeem started wearing his dad's old chain.

"Check you out with the fresh ice! I see you've been stackin' your bread up, huh?" Drastic said.

"Nah, it's not new. I didn't get this with my money. It was my pops. It's the only thing he left me before he split," Akeem said.

Drastic shook his head, smiled, and held the medallion. "Well, you're lucky. At least your pops left you something. With most niggas around here, once their pops dips, they're left with nothing." He continued holding and admiring the medallion.

"This shit is hot. I like the king chess piece, too." Drastic faced Boogie and said, "Don't this shit look like something I would rock?"

Boogie Brown nodded.

Drastic looked at Akeem skeptically. "Everything has a meaning. What statement are you tryin' to make by wearing this? What? You the king now, 'Keem?" Drastic asked.

"Nah, I'm not the king. Maybe one day, if I'm lucky, when you retire from the game, you'll pass it down to me, but I know you run everything around here," Akeem said.

Drastic smiled. I guess Akeem passed his test and answered how he wanted.

"That's right! *I'm* the king," Drastic said.

He patted Akeem on the shoulder and continued, "You're smart, and it's only because you haven't forgotten that I'm the HNIC around here, I'm gonna let you keep your chain."

Akeem nodded, but I knew he wasn't feeling that. In all honesty, if Drastic wanted his chain, he could take it, and there'd be nothing any of us could do about it. I guess now and then, Drastic had to flex and make sure we all understood who was on top of the food chain.

Akeem and I were finishing up doing hand to hands with fiends on our usual corner at the Twelfth Street deli. Daunte motioned for another fiend to follow him to the side of the bodega to do another discrete transaction. Drastic's Suburban drove by us. He and Boogie parked across the street, smiling while they leaned against his ride, watching us.

"That's what I like to see! My boys out here hustling hard! Yo, hop in. Come with me for a minute. I wanna show y'all something," Drastic shouted. Daunte finished handling his business.

"Yo, hold down the corner for a minute. I need them to handle something for me," Drastic said.

Daunte nodded.

We climbed into the back of his truck. The Notorious B.I.G.'s "Ten Crack Commandments" blasted through the speakers. Akeem and I bobbed our heads to the music. Drastic turned it down for a second, turned in his seat, and faced us. "This shit here needs to be your new mantra. Everything this brother is sayin' is the truth. Memorize this shit, apply it to the streets, and you'll go far in the drug game."

Boogie Brown drove us to 41-15 Twelfth Street. We rode the piss-smelling elevator to the sixth floor and took the steps to the roof. Off to the side in a secluded corner of the roof, Taevaughn was there with six of Drastic's new runners huddled around two corner boys who had one of the old-time dealers kneeling in gravel in his underwear with his mouth, hands, and feet duct-taped. The bruises all over his body were signs that they beat his ass before we got there.

Drastic scanned the faces on the roof and said, "I've noticed he's been coming up short on a lot of his packs lately. I did my research and found this cat had been stealing from me. If I let that shit slide, other motherfuckers will think I'm soft and think they can do it, too. I gotta make an example outta him."

He smiled and pulled out a dingy black revolver. "Boogie and Taevaughn already put in their work over the years, and I'm not trying to get my outfit dirty today, so which of you young niggas wants to step up to the challenge and handle this problem for me?"

Again, Drastic scanned the faces on the roof and stopped at me.

"What's up, Jalen? You ready to step up and be the man? You ready to put in some real work today?"

I knew this was a test and an important moment, but I couldn't kill this guy. I didn't even know him. Holding guns, delivering packages, and selling dope to fiends was one thing, but I wasn't a killer.

"Nah. straight up, I'm not ready for that yet," I said, trying to sound tough while still being honest.

Drastic smirked and turned to the two goons holding the guy. They both shook their heads. As Drastic looked around, everyone was shaking their heads or averting their eyes.

"You mean to tell me all y'all niggas is pussy?" Drastic asked.

Finally, Drastic faced Akeem. "What about you, 'Keem? You ready to pop your cherry and get your hands dirty today?"

Akeem was stone-faced, but there was something in his eyes, a darkness that I'd never seen before and it scared me.

Akeem reached into his jeans back pocket, pulled out a pair of black baseball gloves, and put them on.

Drastic nudged Boogie Brown. "What, you some type of hitman now? You got your Little League gloves out," Drastic laughed.

Akeem took the gun from Drastic and pressed the barrel against the man's temple. Drastic smiled and nodded. Without hesitation, Akeem pulled the trigger and shot the man point-blank in the head. The two goons holding the guy looked just as shaken as me. Their eyes widened, and their hands trembled. I couldn't stop my legs from quivering.

Akeem handed the gun back to Drastic without seeming the least bit fazed by what he did.

"Damn, little homie. I was just fucking with y'all. I didn't think you'd actually do it."

Drastic shook Boogie Brown excitedly. "Oh shit! I got myself a new shooter!"

Boogie had a slight smirk. Drastic clapped his hands.

"I don't want you having any remorse. This shit needed to be done. When you get to my position, niggas will try to test you to see if you're weak."

Still shaking, I asked innocently, "But if people wanna test *you*, why didn't *you* shoot him?"

Drastic laughed. "Seeing that you're still wet behind the ears and don't know better, I'm gonna let you slide this one time without fucking you up for questioning me."

I swallowed a lump in my throat at his comment as he continued. "All of y'all remember this and remember it good. When you run shit, you have your soldiers do the dirty work."

We all nodded.

Drastic looked at Akeem and said, "I need you to be stone-cold when dealing with stickup kids, fiends, and snakes."

Akeem nodded.

"This is good. This means you can put in more important work for me and make more money. You're good with that, right?"

"I'm down for whatever," Akeem said.

Drastic handed Akeem back the gun.

"Keep it. Since you broke your cherry with your first body, it's a rite of passage that you keep the gun. This is my gift to you."

Akeem tucked the piece into his book bag.

Drastic snapped his fingers and pointed to his goons. "You two, chop his body up, stuff his ass in contractor bags, go to the park, and get rid of it in the water."

Then he clapped his hands. "Ticktock, motherfuckers. Get going."

His flunkies nodded.

"Make sure you put weights in the bags so that shit doesn't float to the top and the cops find it. Taevaughn, go with them, so they don't fuck it up," Drastic said.

Everyone else on the roof was still shaken except Akeem, who still didn't seem fazed. I looked at Akeem like a brother, but I couldn't lie. Even I was afraid of him after seeing that.

Later that day, Akeem and I sat alone on a bench at Queensbridge Park. Akeem was staring off, looking at the Manhattan skyline. The look in his eyes was cold and empty. I couldn't front. It scared me a little. What happened earlier was still heavy on my mind, and I couldn't get the sight of that guy he shot out of my head.

"Yo, 'Keem?"

"What's up, J?"

"You all right?"

He looked surprised by my question. "I'm good . . . Why wouldn't I be?"

"You just shot that guy without question or hesitation. How can you be so calm and act like nothing happened? I didn't even do anything, and I can't stop thinking about it. I know it's gotta be on your mind."

Akeem looked up at the sky and said, "It's not. It was easy for me. I felt nothing."

"Nothing?"

"When I saw that guy on the roof, I thought about the guy who killed my pops and imagined the cat I was shooting was him."

I slowly nodded. "I get that, but you're not worried about God?"

Akeem didn't take his eyes off the sky. "There is no God. Would God take both of our dads from us or let your brother get cancer? Would God put our moms in fucked-up situations where they have to struggle and work all the time to survive? No. We're our only salvation. If it takes dropping losers like that guy on the roof to make sure my moms and Ebony don't have to suffer money-wise, I'll gladly take the sin and deal with the consequences if or when I see God."

"You weren't scared at all?"

"I'm not scared of anything."

CHAPTER 32

TIME 4 SUM AKSION

Once Drastic realized Akeem wasn't afraid to kill, he used Akeem and me as his enforcers behind Boogie. Boogie had us lift weights daily and do dips and pull-ups in the park. Boogie taught us how to box, wrestle, and shoot guns so we'd know how to handle ourselves in any situation we'd come across in the street.

Months passed. 'Keem and I weren't the same scrawny, gangly boys as before. We were solid now. I knew I was physically intimidating, but Akeem took it to another level and was close to being the same linebacker size as Boogie. He put all his anger and hate into hitting the weights, but it wasn't enough that we looked the part. Drastic wanted to know that we could act it, too, by fucking up anybody that shorted him.

We were on the corner of Fortieth Avenue and Twelfth Street when Drastic tested us.

"I swear to God, man, Neville's crew got the drop on us. The motherfuckers came outta nowhere and took everything. We wouldn't cheat you. You know that," one of the corner boys said.

"Y'all niggas is that pussy that you let those punks chump you, and they're still breathing? I'm not taking that loss. They have my shit, which means y'all owe me my money *and* what they took," Drastic said.

Boogie reached for the butt of the revolver tucked in the back of his waistband, but Drastic shook his head and smiled.

"I'm feeling generous today. I should have my boy, Boogie, off you right now, but I'm gonna give y'all a chance. The two of y'all are gonna fight a fair one with Akeem and J here. If y'all win, all is forgiven. Lose? I'll want all my money by the end of the week, or Boogie will definitely end both of you. Sounds fair?"

They reluctantly nodded.

Before we could square up and brace ourselves, the two corner boys swung at us like they were trying to knock our heads off. I blocked the haymaker and tagged the guy I was fighting with a jab and a right cross that left his knees wobbly. After that, I tagged him with two more wild haymakers, which floored him.

"All right, damn. Chill. You got that," he yelled, holding his hands up for me to stop.

Drastic laughed.

"Fucking pussy. No wonder they robbed y'all. The two of you can't even beat some fucking kids," Drastic said.

I looked over, and Akeem was stomping on the guy he was fighting so badly I thought he was gonna kill him. Finally, Boogie grabbed Akeem, stopping him. The man's face was covered in blood, his eyes were swollen shut, and his nose and lips were busted. Boogie dragged the guy Akeem was fighting next to mine.

Drastic kneeled over them and said, "Have my fucking money by the end of the week, or this ass whoopin' will feel like a blessing compared to what I'll have them do to y'all next."

Then Drastic looked at us. "Y'all ain't done. We're gonna pay a visit to Neville's crew that robbed them and return the favor."

Drastic took us to the corner of Fortieth Avenue and Vernon Boulevard. Neville's goons were standing on the block when we snuck up, beat the shit out of them, and took their stash and money.

Realizing this was turning into a seesaw battle, Neville set up a meeting with Drastic to squash the beef. Since his guys started it, Neville agreed to squash the beef and not retaliate for jumping his guys. Despite getting everything back, plus some, I never saw those two corner boys, Akeem and I fought again.

The more dirt Drastic asked Akeem and me to do, the more ruthless Akeem became. I handled my business, but 'Keem liked the fearsome reputation he was building, and word spread quickly around the hood that he wasn't the one to mess with. With that reputation came more trust from Drastic, and since I was Akeem's right-hand man, Drastic kept me around for the ride and taught us more.

Our next lessons were to learn how to cook, cut, weigh, and bag dope. I remember the first day he taught us. That day, 'Keem, Daunte, and I were working at our usual spot on the corner of the Twelfth Street deli. Business was slow, and the three of us leaned against a black fence, talking shit and cracking jokes. Then a man dressed in tan khakis, a dress shirt, and a tie approached us.

"How are you doing today, Brother Daunte?" he asked.

"I'm good. What you need, Brother Monterey?"

I eyed the man. He was dressed decent enough, but I could tell he was in the early stages of becoming a fiend.

"I'm low on funds this week, but I get paid next Friday . . . Between work and problems going on at the church, I've been stressed out—"

"No disrespect, Brother Monterey, but I'm working, so you're gonna have to get to the point."

"I was wondering if you could do me a solid this one time and spot me a quarter ounce on credit. I'll pay you back as soon as I get my check. You know I'm good for it."

Akeem was reading Donald Goines's book, *Dopefiend*. He overheard the conversation, shook his head, and went back to reading. I looked at Daunte and quoted the sixth commandment from the "Ten Crack Commandments" song. *"Number six, that goddamn credit? Dead it. You think a crackhead is paying you back? Shit, forget it."*

Daunte sighed and rolled his eyes.

"I know the damn song. Brother Monterey isn't a crackhead. He just dabbles with the shit."

"That's how they all start. Stick to the rules," Akeem said.

"If it were anyone else, I would, but he's known my family and me since I was little. He wouldn't do me dirty."

"If he shorts you, that's on you," I said.

Daunte reached into his hoodie pocket and handed Brother Monterey the dope.

"I'm trusting you. Don't screw me over, or I'm gonna forget you were nice to me growing up."

Brother Monterey's eyes were fixated on the dope. He couldn't stop nodding. "Yes. Yes. Don't worry, Brother Daunte, I got you."

"I'm serious. Don't make me have to come looking for you for my money. All that church shit will go out the window, and I'm gonna put my hands on you."

"That won't be necessary."

"What's up, Drastic?" Akeem asked, facing Drastic before he could creep up on us.

Drastic was making his rounds, checking his corners. Brother Monterey's eyes widened, and he looked nervous.

"My man! That's what I'm talking about! Look at you, paying attention to your surroundings and shit. But don't get lost in that book," Drastic said.

Akeem smiled.

Brother Monterey took off running nervously.

"Yo, what the fuck was that? I didn't see no money exchanged in that transaction. I'm not running a charity out here. You better not be out here giving my product out for free, Daunte. I ain't taking no shorts."

"Nah, it ain't like that. That guy has been a friend of my family's since I was a baby. He's good for it. He's gonna pay me back on Friday when he gets paid," Daunte assured him.

"Nigga, I don't run my operation on credit. Go get me my money."

"Don't worry. I got all your money for you. I'm gonna front what he owes."

"Don't make this shit a habit. You owe me double if I hear he didn't pay you back. You understand?"

"Yeah."

"And 'Keem, J, y'all are supposed to be out here working with him. So why didn't you stop him?"

"Before he even handed the dude the product, I told him the sixth commandment," I blurted out.

Daunte looked at me, irritated that I dimed him out.

"What? Don't look at me. That man is never gonna pay you back."

"You'll see," Daunte said.

Drastic shook his head. "You said he's a friend of the family, right?" Drastic asked.

"Yeah," Daunte said.

"If he's so close to the family, why did he come to you and not Shyne?"

Daunte shrugged and had no answer for that.

"He came to you because he knew your gullible ass would break easily and give in, stupid."

Daunte sighed like he had just realized that Drastic was right. Drastic turned to Akeem and me. "You two, come with me."

He faced Daunte and said, "You stay your ass right here and keep working this corner. If you see your friend again, hopefully, you can get that dope back. My guess is he's smoking that shit up as we speak."

Then he turned back to 'Keem and me. "I'm really feeling how you and J have been moving lately. It reminds me a lot of Boogie and me when we were coming up. I'm gonna school y'all about everything in this drug game and how to survive in these streets the proper way, so you don't get suckered like this cat," he said, pointing at Daunte.

He continued. "Most importantly, y'all need to know everything about the product you're selling, so come with me and keep up. We're going on a little field trip."

We nodded and walked with Drastic to a building a block away. We entered a rundown apartment. Boogie Brown was in the kitchen at the stove wearing a mask and hospital-type latex gloves.

"You live here?" I asked.

Drastic laughed and said, "Fuck, nah, shorty. Does this look like a place I'd stay at? What's the fifth commandment?"

"Number 5, *never sell no crack where you rest at. I don't care if they want an ounce; tell 'em 'bounce!'*"

"Exactly! So, to answer your question, nah, man, this is a trap house. It belongs to a fiend me and Boogie pays with dope, so we can use his apartment to cook the work. Remember that fifth commandment. It's one of the most important in the game. Keep where you rest your head at private."

As soon as he said that, a man rushed up to him. The man's cheeks were sunken in, he had an unkempt Afro, a musty body odor, and his dingy clothes hung loosely from his rail-thin body.

"Is it ready yet?" the man asked.

"Yo, back up off me. Keep bugging me, and I won't give you shit. Now, get out of my fucking face and go somewhere."

The man sucked his teeth and started pacing.

"Now, where was I?" Drastic asked.

Drastic pulled out a box of vials, a scale, a razor, a cutting board, and a ceramic plate from an ottoman in the living room. He placed them on a small table, faced us, and said, "Follow me."

We did as he said. Then Drastic reached in his pockets. "Here, put this shit on," he said.

He tossed us masks that covered our mouths and noses.

"We're going in the kitchen, and I don't want y'all getting high off this shit and trippin' out before I teach y'all about it. So never handle this shit without a mask or gloves. You don't want to end up breathing in this shit."

We all put on our masks and stood beside Boogie at the stove.

"You see how Boogie is stirring that shit?" Drastic asked.

We nodded.

"Stirring it helps change the coke into crack."

Inside the pot, the coke looked like a thick liquid. Boogie took the pot off the stove and switched on the cold water tap, allowing the thick liquid to mix with the water until it hardened. Next, Boogie walked to the table, took the crack out of the pot, and placed it on the cutting board. He cut the crack into small rocks with the razor and put them all on the ceramic plate. He weighed a small fraction of the rocks and filled the vials with them.

The fiend walked up to him with his hand out.

Boogie tossed him a vial and said, "Hhhhheeeereee."

The fiend's eyes lit up, and he wasted no time putting the crack into his pipe and smoking it where he stood. He took a hit, and dark gray smoke came out of his pipe and nostrils. The man looked like he was in total ecstasy.

Drastic smiled.

"It's cool to do a line or two occasionally, but you want to keep that shit under control, or the shit you're selling will end up owning you, just like this guy. He used to sell for me; now, he's one of my best customers."

Drastic walked over to a coffee table and made a four-inch line of coke on the glass. Then he sat down at one of the folding chairs at the table and rolled up a dollar bill.

"You wanna try this shit, 'Keem?" Drastic asked.

"Nah, I'm straight," Akeem said flatly.

"What about you, J? This shit will put hair on your little nuts." He laughed. "You down to try it?"

Drastic pointed to the line of coke and handed me the rolled-up bill to snort it. I reached for it, but Akeem batted my hand away. Then he faced me.

"Don't be stupid. Do you see him doing the shit? He just told you that guy used to sell for him. They call that shit 'dope' for a reason. You never hear any success stories of niggas making it who do that shit. All you hear about is their downfall. I'm not going out like that, and I don't want any of my people going out like that either, you understand?"

As soon as Akeem finished talking, the fiend near us staggered around the apartment, dropped to the ground, and drifted off.

Akeem faced me and said, "You see that shit? You want that to be you? Don't touch that shit, even out of curiosity. I've seen it steal too many people's souls around our hood."

"Yo, Boogie, you hearing this? Listen to this lil' nigga sounding like an after-school special." Drastic laughed.

Boogie chuckled and continued weighing and packing the crack in the vials.

Drastic turned back to Akeem and said, "Riddle me this, genius. If I sent you out to pick up some product for me, how would you know if the shit was legit and not just flour?"

Akeem looked deep in thought for a minute, then said, "I'd bring a fiend with me. After talking to the supplier in private, when it came time to test it out, I'd bring out the fiend, let him try it out, and tell me if it's crap."

"You're always surprising me, 'Keem. When I'm done running this hood, you will be the man one day."

CHAPTER 33

CAN IT BE ALL SO SIMPLE?

Every day when I look at my sons, I see Mo. Some days, I see traces of me in them, but mostly, they're the spitting image of their father. They have his deep brown eyes, strong cheekbones, full lips, and dark chocolate skin tone. There was no doubt both of my boys inherited their father's height. Jalen was already six feet.

But as the days passed, I noticed a shift in Jalen. He began to feel less like my son and more like a stranger. Lately, he had been hanging out in the streets all the time, and he barely graduated from junior high school because his attendance was terrible. With Carina and me working, it was even harder to ensure he got to school on time, or at all. I was afraid I was losing him. Changes in how he dressed, talked, and acted worried me and showed me he was gravitating toward and becoming more influenced by the streets. I knew I had to save him before the streets completely consumed him.

Jerami was sitting in the middle of the living room floor with his eyes glued to the TV, playing some fighting game on PlayStation. He didn't even look up from the screen once. Instead, he was too busy mashing buttons on his controller to acknowledge me.

"Hi," I said.

He didn't answer.

"Hello," I said louder. "You don't hear me talking to you?" I asked.

"Sorry. Hey," Jerami said.

There was no enthusiasm in his voice. He didn't even bother looking at me. Finally, I sighed and asked, "Where's your brother?"

"Gone."

"Gone where?"

He shrugged.

"Isn't Carina off today? Where's your aunt?" I asked.

"I don't know."

"Your brother and Auntie be leaving you home alone like this a lot?"

"Yup."

I shook my head, scared that Carina was falling back into her hoeish ways, and worried that Jalen was out in the street doing God knows what.

Lately, Jalen was hanging out with the wrong crowd. I've seen him with men much older than him, and who knows what they were teaching or influencing him to do. I've had plenty of talks with him about the dangers of being around those losers on the corner and ruining his future, but it felt like everything I said went in one ear and out the other.

"I'm going to look for your brother," I said.

Jerami shrugged and continued playing his game.

"Did you do your homework?" I asked.

"Nope."

I took a deep breath and exhaled slowly, annoyed that now I had to get on both of my sons' cases about school.

"Then turn that game off and get to it before I take that system away for a month."

"Uh, OK, OK," he said.

I walked out of my building and looked for Jalen. I went to look over by the basketball courts where he and the neighborhood riffraff usually congregated. Luckily, I was right and found him sitting at the small square concrete chess tables by the basketball courts with Akeem and some other boys their age, but right next to them were older men. I've seen them hanging around with the boys before, and I didn't like that. I didn't need those men in Jalen's ear, influencing him to do God knows what.

I immediately saw the annoyed expression on Jalen's face when Akeem nudged him that I was headed toward them.

"Jalen," I called.

He rolled his eyes, sucked his teeth, mumbled something under his breath, and ignored me.

"Jalen," I repeated.

"What, Ma?" he said with an attitude.

"Well, hello to you too, Sonshine. You didn't hear me call you the first time?"

He didn't answer me.

"It's getting late, and you need to come home. It's a school night," I said.

That got a laugh out of all the other boys and men sitting around with Jalen.

"Ma, I'm chillin' with my boys right now. You're embarrassing me."

"Do I look like I care? You can hang out another time with your friends. Right now, I need you home."

The older men were eyeing me, and I felt very uncomfortable.

"Don't sweat it, J. We'll see you tomorrow," Akeem said.

"Thank you, Akeem. Tracy might be at work, but I know if she were home, she'd want you in the house, too."

"I hear you, Mrs. Juanita, but I get bored sitting in the house. I keep busy being out here."

Rolling my eyes at the older men still eyeing me, I said, "With the company you keep, I'm not so sure you'd get into less trouble out here than you would being bored at home. Plus, you can always hang out with Ebony."

"She's with Bill, doing nerdy school stuff."

I laughed. "Even more reason for you to be around her, don't you think?"

Akeem looked like he was trying to hold back a laugh.

"I remember when just the thought of Bill looking at Ebony had you ready to whoop him."

That got a laugh out of him.

"Trust me, Mrs. Juanita, I'm still protective of my twin, but me and Ill Bill are cool now."

Jalen was sulking beside the older men, who were laughing and teasing him.

"Aren't you guys kind of old to hang out with teenage boys?" I asked them.

"You got us all wrong, Ms. We're taking them under our wing and teaching them how the world works," one man said.

"Yeah, I'm afraid of the lessons you're teaching them."

I faced Akeem. "Stay out of trouble. Jalen and I are going home," I said.

Jalen moaned and groaned, but I didn't give a shit.

"Uh-oh, Mommy said it's time to go in," the men said, heckling Jalen, with one man pretending to beat the other with a belt.

Jalen gave them the finger, and I playfully tapped him upside his head. Then we headed to our building, and Jalen kept complaining.

"You embarrassed me in front of my boys. Why couldn't you just leave me alone?"

"Because I don't like the company you keep, Jalen. You need to be around kids your own age and not hanging around those old losers who've done nothing with their lives," I said.

We walked into our building, and I checked the mailbox inside the lobby. Besides the usual junk and bills, there was a letter from Jalen's school. I immediately opened it and frowned when I learned Jalen was failing nearly every class but gym and English.

I looked at him and waved the letter.

"What?" he asked.

"This letter came from your school saying you haven't been going to your classes in weeks. You're failing nearly everything."

Jalen rolled his eyes.

"So?" he responded.

I looked at him like he had lost his damn mind.

"So? So? If you can do well in English, you can do the same in all your classes. You're too smart for this, Jalen. What makes that English class so special that you can't do the same with your others?" I asked.

"Mr. Sealy makes the class interesting and shows us how it applies to actual life, unlike the other classes where I'm sitting there learning things I'm never gonna use."

"Do you want to end up like those men you were sitting outside with? Sitting around kids, not doing shit with your life? Go to school, Sonshine."

I stayed on Jalen's ass about school all the time, but I wasn't breaking through to him. The streets had their hooks in him, but I refused to give up.

I had my suspicions about Jalen. He had a cell phone but didn't have a job. So who paid that bill? I walked into the boys' room to gather their dirty clothes for the Laundromat, but in reality, it was my subtle way of snooping around and seeing what trouble Jalen was getting himself into.

When I walked in, I immediately spotted empty weed bags and cigarette butts on Jalen's side of the room. Jerami's clothes were neatly put in his hamper, but Jalen's dirty, unfolded clothes were sprawled out and scattered all over the floor. I scooped them into a crumpled pile and tossed them into my laundry bag.

While at the Laundromat, I emptied the boys' pants pockets before putting them in the washing machine and found a wad of money and weed bags in Jalen's pants. I didn't want to believe what Officer O'Sullivan, said about Jalen selling drugs in the past, but this was a lot of money and weed.

When I got home from the Laundromat, I was folding the clothes in the living room when Jalen came home. He walked past me and sat on the couch, smelling like weed and cigarette smoke.

"I'm not dumb, Jalen. You reek of weed and cigarettes. You're too young to be smoking anything."

"Really, Ma, isn't that the pot calling the kettle black? Who do you think I picked up the habit from?"

"I smoke, but I'm an adult. You're still a little boy. So you don't need to do anything that can affect you while you're still developing."

"Don't worry about me," he said.

"Don't tell me not to worry. You're my son, my firstborn. I'll always worry about you. I already have one son battling cancer. I don't need two."

"How about this? I'll stop smoking when you stop smoking."

"Little boy, this isn't up for negotiation."

"I get most of my cigarettes out of your packs."

"First off, you shouldn't be stealing, and second, you shouldn't even be able to buy cigarettes. It's illegal, but speaking of illegal, why do you have weed and all this money in your pockets?" I asked, tossing the wad of money to him.

"What were you doing going through my stuff?" he asked, his voice cracked as he quickly pocketed the money.

"I was doing laundry. You're welcome, by the way, and it was in your pockets."

Jalen rushed to his room. I followed him, stood in the doorway, and watched him frantically look in his dresser drawers and under his bed.

"I noticed you have a cell phone. You don't have a job, Jalen. So who's paying that bill, and where are you getting all this money from? Tell me you're not stupid enough to be selling drugs."

He ignored me and kept searching for whatever he was looking for.

"Ma, where is . . . the stuff?"

"I threw it out. You don't need to be having drugs, anyway."

"What? Ma, that wasn't yours to throw out—that wasn't mine!" he yelled.

"Boy, you don't pay no damn bills in this house. So don't you dare yell at me or tell me what I can or cannot throw out in my house. I don't allow drugs in here, and you know that."

"That wasn't mine for you to throw out. Now, I gotta put up the loot for what you did."

I was taken aback by what he said. More and more, I was beginning to see that my son was selling drugs, but I didn't want to believe it. *Not my son!*

"Well, you have plenty of money in your pockets to pay whatever debt you owe. So let this be a lesson for you."

Jalen sucked his teeth.

"Man, fuck this. I'm out," he said, leaving his room and heading for the front door.

I stormed after him. "Boy, don't you curse at me. Where do you think you're going?"

"Away from you. If you're not gonna respect my privacy and throw my stuff out, then I don't need to be in your house. I'm out!"

I walked over to him.

"Boy, if you don't shut up and sit your narrow behind down—"

"Whatever."

"Sonshine, wait—"

Before I could finish my sentence, Jalen was out the door and running down the steps. I didn't know where he was going or when he was returning, but I questioned if I had gone about everything too strongly.

CHAPTER 34

YOU GOTS TO CHILL

I was too pissed and couldn't listen to any more of my mom's bitching. She threw out at least three hundred dollars' worth of weed, and now I had to take that money out of my cut. I needed to clear my head and get out of that apartment, so I called Akeem.

"Yo! Where you at? Walk to the corner store with me real quick," I said.

"Nah, man. I'm at Nia and Rita's place. Their grandma got admitted to the hospital, and Kiera is going out, so I'm chilling out here to keep Nia company tonight since she was feeling lonely," he snickered.

"Yo, my mom found my weed stash and threw that shit out," I said.

"That's fucked up," he said, sounding like he wasn't paying me no mind.

"Yeah, man. I gotta put up that money now."

"True, but at least she didn't find the hard shit. If she threw out the dope, then you'd really be fucked. Be thankful she only found the weed."

I heard him kissing Nia on the other end. He came back to the conversation with me and said, "Yo, Rita said she's feeling lonely too . . . You need to come through and keep her company over here."

"Word? I'm on my way," I said.

I got to Nia and Rita's apartment, and as soon as the door opened, Rita was all over me with kisses. Nia was in their bedroom with Akeem. The door was closed, but I could still hear Nia's loud moaning. I guess hearing Akeem and Nia going at it got Rita hot, and she wanted the same.

She grabbed me by the hand and led me to her aunt's room. We stripped each other naked and spent the rest of the afternoon and evening sexing each other up. I know Ma expected me to tuck my tail between my legs and come home eventually, but I wouldn't give her that satisfaction. Being in the streets and hanging with my friends was always better than going home and dealing with her mouth. So I didn't care if I ever went home again.

CHAPTER 35

SO WHAT'CHA SAYIN'?

I forced myself to keep my eyes on the documents before me, but truthfully, I was just staring at the papers without seeing them. The whole time I was at work, I went through the motions.

I couldn't focus and wanted to be anywhere *but* here. I was too busy worrying about Jalen since he never came home last night. I left work on time for a change, and as soon as I got near my building, I called Tracy, and she agreed to meet me out front for a cigarette. When she stepped out of the building, she looked as distraught as I was. I took a long pull of my cigarette and blew the smoke out of my nostrils. Then I faced Tracy and said, "Jalen is stressing me out. He didn't come home last night. I don't know if he's locked up, lying up in a hospital, or dead in a ditch somewhere."

Tracy took a drag on her cigarette, exhaled, and said, "I'm in the same boat as you. Akeem hasn't come home either."

"I can't live like this. I need to know that he's OK . . . I'm gonna look for him."

"Queen, you're not gonna go by yourself. Chances are, wherever yours is, mine is, too. I'm coming with you."

"What about work?"

"My nerves are too shot worrying about this boy to deal with patients today. I'm calling in."

Tracy and I walked around the neighborhood asking everyone and anyone we thought would know where Akeem and Jalen were. Finally, we approached some boys around our sons' ages leaning against a fence on the corner of the grocery store. They said they'd seen them by the bodega on Twelfth Street, but that was pretty much it. We learned from the limited information we gathered that our boys were alive, not locked up or in the hospital, but didn't want to be bothered or found.

We walked to the Twelfth Street deli, but they weren't there. Then we walked toward the Laundromat on Fortieth Avenue and Tenth Street, where I saw some brothas who usually hung out with the boys by the basketball courts. The men were leaning against the sidewall of the Laundromat. The way they were ogling us, I felt a bad vibe from them. I pushed those jitters aside, ignored the corny pickup lines they were laying on us, and asked them if they'd seen the boys.

One of the brothas with a Jheri curl and gold tooth said, "Nah, I ain't seen 'em, but fuck finding those two. What y'all ladies trying to get into tonight?"

"The only thing we're interested in is finding our sons. Thank you," Tracy said.

When we realized this was another dead end, we walked away. I looked behind us and saw the man and three of his friends push themselves off the wall and start following us.

"Baby, y'all look stressed. I got something that'll help with that tension," one of the snaggletoothed brothas said, grabbing his crotch.

"I said we're not interested—"

"Bitch, you better stop playing hard to get before I bend your ass over and *make* you interested. Now, both of you, come here," the Jheri curl brotha yelled.

Tracy and I were so desperate to find our sons that we weren't thinking about the dangers we could experience looking for them by ourselves. We put some pep in our step and picked up the pace, but the men closed in on us.

"Yo, what the hell are y'all doin'?" Bill yelled.

Bill was holding hands with Ebony and headed our way coming up the block. The men stopped in their tracks. Tracy and I breathed a sigh of relief. Ebony ran up to us.

"Ma, are you OK?" she asked.

"I'm good, baby. Juanita and I are just looking for your brother and Jalen."

Ebony and Bill exchanged a look.

"Ma, neither of you should be out here looking for them. It's not safe. What if they robbed you, raped you—or worse?"

"We see that now," I said.

Bill walked up to the men.

"Yo, Ill Bill, we didn't know they were with you," the man said.

"*With* me? Are y'all crazy? Do you know whose mothers those are?" Bill asked.

"We figured they were just bullshitting and lying, looking for some dope—"

"If you would've touched them, that would've been your ass."

"My bad, my bad—we didn't know."

"Leave them alone. As a matter of fact, don't even *look* at them. I will keep this shit on the hush so that Akeem and J don't flip out, but if you ever see these two ladies again, keep walking and don't say shit to them."

Bill faced the other men. "Does everybody got that?" he asked.

They nodded and walked back to the corner they were hanging out on.

"Mrs. Tracy, Mrs. Juanita, what are y'all doing dealing with those guys?"

"Bill, we're looking for Jalen and Akeem. They didn't come home, and we were worried," Tracy said.

Bill and Ebony looked at each other and shook their heads.

"Ma, Akeem and Jalen are fine. They're both being stupid right now and would rather be out in the street, doing their own thing, than listen to you two," Ebony said.

"Well, I'm not running a bed-and-breakfast. Jalen can't pick and choose when he's coming home. If you see him, you tell him to bring his ass home," I said.

"I understand, Mrs. Juanita."

Ebony looked like she had more to say, but she was conflicted.

"Ebony, if you know where the boys are, you need to tell us," Tracy said.

"I'm not a snitch, but if I were you two, maybe I'd check to see if they were at Nia and Rita's house."

"Where do they stay at?" I asked.

Ebony was hesitant.

"Ebony, we don't have time for games. What's their address?"

Ebony sighed and said, "They live at 40-15 Tenth Street, Apt 1C, but you didn't get that from me."

"Thank you, Ebony. One last thing, why were those men so afraid of Akeem and Jalen?" I asked.

"That's something you'll have to ask them, Mrs. Juanita. I'm sorry."

That didn't sit well with me. I worried about what Jalen and Akeem had gotten themselves into. The expression on those grown men's faces was absolute fear. Why were those men so scared of our sons? For now, I put those thoughts aside, and Tracy and I went to the address Ebony told us about.

We knocked on the door. I noticed the peephole turn dark, then go back to light again. Then I heard movement and muffled voices inside.

"Who is it?" a woman's voice asked.

"Juanita and Tracy. We're Jalen and Akeem's mothers," I said.

"OK. What do you want?"

"Are our sons in there?" Tracy asked.

"No," the woman said a little too quickly, which made me suspicious.

"Can you open up and talk to us face-to-face, so we're not shouting our business in the hallway?" Tracy asked.

"Nah, I already told you they ain't here, so there's nothing else to talk about," the woman said.

Tracy and I tried our best to keep our composure and not bark at this woman, since we wanted her to listen.

"If you see them, please tell them to come home?" I asked.

"I doubt I'll see them, but if I do, I'll let them know."

"Thank you," I said.

Tracy and I walked out of the building feeling angry and defeated.

"I don't know who that woman was, but I bet you our boys are hiding out in there," Tracy said.

"I think so too. At least we know the boys are alive. Let's go home. They have to come home eventually," I said.

Tracy nodded.

I put on a brave face, but I was still nervous inside. The safest place my son could be was at home with me.

I was tired of fretting and wanted a much-needed release, so I called Miles over. I haven't expressed it to him verbally, but I appreciated him comforting me through all my drama, listening to me, and mostly being my peace when my life was filled with chaos.

I'll admit that I didn't always see Miles in my long-term plans. At first, I saw him as a short-term fling to break up the monotony of my boring life. Maybe a possible part-time companion to go with me whenever the firm had events and occasionally movies and dinner dates, but so far, our "friends with benefits" was still going strong.

After I finished helping Jerami with his homework and I put him to bed, Miles knocked on the door. I opened it quickly.

"Hey . . . You look stressed," he said.

"I am."

"You wanna talk about it?"

"Nope. I need you."

I held his hand and led him to my bedroom. I quickly undressed him and pulled off my own clothes. I didn't want to talk. I didn't want to think. I just wanted a release from the stress over my situation with Jalen. I pushed Miles onto the bed, straddled his lap, licked my palm, and stroked his manhood. He quickly rose in my hand, and his moans helped get my juices flowing. I slid his length inside me, and my eyes fluttered.

I was in complete ecstasy, rolling my hips and plunging myself down hard and fast, loving the feeling of Miles's meaty dick filling me. His hands were on my hips, grinding with me.

"Mmmm," I moaned.

I leaned forward, my breasts tight against his sculpted chest, as I felt his breathing get heavier with his face buried in the crook of my neck. I felt the beautiful, tingly sensation of an orgasm building, radiating all over my body, and I knew I was close. I quickened my pace, and my eyes rolled back at the mind-numbing euphoric release my body desperately needed.

I came strong. I came hard. But as soon as that beautiful feeling subsided, my thoughts returned to my children. I know Miles didn't get off yet, and I tried to relax, rein in my thoughts and emotions, and stay in the moment, but Jerami and Jalen were heavy on my mind.

"Take me from the back," I said. Miles looked too happy to fulfill my request. We switched positions. I knew this was his favorite. The combination of my moaning and pushing back on his thrust always pushed him over the edge. I stepped it up a notch, so he'd come faster, and then I could pretend to fall asleep and mull over my thoughts. Like clockwork, he was done in two minutes. I rolled over on the side of the bed and lay on my back. Miles grabbed my left hand in his, kissed it, slid his arm around me, and held me close. I nestled against his chest and sighed.

"I don't know what I'm going to do about Jalen. He's failing nearly every class and barely goes to school at all. And now, he's doing God knows what in the streets."

Miles sighed and took his arm from around me. He rolled onto his back and stared at the ceiling.

"What's wrong?" I asked.

"Nothing."

"You're huffing and puffing, so it has to be something."

Miles sat up in the bed and said, "Maybe it's time just to accept that he's already set in his ways, and nothing you do is going to change that."

Hearing him say that made me sit up straight in bed. "I'm never going to accept that. I'll never give up on my son."

"Baby, I'm not saying to give up on him entirely, but there comes a point when you have to be realistic and understand that whether Jalen turns out bad or good, you gave it your all and did everything you could possibly do. You beat yourself up over Jalen, and it's not your fault he's acting up."

I looked at Miles in disbelief. Listening to his response felt emotionless and cold. Miles, not understanding why I was so concerned for my son, hurt. I was disappointed in him. I felt like he didn't get it, like he didn't get me.

"Maybe it's a mother thing, or maybe you don't get it because you don't have children yet, but there are no lengths I wouldn't go to make sure my son is on the right path."

"Baby, I get it. But—"

"There is no *but*. He's my firstborn. You're not grasping how I'm feeling and what I'm going through, and I really don't want to discuss it if it makes us argue."

Miles turned his back as if he was too mad to even look at me.

"Before we both say things we'll regret, why don't we call this a night and talk again tomorrow?"

That made him turn around.

"You're kicking me out?" he asked.

I didn't answer that. Usually, I loved being around him, but I was emotional about Jalen not being home, and he wasn't making things better.

Miles shook his head. He sighed, sat up, and swung his feet to the side of the bed. "You know, no answer *is* an answer," he said.

He dressed, kissed me on the forehead, and left without saying anything. I lay in bed, feeling stressed all over again. Instead of dick this time, I settled on having a cigarette and spent the rest of my night worrying about Jalen.

CHAPTER 36

ONE TIME 4 YOUR MIND

"I don't appreciate your mama coming here, knocking on my door, and interrogating me," Kiera said.

I rolled my eyes. Akeem and I sat on the couch, cuddled up with our girls. I had enough of hearing shit from my mother, so I didn't want to hear shit from a crackhead when I felt at peace here. I reached into my pants pocket and tossed her a vial of crack.

"Are we good now?" I asked.

Kiera smiled and stared at the vial in her hand. "Yeah, yeah. We're good. Stay as long as you want."

Nia frowned and said, "Please don't support my auntie's habit. If she gets it outside on her own from other dealers, that's on her, but I don't like knowing my man and his best friend are helping her slowly kill herself."

"It ain't his fault that she got caught up with smoking the shit. What difference does it make if she gets it from him or any other brother on the street?" Rita said.

"The difference is me not seeing it happen in front of my damn face," Nia replied.

For a second, Nia looked as if she was going to say something else, but it passed, and she kept her words to herself. The rest of the night went smoothly, but I knew this conversation about Kiera's habit would come up again soon.

The next morning, I dropped by Mom's apartment, hoping she and Aunt Carina were at work so I could slide in, grab some things, and be out. I jumped when I saw Jerami playing video games in the living room.

"Bro, what are you doing home? Your ass should be in school," I said.

"I didn't feel like going today. It's boring," he said.

I laughed at that because I felt the same way.

"Trust me, I get it, but you're too little to be skipping school this early," I told him.

Jerami waved me off and kept playing his game.

I went to my bedroom and picked up some boxers, clothes, and kicks to match my outfits. Then I grabbed my favorite washcloth, toothbrush, and deodorant from my dresser and stuffed them in an old book bag.

Jerami stood in the doorway.

"You going out again?" he asked.

"Yeah."

"Can I come?"

"Nah, you can't come where I'm going."

"When are you coming back?"

I didn't feel like hearing another nagging lecture from Ma, so I told him the truth. "I don't know, little bro."

"Oh," he said. He looked like something was bothering him.

"Why? You miss me or something?"

"No."

I wadded up a shirt and playfully threw it at him. It hit him in the face, and he laughed and threw it back, but I caught it and packed it. His smile faded.

"What's up?" I ask.

"This kid Lamont keeps teasing me and talking foul about Dad. He's short, so I snapped back on him about that, but the kids in the schoolyard laughed harder at his 'dead dad' jokes."

I didn't like hearing anyone talking foul about our father, plus Jerami needed to learn to fight if he was ever going to get respect and survive around here, so I said, "The next time he talks shit, bust him right in the nose and stomp him out. Once you make an example outta him and everybody sees the ass whoopin' he got, nobody else will fuck with you. You understand?"

Jerami nodded.

"Good! A'ight, bro. Keep your head up, go to school, and I'll check on you again soon. Don't let cats around here think you're not going to school because you're scared of that punk. In the meantime, here."

I pulled out a C-note, and his eyes lit up.

Jerami reached for it, but I pulled it back. "You'll only get it if you go to school and do what I told you."

Jerami grabbed his book bag, put on his shoes, and said, "Bet!"

I handed it to him.

"Thanks, Jalen!"

"Don't worry about it. Buy yourself something nice, but I need you to do me a solid."

"What?"

"Don't tell Ma I was here."

"No doubt."

We walked out of the apartment. My bro was headed late to school, and I was glad I was in and out of the apartment without having to deal with Ma.

CHAPTER 37

READY OR NOT

"Boss lady, you have a call on line three," Francisco said over the intercom.

I was in my office looking over a document for a folder I was rushing to prepare for Francis.

"Thanks. I'll take it in here."

I picked up the receiver and clicked on the blinking red light lighting the phone.

"Wayne, Rothstein, and Lincoln. This is Juanita Wilson speaking. How can I help you?"

"Good morning, Mrs. Wilson. This is Principal Green from P.S. 111."

"Hey! How are you? Wait . . . Oh, God. Jerami isn't sick, is he?" I asked, concerned that his cancer might've come back.

"No . . . He's not sick, but he has had problems lately."

I sat back in my chair, curious about what these problems could be and why I was just now hearing about them.

"Problems like what?" I asked.

"Well, for starters, today, he broke one of his classmate's noses and beat him up pretty badly."

"What? Jerami did that?" I asked, surprised.

"Yes. Lately, he's been either late to school or absent completely, and when he is present, he's been very disruptive in class and argumentative. He's been sent to my office a lot recently. At first, I excused his behavior because I know he's gone through so much, but when he was sent to me today and expressed that he feels school is for suckers and doesn't need it, I knew I needed to talk with you immediately."

"He said that?"

"Yes, I was surprised, too. When I asked him why he thought that was true, he told me his brother doesn't go to school, and he makes a lot of money."

I was livid. I needed to correct this problem before I had *two* kids failing in school. I was more upset with Jalen than Jerami because I knew his big brother's actions influenced Jerami.

"I'm sorry for everything, Principal Green. I will straighten Jerami out as soon as I get home."

When I walked in the door, Jerami was sitting in front of the TV playing his damn video games.

"Turn that shit off now," I yelled.

Jerami huffed and puffed but did as I asked. Then he plopped down on the sofa with his arms folded.

"What is going on with you at school?" I asked.

"Nuttin'."

"Don't give me that. Your principal said you're often late or absent, and when you're there, you're acting up in class. Did you tell her today that you feel like school is for suckers?"

"Well, it is."

I shook my head. "This isn't like you. Why are you acting like this?" I asked.

"Jalen does the same thing and—"

"Jalen is headed down a bad path, and you don't need to follow him to it. Do you realize you broke a boy's nose today? Our heads have just gotten above water. Do you understand that if his mother sues me, we'll be right back where we were?"

"Lamont was saying foul things about Dad. Jalen said if he did it again, to pop him in the nose, and he'd think twice about talking slick again."

I was taken aback by that. "What? Have you seen your brother?" I asked.

He looked like he regretted blurting that last part out. He looked down at his hands.

"Boy, you better answer me."

Jerami sighed. "Yeah, he came home for a second, got some clothes, and left again."

"Did he say where he was staying or when he was coming back?"

"Nope."

"When did this happen?"

"This morning."

"And you're just *now* telling me this?"

"I didn't wanna be a snitch."

"Well, since you're being so loyal to your brother, your video game and TV privileges are gone for the rest of the week."

"Ma—"

"Nope. Do your homework. I'm gonna cook dinner; after that, you can wash up and go to bed. Now, you'll have a few days to think about what you did and why you're being punished."

"This isn't fair."

"Save it. Get your homework done."

Jerami stood up, stormed to his room, and slammed the door.

I sighed and started to make dinner to take my mind off my stress. It was bad enough that I was still worried about Jalen's whereabouts and his going to school, but now, his shitty mindset was influencing Jerami. I needed Jalen to come home so I could talk some sense into him.

I was in my living room channel surfing on the couch, praying that Jalen would stop this nonsense and finally come home. Meanwhile, Jerami was fuming in his room. He barely ate dinner and slammed his door afterward, but he'd get over it.

I heard a knock on the door and hurried to see if it was Jalen. I sighed when I saw it was Miles.

"Hey, babe . . . Don't be too excited to see me," he said sarcastically.

"It's not that. I had to pick Jerami up from school today because he broke a bully's nose. Jalen told him to do it, so now he's following everything Jalen does. I'm trying to nip it in the bud now and thought you were Jalen."

"Yeah, that sucks, but on the bright side, I have the perfect night planned for us," he said.

I was annoyed because I felt like he blatantly disregarded everything I had just said. "Um—"

"I know how much you wanted to see that play *Fences* on Broadway, so I worked my magic, pulled some strings, and got us two tickets for tonight's show."

"Miles—"

"I know Carina is supposed to be home soon. I figured we could ask her to watch Jerami. If she can't do it, I'd offer to pay Debbie to watch him for the night. I know you told me she's been sick lately, but if she wasn't up to it as a last resort, you could put Jerami to bed early, and I figured—"

"Miles . . ."

"—Jerami is old enough to watch himself. I want to be with you tonight, Juanita."

"Miles, I appreciate the gesture. I really do, but I can't go with you tonight. Jalen still hasn't come home, and it's been two days. According to Jerami today, Jalen has already slipped in and out of here to avoid me. I need to talk to him. I need to convince him to stay home. I can't risk missing him stopping by if and when he decides to come home."

Miles sighed, rubbed his hand down his face, and shook his head. "How do you even know he's coming home tonight?"

"I don't—"

"Then why are we going to miss out on having a fun, stress-free night on the possibility that he *might* come home?"

I didn't like his tone or his attitude. "I don't expect you to understand, but I'm a mother and am worried about my sons. Who are you to assume that my sister or my friend will just watch Jerami on such short notice? Like I said, I appreciate the gesture, but something like this needs to be planned first. I can't just get up and leave to go places whenever I want to."

"Fine . . . I'm gonna go, but this is getting really old, Juanita."

"I'm sorry you're disappointed. This isn't how I wanted to spend my free time after a long day at work, either. You know I'd rather be out having fun with you, but I need to be here for my kids tonight."

"I don't ask you for much. All I ask for is a little bit of your time, and you act like that's too much."

"Sorry."

"Yeah . . . I'll call you later. I guess I'm gonna take a loss on these tickets." He sighed, shook his head, opened the door, and let himself out before I could respond.

Lately, he's been getting aggravated and impatient with me whenever I need to cancel plans because of my kids. He's told me a few times it frustrated him that things between us have moved so slowly. *I get it.* After our last time being intimate, I realized my lack of availability was causing arguments and problems. I knew he was mad, but my major priorities were my kids. Everything else either came second or had to wait.

CHAPTER 38

VERBAL INTERCOURSE

I slowly turned the key to my mom's apartment door around four in the morning, eased the door open, and quietly snuck inside. For the past three nights, I'd been hustling and partying with 'Keem, Nia, and Rita. My goal was to creep in, grab some more clothes, and bounce without waking up my family. I wanted to avoid hearing Ma's mouth and her questioning where I'd been at all costs.

I tiptoed into the living room and saw Auntie lying beside Ma, snoring hard, stretched out on the pull-out couch mattress. Auntie was dressed like she just came home from clubbing, and Ma was wearing her work clothes, I guess she stayed up late waiting for me to come home. *Sucks to be her.* I changed clothes and was out the door before she or my aunt woke up and realized I was there.

The past three nights had been great, with Rita and me sexing up each other. After the first night, Nia got on all our cases about going to school, so to get her off our case, Akeem and I went to Mr. Sealy's class, but that was about it. After his class, we hustled on our usual corner and spent the rest of our nights with our girls.

Things were great until the fourth night when my pillow talk with Rita told me it was time to go home. That night, after an intense sex session, Rita was lying on my chest in bed and asked, "Where do you see yourself in five years?"

"I don't really know. I never put much thought into it, truthfully."

"Well, off the top of your head, where do you see yourself?"

I didn't know what kind of answer she was looking for, so I went with the safe, bullshit answer I thought she wanted to hear.

"I see me still being with you and treating you like the queen you are."

She didn't seem moved. "Touching, but besides that, where do you see yourself?"

"I don't know. I guess I'll keep hustling with Akeem and stack my money until I have a fat ass nest egg to retire on."

Rita didn't look impressed. "That's it?" she asked.

"Yeah, I guess. Where do you see yourself in five years?"

"I don't see myself with someone that's not going places. Akeem told Nia he plans to run shit in the next few years. That's the type of plans you should have, Jalen."

I didn't know what to say. I lay there speechless. Seeing that, Rita continued, "Look, I don't share my time or body with losers or bum-ass niggas. Nia loves Akeem because he's goal-oriented and is going places. I want my man to have goals, too."

"I get that, but it's not like I'll be sitting around doing nothing. He won't be running shit by himself. If he's running the show, I'll be there with him as his right hand," I said.

She raised her head off my chest and looked disgusted with my answer. "Why be Robin when you can be Batman? You should never strive to be number two. You should always want to be the head."

"Akeem's like my brother. I'd never fight him over power. It wouldn't be like I'm under him. We'd be running shit together."

"I know that's your man and all, but if you don't want to fight him, make him take a backseat so you can run shit."

I slowly moved her head to lie back on my chest and put her mind to ease for the time being.

"Baby, chill. I still got some time. You gave me a lot to think about, so I'll branch off and do my own thing once I learn everything."

"That's what I'm talking about. Don't lose sight of that goal, though. I know how you get when it comes to Akeem."

I didn't like her making me sound like I was some scrub or a pussy. I didn't want to fight with her, but I was pissed off by what she said and where this conversation was going. The handwriting was on the wall that our relationship probably wouldn't last forever. But one thing was for sure . . . This was going to be my last night here.

"So, we know that it's Macbeth's wife that goads him into killing the king and taking the crown for himself. This book has a lot of lessons in it. There's a lot to unpack here. What are some of the things you guys have taken from it?" Mr. Sealy asked.

Akeem and I were in our English class, and the book we were reading, *Macbeth*, was hitting too close to home. I kept thinking about Rita and her plans for me. In my mind, she was like Lady Macbeth, wanting me to be the one to run shit when that was never really a goal of mine.

Akeem raised his hand, and Mr. Sealy called on him.

"Like in the streets, you gotta keep your head on a swivel. You never know if your own man is gonna do you in," he said.

"Good observation! Jimmy, what did you get out of it?" Mr. Sealy asked, picking on another kid.

"You can't be too confident and cocky. After talking to the witches, Macbeth thought he couldn't be touched, and his cockiness was his downfall," Jimmy said.

"Very good! Jalen, you're quiet today. What lesson did you get out of the book?"

"Um, I learned you should be your own man and not be easily persuaded," I said.

Jameela, a girl in our class, sucked her teeth.

"Do you have something you want to add, Jameela?" Mr. Sealy asked.

"Yup, I'm tired of all the boys here acting like it was the witches' or Lady Macbeth's fault that Macbeth killed the king."

"Go on."

"I see it like this . . . In our neighborhood, we got all types of drugs and crime around here. People can say all types of things to influence us to be a part of that, but it's up to us to navigate through it. So what if Macbeth had those people talking in his ear? He didn't have to listen to them and make all those mistakes. He was weak, and at the end of the day, it was up to him to own up to his mistakes and deal with the consequences."

"Excellent! You guys are on the money today! Great observations!"

Discussing this book was eating at my conscience. I didn't want to lose Rita, but at the same time, I knew she would eventually want me to go against Akeem and branch out to run the hood myself. If there was one thing I knew for sure, I wouldn't make the same mistake Macbeth did. There was no way I'd ever go against Akeem. He was like a brother to me. I figured I'd fill her head with what she wanted to hear for the time being, but eventually, I knew I'd lose her.

The bell rang, and Akeem and I rushed out of school to head to the corner to set up shop and get our hustle on. I made up my mind on the corner and told Akeem that once I was done there; I was going to Nia and Rita's to pack my shit and go home. It was time.

CHAPTER 39

SOUND OF DA POLICE

"Boss lady, you have a call on line one . . . I don't want to scare you, but it's the police," Francisco said over the intercom.

I was in my office. The first thought that came into my head was something had happened to Jalen. My mind kept telling me something wasn't right. As soon as I opened my eyes this morning, I checked my cell phone for missed calls, but there was nothing. I prayed that this wasn't bad news about him.

"What? You gotta be kidding me. Damn. OK, I got it in here. Thank you," I said.

I picked up the receiver and sighed before I clicked on the blinking red light. My first thoughts were, what did Jalen do this time? I hoped he didn't do something too bad that could land him in prison. I was nervous.

"Wayne, Rothstein, and Lincoln. This is Juanita Wilson speaking. How can I help you?"

"Good evening, Mrs. Wilson. This is Officer O'Sullivan—"

"State your business, Officer."

"After arresting your sons and their friends, I thought we were close," he said, laughing.

I didn't find shit funny. I also realized he said, "sons."

"Why are you calling me?" I asked.

"Well, I guess you won't win any mother of the year awards. I picked your youngest son up for shoplifting at the Blockbuster video on Steinway."

I closed my eyes and exhaled. Then slowly, I opened my eyes again and couldn't believe that Jerami was getting progressively worse.

"Your mother of the year comment wasn't needed or professional," I said.

"Maybe not, but it doesn't mean it isn't true."

"Well, you can keep your comments to yourself. I'll be there at the precinct to pick up my son in a few."

I hung up, dropped everything I was doing, and headed to the precinct.

It felt good leaving without hearing any shit from Francis for a change, but I didn't need this shit right now with Jerami. It was bad enough that Jalen hadn't been home, and I had to worry about him getting in trouble with the cops, but now Jerami was following in his brother's dumb-ass footsteps.

When I arrived at the precinct and entered the juvenile room, tears were streaming down Jerami's face. The prick cop O'Sullivan was filling out paperwork.

"Ma!" Jerami said, happy to see me.

"Don't get excited. Depending on what Mr. O'Sullivan—"

He cleared his throat. "*Officer* O'Sullivan," he said, correcting me.

"Whatever. Depending on what this cop says and how you act will determine if I take you home or leave you to rot in Spofford."

That wiped the excitement off Jerami's face.

It was an empty threat. There was no way I'd let him go to Spofford after seeing how Jalen looked after his brief stint there, but I needed to make him sweat a little.

"Mommy, please—"

O'Sullivan was smiling, which only made me angrier.

"Don't 'Mommy' me. Why the hell were you stealing, Jerami?"

He shrugged and looked at the floor.

"Boy, you better answer me."

O'Sullivan was chuckling now. I didn't appreciate being this cop's amusement, so I put chewing out Jerami's ass on pause until I signed whatever I needed to get him out. Once we left the precinct, it'd be on. I faced Officer O'Sullivan.

"I know you're getting a kick out of this, but how would you feel if the shoe was on the other foot, and a Black officer was laughing at your son who was arrested?"

"I don't worry about hypotheticals and what-ifs. Fortunately for me, I don't have kids, and if I did, they'd never be in that situation."

Frustrated at his smug answer and attitude, I asked, "What do I need to sign to get my son out of here and away from you?"

O'Sullivan took me to the desk officer and explained everything. I signed the necessary paperwork to release Jerami, and we left the precinct.

As soon as our feet touched the sidewalk, I immediately let Jerami have it. We argued while we walked from the precinct to the train station.

"What the hell is the matter with you? You know better than to steal. You saw your brother in handcuffs before. I thought that would be enough of a deterrent to stop you from ever being in them, but I guess not. So why are you stealing anything? If you needed something, you could've asked me," I said.

"You treat me like I'm still a baby. I'm not a baby anymore. You and everybody else act like I can't do stuff by myself. I stole that stuff because I wanted to sell it and prove to everybody that I can make money on my own like Jalen does," he said.

"All money isn't good money. You shouldn't be stealing—period! Jalen is not the role model you should be following. Your father and I raised you and Jalen better than this."

Jerami sulked. We got to the station and hopped on the train, but I wasn't done with him yet.

"Did you see that cop laughing in there when I was talking to you? To him, you're just another stupid, stereotypical nigger stealing stuff. You're entertaining to him; every time he arrests boys like you and your brother, you make him richer. He doesn't care about you or any boys that look like you. Whenever you do stupid shit like shoplifting, you automatically reinforce the stereotypes he already sees you as."

Jerami's response was simple but disappointed and hurt me just as easily.

"So what? I don't care what anybody thinks."

After he said that, I didn't want to talk to him anymore. I couldn't believe that this was my baby talking like this. In silence, we rode the rest of the train and walked home. We walked into our apartment, and Jerami turned on the TV and reached to power on the PlayStation.

"Boy, have you lost your mind? You're not playing any games for a long time. Matter of fact ..."

I snatched the wires and power cord from the back of the TV and wall, walked to my bedroom, and threw the system on my bed. When I returned to the living room, Jerami was sitting on the couch with his arms folded.

"I hate you!" he said.

I couldn't take it. It was bad enough that I felt like Jalen didn't love me, but to hear Jerami say that after everything I sacrificed for both of my sons, it hurt too deeply. I burst into tears. Suddenly, I heard the door locks clicking and thought, *What else can go wrong?*

CHAPTER 40

MY BLOCK

I walked in the door and saw Jerami pouting on the couch with his arms folded and Ma standing in the living room in tears.

"Boy, where have you been?" she asked.

"Out."

"I can't take this."

I sighed, figuring Ma was being overdramatic as usual, and asked, "What's going on?"

"I just got back from the police station. I had to pick up Jerami because he was arrested for shoplifting. His grades are slipping. He doesn't want to go to school. He's getting into fights, and now he's stealing."

"What?"

Ma shook her head. "I can't go through this again. I went through it enough when you were doing it. You boys are making my blood pressure go up, and I don't need this right now. *You* talk to him. I can't get through to him."

She walked to her room and slammed the door. I turned to face Jerami.

"Yo, what are you stealing shit for? You know if you ever need dough, I always got you. You don't need to be stealing."

"I know, but Drastic said you started out boosting and doing drops too—"

That caught me off guard. "Wait, what? You're out here doing this shit for Drastic?" I asked.

"Yeah, I want to make my own money like you."

Drastic never told me he was talking to my brother, and he damn sure never told me Jerami was working for him. My bro wasn't built for street shit; he wasn't even fully cured of his cancer yet. The whole situation made me think of what Joe said to me.

"As soon as one of y'all gets arrested, he can always find more dumbasses like y'all because you're expendable."

"Hold up. Start from the beginning. How did this shit even happen?" I asked.

"One day after school, Auntie wasn't around, and I went to the basketball courts to look for you. Drastic saw me and asked if I was your brother. I said yeah, and he asked me if I wanted to make some quick money. He told me you started out the same way, so I said yeah."

I don't like this shit at all. "You working for Drastic—that whole shit—ends today. You understand me?"

"But why? You work for him, and you're doing good. I want to be like you."

"You need to be *better* than me. You need to be in school, not doing drops or stealing shit. You're too smart to be out here in these streets."

"You're smart too. If you did everything I'm doing, why are you telling me I can't do it?"

"I do this shit because I need to. You're smarter than I was at your age. You don't need to be in the streets. You need to focus on school, and if you need money for something, I'll help you get it."

"I don't want anyone to help me anymore. I wanna help myself."

I understood that, but I didn't want him getting in trouble. "Look, I get it, but from now on, your job is gonna be school. I'll give you twenty dollars for every test you get at least 75 percent on. Deal?"

Jerami lit up. "Deal!"

I didn't want Jerami working for Drastic and planned to stop that shit ASAP, but I had to tread lightly. If I came too hard at Drastic, he'd beat my ass, maybe even kill me and force Jerami to work for him more out of spite.

I gave Akeem and Daunte the 411 on what was going on the following day when we went to one of Drastic's stash spots. We had been to lots of them, but this was the first time he told us to meet him at apartment 3A at 41-08 Vernon Boulevard.

"That's kinda fucked up that he never told you he had Jerami working for him," Akeem said.

"Word!" Daunte added.

"Right. I thought the same thing," I said.

"Definitely bring it up to him, but be careful how you say it. If he thinks you're disrespecting him, that'll be your ass," Akeem warned.

"I know."

We knocked on the door. Boogie opened it and signaled us to follow him. It was a nice two-bedroom apartment that looked different from Drastic's usual trap spots. He had nice leather furniture and a giant screen TV in the living room.

We walked into one of the bedrooms. Drastic was in a tank top and basketball shorts, picking out his pants and sneakers for the day from his closet while Boogie started ironing a shirt for him.

"Yo, this place looks way better than your usual dope houses," Daunte said.

"That's because this isn't a dope spot, dumb dumb. I rarely stay in one location, but when I need to be away from everyone and everything, I stay here."

Drastic looked at us collectively and said, "Only a select few know about this spot, so consider yourselves fortunate. But if I hear y'all blabbed and told anyone about it . . . God help you."

We nodded. Drastic faced Daunte.

"Yo, dumb dumb. Move my truck," he said, tossing him the keys.

Daunte sucked his teeth.

"Is there a problem?" Drastic asked.

"Nah."

"Then move my shit without the extra sound effects with your disrespectful ass," Drastic said, nudging Boogie and laughing at Daunte.

Daunte did as he was told.

"Me and J need to re-up," Akeem said.

"Link up with Taevaughn. I don't keep work in this apartment. I don't need the cops raiding this spot or cats creeping up on me to rob me," Drastic said.

"No doubt," Akeem said.

Drastic went back to looking in his closet for the right pair of sneakers and pants to match his shirt. Akeem mouthed to me to talk about the Jerami situation.

"So...I was talking to my little brother, and he said he's been putting in work for you..." I said.

Drastic stopped what he was doing and looked at me. "Yeah, and?"

I was silent for a second, thinking of the right way to get my point across.

"I don't got all day. Speak your mind, J," Drastic said.

"How come you never told me about that?"

Drastic walked up to me and got in my face. "First of all, who the fuck do you think you're talking to?" he asked.

I averted my eyes.

"Nah, don't act like a pussy now. *Look* at me," he said.

I did what he asked.

"Second, and this is really important to remember, *who's* running shit around here, me or you?"

"You," I answered meekly.

"Good answer, and don't forget that shit. Now, when it comes to my money, I'll recruit whoever the fuck I want. You understand?"

"Yeah...It's...It's...It's—"

"You're irritating the shit out of me. Speak up and get to your point."

"It's just my moms is on my ass about it, and I don't really want him doing anything that'll get him in trouble. He's been getting in trouble at school, and he got bagged by the cops already—"

Drastic grabbed me by my shirt and said, "Nigga, are you asking me something or tellin' me?"

"Nah, Nah. I'm-I'm—" I stammered before Akeem stuck up for me.

"He wants to know if you could do him a solid and keep Jerami out of the street shit. His lil' bro is still recovering from his cancer treatments, and his mom has been nagging extra hard because she's blaming him for being in the streets."

Drastic looked at me. "Is that true?"

"Yeah."

"Why should I care?"

I quickly searched my mind for a good reason and settled on something I thought he'd like. "Because of the seventh commandment. *#7 This rule is so underrated, keep your family and business completely separated.*"

Drastic laughed. "You're learning, kid. All right, let your lil' bro know that I'm cutting him off because he got caught by the cops."

I nodded and said, "Thanks."

I was grateful he wouldn't use Jerami anymore, but I was still mad that he did that behind my back, and I didn't have a clue.

Daunte walked into the apartment and handed Drastic his truck keys.

"You parked my shit in a spot where I'm not gonna get a ticket, right?" Drastic asked.

"Yup," Daunte said.

"If I get one, I'm gonna fuck you up."

Daunte swallowed hard. "Let me see if I can find a better spot," he said.

"Yeah, you do that."

Daunte rushed out of the apartment.

"The kid got heart, but he's kind of slow like his cousin, Shyne," Drastic said.

"Why didn't you just have Shyne move your truck?" Akeem asked.

"Nah. I don't let that nigga touch my shit anymore after the absent-minded motherfucker almost got me locked up."

"What happened?" I asked.

"When I was first coming up, the cops were eyeing Boogie and me hard, and I didn't want either of us to get bagged having shit on us, so I told Shyne to take my truck and do the re-up for us. The nigga made it back with no problems but didn't tell me he never took the shit out of my truck. I drove around all day thinking I was clean and the work was already in my crib until I went to put something in the trunk, and the cops crept up on me. I lucked out. I closed the trunk just in time, so the pigs only thought to frisk me but not search the trunk. If the pigs came a minute earlier, I would've been doing serious time because of his dumb ass."

"Damn," I said.

"Yeah. After that day, I don't let Shyne near my truck anymore," Drastic said.

Someone knocked on the door. Boogie went to open it. When he came back to the bedroom, two girls followed him. LaShonda and Terria were 'Keem's and my ages. We knew them from school. They were both wearing short skirts and tight shirts.

"A'ight, boys. Y'all gotta bounce. Me and Boogie got some pussy we're about to get into, and we don't need an audience," Drastic said.

"Aren't they too young for—" I started to say, but Akeem nudged me.

"J, get to stepping before you say something that makes me fuck you up and change my mind about your brother. Nigga, are *you* too young to work for me?" Drastic said.

I shook my head.

"I didn't think so. Find some cause and get outta my face."

LaShonda and Terria took off their shirts and were completely topless, which made Drastic smile and wave us off. Akeem pushed me out of the bedroom door.

"Yo, 'Keem. I know your fine-ass sister is into the white boy, but put in a good word for me. You know I like 'em young and fresh. I'll treat her nice," Drastic laughed.

Akeem looked pissed, but he didn't say a word. We just left the apartment. I was glad I convinced Drastic to leave Jerami out of the street shit.

CHAPTER 41

EX-FACTOR

With all the stress I had with Jalen not being home and Jerami acting up, I needed a night to take my mind off things, so when Miles asked to take me on a Friday night date, I didn't hesitate to say yes.

We went to Frankie and Johnnie's on West Forty-Sixth Street in Manhattan. The decor and atmosphere of the restaurant were definitely impressive, but my attention kept cycling between thinking of my boys and being on my date. We ordered and were laughing and enjoying each other's company, but at some point, I must've spaced out because the next thing I knew, Miles was snapping his fingers in my face.

"Juanita, are you even listening to me?"

"Sorry, I have a lot on my mind," I said

Miles sighed. "Let me guess. You're thinking about your kids."

I didn't like that he looked bothered by the fact that he knew they were on my mind.

"I am—"

"They're fine, Juanita. Carina is watching them. You can enjoy a couple of hours for yourself for once."

"I'm always concerned about my boys, but right now, I'm worried that Jalen is having too big of an influence over Jerami, and I don't know how to stop it."

Miles looked unmoved by my statement. He sat back in his chair, sipped his wine, and shook his head. "Did you ever think that maybe Jalen is too far gone? Or maybe you're too busy trying to save him, and he doesn't *want* to be saved?" he asked.

"He's not too far gone, and even if he was and didn't want to be saved, I'd never stop trying."

The waiter returned with our meals and placed them in front of us. Then he refilled our wine. I forced a smile and pretended everything was lovely, but I was ready to explode inside.

Miles looked at me over his wineglass and asked, "Where are we going with this? I'm always competing with something. First, I had to be patient because your son was sick. Then I had to be patient because of your career, and now, you're telling me I have to be patient because your oldest is acting out. Why do I always have to come in second place in our relationship? When is it going to be our turn without other...*obstacles* getting in the way?"

I dropped my fork on my plate and wiped my mouth with my napkin. He just made me lose my damn appetite. His tone and demeanor automatically raised my defenses.

"*Excuse* me?" I said.

When he realized how bad that shit was to say to me, I immediately saw the regret on his face.

"I'm so sorry that my kids are such an inconvenience to you, and your feelings are hurt."

"I didn't say that."

"Not in those exact words, but you *definitely* said it, and I'm tired of it. What would you like for me to do, Miles?"

He hemmed, hawed, and stammered, trying to plead his case. I was tempted to walk out and leave his ass there, tripping over his words, but the last thing I wanted to do was make a scene at this restaurant. He was about to spew another weak excuse, but I cut him off.

"Fuck you, Miles. I can't believe you right now. You're so fucking selfish."

He instantly had a look of frustration that told me he didn't want to be a part of the argument he knew was coming. I know he felt the eyes of all the staff and patrons zeroed in on our spat.

"Let's not do this here, please," he asked.

I nodded and kept quiet.

Miles tried to steer our conversation away from our drama by being overly nice with compliments and attempting to make me laugh, but he was wasting his time. His comments had already soured my mood, and I was already checked out emotionally. After we finished eating, I wanted to end this train wreck of a date.

"Can you take me home, please?" I asked.

Miles reluctantly signaled for the waiter to bring the check. He paid the bill and reached for my hand as we walked out of the restaurant, but I batted his hand away and folded my arms as we walked to his car.

We rode the rest of the way to Queensbridge in silence, both of us lost in our thoughts. During the ride home, I sat slumped down in the passenger's seat, arms folded, facing the window with my eyes focused on the streets outside.

Miles parked near my building, turned down the radio until it was low enough to talk over, and broke the silence.

"We need to talk," he said sternly.

I sighed, bracing myself for a conversation I wasn't prepared to have tonight. "Miles, just stop. Not now. Not tonight."

"Then when? I was patient when Jerami was going through cancer. Now he's better, and you're still pushing me to the side like our relationship isn't shit, like things with me aren't important."

"My kids will always come first. You should know that by now."

Miles held my hand. "Juanita, listen—"

I yanked my hand free. "There's no point in listening to someone who doesn't listen to me," I said.

"Can I come inside?" he asked.

I didn't respond to his question or wait for him to come around to my side of the car and open the door. I pulled the latch, got out, slammed the door, and power walked to my apartment building. Miles quickly got out of the driver's side, shut the door, and trailed behind me. Out of the corner of my eye, I saw he was right behind me, doing his best to catch up.

I opened my building door, hoping it would close quickly, but Miles was right behind me. I rushed up the stairs to my floor.

"Juanita, please. Can I come in for a minute? I don't want us to end our night like this."

I didn't answer him. I just opened my apartment door and walked in. Miles caught the door before it closed behind me and walked in. I didn't know where Carina was with the boys, but I was glad they weren't here for our fight.

"Juanita, you're a brilliant woman. You're a good mother, and I know you only see the good in your kids, and I'm not saying that Jalen can't change, but I think it's important that you also keep an open mind that there's a chance that he won't."

"What's your point?"

Miles rubbed his face and sighed. "My point is you have a lot going, and I don't want you missing out on life and opportunities, worrying about your sons, who might be too far gone."

I didn't say anything. I just let him continue.

"Do you know how many moms I see every weekend at Queensboro Plaza station wasting their time waiting on the Q100 bus to Rikers to see their kids? All those women are in denial, believing that their kids can do no wrong or feel like they failed them somehow. They waste years of their lives worrying about these ungrateful children and spend money they don't have on their books in prison. Those same kids don't give a shit about the stress and pain they bring their mothers. I'm afraid if you're not careful, that will be you."

"Is *that* how you see me? Some stupid woman that will waste her time and money on lost causes?"

There was a long pause between us, a knowing pause that showed us that our relationship had reached its expiration date. Him not responding spoke volumes. It took me some time to learn that, like perishable goods, relationships can expire too, and sometimes, expiration dates are needed for growth. Not everyone will make every chapter of your life, and I was unsure whether Miles would survive the next chapter of mine after this night.

I liked him a lot, but if this would constantly be a problem with us, and he couldn't understand that my kids would always take precedence and be my number one priority, it was time to end our relationship before we wasted more of each other's time.

"All I'm asking is when is it going to be *our* turn? I thought maybe one day we could move in together and have a future, but there's always something. When can we enjoy being with each other without always feeling like there's some limitation? Look, at some point, you're going to have to decide whether you want me in your life full-time or not at all. It's not fair to keep me around part-time because it's convenient for you. I deserve more than that."

I shook my head at his ultimatum. "No one is making you stay with me. We don't even have a title, so I don't know why you're acting like I'm holding you back from something."

"We're adults dating each other exclusively. Only kids give titles of boyfriend and girlfriend. I didn't feel the need for us to have a label. I just wanted to be with you and figured you felt the same."

"I made it very clear that I didn't want a relationship every time you brought it up. Obviously, you want more than I can give you."

"You don't mean that. You're mad right now, but when we're not fighting, and we're together, I know you feel the same way I feel. I love you, Juanita. Please don't push me away out of anger and spite."

My lips trembled. I was too damn emotional. "I . . . I think you need to find whatever you're looking for with someone else because, clearly, you're not gonna find it with me. My kids will always take precedence over any relationship I have, and that seems to be too much for you."

Miles looked taken aback and deeply hurt by my words. He wiped his palms down his face and reached for my hand, but I didn't give him that privilege and snatched my hand away.

We stood there and stared silently at each other for a long while. The pain in his eyes mirrored his voice when he finally broke his silence and said, "I've been nothing but good to you since we met. I know what I bring to the table, and I don't deserve you pushing me away, but trust me when I say I'm not afraid to be alone. Take care of your boys . . . I'll see you around."

I opened the door for him without saying a word. I pointed toward the hallway. With his head down, shoulders slumped, Miles shook his head and walked out without looking back or saying another word. I shut the door behind him, turned, and slowly fell back against my apartment door, sobbing with my arms wrapped tightly around myself. Minutes later, I heard a commotion behind the door and opened it, thinking Miles had come back, but it was Carina and the boys holding bags from the Chinese restaurant. Carina looked into my red-rimmed eyes and asked, "What did I miss?"

The next morning, I pulled a cigarette from my purse, lit it, and leaned against the black iron fence.

Tracy walked out of our building and playfully bumped me when she saw me sulking.

"Where's Debbie?" she asked.

"She wasn't feeling well this morning."

"How'd your date go last night with your big-dick lover?"

"Uneventful," I said, dryly.

"You're salty this morning. What's gotten into you, or should I ask what stopped going inside of you?" she joked.

"I don't wanna talk about it."

"C'mon, spill it. What's got you all cranky?"

"Nothing important . . . Let's talk about something else."

"Judging by the vibe you're giving off; I'm guessing this attitude is because of Miles."

"Queen, please. Let it go."

Tracy stared at me for a moment. "Bad breakup?"

"Something like that."

"Fair enough, I won't push. I'll drop it."

With my free hand, I gave her hand a friendly squeeze. "I'm sorry for being a bitch. I just had a long night, and it's all too much to talk about before I head to work. To make a long story short, I don't think I'll be seeing Miles anymore. He'll never get that my kids will always take precedence over him."

"I understand, Queen. I got your back."

Slowly but surely, I felt Miles distancing himself from me. We didn't go on another date after our fight. The excuses started soon after. Suddenly, he had to work late all the time, and he was too tired to stop by my apartment. Our phone conversations went from less frequent to nonexistent, but I mentally prepared myself for this on the night we fought.

I called him occasionally, but when he stopped returning my calls, against my pride, I stopped by his apartment a few times. Once I accepted that he wasn't responding anymore to my attempts to reach out to him, I gave up on our relationship or whatever it is you would call what we had.

When something went wrong with the radiators, and the heat stopped working, or an outlet didn't get power to it, there were no more quick responses to fix it anymore. When the elevator in my building got broken by the other tenants again, nobody came to fix it anymore. That let me know that Miles no longer cared, and we were really over.

I pushed down what I felt for him. Being alone after Mo's death taught me patience, selflessness, and resilience. I couldn't lie to myself and say I wouldn't miss Miles, but in time, I knew I'd be OK. If having a relationship with a man meant neglecting my children, I'd be just fine being alone.

CHAPTER 42

LIVIN' THE LIFE

Mayor Giuliani was pushing the cops hard to crack down on drugs, so the pigs were on everybody's asses more than usual. After a major drug bust that had Rasheed, Naleighna, Joakim, Erica, Buddha, and a bunch more of Drastic's top generals and lieutenants shipped off to prison, Drastic was acting way out of character, switching up stash spots, trap houses, and had us posted up in different locations and corners to throw off the cops. He was always a scary guy, but lately, the way he had been moving and acting all paranoid, it looked like he was having a hard time figuring out who was friend or foe. That made him more dangerous and ruthless.

Corner boys, runners, and shooters were getting locked up left and right. Money was slowing up on the streets. Drastic was extremely paranoid and kept things close to the cuff with Boogie, Taevaughn, Shyne, Daunte, Akeem, and me.

Since 'Keem and I were now extremely valuable to his organization and two of the few people he trusted, he spazzed out on us one day about not wanting us to waste our time going to school anymore.

"What the fuck took y'all so long? Where the fuck y'all been?" he yelled.

"We had school," Akeem said.

"Nigga, fiends don't wait to get high because y'all are in school. If they can't get it from you, they'll cop it from the next man, and if they're copping from somebody else, I'm losing money, and *that's* a problem. Get my money."

A police car drove by us slowly.

"I don't like how shit is moving out here. I can't afford to lose any more soldiers. I need people I can trust to move this weight heavier and smarter. Y'all been part-timing, and that's not gonna fly anymore."

"We do the bare minimum in class to keep our moms off our backs. What do you expect us to do? When we're not in school, most of the time, we're handling our business and working," Akeem said.

"Y'all not pulling your weight. You want to work part-time? Flip burgers after school at Mickey-D's. If you're trying to get this money with me, you need to be all in. If you can't handle that, step off, and I'll find new soldiers that can. I can't have you two out here half-assing, so either y'all are in, or you're out. What's it gonna be?"

Akeem looked at me.

"We got into this together. Whatever you say, I'm down with it a hundred percent," I said.

Akeem nodded.

"Me and J are wit' it," Akeem told Drastic.

"Good. Y'all needed to dead that going to school shit, anyway. You'll learn more from what I'm teaching you than you'll ever learn in that stupid-ass place."

We nodded hesitantly. We knew our moms would give us shit about missing school, but whatever. We'd figure it out and deal with it.

Akeem and I focused solely on grinding and making money and stopped showing up to Mr. Sealy's class. Since we were constantly missing assignments and skipping our other classes anyway, we dropped out of school altogether.

Working the corners, we didn't have time for basketball anymore, either. We still went to games to cheer for our boy, Bill, but our playing days were over. We were men now.

I gotta give Ma credit. She was on my ass all the time, but it didn't matter. My mind was made up. I was done with school.

I walked into our apartment, tired from hustling all day, and knew I was in for some shit when I saw her in the living room with Auntie.

"Sit down, Jalen," Ma said.

"What now?" I asked.

I'd only been in the apartment for a minute, and Ma was already giving me shit, making me wish I hadn't come home.

Auntie stood up and sat on the arm of the sofa so I could sit next to Ma. I rolled my eyes, plopped down next to her, and yawned.

"Am I boring you?" Ma asked.

"A little."

"What's wrong with you?"

"Nuttin'."

"Nothing? Your school called and said you haven't been going to your classes at all."

"And?"

Mom sighed. She looked like she was about to scream at me but caught herself. She opened and closed her hands repeatedly, and I knew she wanted to smack the shit out of me, but she reined in her emotions, knowing hitting me would only shut me down more. She put on a patient expression and said, "You're setting a bad example for Jerami, and now, he's been acting out in school."

"What does Jerami acting up have to do with me?"

"Jerami is impressionable. He looks up to you. He sees you not going to school and thinks it's the cool thing to do, but both of you need an education so you can have a future. I'm trying to talk some sense into you—"

"I'm not trying to hear you talk to me about school. I'm done with that," I said, staring at the ceiling, annoyed.

"I don't even know who you are anymore. Do you think you're a man now? You're a damn fool. You think dropping out of school in ninth grade is a smart move? How do you expect to get a job without an education? Boy, don't be stupid. Your father, God rest his soul, was all for education, and you know that."

That last part she said, hurt, but I couldn't let that fuck with my decision. "I'll be a'ight."

"You'll be a'ight? What skills do you have? Who will hire you with no schooling, skills, or experience?"

"You went to school, and how well did that work out for you? We still live in Queensbridge, and you're still broke. I don't have to go to school to do that. Look, no disrespect, but I don't want to be like you, educated and working a shitty job I can't stand."

I knew that would hurt her, and I didn't care.

SMACK! Mom slapped me, and my eyes shot daggers at her. I was fuming and went back to staring at the ceiling to calm myself.

"We might not live in the best of neighborhoods, but you're not homeless, sleeping on the streets either. I bust my ass every damn day to keep a roof over your and your brother's heads. I don't make a ton of money, but it's because of my education that I have a respectable, honest job that provides for all of us while you're running the streets with your hoodlum friends."

I continued to stare at the ceiling. Ma grabbed my face and forced me to look at her. "Every damn day, I work for bigoted white men that think I'm nothing. To them, I'm not shit. Men like them run this world, and they don't think you're shit, either. When boys like you quit school, you only reinforce the stereotypes they already think about us." She shook her head and continued.

"Every damn day, I have to work harder than everyone at my job to prove I didn't just get it because of affirmative action. I work to show those bigoted white men that just because I live in the projects doesn't mean I'm worthless."

"Ma—" I tried to cut in.

"No, you need to hear this. I need you to want more out of life and not live it believing there's nothing more than these projects. Don't be a statistic. Be the man your father would've been proud to see growing up."

"You just proved my point. You're barely making it. I don't need to prove anything to those white people, and neither do you. Even if I went to school, it wouldn't change how they see us, anyway."

Mom shook her head, disgusted with my response.

"I'm done with school. You can talk to me until you're blue in the face, and you can drop me off every day and make sure I walk in the building, but unless you're gonna sit with me in every class and spend the entire day with me, as soon as you leave, I'm gone. There's nothing that place can teach me that I can't learn on my own."

Mom threw her hands up in frustration, stood, and left. I heard her bedroom door slam behind her. Aunt Carina sat next to me.

"You just don't get it. Your momma, and I don't always see eye to eye on a lot of things, but I'm with her on this one. You need to finish school. She only wants the best for you."

"I want the best for me too, and school, ain't it."

"Do you want to be a fuckup like me? Sleeping on a couch and not having shit? Your momma wants you to make something of yourself, do better than she and your father did, and move on from this neighborhood."

I tuned her out, grabbed the remote off the coffee table, turned on the TV, and flipped through the channels while Aunt Carina kept talking.

"You're failing out of school. You're always out in the streets. She might be blind to it, but I know you're dealing."

That caught my attention. I turned and faced her.

"Didn't think I knew that, huh? The guys I date talk, and you and Akeem are notorious. Your mother doesn't want you getting caught up in these streets, locked up, or worse. If anything was to happen to you or your brother, she couldn't take it."

"Nothing is gonna happen to me." I stood up, walked out of the apartment, and went outside. Anywhere was better than being home and hearing my mom and aunt bitching.

No matter the weather, Drastic expected us to be outside making him money. Instead of us standing on the corner freezing our asses off, waiting for fiends, and to throw the cops off from seeing us posted up at our usual spot, every day, Akeem, Daunte, and I set up shop in the lobby of different buildings. We had our runners do some intel, picked the locks on a few small metal mailboxes of apartments we knew no one lived in, and hid our stashes in there while we worked.

We leaned against the mailboxes and played craps in the lobby to make it look like we were chilling. We crouched down in a tight circle while Daunte shook the dice. As soon as he let the dice fly, a fiend walked in. Shivering, we hurriedly closed the door behind him.

"What you need, man? If you don't got money, you can walk your ass right back out in the cold," Akeem said.

"Nah, I got money. Lemme get two," he said, digging in the pocket of his dirty jeans and pulling out a dingy twenty-dollar bill.

"Walk up to the second floor. Chill right there until we tell you to come down. By the time you come back, your shit will be ready," I said.

The guy was fidgety. "How do I know you won't just leave with my money?" he asked.

"Do you want this shit or not?" I yelled.

"OK, OK."

We heard the fiend making his way up the stairs, and we quickly took out the work from the stash spot.

"All right, you can make your way back down here," I yelled.

Once he came back, we handed him his shit. We opened the door for him . . . and spotted O'Sullivan and McIvor walking to the building. We quickly locked the mailboxes and acted like we were playing dice the whole time when they snatched the door open. O'Sullivan's eyes darted around the lobby.

"What are you guttersnipes doing here?" he asked.

"Just chillin', Officer. It's cold as hell outside, and we didn't feel like being cooped up in the house," Akeem said.

"I don't buy that shit one bit. You two are hiding something," McIvor said.

"Y'all know the drill. Turn around and place your hands on the wall," O'Sullivan said.

"We didn't do anything," I protested.

"Shut it. Up against the wall," O'Sullivan repeated.

We did as we were told. He kicked apart our feet, spreading our legs before frisking us while his partner, McIvor, watched.

"When dealing with these monkeys, sometimes it's best to shake the tree they're in and see what falls," O'Sullivan said.

"You're not a housing cop. Why are you even here?" I asked.

"It's called 'Reasonable suspicion,' asshole. That crackhead, Tobias Wilkins, that I know you sold shit to, has done time for burglary and home invasions. We know he doesn't live here or have family here, so that gives us reasonable suspicion to check out the situation," McIvor said.

That shut me up.

"Speaking of which, you punks don't live in this building either, isn't that right?" O'Sullivan asked.

I kept quiet.

"Do me a favor and read that sign by the door. As a matter of fact, *I'll* read it. None of you dumbasses go to school, so you probably can't read. It says, '*No Loitering and No Trespassing. Violators caught loitering or trespassing in or around the building premises will be arrested by the NYC Police Dept. Owners and the Police Dept will prosecute violators to the fullest extent of the law,*'" McIvor said.

"So, with that being said, all of you are under arrest for trespassing, but maybe we can let it slide if you tell us where your stash is," O'Sullivan said.

None of us answered him.

"I figured none of you would talk. Well, put your hands behind your backs."

We got arrested. We were lucky we listened to Akeem and had the stash hidden and locked in the mailboxes instead of on us. If we got bagged with the drugs in our pockets, our case would've been a lot worse, and we'd probably have to do time. Luckily for us, we only had to pay a fine.

Even though things worked out, that didn't stop my mom from bitching.

"You keep hanging out in these streets; next time, you won't be so lucky. That cop has it out for you, and sooner or later, he'll arrest you for something that'll stick," Ma said as we left the court.

As usual, her words went in one ear and out the other. Seeing that I wasn't paying her any mind, Ma shook her head and said, "Boy, if your father could see you now."

I glared at her. She knew bringing up my dad would strike a nerve and was a sore spot with me. I sped up, walked away from her, and left her talking to herself.

"What bullshit are you reading now?" Drastic asked Akeem.

Shyne, Daunte, Drastic, Akeem, and I were sitting on a bench in front of our building.

"*The Invisible Man*," Akeem said.

"You ain't in school no more, nigga. Why is your young ass still fucking with books? You always got your head in these shits when you need to keep your mind on getting this paper. I keep tellin' you, a street smart nigga will always out-hustle a book smart nigga any day."

"That's why it's good to be both."

"You forgot who you're talking to? What are you sayin'? You know more about this game than me now?"

"I'm not saying that—" Akeem said.

"I know you're not, because your young ass still doesn't know shit. You need to stop reading and keep your head on a swivel, so you don't get bagged by the cops," Drastic pointed out.

"Yo, speaking of which, who's this goofy cat looking at us and walking over here? Is that an undercover?" Drastic asked.

Akeem and I groaned and sucked our teeth when we saw Mr. Sealy walking toward us. I turned to Drastic and said, "Nah, he's cool. That's our English teacher, Mr. Sealy."

"That nigga ain't cool with me—"

"He's a good dude. He probably wants to talk to us about going back to school. Don't worry. We'll handle it."

"I ain't worried about shit. You got five minutes."

Mr. Sealy was getting closer to us.

"Akeem. Jalen. I haven't seen you guys in school in weeks. I wanted to check on you two to make sure everything was OK," Mr. Sealy said.

"Is this nigga for real? Tell me I'm buggin', and this after-school special motherfucker isn't here making house calls. Get him the fuck outta here before I do it for you," Drastic said.

As soon as Mr. Sealy stepped closer to us, Shyne and Daunte pulled out their guns and aimed them at Mr. Sealy. Mr. Sealy put up his hands and slowly walked backward. Akeem and I rushed over to him.

"Whoa, whoa, whoa. Be cool. We got this," Akeem said to everyone.

I walked Mr. Sealy to the curb, and Akeem rushed over to us.

"Yo, Mr. Sealy. What are you doing here? You can't come around here like that," I said.

"You two haven't been coming to school anymore, and you're both too smart to waste your talents. I've seen too many young brothers get caught up in street nonsense, and I don't want that to be y'all."

"Mr. Sealy, you need to go before you get hurt. It's badass that you came here to talk to us, but we're working," Akeem said.

"Do you boys trust me?"

We nodded. "Of course, Mr. Sealy, but—"

"Then trust and understand that I've got the two of your best interests at heart, and I wouldn't lead you wrong."

"We get that, but school just isn't for us anymore. Sorry," Akeem said.

Drastic was yelling at Shyne and Boogie. He was getting more impatient by the second. Akeem and I shoved Mr. Sealy to get him to move faster before Drastic lost his shit completely.

"Seriously, you need to get out of here before this cat starts flipping and kills you. Get out of here," I said.

Mr. Sealy slowly walked away with his head down. I was getting too used to people that cared about me being disappointed with me.

CHAPTER 43

THE MESSAGE

Daunte, Akeem, and I were in front of the Twelfth Street deli, as usual, when we saw Joe walking to the Chinese restaurant next door.

"Jalen, Akeem, I see Drastic completely turned you two into his little minions," Joe said.

"It beats making scraps working at your shop," I replied.

Joe got right in my face. "Youngster, you better respect your elders. Kid or not, friend of your mother or not, I'll knock you the fuck out," he said.

I yawned and pretended I didn't care and wasn't afraid, but I was shitting bricks.

"You go right ahead. All you boys are headed on a one-way trip to prison, and you're all too stupid to realize that you're killing and selling poison to your own people."

"Man, you ain't no saint. You used to be in the game, too, doing the same shit. What are you talking about?"

"When I was locked up, I had nothing but time to realize what I was doing was wrong. I'm trying to talk some sense into you knuckleheads, so you don't make the same stupid mistakes I did. If shit isn't bad enough, you little dummies waste every cent you get on stupid shit," Joe said.

"Go on with that, old man," Daunte said.

"You don't know what you're talking about. How are we wasting our money when we got everything we want? Fast nickels are always better than slow dimes," Akeem said.

Joe shook his head. "Youngster, since you're all so green and still wet behind the ears, I'll school you to some game. Y'all waste your money buying clothes and jewelry, but you don't save anything. I bought my fair share of shit when I was young, but I saved money for a rainy day, too. When I came home from doing my bid, I had money to fall back on to open my own business, but look at y'all. If you stopped hustling for a week, all of you would be broke without a pot to piss in. You guys are all wearing flashy shit without making sure your mamas are straight. Tell me I'm lying."

He had a point, and none of us could argue with him about that. We all stood there in silence.

"See? Y'all quiet now. There's no reason why your mamas should still be broke and struggling if you're pulling in money. Now, realize this, if your savior, Drastic, ever got locked up, y'all wouldn't have shit anymore. Smarten up. If you're still gonna hustle, at least save some money, and take care of your mommas, so if shit hits the fan, you have an exit plan, and your family is good. With that, I'm gonna go on in this here Chinese spot and get my dinner. I leave y'all to marinate on those gems of knowledge for a while."

Joe left. Daunte and I were waving him off and talking shit, but Akeem looked deep in thought.

"Yo, what's wrong with you? Don't tell me you're taking what that old man said to heart," Daunte said to Akeem.

"Joe talks a lot of shit, but there's truth to what he's saying," Akeem replied.

"How you figure?" Daunte asked.

"He's right. We gotta be better with our money. How will we ever level up if we don't stack our dough?" Akeem said.

Daunte and I laughed.

"Don't let that old man mess with your head. As long as fiends are lining up to get the shit we're selling, we'll never be broke. Let him stay in his wack-ass barbershop, cutting hair," Daunte said.

Across the street, I saw Brother Monterey walking fast, like he was trying not to be seen. I blew up his spot and told Daunte.

"Ay, yo! There goes your boy," I said, pointing out Brother Monterey.

"Hey, where's my fucking money?" Daunte yelled.

"I'm gonna get that to you as soon as I get paid," he yelled. He looked frail, and it was apparent he was turning into a full-fledged fiend.

"You told me that shit last time. I'm not playing with you. You better have my money the next time I see you."

Brother Monterey waved him off and ran away. Out of nowhere, Boogie and Drastic rolled up in his truck. Daunte sucked his teeth and sighed because Drastic saw the whole interaction between him and Brother Monterey.

"Daunte, you stay your ass right there. 'Keem, let me holla at you," Drastic said.

'Keem walked up to see what he wanted. I was in hearing distance but stood to the side and pretended to mind my business so I didn't look nosy.

"Word on the street is your boy Draper is selling Neville's shit on my corners on the low. I'm not having that. Take a ride with me and bring J."

Akeem signaled for me to come over.

"Yo, J. We got shit to handle," he said.

I nodded, and we got in the back of Drastic's truck.

"Yo! What about me?" Daunte asked.

"Until you collect on what that nigga owes, your ass is gonna stay right there."

Daunte sulked and leaned against the front wall of the deli. Boogie started driving, and Drastic turned in the front passenger seat to talk to us.

"We're going to do a little investigation on your boy, Draper. Word on the block is he's selling product on my corners on the low. If it's bullshit gossip, everything will be cool, but if what I heard is true and I catch this cat being grimy and selling on my corners, that's his ass, and I'm gonna have to make an example outta him," Drastic said.

"Yo, stop the truck," Drastic ordered.

Boogie pulled over and put the car in park.

"I know this little nigga isn't selling on my fucking corners."

We all followed Drastic's line of sight and saw Draper standing discreetly against the side of 41-03 Tenth Street, doing hand to hands with a fiend.

"Nope," Drastic said.

"You want me to—" Boogie started to say.

"Nah, 'Keem, Jalen, handle that nigga."

We hopped out of the back of the truck and crept up on Draper. As soon as he saw us, he started to run, but Akeem caught him by his hood and threw him up against the small, black metal fence.

"Are you fucking stupid? You know you can't be selling shit on Drastic's blocks," Akeem said.

Out of nowhere, Drastic hit Draper with a right cross that floored him.

"Enough talking. Whoop his fucking ass," Drastic said.

Draper crawled backward on the sidewalk, raising his hand to protect his face. "Please, I was just tryin' to make a little money—"

Drastic cut him off abruptly. "Shut the fuck up. Don't give me that shit. Don't try to cop a plea now. Take your ass whoopin' like a man," he said.

A crowd gathered to watch Akeem and me beat Draper's ass. Drastic loved it, and when he saw enough, he waved us off and looked at the crowd.

"Let this be a lesson to all of y'all. Anyone that I catch crossin' me is gonna get it worse than this nigga here. The next person I catch is gettin' laid down; that's my word. Try me if you think it's a game," Drastic challenged.

He walked up to Draper and punched him repeatedly. It got so brutal that some of the crowd that was watching averted their eyes; others just left.

As bad as it was, Drastic knew that nobody was crazy enough to call the cops or report him. Draper's eyes were puffy and swollen. Draper was barely conscious, but Drastic held him by his shirt and continued to punch him. When Drastic was finally done, we all walked up to him and returned to his truck.

Before Boogie started the car and pulled off, he looked at Drastic and asked, "Hhhow dddid you hear abbbout him selling?"

"I have my ways. I got eyes and ears all over," Drastic said with a smirk. He gave Boogie a weird look and said, "It's always the ones you least expect that be plotting against you to take your spot. I don't know if cats around here are taking my kindness for weakness or if they're just crazy, but before this day is over, I'm gonna make another example out of some-body to remind everyone around here that I'm not the one to fuck with."

Drastic turned and faced us, then turned back to Boogie. "Drive them back to their spot."

Boogie nodded.

When we got back, Drastic pulled out his roll of money and hit Akeem and me with three hundred dollars each.

"Both of y'all take this. Y'all did good today. Keep your phones on. I'm not done yet with my spring cleaning."

We nodded, and I wondered who was next on his hit list.

"You're a damn cheater," I yelled, mashing the buttons on my PlayStation controller.

"I don't cheat. You just can't touch me in this game. I'm too nice!"

"Whatever."

We both laughed.

We were chilling in Akeem's room playing *Tekken 2* when his phone rang. Since it was a cordless phone, and he was trying to hold his controller and talk, he put it on speaker and said, "Yo, talk to me. Who's this?"

"Nigga, what the fuck you mean, who's this?"

"My bad, Drastic. I didn't look at the number. What's up?"

"Where are you right now?" Drastic yelled.

"I'm chillin' at home with J. What's up?

"Both of y'all bring your asses to 40-01 Vernon Boulevard, apartment 5B, now."

"What's up?"

"Nigga, this is business. I don't talk shop over the phone. I need you to take care of something for me. You're about to make a come-up. Now, bring your ass." Drastic ended the call.

Akeem sighed. "Come with me to see what this cat wants really quick," he said.

I nodded.

We went to the apartment we were told to go to. Loud music was blaring from behind the door. The door flung open as soon as we knocked, and Drastic stood there covered in blood.

"Hurry up and bring y'all silly asses inside," he barked.

We stepped inside and saw Boogie Brown lying naked on a plastic tarp, gagged, with his hands and feet duct-taped, bleeding. There was a baseball bat next to him. Drastic lowered the volume on the stereo.

"This motherfucker has been doing deals on the side behind my back," he said.

Drastic kicked Boogie Brown in the stomach. Then he leaned over and pulled down the gag in Boogie's mouth.

"Nigga, you already know nothing goes down around here without me finding out about it." Then Drastic turned and faced us.

"I've known this nigga since we were in diapers, and he's been plotting to take me out. Friend or not, I can't look soft in these streets. I gotta make an example out of him."

Boogie was whimpering on the floor. His arms and legs were visibly broken. Drastic pulled a loaded .45 from his waistband and handed it to Akeem.

"Pppllease, man, please. Yyyou know mmmmeee. Yyyou're lllike a brother ttto me, man. I wwwwooouldn't do you dirty like that. I wasn't trying to overthrow you, man."

"Oh, now, you want to be all apologetic and shit."

"IIII wwwwas just ttttryin to mmmake a little extra mmmmoney on the ssside, that's it, IIII sssswear," Boogie pleaded.

"Shut your lyin', stuttering ass up. Nothing moves around here unless I get a piece, and you know that. I'm not having that shit, and I ain't tryin' to hear it either," Drastic said. He turned to Akeem. "It looks like you're the only one I can trust, 'Keem. If you take him out, you'll take his place as my right hand. Handle your business."

"I thought if anything, Taevaughn would be next in line," Akeem said.

"Do you see him here? I didn't ask him to do this. I'm asking you. Do you want the spot or not?"

Akeem walked up to Boogie and pulled his black baseball gloves from his back pants pocket. He slowly put them on.

"Nigga, enough with the fucking gloves. This ain't batting practice. Stop stalling and shoot this motherfucker," Drastic said, shoving the gun in Akeem's gloved hands.

"Akeem, ddddon't sssshoot me. IIII uuused to bbbbeee wwwwhere you're standing. Oooone day, this ccccould be you, mmmman. He's crazy, please—"

"Don't go getting soft on me now, 'Keem," Drastic said.

Drastic cranked up the volume on the stereo. I haven't seen it often, but Akeem looked apprehensive about pulling the trigger on Boogie. I guess Boogie's words had an effect on him.

Akeem stood behind Boogie, the gun shook unsteadily in his hand with his finger lightly touching the trigger.

"What are you fucking waiting for? Fucking shoot him," Drastic yelled.

Akeem steadied his shaking hand, took aim, and did as he was told, shooting Boogie in the back of the head at point-blank range. Blood splattered all over the tarp Boogie was on. The deed was done, and there was no coming back from this now. Akeem tossed Drastic back his gun. I couldn't stop myself from shaking.

"Good. You're my right hand now," Drastic said.

He looked at me and laughed. "Yo, J, I see you still aren't built for this shit, huh?"

I nervously shook my head.

"Just remember, if you snitch, you'll end up just like Boogie, and I'll have 'Keem be the one to off you. You understand?"

"I don't snitch," I said.

"Good, keep it that way."

He faced Akeem. "All right, y'all gotta bounce. Get rid of that gun and catch up with me tomorrow morning. For now, get outta here. You done came up, Akeem. Don't let me down."

"I won't," he said.

"Good."

Drastic took out his cell phone and made a call. "Yo, Tae. I need you to get rid of this body . . . Yeah, Boogie had to go. Hurry up."

Akeem and I closed the door behind us. I questioned what the future had in store for us.

The next day, Drastic called a meeting between Forty-First Road and Twelfth Street at "Baby Park."

I felt bad for Boogie. He was always good to me and 'Keem and taught us a lot. On the other hand, Drastic didn't look like he missed a beat even though his supposed best friend was gone.

Drastic whistled to get everyone's attention. Shyne, Daunte, Taevaughn, Akeem, and I stood beside him while the other corner boys, runners, and street soldiers gathered closely. We formed a circle and quieted down to hear what Drastic had to say.

"As y'all might have heard, Boogie Brown is no longer with us. It's sad, but the show goes on. Let this be a lesson to everyone that it doesn't matter who it is; if I catch you doing shady shit behind my back, I won't hesitate to take you out. Now, with Boogie gone, I need someone I can trust to be my new second in command . . ."

Taevaughn smirked and stepped up, confident that the person named to be the new right hand would be him.

"I put a lot of thought into this decision, and my new right hand is gonna be 'Keem."

Everyone looked at one another. There were some murmurs, but mostly, everyone kept their comments to themselves. Taevaughn looked pissed.

"What? What the fuck do you mean this punk-ass little boy is going to be next in command? I've been loyal and held you down when the cops were wilding. I handle your dirty work. Shit, I got rid of Boogie's body for you when you put him down, and *this* is how you do me?"

Drastic walked up to Taevaughn and hit him with a jab to the bridge of his nose, followed by a straight right hand to the jaw that floored him. Then Drastic stood over him.

"I warned you before about questioning my decisions. Don't make me have to make an example out of you in front of everyone, too. Straight up on the real, I value you and appreciate what you do, but don't ever think you're irreplaceable. Play your position, and if you ever come out of your face like that again, I'll have 'Keem lay you down. Now, pick yourself up, shut the fuck up, and fall in line."

Handling things without Boogie around was definitely a learning curve that Akeem and I had to pick up quickly. Drastic had no patience. He wanted things done HIS way and demanded perfection.

Drastic had a different approach to using Akeem as his right hand than he had with Boogie. This time, he used Akeem more as his primary enforcer than his friend and bodyguard. I guess he kept me around as a backup. Drastic made it clear that he was doing things differently one day after we finished driving around, checking all his corners with him.

"Yo, I'm letting y'all out right here. I'm gonna check y'all later. I gotta date with some pussy," Drastic said.

We got out of Drastic's truck, and Akeem asked, "Which place are you crashing at?"

"Chill, 'Keem. You don't need to know all that. If I need you, I'll call you," he said.

"No disrespect. I wasn't tryin' to be nosy. I was just asking in case shit popped off."

Drastic sighed. "I get it, and your heart is probably in the right place, but if there's one thing I've learned from dealing with Boogie, it's that having niggas around you all the time makes it too hard to recognize the real from the snakes. Boogie got too comfortable and thought he knew all my moves. Not saying that you'd do the same foul shit he did, I trust you, but I'm not gonna make the same mistakes I did with him with you."

After those words that day, Akeem and I understood why he was so cautious and paranoid, but he surprised us when he gave us our newest and scariest responsibility, being his muscle when he had to re-up with his supplier.

We were watching TV at Drastic's apartment at 41-08 Vernon Boulevard when he walked into the living room and said, "Yo, cut off that shit. I need you to make this run with me."

Akeem nodded.

"J, come on, we're out," Akeem said.

Drastic looked like he was going to tell me to stay back, but instead, he said, "Yeah, come on. This way, we have strength in numbers in case shit goes left."

". . . Why would things go left?" I asked.

Drastic waved me off and tossed Akeem the keys to his ride. "This'll be another driving lesson for you. Remember, you fuck up my car; I'm fucking you up." He laughed.

"Yo, slow down before your nondriver's-license-havin' ass gets us pulled over," Drastic said.

It was after midnight. Akeem and I were riding up front while Drastic rode shotgun behind me in his truck. Drastic had Akeem drive and park in a dark corner of the abandoned C.N. West chemical factory near Queens

Plaza. The streets were deserted, and there weren't any signs of cameras, people, or cops nearby.

The truck was idling, and the lights were off. Mobb Deep's "Give Up the Goods" played low in the background while we waited for Drastic's connect.

"You're always being studious and shit, right? When you used to go to school, did you learn how to speak any Spanish?" Drastic asked Akeem.

"Yeah."

"How good can you speak that shit?"

"I know enough not to get jerked if we cop work."

"Good. I do business with these cats, but I don't really trust them, especially when they start yapping in Spanish."

Drastic sounded sad when he said, "I used to bring Boogie to this run...Now I'm bringing you and J with me to watch my back. Can y'all handle that?"

We nodded. I turned and faced Drastic. I couldn't tell if his expression was nervousness or anxiety, but the way he bounced his leg made me think he was as on edge as I was. Akeem, as always, looked calm and collected.

Three Hummer trucks pulled up across from us.

"Should we get out?" I asked.

"Nah, wait 'til they give us the signal," Drastic said.

"What's the signal?" I asked.

One truck flashed its high beams at us and revved the engine.

"That's them. Yo, 'Keem, kill the engine."

Six men stepped out of the Hummers holding guns, while two other tall men, one with a cigarette and one with a scar, approached us. All of them were Hispanic.

"Good to see you again, Drastic. You look well," the man smoking the cigarette said.

"What's up, Wilfredo? You know how I do. I don't let anything hold me down. Let's hurry up and get down to business," Drastic said.

"You're acting all fidgety and shit. Why are you in a rush? Who are these *cabrons* you have with you?" the man with the scar asked.

"*Cuida tu lenguaje. No soy el carbón de nadie*," (Watch your mouth. I'm nobody's dumbass) Akeem fired back.

Wilfredo laughed and looked impressed by Akeem's response while the guy with the scar and 'Keem sized each other up.

"Ernesto, *se amable con nuestros clientes,*" (Be nice to our customers) Wilfredo said before facing Akeem.

"My right hand, Ernesto, is cautious when meeting new people, and so am I. It's nothing personal. My men are gonna pat you down and make sure you're all on the up-and-up before we go further and do business. Drastic knows better than to bring new faces to our meeting unannounced, so this is on him."

Drastic looked at us and nodded that everything was fine.

The men patted us all down, checked us to see if we were wearing wires, and removed the guns we had on us.

"Where is Boogie today?" Wilfredo asked Drastic.

"Boogie is no longer with us. He did some foul shit and had to be handled."

"That's the cost of being the boss, but can these new guys with you be trusted?" Wilfredo asked.

Ernesto glared at me. I swallowed hard, intimidated by his intense gaze.

"These are my boys, Akeem and Jalen. They're legit. They wouldn't think of fucking you or me over. Akeem is my new right hand."

Wilfredo nodded.

"How much product do you want?" he asked.

"Ten keys," Drastic said and tossed a duffle bag over to Wilfredo.

"It's all there, straight cash," Drastic said.

Wilfredo smiled and handed the bag to one of his goons to count. Once his goon nodded after being satisfied with the count, the goon went to one of the Hummers and emptied the duffle bag inside the truck. The goon returned and tossed the duffle bag back at Drastic's feet.

Drastic pointed to me and said, "The work is in there. Grab it and load it up."

I did as I was told while Drastic got in the driver's seat of his truck.

"Always a pleasure. See you again soon," Wilfredo said.

We pulled off, and I felt like Akeem, and I finally made it to the big time.

For most people, when they first start getting money, they buy nice, flashy rides. Even I had a 3 Series BMW, but not Akeem. After Drastic pushed for us to get our driver's licenses, Akeem bought himself an old 1972 Chevrolet Chevelle and fixed it up. His reasoning was souped-up cars drew too much attention, but old, hooked-up cars were less attention-grabbing. We made way more money than being corner boys, and everybody around the hood knew it.

Bill wanted to get down with selling with us, but Akeem always shut that thought down quickly. Akeem and I were sitting in the front row in the stands at one of Bill's games at the high school, and he was putting on a show, dropping fifty points on Aviation High School. When it was over, we walked onto the court and congratulated our boy.

"Damn, kid! You represented hard for the 'Bridge today!" Akeem said.

"Thanks, but I really need to dead this basketball shit. It's not like I'm gonna make it to the NBA. I need to be on the corner with you guys," Bill said.

"Nah, B. You're meant to do more in life than what we're doin'. You're smart. Keep your head in the books. The street shit ain't for you."

"You're making good money, though. I'm broke. My mom barely has money to buy groceries after paying all the bills, and she doesn't want me to quit playing ball to work because she says she wants me to enjoy life while I'm young."

He put up a good fight and had good points, but I knew 'Keem wasn't having that. He slapped a wad of cash in Bill's hand and said, "If you need money here and there, I got you."

"Nah, I'm not cool with that. I'm no charity case," Bill said, reaching to hand Akeem the money.

Akeem wouldn't take it. "It's not charity. You got my back, and I got yours."

They gave each other a brotherly hug, and after that conversation, every other week, 'Keem slipped money under Bill's door to help his mother buy groceries. Akeem never said anything, but I know he was trying to keep Bill's hands clean for Ebony.

CHAPTER 44

ALL THAT I GOT IS YOU

"Checkmate!" Akeem said confidently.

Akeem and I were at the chess tables near the basketball courts by our apartments. Drastic decided to play a quick game of chess with Akeem while he was making his rounds.

"That's the first time he's ever beaten you," I said.

"Yeah, yeah, even fiends get a lucky day sometimes. Don't get too excited," Drastic said.

Nia and Rita were headed toward us. Rita approached me and gave me a quick peck on the lips. Nia came over to 'Keem and sat on his lap.

"Hey, baby," Nia said.

"Hey," Akeem said, setting up the chessboard again.

"You kickin' ass?" Nia asked.

Akeem smiled. "You know this!"

Akeem directed Nia and Rita's attention to Drastic.

"Ladies, this is our . . . boss, Drastic. Drastic, this is my girl, Nia, and J's girl, Rita.

Nia and Rita greeted him, but Drastic was more interested in Nia. He was eyeing her shape hard, and Akeem noticed.

"So, Drastic, I heard you got that work. I'm looking to get put on. What's up?" Rita asked.

"Rita!" Nia said.

I was mad about Rita's question too. I've seen firsthand how Drastic used women in his trap houses, and I didn't want my girl working butt-ass naked, packaging dope in front of Taevaughn.

"You want in on this shit, shorty?" Drastic asked.

Akeem patted Nia's thigh, so she'd get up from his lap.

"Baby, can you and Rita give us a minute? Y'all go kick it at your crib. Me and J will be there after we finish chopping it up with the boss," he said.

At first, Nia looked taken aback by 'Keem's dismissal, but she didn't fuss or argue. Instead, she nodded and signaled to Rita to head out.

"I don't wanna go anywhere. I'm trying to make moves here," Rita said.

"Go on with your sister. When the time is right, shorty, we'll talk," Drastic told her.

Rita looked disappointed but nodded, kissed me again, and walked home with Nia.

Drastic smiled and said, "I got time for another one. Set up the board, but this time, let's play for something. Let's see how good you are when something is on the line."

"What are we playing for?" Akeem asked.

"My truck for your chain, straight up."

"Nah, this was my pop's—"

"Nigga, you're getting the chance to get a truck, and you're turning it down? Don't be stupid."

"A'ight, bet!"

"You sure you wanna do that?" I asked.

"Stay out of this, J. This is between me and 'Keem," Drastic said.

Akeem put his chain on the side of the table, and Drastic put the keys next to them. They started playing another game. Drastic had an amused expression on his face.

"You must be really feeling this chick, huh?" Drastic asked, trying to get a rise out of Akeem.

'Keem didn't answer; he kept his eyes on the chessboard.

"How come you never brought her around me before, huh? Maybe instead of your chain, I should've bet you for some of that pussy."

Akeem stayed quiet, but he was making silly mistakes, losing pieces, and it was written all over his face that Drastic's words were getting to him.

"She's a pretty little thing. You better treat her right. You don't want a smooth nigga like me to scoop her up and turn her young, thick ass out," Drastic laughed.

That last bit definitely hooked Akeem. He was noticeably pissed and moved a piece that caused him to lose the game.

"Checkmate!" Drastic said.

Akeem looked at him like he wanted to kill him, and I could see from Drastic's face he loved seeing that expression on him.

"Awww, don't make that face, 'Keem. I'm gonna let you have her," Drastic said.

Drastic snatched the chain from the table and walked away, snickering. Then he stopped, turned around, and walked back to us.

"A word to the wise, 'Keem. Never let a nigga see they can press your buttons. I made a few slick comments about your lady, got in your head quickly, and made you lose the game. This street shit is like chess. Even if someone fucks with your Queen, you can't let that rattle you. If you want to be the man one day, let this be a lesson that you can't let a nigga see he got to you."

Drastic chuckled and used the bottom of his shirt to shine the medallion on Akeem's chain.

"Now, whenever you touch that empty spot where your chain used to be, remember this. Hopefully, this was a learning experience for you today, and if not, I'll keep making bets with you for stuff and take all your shit. Thanks for the chain. I'm calling it a day. I'm meeting up with one of my girls. I'm gonna check y'all later."

Drastic walked away laughing. Akeem sat at the table seething and slapped the chess table hard.

"I gotta get my chain back," he said.

"Yeah . . . I tried to stop you, but he wasn't having that," I said.

"He made me get caught up in my feelings. That ain't gonna happen again." Akeem put all the pieces in a plastic bag and said, "Come on, let's go."

"You wanna head over to Nia and Rita's?" I asked.

"Nah, not yet. I don't want Nia to see me mad like this. She'll keep bugging me to talk about it, and if I tell her what happened, I'll never hear the end of it. Let's kick it at your place until I cool down."

"Nah, man, you know I hate being in my apartment. Let's just chill at yours."

"Nope. Twin is there, and the first thing she'll notice when she sees me is that my chain is missing. I don't want to have that conversation with her right now."

"I get it. Let's not stay too long, though. I'm not trying to deal with my moms right now."

We walked to our building. Mrs. Tracy and Ma were outside, leaning against the fence in front of our building, smoking a cigarette. As we headed up the path to our building, Akeem hugged and kissed his mom.

"Hey, Ma," he said.

"Hey, baby."

Ma smiled and said, "Hey, Sonshine."

She spread her arms wide for a hug, but her smile faded quickly once I rolled my eyes and walked past her without saying shit like she didn't exist. I heard her say, "Excuse me, Tracy. Usually, I let his rude ass slide, but not today. I need to straighten out this boy. I've had enough of his bullshit, and it needs to stop now. Every day he tests my patience, and I'm sick of it."

"I understand completely. Handle your business, Queen," Mrs. Tracy said.

I ignored them and walked inside the building.

Akeem caught up to me and, while we walked up the steps to my apartment, said, "Yo, J, you need to ease up with doggin' out your mom like that."

"Why? If she didn't nag my pops to go to the store, he'd still be alive."

"You need to cut her some slack. I see how hard shit is for my mom, and she doesn't have to deal with taking care of a kid with cancer like your mom does. Your mom didn't pull the trigger that killed your pops. If you want to be mad at somebody, be mad at the nigga that killed him. You're lucky you got a mom that cares. Our moms might not be perfect, but they're all we got left."

"Yeah, well, my mom wouldn't have to struggle so hard if my dad was alive, and he'd still be here if it wasn't for her."

Akeem shook his head. "What was the last thing your pops said to you before he died?" he asked.

He knew the answer. Over the many times we talked about our dads, he knew the last thing my dad said was, "Take care of your mom for me."

"You know what he told me," I said.

"Exactly. So, stop doggin' her out and do what he asked you to do."

I didn't respond. I opened the door to my apartment. About a minute later, Mom walked in, pissed.

"Akeem, I need to talk to my son. Alone!"

"No problem, Mrs. Juanita," he said.

Akeem faced me. "Yo, J. I'll catch up with you later."

I nodded, and as soon as he left, I stood up from the couch and headed toward my room. Ma was right on my tail down the hallway.

"We're *going* to talk," she yelled.

I walked into my room and slammed the door in her face.

"Get back here! Don't you walk away from me when I'm talking to you," Mom yelled.

She flung open the door and said, "From now on, you will *not* slam another door in this apartment. Do you understand me?"

I sucked my teeth, lay on my bed, and stared at the ceiling. Mom grabbed me by my shirt and brought me face-to-face with her.

"Look at me when I'm talking to you, little boy."

I rolled my eyes. "Whatever," I said.

She let me go and smacked me. "Boy, have you lost your mind? Don't you 'whatever' me. Who do you think you're talking to?"

I turned my head. Ma grabbed me by my jaw and made me face her. "I don't appreciate my own son treating me like I'm a piece of shit. I'm your mother, dammit, and we're gonna talk."

"Talk about what?"

"Your funky attitude you have with me all the time. All this pent-up anger you're holding in. I don't deserve to feel the wrath of it. I work too damn hard for this family to have you disrespecting me like you do. It needs to stop, and it's gonna stop *today*."

I stayed quiet, and we stared each other down for a while. Finally, Ma shook her head and said, "I wish your father was here to straighten your ass out. How long are you going to be like this? What? Are you going to hate me forever?"

I sucked my teeth and shrugged.

"I asked you a question, Jalen."

I looked her in the eyes and said, "I don't know; maybe."

"I'm not putting up with this shit anymore. It's not my—"

This was it. Today was the day I let out all the anger I'd bottled up inside me for so long. I cut her off abruptly.

"I treat you like shit because it wasn't the bullet that killed him. It was *you*! You nagged him and made him go to the store for bullshit. *You* could've cooked something else, but *you* had to have everything *your* way. *You*! *You're* the reason he's dead. Our family wouldn't have to suffer if it weren't for *you*."

Her face softened. "Jalen—"

"No! Don't say shit. Why did God have to take my dad, huh? I wish he would've taken you instead."

The words left my mouth before I realized what I had said.

She looked taken aback by what I said. Her eyes got misty, and their sadness showed I hurt her, but *good*. I knew I had gone too far, but I couldn't help it. I was too angry.

After the hurt and shock of what I said passed, Ma said, "Since the day he left us, I've felt nothing but regret and responsibility for his death. A piece of me died with him, and it bothers me every day, but nothing I say will bring your father back. I'm trying, Jalen."

I chuckled. "Trying. You're 'trying' ain't good enough. Where were you when I needed you? When kids used to pick on me, where were you? When I just needed someone to talk to because I missed Dad and was scared, where were you?"

"Where was I? I was busting my ass going to work every damn day, working a job I fucking hate to make sure you had clothes on your back and food on the table. *Where was I?* I was waking up early and coming home late, taking your brother to chemo and doctor appointments, and doing everything I could to make sure we didn't lose him too. Your father's death broke my heart and drained all of us, but every day, I made time to talk to you. If you needed to say something to me, you could've talked to me anytime. Don't act like I wasn't there. I've *always* been here for you, and I will not let you guilt-trip me into feeling like I haven't been."

"Here for me? You didn't give a shit about me. You think sitting on the edge of my bed and having a shallow five-minute conversation about how my day went was being there for me? Stop it! The world revolved around Jerami. I was just here for the ride. Even when Jerami wasn't at the hospital, you might've been home, but you weren't there for me. You were catering to your job and Jerami every second."

"You're always quick to criticize everything I don't do, but you *never* appreciate anything I've *done* for you. When I try to talk to you, you shut me out. You treat talking to me like it's a chore for you. You ever wonder how you're able to watch cable when I'm 'catering' to my job? You don't pay any damn bills around here. *I* pay that bill. You know that PlayStation you enjoy playing with? You don't know what I sacrificed to buy that for you and your brother. I've gone without plenty of times to make sure you and your brother are taken care of before ever thinking about buying things for myself and not once do I get a thank-you."

"You do all that stuff for Jerami. You don't love me."

"How could you look me in the eyes and say that to me? You're my firstborn, my Sonshine. I love you more than anything in this world."

I sucked my teeth. "Sonshine. Why do you call me that stupid name, anyway?"

"The day you were born, it was pouring outside, and you decided to come a month early. I was in labor with you for hours. Your dad and I were scared that we weren't strong enough to be good parents to you, but we were determined to give you the best life we could and were excited to meet our firstborn. I pushed and pushed, and suddenly, the rain stopped. The sun broke through the clouds, and you finally decided to come out. The West Indian nurse in the delivery room smiled, pointed at the window, and said, 'Ya see how the sun started shinin' as soon as your boy came? Dat's the Lord tellin' you ya son is gon' always be a blessin'.' She was right.

"Before your father passed, when days were hard for both of us, coming home and seeing you smile was like sunshine and made our days better. *That's* why I gave you that nickname. I thought in the darkest times and our rough patches, with your father gone, you'd really be the light for me at the end of the tunnel. When you were a baby, I laughed when you splashed around in the tub and held on tight to my finger when changing your diapers. It made me so happy just feeding you and watching you fall asleep on my chest."

There was a smile on her face, but it slowly faded, and her eyes got red-rimmed as she went on.

"I loved you more than anything in the world, but my little boy grew up, and instead of being my light, lately you've been nothing but darkness for me. It hurts my heart, and it's killing me that my son disrespects me openly. It kills me that you don't appreciate anything I do for you and our family. It kills me that my own flesh and blood, my firstborn, acts like he hates me and treats me like I'm less than a stranger. It's killing me . . . YOU'RE KILLING ME."

Tears were streaming down her face. Mom's chest heaved up and down as she wrapped her arms around herself and wept. All the anger left her face. Her shoulders were hunched, and she looked so deflated and defeated. I don't know why, but tears were rolling down my face out of nowhere. I thought about how good we were together before Dad died; how we used to laugh, talk, and were so happy and loving toward one another back then, and looked at where we were now. The truth was, I didn't like seeing her in pain, knowing I made her break down like this.

"Yo, J, you need to ease up with doggin' out your mom like that. You need to cut her some slack. I see how hard shit is for my mom, and she doesn't have to deal with taking care of a kid with cancer like your mom does. Your mom didn't pull the trigger that killed your pops. If you want to be mad at somebody, be mad at the nigga that killed him. You're lucky you got a mom that cares. Our moms might not be perfect, but they're all we got left."

I thought about what Akeem said and how hard Ma tried to balance work and being there for Jerami and me, especially dealing with his cancer. It took all that and seeing Ma break down from me being an asshole to realize what I was doing was wrong.

I felt a tightness in my throat and my eyes getting moist. I closed them, and tears streamed down my face. I couldn't control it and surprised myself when I wrapped my arms around her shoulders, hugged her, and wept with her.

"I'm sorry, Ma. I just miss him so much, and every time I think of him, I end up taking my anger out on you."

Ma pressed her forehead and nose against mine. "I know. I miss him every day, too."

Months passed, and after that day, our relationship improved. It didn't happen overnight, and I still did what I wanted to do, but I eased up on how I talked to and treated her. I remember Joe said, *"You guys are all wearing flashy shit without making sure your mamas are straight . . . There's no reason why your mamas should still be broke and struggling if you're pulling in money."*

I took his advice and started giving my mom money to help out around the house. She never took it because she questioned how I could have so much money without a job, but since she wouldn't take money from me, I usually hid it in her jewelry box on her dresser. Things weren't perfect, but they were a lot better with Ma and me now.

CHAPTER 45

KICK IN THE DOOR

"Yo! Move my truck across the street. I'm not trying to get another ticket for no alternate side parking bullshit," Drastic said, tossing his keys to Daunte.

Daunte nodded.

"And don't forget to lock my shit. I found my truck unlocked the last couple of times you moved it. If I get a ticket or somebody steals some shit outta my car, that's *your* ass."

Daunte looked shook when he said, "I got it. You don't gotta worry."

"I'm not worried about nuttin'. If I find my shit unlocked, *you're* the one that's gotta worry."

Daunte leaned in and asked, "Y'all mind coming with me to find a spot for him?"

"Yeah, we'll roll with you," Akeem said.

We had some time to kill before we met up with Nia and Rita since they were in school, so we rode with Daunte looking for a parking spot, but the streets were lined with cars along every curb for at least seven blocks.

Akeem pointed and said, "Yo, that car is pulling out. Park this shit there."

Daunte pulled into the spot. Akeem pointed again, "Yo, isn't that the fiend that stiffed you for money?"

"Yeah, that's him. I'm gonna fuck him up," Daunte said. He slammed the door and shouted, "Hey, Monterey."

The man turned around and started backpedaling.

"Where's my fucking money?" Daunte yelled.

"Hey, Brother Daunte. I...I don't got it right now, but I'm gonna get it to you. I swear.

"Nah, I don't wanna hear that shit. You've been ducking me for months, and I ain't no sucka. I want my money today."

The man bolted down the block, and Daunte ran after him. Dealing with Monterey, Daunte was too distracted and forgot to lock the truck. I locked it, but Akeem stepped out and quickly unlocked it.

"Leave it," Akeem said.

"Daunte is our boy. Drastic will beat his ass if he finds his car open."

"Don't worry about that. Trust me; he won't."

Akeem opened the back passenger door and pulled a brown paper bag from his back pocket. His hands were working busily, and it looked like he shoved something underneath the backseat on the driver's side.

"What's that you put back there?" I asked.

"Nothing, and don't say shit about it to anyone either, you hear me?"

"I wasn't gonna—"

"Good. Just trust me."

I nodded.

Akeem walked behind Drastic's truck and broke one of the taillights. Whatever was going on, I knew it would all make sense eventually. Akeem never did anything without thinking first or having a plan.

We spent most of the day cooking up the product Drastic gave us earlier and selling some right after. Once we were done, we walked to Nia and Rita's place, and on the way there, it looked like the whole hood was gathered in the street.

Drastic was pulled over by O'Sullivan's unmarked patrol car. O'Sullivan walked to the driver's side to talk to Drastic while his partner, McIvor, inspected the truck with his flashlight. McIvor pressed it close to the tinted window to look at the backseat. O'Sullivan tapped on the window and motioned for Drastic to roll it down. Drastic cut off his engine and lowered the window.

"License and registration, scumbag," O'Sullivan said.

Drastic opened his glove compartment, reached inside, and handed O'Sullivan his documents.

"I guess you guys haven't reached your daily quota of harassing niggas today, huh?" Drastic asked.

"Not yet," O'Sullivan chuckled.

"What bullshit are y'all trying to hit me with now?" Drastic asked.

"You got a broken taillight, jerkoff," O'Sullivan said.

McIvor whistled to get O'Sullivan's attention.

"You got something over there?" O'Sullivan asked.

"Yup, I think so. Tell homeboy to roll down his back windows," McIvor said.

"You heard him."

Drastic sighed and did as he was told.

"Bingo!" McIvor said.

"Step out of the vehicle," O'Sullivan yelled.

"For what? Come on, now. You've been trying to catch me holding for years. You know I'm too smart to be riding dirty and have anything incriminating in my car; all my shit is clean and legit here."

O'Sullivan tugged on the handle, opened the door, and yanked Drastic to the street. He dragged Drastic's face across the pavement as he pressed his knee into his back, pulled his arms behind him, and slammed metal handcuffs tightly on his wrists. Drastic squirmed and struggled to break free, jerking his body in the opposite direction as the officers led him from the street to their patrol car.

"Get the fuck off me, man. I want a fucking lawyer," Drastic screamed.

"Stop resisting," Officer O'Sullivan said, hitting him on the back of the legs with his nightstick.

McIvor searched the truck and pulled a black .45 semiautomatic and a kilo of cocaine from a brown paper bag under the driver's seat.

"I saw the gun handle first, but the coke is a bonus," McIvor said.

"Ahhh. Y'all are fucked up. Y'all planted that shit on me, man. That shit ain't mine. I don't keep heat on me, and y'all know that," Drastic yelled.

"We didn't plant shit. All you drug dealers slip up eventually—no more short kiddie stints at Rikers for you. You're going to big-boy prison now," Officer McIvor said.

"We've been building a case against you for a long time. Finding you with drugs *and* a weapon is the icing on the cake. Watch your head, asshole," O'Sullivan said, banging Drastic's head on the door frame as they stuffed him in the backseat behind a Plexiglas shield in the patrol car.

Akeem rushed over to them. "Yo, Drastic, I'll hold your wallet and ice for you, so they don't voucher your shit at the precinct," Akeem said.

"C'mon, O'Sullivan, give him my shit to hold for me," Drastic said.

O'Sullivan rolled his eyes and handed Akeem all of Drastic's money and jewelry. Akeem smiled big when he got his dad's chain back.

"All right, back up," McIvor yelled, closing the door to the patrol car.

Through the car's back window, Drastic didn't have the tough, confident look he usually wore. Today, he looked like a scared, helpless little boy. Tears were streaming down his face.

Everyone watched. Some were happy to see Drastic go down. Some were depressed because they'd need a new way to hustle to make ends meet. Once the police car drove off, everything went back to normal. I couldn't read Akeem's face.

We walked back to Akeem's apartment. He didn't miss a beat. I was afraid of what fate had in store for us.

"That's fucked up that the cops set him up like that," I said.

We were in Akeem's room, and he was quietly playing himself in chess.

"Maybe this is a sign that we should get out of the game while we can," I added.

Akeem smiled. "Nah, we're good. Drastic got what was coming to him; trust me on that."

"Why do you say that?"

He laughed to himself like he knew something that I wasn't getting. Without taking his focus off the chessboard, Akeem said, "He was right about one thing."

"What?"

"Someone planted that dope and gun in his car."

I already knew the answer but wanted to hear him say it. I needed to understand. "Who?" I asked.

Without taking his eyes off the game, Akeem calmly said, "I did."

"Why? He was like a hero to you—"

"You gotta move on from your heroes eventually, right?"

"Drastic taught us everything we know about the street. He gave us money when we were dead broke. Why would you cross him?"

I wanted answers to all those questions, but I also wondered, if he could do that to someone he was close to and admired, could he do that same shit to me?

Akeem reset his chessboard. He looked at me with all seriousness and said, "Drastic never gave us shit. We used to think Joe was all talk when we were at the barbershop, but truth be told, he was right. We put in the work by doin' Drastic's dirt. When we started out, we stole for him, and he gave us scraps. Whenever we got busted, we were on our own. He didn't give a fuck about you or me. Him being cool with us was part of his way of manipulating and controlling us. We weren't special; he targeted us. He was an opportunist. He knew we only had our moms, and neither of us had our pops at home. We were desperate for money, and he used what he knew about us to hustle us."

I heard Joe's voice echoing in my head. *"You two are so dense that you don't even see when you're being hustled. Do you ever see this cat Drastic on the corners selling? Do you see him snatching purses or doing any of the other dumb shit he has you and all these other niggas around here doing? No."*

I nodded as Akeem continued.

"His game was simple. Keep us needing him and teach us just enough to gain our trust and make us think he cared. He wanted to keep us under his thumb and stay dependent on him for loot forever while he got rich off our backs. He liked that we did his dirt so he could keep his hands clean."

"You're probably right, but was it worth doing him dirty like that?"

"Before you go thinking I'm the devil and he was some type of saint, you need to know the truth about him."

I looked at him skeptically. "And what's that?" I asked.

"He admitted to me that he was the one that shot your pops."

"What?" I balled up my fist and searched his face to see if he was lying, but I saw nothing. I didn't know what to believe. I've seen Akeem kill without blinking an eye. He set up his idol to go to prison and didn't miss a beat, but he never lied to me before; at least, I didn't think he had. In this case, I was sure he was telling me the truth, but I needed to know more.

"What do you mean?" I asked, my breathing choppy.

"He slipped one day and told me that when he did it, he didn't really want to kill the dude he was shooting at. He just wanted the hood to see that he'd shoot anyone who was disrespectful to him. He was letting off shots wildly, and one hit your pops."

I turned my head to hide the tears welling up in my eyes. "Why didn't you tell me this before?" I asked.

"Because it was hard enough trying to move without showing my hand. I figured if I put you on to what was going on, you either wouldn't do anything about it, or you'd do something crazy and get yourself hurt, maybe even killed. After he told me what he did, I waited until we learned everything we needed to know from him. Once I got in with his connect, there was nothing else we needed from him. I had this shit planned out for a while and knew when the time was right, O'Sullivan would pull him over for any little thing wrong he saw on Drastic's truck."

I kept quiet, looking at the floor while he continued.

"Today, when Drastic told Daunte to move his truck, I knew it was now or never, and this was the perfect opportunity to set my plan in motion, so I took it. I broke his taillight and put the dope under his seat. Remember that gun he told me to get rid of the night I killed Boogie?"

"Yeah."

"Well, I got rid of it all right . . . right in that nigga's truck today. I wore gloves that night with Boogie. Drastic didn't. His prints were all over it. I put that and the dope in his truck this morning. Then I used a payphone to give the cops an anonymous tip that a man with a cracked taillight was driving down the block selling drugs out of his car. The rest, you already know."

I slowly nodded.

"This street shit is like chess, and sometimes, you must sacrifice some big pieces to get the win. It bothered me that Drastic could laugh about killing your dad behind your back but smile in your face. I also wasn't feeling that he hid that he had Jerami working for him while he had you doing dirt for him. The bastard probably thought he was doing you a favor by cutting Jerami off."

I just nodded. All of this was just too much for me to process. Akeem continued.

"Drastic knew Boogie for years. That was his best friend, his right hand, and he had me kill him without flinching. If he could have his own friend, Boogie, killed, a guy he said was like a brother to him, that meant neither you nor me were shit to him. I killed two birds with one stone. I got payback for you, and now, with him gone, this puts me on top. The pawn finally becomes the king, and I'm bringing you to the top with me."

We high-fived.

"I'm with you every step of the way," I said.

"Let's do this."

Everybody who showed love to Drastic when he was the king on the streets forgot about him once he was locked up. Word on the street was even his so-called friends he grew up with never visited, wrote to him, or put money on his books in prison.

It was bad enough that the cops found drugs in Drastic's truck, but the gun they found not only had his fingerprints all over it, but it also traced back to five homicides.

The judge denied Drastic bail after his arrest. When he went to trial with his priors on top of everything else he was charged with, the judge showed no mercy. Drastic was sentenced to life in the Sing Sing correctional prison upstate without the possibility of parole.

Akeem's reign caused a divide between those who accepted him as Drastic's successor and those who didn't want to see him running shit because they thought he was too young. It wasn't long before some small-time dealers and even some of Drastic's old goons tried to test him. I remember the first time was when 'Keem called his first meeting in front of the handball courts on Forty-First and Twelfth Avenue.

"We all know, Drastic got bagged by the cops. It's tragic, but that's the nature of the beast; business still gotta go on. I know it's been dry out here for a minute, and getting our hands on product has been hard, but

I already set up a meeting with the connect, and I'm gonna continue running shit so we all can eat."

Taevaughn tossed up his hands and laughed at 'Keem. "So, you're the boss now, huh? You got to be kidding if you think you're gonna be running the show now."

"Does it look like I'm playing? I'm not asking if I can run shit. I'm *telling* you I'm running things now," Akeem said defiantly.

"Fuck this. I put up with your shit when Drastic was on top, but I ain't taking orders from no punk-ass kid now," Taevaughn said.

Akeem stepped up to him. "You challenging me, big man? Who should call the shots? You?" Akeem asked.

"Damn straight, nigga."

Taevaughn spat and faked like he would hit 'Keem, but 'Keem didn't flinch. "I should beat your ass and make you give up that connect. What you gonna do about—"

BAM!

Before Taevaughn could finish his sentence, Akeem was whooping his ass in the street. Some of Taevaughn's boys tried to jump in, but Daunte and I lifted our shirts to let them see we were holding to keep the fight fair.

Taevaughn screamed as Akeem whaled on him. It got to the point Shyne, Daunte, and I had to pull 'Keem off Taevaughn before he killed him.

"Anybody else wanna test me or voice their fucking opinion?" Akeem asked.

Some of Taevaughn's boys picked him up, but he yanked away. "Man, fuck this shit. Y'all can stick with this kid if y'all want, but me and my people are out," he said.

"Enjoy being broke, nigga," Akeem expressed.

"You ain't the only one that got that work," Taevaughn said.

"As long as you stay off my corners, I don't care how you make money. Just know if it comes on my blocks, I'm taking your money, your life, and your product. Try me if you think it's a game."

Those who hated Akeem decided to work for Neville. What Akeem and I didn't know was the same way Drastic was teaching us, Neville was grooming Draper to one day replace him. Months passed, and while Akeem was on the rise, Neville retired from the game and handed everything over to Draper. Even though Draper and Akeem were the same age, the men who left Akeem to link up with Neville stayed with Draper out of spite.

CHAPTER 46

JALEN

THE WORLD IS YOURS

It was around 2:00 a.m., and Akeem and I were at the abandoned C. N. West Chemical Company near Queens Plaza, trying to re-up without Drastic for the first time. On the drive here, Akeem told me that the day Joe schooled us about being dumb and not saving our money, he took his advice and realized that if he wanted to branch out and be his own man one day; he needed cash to be taken seriously, so he started saving.

Wilfredo, Ernesto, and his soldiers pulled up and stepped out of their trucks. We got out of 'Keem's car.

"Usually, Drastic is here when you need to re-up. Why did he have you make the call? Where is he?" Wilfredo asked Akeem.

Wilfredo signaled to his soldiers to search us.

While we went through the routine, Akeem said, "Drastic's dirt caught up to him. He's doing life in Sing Sing and isn't gonna be around. I wanted to see if we could continue where you and him left off."

Wilfredo laughed and said, "Is that right? I don't think you have the money to continue doing business on this level with me, kid, and I don't give product on consignment to small-timers."

"I wouldn't play myself or waste your time by not coming correct and having your money," Akeem said.

I reached into the backseat and grabbed our usual duffle bags for the re-ups. I opened them, showed the cash to Wilfredo's soldiers, and tossed it to them for inspection. I tried to look tough, but I was scared. I worried that they would just kill us and take the money.

Wilfredo's soldier nodded and said, "It's all there."

"Good," Wilfredo said.

Ernesto didn't look moved that we had the money. "So what if they saved their little chump change? They're just a bunch of punk kids. They aren't ready to move big-time weight," Ernesto said, glaring at 'Keem and me.

Wilfredo looked at Akeem skeptically. "What makes you think you can fill Drastic's shoes?"

"Me and my right hand, Jalen, learned everything from Drastic and Boogie."

"What makes you think that?"

"If we didn't, Drastic wouldn't have trusted us enough to introduce us to you."

Wilfredo smirked but didn't respond. Instead, he waved to Akeem to continue talking.

"Drastic trusted us and our ability to hold things down. He made me and J enforcers because he knew we understood the business and we're not afraid to get our hands dirty. We learned a lot from Drastic and Boogie, but we also learned from their mistakes. We know what worked and what didn't from them, and we won't fail," Akeem said confidently.

"You've got balls, kid, and that's good. Those are some strong words, but Ernesto is right. You and your boy are just niños. Why would Drastic's crew fall in line and listen to the two of you?"

"Either they'll respect me and J for helping them eat, or we'll make them respect us."

"Internal fighting hurts business, and if I agree to hand over product to you, I'll want my money whether you're winning your little war or not."

"And if you give us the opportunity, getting your money will always take precedence."

Wilfredo nodded and looked pleased with 'Keem's answer.

"Right now, we'll do things business as usual, but this will be your probation period. If you come up short with my money, that'll be your ass and the end of our arrangement. You boys understand?"

"Yup," we said in unison.

Wilfredo turned to his soldiers and said, "All right, get these men their product."

Akeem took over the reins of Drastic's crack operation and applied every bit of knowledge Drastic taught him. 'Keem knew all of Drastic's stash spots and how he handled business, so for the most part, the transition went smoothly because he kept everything the same. One problem that came with street success was constantly being watched and harassed by the cops.

Akeem and I were walking on Vernon Boulevard when an unmarked skidded up on the sidewalk. O'Sullivan and McIvor hopped out.

"All right, homeboys. Y'all know the drill. Get against the car and spread 'em," McIvor said.

Akeem and I rolled our eyes and did what we were told while they frisked us.

"Word around this zoo is you're the new HNIC around here," O'Sullivan said to Akeem.

"I don't know who told you that lie," Akeem replied.

"Don't play fucking dumb with me. You punks are like weeds. We get rid of one and two more sprout in its place."

O'Sullivan faced me. "And you, we haven't seen Boogie Brown around. I'm sure he's lying in some gutter around here. Your boy Akeem here will eventually go down just like Drastic did. You wanna end up like Boogie?"

I felt that comment.

"Man, why are you harassing us? We were minding our own business, and here you come fucking with us," Akeem said.

O'Sullivan jabbed Akeem in the stomach with the end of his nightstick, and 'Keem dropped to his knees.

"Speak when spoken to, turd," O'Sullivan said

I averted my eyes and kept my mouth shut.

"The strong silent type, huh? Boogie was the same way; remember that. History with you people around here always repeats itself."

After frisking us and seeing that we didn't have shit, they continued threatening us.

"Where's the stash, you little shit? I know you got something on you," O'Sullivan said, with gritted teeth.

"I keep telling you we're good. It's you that keeps believing we're not. You ever think that maybe we learned from Drastic's mistakes?" Akeem asked.

"Keep playing stupid. You people always slip up, and when you do, we'll make sure you get a cell right next to him upstate," McIvor said.

"Back when you were just baby dealers, we only fucked with you a little bit, but get used to this because every time we see you two, we're going to be all over your asses like flies on shit. See you next time, jigaboos," O'Sullivan threatened.

O'Sullivan and McIvor got back in their car and sped off. Akeem faced me.

"They got us in their crosshairs, so we gotta move smarter if we don't want to get bagged like Drastic," he said.

"We'll make sure the youngins hold the weight and weapons—"

Akeem cut me off. "I want you to keep your hands clean, too. We'll use our soldiers for everything unless I need to prove a point and handle something directly."

"But—"

"One day, we're gonna retire from the street shit. We need to be clean to do that. I'm running this shit, so if I gotta get a little dirty, it is what it is, but that's on me—not you."

I nodded.

When you're coming up in the streets, nobody wants to see you doing better than them, and they'll do anything to bring you down. Akeem learned quickly that the "crab mentality" in the hood was real.

For months, Akeem fought and shot anyone who opposed and challenged him. The drama and bloodshed drew a lot of attention from the cops, and the blocks were hot, making it hard for us to make moves, but Akeem stayed true to his word and made sure Wilfredo always got his money in full and on time.

While Akeem had no problems handling things on his own, he learned from Drastic that nothing moved in the hood without the old-timers getting their kickback, so he made sure to continue in Drastic's footsteps and followed suit. With that done, Akeem also had them as added protection.

Akeem was a scary dude when he was in the street. He was a different person entirely, but he never let Bill, Nia, or Ebony see the brutal side of him that me and everyone in the streets saw. His temper was short, and he was quick to make an example out of people, qualities he learned from being around Drastic.

This became blatantly obvious one day when 'Keem brought me to a roof where he had Daunte, Shyne, and four of his newest dope boys up there to deal with a fiend that stole from him. Like Drastic used to do,

Akeem had the fiend beaten up, gagged, and duct-taped. I looked around and realized we were on the same roof where 'Keem caught his first body.

Akeem put on his baseball gloves, looked around at everyone on the roof, and said, "We got a problem here. This nigga stole from me, and I'm not having that. How are we gonna handle this, huh? Who's tryna earn their stripes today?"

Nobody answered him.

Akeem pulled out a gun he had tucked in the back of his waistband. The fiend flinched and cried at the sight of the pistol waving close to his face.

"I should cut off your fucking hands for stealing from me," Akeem said.

The man struggled to plead with Akeem through the gag, but I couldn't understand what he said. I'm sure Akeem didn't care, anyway.

I folded my arms and acted hard, but I was shitting bricks on the inside.

"Time to handle business," I said, my voice sounding strong.

I prayed he didn't ask me to kill the guy. I wasn't afraid to fight or shoot, but I wasn't a killer. Deep down, I think 'Keem knew that too.

Akeem shook his head.

"Nah. Me, Daunte, and J already put our work in, so we're not trying to get dirty today. Which one of y'all are gonna step up and handle this problem for me?" Akeem said, offering the gun.

The boys looked scared. It was obvious they weren't ready to do what he was asking.

"Shyne, you wanna handle this for me?" Akeem asked.

"Nah, let one of the new bucks do it," Shyne said.

"Fair enough."

Again, nobody stepped up. Finally, Akeem laughed and said, "If you want something done, you gotta do it yourself."

Akeem smashed the butt of the gun down on the bridge of the fiend's nose, whaling on him until his body was limp and lifeless. Everybody on the roof was shook, including me.

"Shyne, Daunte, y'all know what to do. Get rid of him," Akeem said.

"You got it," Shyne replied.

Later that day, Akeem and I sat in Queensbridge Park.

"Yo, you're a scary dude sometimes," I said.

Akeem chuckled and said, "I know. I gotta be like that and play that character when I'm out in these streets, but it's not who I really am. You,

Nia, Bill, and my sister get to see the *real* me. You're the only people I can be myself around, but I have to put on a façade when I'm dealing with these cats in the street."

I nodded while he continued.

"If I show weakness, they'll think they can cross me and take me out. For now, I'll play the bad guy until I have enough loot for me, you, my mom, and Ebony to retire off of. Then I'll put this street shit behind me. For now, I gotta do what I gotta do."

We sat there staring at the water. Since we were kids, I promised 'Keem that I'd never cross him, and we made a pact to always have each other's back, but in the back of my mind, I worried that one day he could turn on me like Drastic did to Boogie.

"I'm being straight up with you. I don't want us to end up the way Drastic and Boogie did," I said.

"We won't. You're one of the few people I can be real around, and that means something to me. I got your back, and you got mine. As long as we always keep it real with each other, we won't go that route."

"No doubt."

We gave each other dap. Akeem was scary at times, but he was still my boy, and I had his back no matter what he did, because I knew he was the same way with me.

When Neville was in power, he and Drastic had already established their territories to keep the peace between their crews and business flowing. Neville had corners in Ravenswood, but mainly stayed on his side in Astoria. With Draper coming into power, everyone figured things would remain the same, but as usual, Draper was trying to show out in front of his boys.

Word got around to Daunte, 'Keem, and I, that Draper wasn't feeling running his operation out of Astoria and didn't like being away from Queensbridge. Rumor had it Draper was trying to set up shop quietly in his grandparents' building at 40-02 Tenth Street instead of in Astoria, where Neville used to run shit. The three of us walked up to him, sitting alone in front of his grandparents' building, smoking a cigarette.

"You lost or something?" Akeem asked.

Draper stood up and got in Akeem's face. "Do I look lost, nigga?" he yelled.

"That's tough words for a guy sitting out here by himself."

"Everybody around here knows who I am, and nobody in their right mind would think to fuck with me."

"I'm hearing you're getting real comfortable in this building. If you're visiting your fam, that's cool, but if I find out you're trying to set up shop out of here, we're gonna have a problem."

"You ain't the boss of me. I don't care what Drastic and Neville agreed on. That was the past. This is a new era, and you're not gonna punk me on where I handle my business—"

SLAP!

Akeem smacked the shit out of him. The block was busy, so a lot of people saw it. Akeem grabbed Draper by his shirt. "I'm not playing with you. If I catch you or any of your boys around here hustling, I'm gonna put you in the ground myself." Then Akeem shoved him and let him go.

Daunte and I were so focused on what was going down that we didn't notice a man creep up behind us. At first, I didn't recognize him because he looked like a full-fledged fiend, but when I took a closer look, I realized it was Brother Monterey.

"Excuse me, Brother Daunte—"

"Get the fuck away from me. You're never getting shit from me again," Daunte yelled.

"Don't be like that. I paid you back, didn't I?"

"Yeah, after ducking me for months and me beating your ass to take it from you."

"You can get it from this chump," Draper said, pointing at Akeem.

Brother Monterey smiled and walked up to Akeem. "Hey, young brother. I'm a little short right now, but I'm good for it—"

Akeem reached in the back of his waistband for his gun. Then, realizing that Akeem was going to kill Brother Monterey, Daunte asked, "Don't worry about it, 'Keem. I got this. How much you got on you, Brother Monterey?"

Akeem looked at Daunte like he was crazy.

"Nah, you're not doing that. I don't care if he's a penny short. If he doesn't have all my money, he gets nothing," Akeem stated.

Akeem faced me and said, "Matter of fact, put the word out. Nobody is serving this man any product. I saw how he had Daunte running around here looking stupid, trying to collect a debt. He's not making none of my people look like that. Let's go."

Brother Monterey reached to grab Akeem's arm to reconsider, but I batted it away before he touched him. Daunte, Akeem, and I walked away. I didn't know it then, but that was the beginning of a war between Akeem and Draper.

CHAPTER 47

MADE YOU LOOK

I walked outside my building and leaned on the fence, waiting for Debbie and Tracy to come out for our usual morning smoke and conversation. I immediately rolled my eyes when I saw Kisha and Joyce outside.

"It's nice to see you too, uppity bitch," Kisha said.

I ignored her and waited for my friends to come outside. They walked out laughing, and Kisha had to ruin the fun by opening her big mouth.

"The party can start now, y'all. Massa done brought the other boujie one and is allowing these two darkies to smoke," Kisha said.

Joyce laughed like it was the funniest joke in the world while the three of us gave them death stares.

"You're always talking shit, Kisha. Why don't you go somewhere?" I said.

Kisha waved me off.

"Word on the street is your welfare is getting cut off soon, and you're gonna have to get a job and work like the rest of us," Tracy said to Kisha.

"I'm gonna be fine. From what I'm hearing on the street, your and Juanita's sons are the new drug kingpins around here. Tracy, I hear your boy is the damn ringleader. Both of you need to mind your damn business. Stop worrying about me and worry about your badass kids."

Kisha looked at Debbie and continued, "Oh, don't worry, white lady. Your precious white son isn't involved in any dirt their black bastards are in, but be careful. Everyone knows Billy is fucking Ebony, so you might have a little mocha grandbaby running around here soon."

"Fuck off, Kisha," Tracy said.

Kisha flipped Tracy off and motioned to Joyce. "Let's go. They bore me today. The boujie bitches aren't putting up much of a fight."

Joyce nodded, and they left.

I faced Tracy. "You think there's any truth to what they're saying? Between the wads of money, I find in Jalen's clothes when I'm doing laundry, him having a cell phone, and buying all types of expensive jewelry and clothes without having a job, they got to be getting money from doing something dirty. Whenever I go into Jalen's room, I find gutted cigars and weed bags all over the floor," I said.

"I've seen the same thing in Akeem's room," Tracy said.

"Do you think they're dealing?"

"I think they might sell some weed here and there to their friends, but I think they're mostly smoking it. I don't think they're selling anything harder than that or are drug kingpins the way Kisha is making them out to sound."

"I'm sure your boys aren't drug dealers, but do you think Billy and Ebony are really having sex?" Debbie asked.

Tracy and I chuckled because we'd seen how close those two were, and there wasn't a doubt in either of our minds that they were fucking.

"I'll talk to Ebony, but if they are being intimate, we need to talk to both of them about safe sex. They both have futures ahead of them and don't need to ruin them by having babies right now," Tracy said.

"What? Babies? I'm not ready to be a grandma yet," Debbie exclaimed.

Tracy and I laughed. Then Tracy wrapped her arm around Debbie's shoulder and said, "Look at it this way. If our babies make babies, then we really will be a family."

That made Debbie smile a little.

"That's true, but I at least want them to finish high school first," she said.

We nodded, laughed, finished our cigarettes, and enjoyed each other's company before I made my way to work.

After a long, stressful day at the firm, I hiked up the stairs and walked to my apartment. I put my key in the door, and in the corner of my eye, I thought I saw something move. Then I felt a shadowy figure hovering over me. I turned around quickly and jumped when I saw a junkie in front of me.

I balled up my fists, ready to knock his ass out and defend myself if he tried anything.

"Excuse me, missus. I don't mean no harm. Do 'Keem and J live in this building? I'm jonesing real bad, and none of their corner boys will sell to me. I just need a little fix to get me through the day. I got money this time, I swear."

The man flashed me some dingy, crumpled-up bills. It hit me that he said none of "their" corner boys would sell to him.

"I...I...don't know who you're looking for or have anything you want," I said.

The man sucked his teeth. "Damn. Their boy Draper told me they stayed here, and I've seen them come in and out of this building a lot, I really thought they lived here."

"Well, they don't!" I said.

The man's facial expression changed, and he got loud with me.

"Look, I know they're in there. I said I got money. Just let me get my fix, and I'll be on my way."

"I already told you. They aren't here. They don't stay here. You need to leave before I call the cops."

The man groaned and started coming closer. I quickly opened my door and rushed inside the apartment. I swiftly put the deadbolt and chain on the door for added security. He kicked and banged on my door.

"Let me in. I know they're in there. Just give me my fucking fix," he screamed.

Jerami was sitting in the living room playing video games. I motioned for him to keep quiet and go to his room. He nodded and did as he was told.

"They don't stay here, and I don't know where they are. Now get away from my door. I'm calling the cops."

The banging and kicking stopped. I took a deep breath and watched the man through the peephole pacing back and forth in front of my door until he left. Fifteen minutes passed, and I needed a damn cigarette.

I cautiously walked down the steps and checked the small windows on the door in front of the building. The junkie was talking to Kisha and Joyce, who were sitting on the benches.

I waited for him to walk away. Then, once the coast was clear, and he was nowhere in sight, I stepped outside, stood in front of the doorway, and nervously smoked my cigarette.

I was hoping to enjoy it without Kisha and Joyce starting shit, but to no avail.

"What's the matter? Is Mrs. Prim and Proper sad because she finally realized her firstborn is a dope dealer? That's right, bitch! You're no better than the rest of us around here."

"Fuck off, Kisha. I'm not in the fucking mood today."

"Whatever, boujie bitch. We already told him Akeem and Jalen live here, so look forward to him coming back to pay you a visit again real soon," Kisha smirked.

I acted like I was paying her no mind, but deep down, I was freaking out. Lucky for me, Kisha and Joyce stopped heckling me and left. I spotted Tracy walking toward our building. It surprised me to see her but I was happy for the company. She looked at me and asked, "You all right?"

"Nope. You left work early?"

"Yeah. Ebony and Billy have an honors awards dinner tonight, so I'm going with Debbie to it later. What's wrong, Queen?"

I handed her a cigarette and my lighter.

"I was coming home from work, and some dope fiend was waiting on my floor by my door, asking if I saw Akeem and Jalen. He said he needed a hit badly and saw them coming in and out of this building, so between that and their friend Draper confirming it, he figured they lived here."

Tracy shook her head and said, "Jesus."

"I know our boys aren't angels. You and I both suspected they were probably selling weed, but that fiend wasn't on no weed; he was a full-fledged crackhead."

Tracy looked like she was deep in thought.

"Kisha is always talking shit about our sons being big-time drug dealers, and I didn't want to believe her, but seeing that junkie told me everything I needed to know. Jalen is selling drugs harder than weed," I said.

"Our boys do everything together, so if that's true, I'm sure mine is, too." Tracy shook her head.

"Akeem is so different from Ebony. He could do anything he put his mind to if he used his smarts for good, like his sister. He isn't bad . . . He just loves the streets like his daddy did."

"What are we supposed to do? If they're doing dirt in the street, that shit can make us a target for their enemies."

"You're right."

Tracy took a drag on her cigarette and continued. "Lately, no matter if I'm coming home from work or going to it, I've noticed the cops driving slowly when they see me, like they know I'm 'Keem's mother and what he's been up to. I have this unsettling feeling that the cops are one day away from kicking my door in, raiding my place, and walking Akeem, Ebony, and me out of this building in cuffs."

"What are you going to do?" I asked.

"I love my son, and I really don't want to, but I'm gonna have to kick him out of my house. I can't have him endangering Ebony and me."

I ashed my cigarette. "I don't know if I can do that. Jalen and Jerami are all I have left. I can't just throw my son to the wolves like that."

"Queen, I get it, but at the same time, you don't want to get caught up in their bullshit, either. I'm not saying this to hurt you, but your husband fell victim to street shit. You have to take a stand and let Jalen know he can live with you as long as he's not dealing out of your house."

"I feel like I failed him. Maybe this all could've been prevented, but I couldn't really stop him from running the streets because of my work schedule, taking care of Jerami, and depending on Carina to watch him. I couldn't miss work and risk not having benefits for Jerami or money to take care of us."

"Akeem and Jalen being drug dealers, has no reflection on who we are as parents nor does it mean it's a failure on our part. We're doing the best we can. They gotta try to do the best they can, too. They can either try to be more than their neighborhood or be consumed by it."

As we leaned against the black iron fence, I looked toward the sidewalk and saw Miles walking hand in hand with a woman to his car. Tracy's lips were moving, but I couldn't hear what she was saying. I was too fixated on Miles and this new woman to pay attention to anything else. *Of course, of all days, this would happen.* Tracy noticed I wasn't listening and followed my line of sight.

I studied their body language, and I won't lie. I felt a momentary pang of jealousy. The woman's eyes raked over his built frame possessively, like she was pleased and proud to be with him, and I remembered when I used to look at him like that.

The way they both smiled in each other's faces and were so touchy-feely, it was evident Miles had moved on, and it hurt seeing him with another woman. With sadness, I watched him open the car door for the woman, and I questioned if I made a mistake, if maybe he was right, and if I had overreacted and mishandled our situation.

Miles was grinning as he walked to the driver's side of the car and saw that the woman had unlocked the door for him.

Miles turned and looked in my direction, as if he could sense me watching them. The smile he wore left his face. Our eyes locked before I had a chance to look away. I looked up again, and he was still staring at me. He nodded, and I returned the nod. At that moment, his eyes were warm, but he quickly averted them and went back to focusing on his new woman. I looked away, not wanting him to see the hurt in my eyes. Miles got into his car and drove off.

I'll admit, I regret pushing him out of my life, but everything happens for a reason. People enter our lives for a season, a reason, or a lifetime. I know he was in mine for a reason, but I wished it were for a lifetime.

To say I didn't miss him would be a lie. Miles had become a part of my life, and while I cherished the time we spent together, seeing him with that woman put things into perspective. He didn't understand that as a parent, especially a single mother, my focus would always be on my children; they would always come first. Seeing him drive off with that woman made me feel like I had closed that chapter in my life.

"Are you OK, Queen?" Tracy asked.

"Yeah, I can't sweat that. We have more important things to deal with now."

After the honors dinner, we let Debbie know what was going on earlier with our boys, and she agreed to keep Jerami for me overnight so Tracy and I could have a heart-to-heart talk with our sons if and when they strolled in late. Around eleven p.m., Akeem and Jalen walked into Tracy's apartment, laughing and joking around. Tracy and I were sitting on her couch.

"What's up, Ma? Why do you and Mrs. Juanita look so serious?" Akeem asked.

"Sit down. We need to talk," Tracy said.

Akeem rolled his eyes, sucked his teeth, and sat down on the couch across from us.

"Do you want me and Ma to get out of here?" Jalen asked.

"Nope. You need to hear this too," Tracy said.

Jalen sat next to Akeem, and Tracy faced her son.

"Some crackhead came by today looking for you two. When he couldn't get his drugs, he tried to force himself inside Juanita's apartment to find y'all."

"What? I'll kill that motherfucker," Jalen said, standing up.

"Calm down. Sit and watch your mouth," I said. Jalen did as he was told, but I could tell he was mad as hell. Tracy went back to talking to the boys.

"Akeem, I'm not going to have crackheads knocking on my or Juanita's door, and I damn sure am not going to have drugs being sold out of my apartment."

"That wasn't supposed to happen, Ma . . . I'll take care of it," he promised.

My heart stopped. There it was. I heard the gossip and rumors about Jalen and Akeem dealing in the past, but I knew *my* son wasn't that stupid. Akeem confirmed it, though.

"You'll take care of it? What the hell does *that* mean? How are you going to take care of it?"

Akeem didn't answer. Tracy continued. "I don't want junkies coming in and out of our building endangering me, Ebony, or Juanita and Jerami. The same way your customers can come here looking for you is the same way your enemies will come, too."

"It ain't like that, Ma."

"Oh, it isn't? The junkie said your boy Draper told him this is where you and Jalen stay at."

"I'm gonna handle that, too. Everyone around here knows not to mess with y'all. Families are off-limits. They know if they attack my or J's families, they got family and people they care about around here too. The same thing would happen to theirs."

"So, you're a big tough guy, and everyone just falls in line, huh? Boy, you really are young and stupid. You think people follow fucking rules when it comes to street shit? Did that crackhead follow the rules today?"

"I said I'll handle it."

"You are your daddy's child, boy," Tracy said, shaking her head.

"I'm not a boy; I'm a man."

"A man?"

"I buy clothes for me and Ebony. I pay for the groceries and hit you off with money for bills. My father didn't do that. Boys don't do that. *Men* do. I'm a man."

"You think giving me dirty money makes you a man?"

"You act like you don't know where my money comes from, but deep down, you always knew the truth. You might hate it, but the money I make helps a lot."

She grabbed the sides of Akeem's face and looked him in the eyes with grave seriousness. "You're following in your father's footsteps and repeating the same damn cycle. I don't want you to end up like him—dead in the fucking street somewhere."

"Ma, I won't. Stop worrying," Akeem said.

"You can't keep that poison here. You...You have to leave."

"Where am I supposed to go, Ma?" Akeem asked.

Tears streamed down Tracy's face when she said, "I don't know, but you can't stay here. You're putting all of our lives at risk, and I don't want to be a victim because of your street drama." She wiped her face with the back of her hand.

"Every damn day, I hold my head down low because our neighbors gossip and talk about you being a drug dealer."

"You don't look ashamed when I'm hitting you off with mon—"

Slap!

Tracy covered her mouth after hitting him.

They both stood there staring each other down.

"I will not be one of those women on the evening news with her head down because her apartment was raided by the cops. If you're arrested on drug charges, Housing will automatically evict us, and I'm not going to let that happen. You're my son, and I love you, but you can't live that lifestyle and stay here."

Akeem nodded. "Fine. I'll leave."

He walked to the kitchen, grabbed some garbage bags from the cabinets underneath the kitchen sink, then went to his bedroom with Tracy, Jalen, and me right behind him. Tracy stood in his room with her hands on her hips while he emptied each drawer from his dresser and closet into the garbage bags. Akeem and Tracy's bickering drew Ebony from her room.

"What's with all the yelling? What's going on?" she asked.

"Your brother has to move out," Tracy said.

"Why?" Ebony asked.

"Because I can't have a drug dealer living in my house."

"Momma, can't we talk about—"

"I know you want to stick up for your brother, but I can't risk us getting hurt or arrested because of him."

"Don't sweat it, twin. Momma's right. Plus, it's time for me to act like the man I say I am and stand on my own two feet."

Ebony sulked while Akeem quietly finished packing and walked to the front door carrying the bags full of his belongings.

Tracy held her hand out and said, "I'm gonna need your key."

Akeem didn't fuss. He calmly took his key off his key ring and placed it in her hand. "I'll see you around, Momma," he said. He turned to Ebony and Jalen, saying, "I'll call y'all in a few."

As soon as he walked out the door, Tracy wept. Ebony stormed to her room and slammed her door. I held Tracy as she cried on my shoulder.

When Akeem and Jalen first started getting arrested, we saw signs that things were getting progressively worse. We knew back then that they were headed down the wrong path, but we downplayed it. *Not our sons.* We could try to turn a blind eye to it and deny it all we wanted, but the truth was . . .*Our sons were drug dealers.*

Deep down, I prayed that the words, lessons, and guidance his father and I had given Jalen throughout his life were still inside him. I questioned if being at home more often would have made a difference and prevented this. I'm sure my constant working contributed to his love for quick money and the street life. Honestly, I felt responsible since I couldn't afford to buy him the things he wanted.

"We're gonna go. I need to talk with Jalen, too," I said.

Tracy and I said our goodbyes, and Jalen and I walked to our apartment. As soon as we entered, I said, "Have a seat."

I grabbed Jalen by the hand. "Sonshine, I don't want you to end up like—"

Jalen yanked his hand from me. "End up like who? Like Dad? Like Akeem's dad? I'll be fine."

"You and Akeem think you're invincible, but it only takes one bad day for you to ruin your life. After losing your father, you should know that by now."

"Just tell me now, are you gonna kick me out like Mrs. Tracy did 'Keem?"

I looked down at the ground and shook my head. "No."

Jalen dug into his pocket and handed me a wad of cash. "Look, I'm sorry," he said.

I shoved his hand away and glared at the money he was holding. As nice as the money looked, and it could definitely help me financially, I couldn't take his blood money.

"I appreciated the gesture, but I never use the money you leave for me."

"That's dumb. Why? What do you do with it?"

"I save every cent for you in case you need bail money, a lawyer, or even worse, God forbid, I need to bury you."

The thought alone of that possibility made me uneasy.

"Don't think like that, and stop saying things like that, Ma."

"How can I not think like that when you're selling that poison in the streets? I don't want to see my flesh and blood locked up like a caged animal in prison or fear that one of your and Akeem's enemies will be waiting to kill us in our sleep."

Jalen stayed quiet and looked at the floor.

I sighed.

"I'm not kicking you out, Sonshine, but you need to change before you force my hand."

I prayed this was the wake-up call he needed to stop this street nonsense before it took his life.

CHAPTER 48

LIVIN' PROOF

The next day, Akeem, Daunte, and I walked over to Draper's grandparents' building, and sure enough, he was there with two guys from his crew. Akeem walked up to Draper. His two goons stepped to Akeem, but Daunte and I flashed the pieces in our waistbands to let them know we weren't fucking around.

"Yo, why all the hostility?" Draper asked, laughing.

Akeem got in his face. "You think sending that fiend to my momma's building is funny?" Akeem yelled.

"Hey, he asked where you might be, and I just pointed him in the direction."

"Keep fucking playing with me, and I'll point some stickup kids in the direction of your fucking grandparents' apartment. 6A, right? That's the apartment your people stay at, right?"

Draper shoved Akeem. "Yo, don't be threatening to hurt my fucking family," he yelled.

"You started this shit, and I'm letting you know I have no problem finishing it. Keep playing with me."

Draper signaled to his crew. "Let's go." He looked at Akeem and said, "This ain't over."

Akeem threw up his hands as Draper and his boys walked off. I stood next to him.

"What do you think he's gonna do next?" I asked.

"I don't know, but I was too sloppy. Drastic used to always stay in and out of different apartments. I was stupid and kept going to my momma's place. I can't make mistakes like that again," he said.

Right after Mrs. Tracy kicked 'Keem out, he quickly began revamping how he ran the organization. First, he moved into Nia's grandma's apartment. Kiera loved the move because, in addition to paying the rent, Akeem also supplied her with enough dope to support her habit on the side. He used Nia's apartment as his primary place but slept at many of Drastic's old stash spots to keep people guessing.

In the past, he would've kept Rita out to keep her hands clean, but now, he put her on. He needed people he trusted and believed Rita would never cross him. He had leveled Daunte up to a lieutenant and had him, and Rita posted up at random spots looking over workers who were packaging the product. Nia tried to have a blind eye to everything. She knew trying to stop Rita and Akeem was pointless, so she didn't try, but she always talked to Akeem about the bigger picture, only doing this until he made enough money to retire from the streets. Rita loved being a part of the drug operation and had no problem quitting school and overseeing all the trap houses full-time. I started feeling like she only saw me and used me for a come-up.

With her learning the business, she constantly got on my case about branching out and being my own man. So far, I stalled her, but putting her on with the organization would only pacify her for so long.

As months passed, the war between Akeem and Draper worsened by the second. Finally, things got so bad that Akeem and Draper couldn't be in the same area without a heated exchange. While Drastic and Neville used to bet on games out of friendly competition, we couldn't enjoy Bill's games because Akeem and Draper were ready to kill each other by the end of them.

Draper was a sore loser and never paid out when he lost a bet. He kept pushing and testing his limits with Akeem, and 'Keem kept checking him. Whenever Draper wouldn't pay his debt, Akeem publicly pushed him around. Whenever 'Keem caught Draper's corner boys trying to sell product anywhere in Queensbridge, he beat the shit out of them, then took their money and product. Draper would hit him back by dropping dimes to the police about areas where our corner boys were, and some of our best earners were getting arrested. With the tension constantly bubbling between them, I knew it was only a matter of time before shit boiled over. This beef wouldn't end well.

CHAPTER 49

GOT UR SELF A GUN

Akeem and I were in his mom's living room watching TV. 'Keem stopped by often when his mom was at work to drop off money, hang out, and see his sister.

Bill and Ebony were at the kitchen table, laughing while working on some school project, when Akeem's face turned serious.

"B, come here for a sec," he said.

Bill rushed into the living room and walked up to him. "What's up?" he asked.

"Sit down. I want to talk to you about something."

"Is everything good?" Bill asked.

"I know you and my sister got something going on, B."

Bill looked scared as hell and started stuttering, trying to explain himself. "It's not–I wasn't trying to–I won't—"

"It's fine, B, relax. You're a good dude, and you're going somewhere in life. I don't want her to be with a guy like me. She deserves the best, and I know you'd give her that type of life. Just don't hurt her."

"I won't."

"I know."

Bill smiled. Akeem patted him on the back and said, "Come, I gotta check on some of my corner boys, and one of these cats has been talking shit about being able to beat you in a one-on-one. I bet him money you'd bust his ass. He should be there now. I'm trying to collect my paper. Can you handle this clown for me?"

Ebony walked in on the tail end of Akeem's sentence. "Don't be pimping Bill out like that," she said.

"I only bet when it's a guaranteed win for me," Akeem said. He faced Bill again. "You coming or what?"

Bill looked at Ebony. She rolled her eyes and gave him a nod of approval.

"Yeah, I'm down."

Akeem, Bill, a few of our shooters, and I were sitting at the small square concrete chess tables by the basketball courts, joking around about how badly Bill beat that corner boy in the one-on-one when Draper walked past us with his boys.

Draper and his goons sat on the benches opposite Akeem, our boys, and me. I couldn't distinguish everything Draper was saying, but I knew he was talking shit. Whatever he was saying, he was acting all animated, grilling us, waving his hands, and pointing in our direction.

"What the hell is your bum ass looking at?" Akeem shouted. "If you got something to say, man up and say it to my face."

"Mind your fucking business. Nobody is talking about you, punk," Draper spat.

"Good, keep it that way. Oh, and I got your punk. You stay talking shit, even though I've been smacking your ass up since we were in junior high."

Draper, needing to save face with all his boys looking on, sprang up off the bench and his soldiers were met by Bill, Akeem, our soldiers, and me. Akeem was right in Draper's grill, but Draper held his ground and returned the stare-down.

"We ain't kids no more, nigga, and you ain't gonna chump me in front of my people. Say something else, and I got something for your big-ass mouth," Draper warned.

"That sounds real gay. I knew you were a homo," Akeem fired back.

Draper shoved Akeem and faked like he was going to punch him.

"What? Was that supposed to scare me? Nigga, you better come harder than that."

Quickly, Akeem faked a punch, and Draper flinched, turning his head and covering his face with his hands.

Akeem laughed, turned to us, and said, "See, I told y'all he was a pussy."

Pissed off and embarrassed, Draper threw a flurry of punches at Akeem, but Akeem blocked them and floored him with a right cross. Draper's lackeys came over to jump in but were met by our crew. Bill jumped in between, putting his arms out to separate them before they killed each other.

"C'mon, 'Keem, chill. Y'all gonna draw attention to all of us and have the cops up our asses," Bill cautioned.

Appearing like clockwork, O'Sullivan and McIvor came out of nowhere and caught us slippin'.

Akeem shook his head. "You called that one, B," he said.

"You all know the drill. Place your hands on the fucking table," O'Sullivan said, kicking apart our feet and spreading our legs.

We did as we were told.

O'Sullivan and McIvor went down the line and cuffed us. Five more officers surrounded us, so there was no use in trying to run. O'Sullivan walked next to Bill and whispered something in his ear that pissed Bill off. O'Sullivan shoved him and shouted, "Get outta here!"

"They were just arguing. Nothing happened," Bill said. O'Sullivan swiftly punched him in the stomach so hard Bill's knees buckled, and he dropped to the ground, gasping for air. O'Sullivan manhandled Bill, yanking him off the ground, and talked to him real close so none of us could hear him.

Bill looked at us. Akeem took his hands off the table and motioned for Bill to calm down.

"I said keep your fucking hands on the table where I can see them," McIvor yelled.

O'Sullivan grabbed Bill by the face and brought his attention back to him.

"Look at me, kid. They don't have futures. They're gonna be stuck in this hellhole for generations to come. I'm trying to keep your record clean so you can amount to something in life and get out of here. I'm nice, but don't take my fucking kindness for weakness."

"I'm not asking for your help, and I don't want it," Bill said.

O'Sullivan punched him in the stomach again.

"I'm not going to say it a third time . . . get the fuck out of here. Your mother is under enough stress with her sickness. She doesn't need this bullshit from you. Go home."

"It's Ok, man, just do what he says. We know you got our back," Akeem said to Bill.

I nodded.

McIvor put Akeem in an arm bar and slammed him on the ground.

"Nobody was talking to you, boy. Let's get something straight. *We* run shit here."

Akeem's face was all scraped up, and his lip was busted and bleeding. Seeing what McIvor did to him, everyone fell in line and did as they were told.

"You see what you staying here caused? If you don't want to see your homeboys get hurt more, go home," McIvor advised.

Bill shook his head and started walking away.

"Now, where were we?"

The officers went down the row, patting us down and running our IDs to check for warrants. Once we came back clean, they uncuffed us and gave us tickets for disorderly conduct.

"All right, mutts, all of you need to disperse right now. If I catch the lot of you gathered around here again, all of you are spending the night in the bookings. Does everyone understand me?" O'Sullivan said.

"Yes," we all said in unison.

"All right; go home, losers. Kill each other another day," McIvor said.

Guys from both our crews started going off in different directions, but Akeem and Draper kept staring each other down. Finally, when the cops saw enough of us were gone, they bounced too.

Draper stepped to Akeem again, but one of his crew stopped him.

"Next time I see you, I'm gonna put a bullet in your ass. Mark my words on that shit," Draper said, with his boy holding him back and walking away with him in the opposite direction from us.

"Yeah, yeah. You're soft!"

"I got your 'soft' right here," Draper said, grabbing his crotch.

Something had to change, or eventually, things would turn deadly.

CHAPTER 50

STREETS IS WATCHING

I couldn't explain it, but I was experiencing the same dark, brooding feeling I felt deep down in the pit of my stomach when I lost Mo. I had this gut feeling that something bad would happen this night, which scared me.

Jalen's cell phone buzzed. He read the display and rushed to take the call in his room. Something didn't feel right. I left Jerami to watch a movie in the living room, stood by Jalen's bedroom door, and quietly listened as he lowered his voice and continued his conversation. Then Jalen lifted his mattress, picked up a gun, and tucked it in the back of his jeans waistband.

"You want to go looking for him? Cool, you already know I got your back…You need to take this cat seriously, though…You're hunting for him, but he might be looking for you too…I got you…All right, cool. I'll meet you in front of our building in fifteen…peace," Jalen said, ending the call.

I immediately figured he was talking to Akeem. I walked into his room, gripped his arm tight, and said, "Where are you going this time of night?"

"Come on, Ma. Don't start. I gotta handle something real quick."

"Something doesn't feel right . . . Don't go out there tonight."

Jalen moved my arm off him. "Ma, you're trippin'. Nothing's gonna happen to me."

"I heard what you said to Akeem, and I know you're about to do something stupid . . . Why do you have a gun in my house?"

"You don't know what you're talking about."

"Boy, don't play dumb with me. I saw you get it from under your mattress. What if Jerami found it and hurt himself or another kid?"

"I don't have time for this right now."

I grabbed his arm again. "You and Jerami are all I have left. I already lost your father. I couldn't take it if something happened to you or your brother. Stay home!" I begged.

He shook me off him. I followed closely behind him as he walked around his room, picking up his keys and wallet.

"Ma, chill. I'll be fine. I'm going to a couple of stores at Queens Center Mall with Akeem, and I'll be right back."

I saw the handle of his gun tucked in the back of his jean waistband again as he put on a black hooded sweatshirt and his black Timberland boots.

I walked in front of him, blocking his path.

"You know that cop O'Sullivan has it out for you and Akeem. If he catches you with a gun, your ass is going to prison to do real time. Is *that* what you want?"

He didn't answer.

"I'm not stupid, Jalen. You're getting ready to fight some boy with Akeem."

He didn't deny it.

I took his hands in mine, squeezed them as I looked him in the eyes, and said, "I had a bad feeling the day your father was taken from us, and I have that same feeling now. I can't lose you too. Please, listen to me. Don't go out there tonight."

"I'm coming right back. Stop worrying," he said, brushing past me. He exited the bedroom with me following him and walked toward the front door.

"Bye, Ma."

"I love you, Sonshine..." My voice trailed off as he rushed out, slamming the door behind him.

My heart pounded as I sat in the living room, frantically waiting for Jalen to return home.

CHAPTER 51

I GAVE YOU POWER

"Where y'all headed?" Bill asked.

We walked down the steps and saw Bill throwing trash down the incinerator.

"This cat, Draper, has been running his mouth, talking about he's gonna shoot me. I'm tired of his shit, and I'm gonna end him tonight."

Bill looked worried. "Nah, both of y'all are just angry. Let me roll with you and J."

"B, you're my man and all, but things might get real out here tonight. I told you before, I need you to take care of my sister. I don't want you getting caught up in street shit."

"Come on, 'Keem, you need somebody in your ear to calm you down. Let me just put on some kicks, and I'll be right out."

"Nah, stay home, Bill. For real. Me and J will handle this."

Bill knew there was no convincing Akeem, so he gave us both dap, and 'Keem and I headed out.

"He's gotta be around here somewhere," Akeem said.

Ma called me on my cell back-to-back. I silenced the calls and sent them to voicemail, eventually just powering off my phone altogether so I wouldn't be bothered with a bunch of calls to come home. Finally, I turned to 'Keem and said, "He probably knows you're looking for him, and he's lying low."

The hood was flooded with cops. Marked and unmarked police cars circled nearly every block we passed. We lay low and ducked behind cars until they passed by. I guess even the cops felt that something bad was brewing and was about to go down tonight.

Akeem and I spent a good thirty minutes looking for Draper. Even though Queensbridge is made up of ninety-six buildings, the entire project is only six blocks long. Besides his grandparents' apartment building and the usual hangout spots, there weren't too many places he could be where we wouldn't spot him.

We asked a few guys around the way that we knew Draper was cool with if they'd seen him, but no one knew where he was.

Ma's words kept running through my mind as I walked with Akeem. Her voice echoed inside my head, saying, *"Come home, Jalen. I don't know what I'd do if I lost you."*

Like Ma, I had a bad feeling about this night, too. I wasn't sure if what she said before I left made me paranoid, but I felt like something terrible was gonna go down. I needed to go home.

"Yo, let's fall back and call it a night. We've been walking around for a while and still can't find this cat. Maybe that's a good thing. Let's get him another day," I said.

"Nah, I wanna get his bitch ass now."

"If Drastic taught us anything, he taught us that when you run shit, you have your soldiers do the dirty work. Just have one of your shooters take him out, and once the deed is done, promote him."

"Drastic was the past. I'm running shit now. I don't want a shooter to do this for me. This shit with Draper and me is personal. I want to clap him myself."

I guess 'Keem saw the skeptical look on my face because he said, "Look, I know you don't wanna be out here all night looking for this cat. Go ahead; you can bounce. That pussy isn't gonna do shit to me. He talks tough, but I've known him since we were kids. His bark has always been bigger than his bite. He doesn't have the heart to shoot me."

"Nah, I'm not letting you handle this yourself. Let's just go home. We'll get him another day."

"Nope. It's the principle of the shit. If I don't handle this quickly or let him slide, other cats around here will think they can say and do anything they want. I got to nip this in the bud today."

"What if he's not alone? I can't let you get jumped. Let me call Daunte and Shyne to meet us here, just in case."

"Ain't nobody gonna jump me, especially when I got my piece on me. I'll be all right. Go ahead."

"Nah, this doesn't feel right, man."

"How about this? If he's alone, I'm handling him. If he's not, I'm not stupid. I'll call you and get the rest of the guys."

"Nah, just come with me."

"You worry too much. I'll be fine. Seriously, though, I'll catch up with you after I handle this."

"You sure, man?"

"J, I don't need you to hold my hand. I got this. I know you got my back. Stop worrying. I'll see you after I slap him up."

"All right," I said hesitantly.

We said our goodbyes. I headed back to my building, and Akeem ran deeper into the hood to find his prey.

On my way home, I stopped by the bodega on Forty-First Avenue for a loosie and a soda. Coming out of the store, I saw Rita and Nia walking toward me.

"Where y'all headed?" I asked.

"Nowhere really, just walking around," Nia said.

"We get tired of being cooped up in that hot-ass apartment looking over 'Keem's workers all the time. Now and then, we need some fresh air. You stopping by later?" Rita asked.

I looked her up and down and licked my lips. "I'm thinking about it," I said.

Rita giggled. "Well, don't get your hopes up. It's my time of the month."

"Where's Akeem? Usually, you two are joined at the hip," Nia joked.

I laughed. "He's out handling his business with Draper."

A serious look came over her face. "And you didn't go with him?" she asked.

"I was, but he told me to head home, and he'd take care of Draper himself. You know how he gets."

"He needs to watch his back around Draper. I heard he's tired of Akeem punking him, and he's got a new gun he's itching to use on him," Nia said, looking worried.

"Akeem's been putting him in his place since we were kids. Draper talks shit, but he doesn't have the balls to step to 'Keem. 'A' will slap him up a bit, and that'll be the end of it."

I turned to Rita. "Anyway, with that being said, my dear, the block is too hot for me tonight. I'm gonna take a rain check on stopping by and just hang out at the crib."

Rita laughed. "You're just going home because you know you're not getting any booty tonight."

"Not totally true," I joked.

"Tell Akeem to call me when he gets in. I know he's not afraid of Draper, but he needs to take him seriously. Draper wants to show everyone around here that he's the man, and he won't hesitate to kill Akeem to prove it," Nia said.

After she said that, that ominous feeling I had earlier hit me again.

I nodded and said, "No doubt."

I kissed Rita and hugged Nia.

Rita playfully slapped me on the ass while I walked away. "Bye, handsome. Call me later," she said.

"No doubt."

I walked away and started dialing Akeem. He picked up.

"Yo! I just found this cat chilling by himself on the benches by 40-09 on Twelfth Street. I'm about to get the drop on him. I'll call you back."

"Be careful, man. I just talked to Nia, and she said the word on the block is he got a gun he can't wait to use on you."

"He ain't gonna do shit. I'll call you back. Peace," he said, rushing off the phone.

I stepped inside my building and checked the mailbox inside the lobby.

BOOM, BOOM, BOOM!

Three loud gunshots echoed throughout the streets. I grabbed the mail, shut the box quickly, and ran up the steps to get to my crib.

Running up the steps, I looked out of the open staircase window in front of me. Between the black iron safety bars, I saw Akeem running toward our building with his gun in hand while Draper shot at him. People passing by screamed and ran frantically in different directions for cover as Draper kept firing.

O'Sullivan's patrol car screeched to a halt and stopped in front of them. I should've followed my intuition. I should've convinced Akeem to go home when I had the chance. Draper quickly dropped his piece to the ground and put his hands up.

O'Sullivan and McIvor focused all their attention on Akeem. Draper quickly seized the opportunity, ran in the opposite direction down the block, and disappeared into the nearby buildings. O'Sullivan and McIvor had their guns drawn as they chased Akeem to the front of our building.

"Drop your weapon and put your hands on your head," O'Sullivan yelled, aiming at Akeem.

Without thinking, Akeem turned around quickly with his gun in his hand. O'Sullivan and McIvor opened fire and riddled him with bullets. The weapon slowly dropped from his hand as he stumbled back and grasped his chest. He collapsed against the fence and slid down to the pavement as thick blood flowed from the bullet wounds in his chest.

Tears streamed down my face as I witnessed my best friend get gunned down. I stood there in shock for a few seconds and didn't come to until I heard somebody charging down the stairs. Bill rushed past me down the stairwell and went to Akeem.

"You gotta tell Mrs. Tracy and Ebony. Hurry up," Bill yelled.

Akeem was slumped against the fence. Bill cradled Akeem in his arms as blood spilled out of Akeem's mouth. I couldn't bring myself to go out there and see my best friend dead just yet.

I needed to tell Mrs. Tracy. I needed to see my mom and let her know she was right about not going out tonight and that I was OK. I flew up the stairs, taking two at a time. I got to my floor and fumbled with my keys in the lock, lucky to be alive.

CHAPTER 52

TAKE IT IN BLOOD

I looked out of my apartment window overlooking the street, hoping that Jalen was returning home. I widened a slit in the blinds, and numerous unmarked and regular patrol cars cruised around the area.

I constantly checked the peephole to make sure Jalen wasn't shot or stabbed and bleeding out on the floor landing. I called him over ten times, but his phone went straight to voicemail, and he didn't bother to call me back. I checked my watch again and paced my living room nervously, waiting for him to come home. What felt like an eternity was actually only thirty minutes.

"Please, God, keep him safe tonight," I prayed out loud.

My prayer was cut short when the sound of gunfire caused me to drop instinctively to the floor, pulling Jerami with me as we took cover behind the couch and coffee table.

"Ma," Jerami screamed.

"Stay down," I yelled.

For a second, I couldn't move. My heart dropped to the pit of my stomach. Then I heard the blaring sounds of approaching sirens in the distance. Carina rushed into the living room. Her worried eyes showed me we had a mutual fear . . . *Something happened to Jalen.*

"Y'all all right?" she asked.

"Get down, girl," I yelled.

Carina dropped down and crawled toward us.

I heard another round of shots in front of our building. My hands shook uncontrollably. My heart went out to my firstborn, and my mind was going to places that scared me. I held Jerami tightly, sobbing uncontrollably. I prayed again that those shots weren't for Jalen. Most of the time, I felt that God rarely heard or answered my prayers, but I desperately hoped he would tonight.

Finally, I heard keys jingle at the door and breathed a sigh of relief when I heard the locks unlatching, and Jalen rushed in. He was panting and crying.

With tears in my eyes, I rushed to him, pulled him into my arms, and hugged him.

"Thank you for bringing him home safely," I mouthed to God silently, staring up at the ceiling.

"I was so scared someone had taken you away from me—" I quickly checked him for any injuries.

"Ma, I'm OK . . . I'm OK . . . but Akeem . . . The cops shot Akeem!"

My heart sank and went out to Tracy. "Oh my God. Is he OK?" I asked.

"I don't know . . . I don't know," Jalen said in a panic.

His hands were trembling as he brought them to his face.

"We were on our way to fight with Draper, but I kept hearing your voice in my head telling me to come home . . ."

Reality hit me. I had to tell Tracy that her son had been shot.

"Stay here. I have to tell Tracy what happened."

"I can't stay. I gotta get back to Akeem. Bill is out there with him. I need to be there."

"Please be careful," I said.

I rushed to Tracy's floor and frantically banged on her door to break the bad news.

CHAPTER 53

FALLEN SOLDIER

I jetted down the steps and pushed the front door open. Then I charged through the crowd in front of the building. The pool of blood around Akeem kept growing, and Bill's shirt was drenched in it.

"Help! Somebody help me!" Bill screamed.

Seeing Akeem's eyes fluttering, my world stopped. Everything felt like it was moving in slow motion, and I couldn't hear anything that was going on around me.

Bill was crying, clutching Akeem to his chest, rocking back and forth. I dropped to the ground beside him, and I couldn't move. People hovered close by. The area around us was being cordoned off with yellow crime scene tape. All types of police and emergency vehicles were parked on the sidewalk and street.

"Come on, man. Stay with me!" Bill shouted.

Akeem tried to talk, but the foamy blood pouring out of his mouth made it damn near impossible.

I sat there, not knowing what to do or say.

Akeem struggled to breathe, taking short, quick breaths, and his eyes were rolling to the back of his head as he strained to stay conscious. In a few seconds, his breathing became thin and shallow, and I watched the guy I saw as my best friend, my mentor, and my brother take one last breath and fall limp in Bill's arms.

The paramedic approached Bill and tried to pry Akeem from his grip.

"He's gone, B," I said.

Bill loosened his grip, and the paramedics took Akeem out of his arms.

They laid Akeem's lifeless body on the stretcher and brought him to the ambulance. The paramedics were working frantically to bring Akeem back to us. I tried to have a little hope that he'd pull through and make it, but I knew the truth.

Akeem was dead.

CHAPTER 54

LIFE GOES ON

It was like déjà vu with my husband all over again. The memory of Tracy rushing to tell me that Mo was shot swirled through my head. The commotion from my knocking drew people to open their apartment doors and step into their doorways.

Tracy swung open her door.

"Damn, Queen, I thought you were the damn police beating on my door like that."

Her smile slowly waned when she saw my face. Her eyes widened.

"What's wrong? What happened? Juanita, did something happen to Akeem?"

"We have to get downstairs. Jalen said the cops shot Akeem."

Tracy's eyes watered. Ebony, who was sitting at the kitchen table doing her homework, hurriedly pushed past me and bolted down the stairs after hearing what I said. Tracy and I followed.

We ran out of our building. Everyone in the neighborhood seemed to be standing outside behind the police barriers, being nosy, gossiping about how Akeem got shot.

"Billy, where's Akeem? Where's my brother?" Ebony yelled. Jalen and Billy were crying hysterically on the ground.

Ebony shook Bill by the shoulders and asked again with her eyes welling up with tears, "Billy, where is he?"

Bill pointed to the paramedics, who were using a defibrillator on him.

"Nooooo!" Tracy screamed.

The paramedics were in the ambulance, moving frantically, working to stop the bleeding, and had an AED attached to Akeem's chest. Akeem's eyes were closed, and his arms dangled from the side of the stretcher.

Ebony and Tracy sprinted over to the ambulance.

"Ma'am, you can't come in here," a paramedic said to Tracy, extending his arms to block her.

Tracy batted his hands away. "That's my son," she shouted as she and Ebony tried to jump onto the ambulance.

While the paramedics struggled with Ebony, Tracy pushed past everyone and ran into the ambulance. She reached for the gurney and tried to pick up Akeem's lifeless body, but the staff and cops pulled her off.

Tracy wept on the ground with Ebony. Then she jumped to her feet, rushed over to one of the random cops that took her out of the ambulance, and weakly pounded on his chest. He didn't stop her. The look of sympathy on his face showed he wasn't worried about her hurting him, and he allowed her to get her frustrations out.

Some of the other cops tried to restrain her; even Ebony tried to hold her back. Tracy finally stopped hitting the officer and looked at her son's lifeless body in the ambulance and his blood on the concrete. She shook off the hands of the officers and EMS workers who were trying to console her.

"Get off me. Get the fuck off me. You murdered my son." Tracy wept, falling back onto the ground.

I blocked out all the chatter and noise around me and rushed to Tracy with my arms outstretched. I tried to help her up to her feet, but she squirmed from my grasp and fell back down to the street.

She was screaming at the top of her lungs and crying hysterically. I wrapped my arms around her and pulled her into a tight embrace. We cried together, and I did my best to comfort my heartbroken friend. But I couldn't stand to look her in the eyes—not when there was nothing but pain staring back at me.

In the back of my mind, I felt guilty. I felt terrible for Tracy losing her son, but also relieved that God hadn't taken my oldest from me. I knew that type of pain, seeing a loved one gunned down in the street. A loss is a loss, whether it's a husband or a son, and both of our losses came from senseless violence.

CHAPTER 55

SIX FEET DEEP

There were a lot of rumors going around after the night Akeem was killed. Some people said they saw Akeem shoot at the cops first. Some said Draper shot Akeem, and the cops were taking the heat for it, but I knew the truth and wished I could've done more to save him that day. I felt guilty because maybe if I had pushed harder, I could've got him to listen to me and go home.

Some people from the neighborhood put candles, flowers, and pictures on the spot where Akeem died. While that was nice, most of the guys around the neighborhood didn't care. They just wanted to know who was gonna step up with a connection so they could keep making their money. I didn't care about money, the streets, or who was trying to run things.

The past few days had been some of the hardest I've ever been through, but nothing compared to this day, the day I finally had to see my best friend put to rest. The funeral was at Gilmore's Funeral Home on Linden Boulevard, the same place where we had my dad's funeral. The whole scene put me further into a depression because it was rainy and gloomy, just like the day I had to bury my dad. Like my dad's funeral, barely anyone came to pay their respects to Akeem.

Bill and Ebony held hands and cried with my mom, Jerami, and Mrs. Tracy in the first pew. Nia, Rita, Joe, and Mr. Sealy sat in the second row behind us. Shyne and Daunte were sitting in the back of the church with a couple of our corner boys and some of Mrs. Tracy's coworkers, who stopped by to pay their respects.

I stood up and followed the line to view Akeem's body. Ebony was sobbing on Bill's chest. As we moved closer to the front of the church, my hands shook, and it was getting harder to keep it together. I knew this day was coming. I knew he was dead and wasn't coming back, but seeing him lying in the casket solidified the finality of everything, and I couldn't take it.

I was now up to view the body. My knees buckled when I looked down at Akeem in the casket. Seeing my closest friend, mentor, and brother lying there, knowing he was gone for good, I fell to the floor, closed my eyes, and sobbed hysterically.

I felt myself being picked up. When I opened my eyes, I saw it was Joe and Mr. Sealy helping me up. I figured they'd be wearing I-told-you-so expressions, but they looked as hurt by the loss as I was.

I cried because I never thought this would happen. I cried because 'Keem and I were both supposed to save our money, retire, and laugh about the crazy shit we did in our youth, but that wasn't an option anymore.

We went to the cemetery with everyone who sat in the first two pews at the funeral home. It was the same cemetery where my dad was buried, which made me even more emotional.

We all put roses on the casket as it lowered into the ground. After the coffin was put in place, Mr. Sealy, Joe, Bill, the cemetery workers, and I filled the hole with dirt.

While everyone else headed back to their cars to go home, I stayed behind and stood in front of 'Keem's headstone. Tears streamed down my face when I said, "I'm so sorry, man. I should've been there with you." Bill and Ebony walked up, hugged me, and walked me to the car so we could all leave and put an end to this sad day.

CHAPTER 56

MOURN YOU 'TIL I JOIN YOU

After the funeral, Debbie and I stopped by Tracy's place to check on her. I knocked on Tracy's door. She opened it and said, "Hey, Queen."

"Hey," I said.

Debbie hugged her.

Tracy let us in. We walked to her living room and sat on her sofa.

"How are you holding up?" Debbie asked.

"I have my moments. I'm just trying to stay strong and be there for Ebony."

"Where is she right now?" I asked.

"She's in her room mourning with Bill."

Tracy closed her eyes like she was fighting back tears as she continued. "Ebony couldn't sleep last night. She said losing her twin was like losing half of herself. I know how she feels because I feel the same about losing my son."

She took a deep breath and exhaled slowly. "Seeing my only remaining child in pain when there's nothing I can do to make things better hurts."

Tracy started to break down again. Debbie and I reached for her, pulled her close to us, and she wept in our embrace.

Someone knocked on the door. Tracy sighed, stood up, and opened it. Nia was standing in the doorway with tears in her eyes.

"Come in, girl," Tracy said.

Nia nodded, and Tracy stepped aside to let her in.

"Where's your sister?" Tracy asked.

"She's checking up on Jalen. She knows he's taking it hard."

Tracy nodded.

Nia was holding Akeem's old duffle bag. "I . . . I have something for you," Nia said.

She handed the bag over to Tracy. Tracy opened the bag, and it was full of money.

"Akeem had this in our apartment. He always told me he wanted to make enough money to take care of you and Ebony, so neither of you would ever have to want for nothing. Here . . . I know he'd want you and Ebony to have this."

Tracy closed the bag, pulled Nia in for a hug, and said, "You keep it. Use it to go to college and make something of yourself. I know my son loved you. Use this money to build a better life for yourself. That's what I want you to do with it."

Tears streamed down Nia's face when she nodded. Tracy hugged her, and then she and Nia said their goodbyes. Once Nia left, I realized how hard that must've been for Tracy.

I know for a fact that as a courtesy, Housing offered to move Tracy to another building once they heard she had lost her son. However, she's much stronger than me because she refused Housing's offer to move her to another building, saying she'd feel closer to Akeem staying where he was taken from her.

Even though I knew she was tough, I couldn't leave her alone when she needed me. Debbie and I spent the rest of the afternoon being there for her, and, as always, I admired my friend's strength.

CHAPTER 57

MEMORY LANE

After the funeral, I came home and locked myself in my room. Jerami knew I just wanted to be alone, so he didn't fight with me when I kicked him out of our room.

Mom and Ms. Debbie were with Mrs. Tracy, trying to cheer her up, and even though I knew I should be mourning with Ebony and Bill, I didn't feel like being around anyone. I just wanted to be alone with my thoughts.

I couldn't take my eyes off the dried reddish-brown bloodstained shirt still in the corner where I left it after taking it off the night Akeem was killed.

I heard a knock on my room door. "What, bro?" I asked.

"Can I come in?" I heard Rita ask.

I quickly stood up and opened the door. "Hey," I said.

"How are you feeling?" Rita asked.

"Like shit."

I stood aside, let her walk in, and closed the door behind her.

"I still can't believe he's gone," I said.

"Yeah . . . It sucks, but life goes on. You gotta keep it moving, you know?"

I didn't like where this conversation was headed and wished I had stayed alone.

"It's not that easy. I can't just get over it like that. He was my best friend," I said.

"I get it, but everything happens for a reason. Maybe this is the universe's way of putting you in a position where you can run shit now without having him in your way. I know you were holding back, but you don't have to now. Now, it's your time."

I shook my head. I knew she liked the prestige and power of Akeem and me being in the street, but I wasn't in the mood for this, and being "the man" was never something I wanted.

"I'm not trying to hear that right now—"

"Well, you *need* to hear it. Akeem is gone, and he ain't coming back. Stop acting like a bitch, sitting here crying and shit. Man up."

I sat on my bed, fuming, looking at her in disbelief. "Do you hear how you sound right now? Akeem hasn't even been in his grave a day, and you're already here talking about me sliding into his spot? Listen and listen good. I told you before, but you weren't listening. I don't *want* that spot. I never have and never will. That spot might be something you think is hot, but being 'the man' is what got 'Keem killed."

"That was him. You're you. You're acting like a scared little boy right now. Yeah, it's sad that he died, but this opened an opportunity for you to make a come-up. Instead, you're acting like you want to throw it away."

"I *am* throwing it away."

"So, what's your plan, huh?"

"I'll figure something out."

Rita stood in front of me, shaking her head. I knew she loved the streets, but deep down, I thought she had love for me too. I guess I was wrong.

"I told you before. I don't date losers. If being number one ain't for you, this ain't gonna work."

I looked at her skeptically. "What are you saying?"

"Maybe it's best to end this and go our separate ways."

I nodded. I was hurt, but Rita never wanted me for me. She only wanted me in the streets. I realized if I stayed in the game and had to do a bid, she'd be on to the next man and leave me in a heartbeat.

"All right. Well, it was nice while it lasted. I guess I'll see you around," I said.

Rita shook her head. "Bye, Jalen."

"Peace."

She walked out of my room and left me standing there, questioning if our relationship ever meant anything to her or if it was even real. Seeing her leave me only magnified the pain of losing my best friend.

The next day, I was sitting on the floor in my room playing myself in chess. Ma opened my door.

"Joe is here to talk to you. You need to talk to someone, Sonshine. Hear him out," she said.

I didn't answer. I just kept my eyes on the board. Joe sat down on the opposite side of the chessboard.

"Hey, youngster. I just wanted to check on you."

I stayed quiet.

"Chess, huh? I haven't played this since I was in the joint," he said.

I closed my eyes and slowly exhaled.

"Set up the board. I'll play you a game, talk to you a little, and I'll leave you be after I say what I need to say."

I did as he asked.

We started playing. Joe brought his queen out early. We exchanged queens, which I thought was dumb, but then I realized after losing mine, I was making a lot of mistakes.

"Youngster, you're playing checkers while I'm playing chess."

"Man, what are you talking about?"

"The game of life is like chess—"

"Yeah, yeah, I'm supposed to think three moves ahead and strategize, yadda yadda yadda. I heard all of that before."

"Youngster, in chess and life, you gotta control your emotions. Your game went to shit once you lost your queen. Yeah, we exchanged pieces, but you didn't realize I did that to distract you."

I think my face showed I was confused, so he continued.

"If you had paid attention to the board, you would've seen that you were one move away from getting a checkmate. I took your queen, you got emotional, and I messed up your head. You stopped sticking to the plan of tryin' to get the win, and you immediately took my queen in retaliation."

I somewhat understood, but he drove the point home further when he said, "The point is, I know your boy getting killed got you hurtin', but don't let that distract you. Word around the neighborhood is it had something to do with that boy, Draper. Stick to the plan. Live your life. Don't get emotional, retaliate against him, and give years of your life to the system like I did."

He moved his rook and ended the game.

"That's checkmate, youngster. I'll leave you with that, but think about everything I said today."

We stood up, shook hands, and he pulled me in for a brotherly embrace. Then he left my room and left me with a lot to think about.

I remembered hearing O'Sullivan say to Bill one time, *"They don't have futures. They're gonna be stuck in this hellhole for generations to come."* That memory brought me back to a conversation I had with Akeem back in the day in the park.

"Did you know my great-grandmother, grandmother, and mother all grew up and lived here in Queensbridge?" Akeem said.

"Nah, I didn't know that."

"Yeah, Ebony is going to break that chain. That shit is gonna end with her. She got the brains to be more than our block. Look at me and you. The furthest we've been from Queensbridge is probably going to Green Acres Mall in Valley Stream. There's a whole world outside of Queensbridge. I already know my future is pretty much set, and I'm gonna be working in these streets like my pops did, but I want more for Ebony."

Thinking about those memories helped me realize I needed to want more for myself, and after Akeem's death and my talks with Joe and Rita, I knew I had two choices. I could stick around the hood, possibly end up in prison or dead like Akeem, or I could come up with a plan B. I went the plan B route.

A week after Akeem's funeral, I went out looking for Draper. Not out of retaliation but to put our beef to rest. I still had to walk these streets, but this beef was bigger than me. My mom and bro didn't need to be messed with over a stupid spat 'Keem and I had with Draper.

With Akeem gone, Draper now had free rein to operate in Queensbridge, and he didn't hesitate to expand his turf. Instead of running his base of operation out of Astoria, he made his new home base out of one of the apartments in his grandparents' building.

I walked to his grandparents' building, convincing myself that it was best to approach him first before his goons came looking for me and things got ugly. Draper was sitting on a bench outside his building, smoking a blunt. One of his flunkies saw me walking toward them and nudged Draper to alert him I was coming.

"Well, well, if it isn't Akeem's old butt buddy, Jalen. To what do I owe this pleasure?"

"You want me to off this nigga right now?" one of the goons asked, reaching in his waistband for his piece.

Draper motioned for him to stand down. "Chill. His name don't hold no weight in these streets anymore. I'll hear him out," he said.

Draper faced me. "Hurry up and state your business."

"We used to be boys, right?" I asked.

"That was a long time ago. We ain't kids no more, nigga," he said. He paused, took a hit of the blunt, and blew the weed smoke out of his nostrils before he continued.

"But I'm a reasonable man. Us being cool now all depends on if you're thinking about coming at me for the shit that went down with 'Keem. You tryna step up and replace him?"

"Nah, I'm done with all that. I don't want any more beef with you."

Draper laughed and pointed at me. "Wise choice." He faced his goons and said, "Y'all hear that? He don't want no more beef with me. This pussy doesn't want to end up like Akeem, so he's calling it quits."

They laughed and pointed at me like I was a sucker. I balled up my fists, ready to rush and knock Draper's ass out, but I thought about what Joe said, *"Youngster, in chess and life, you gotta control your emotions."*

Joe was right. I was done fighting. I didn't want any part of that life anymore. I had to think long term. I unclenched my fists, took a deep breath, and asked, "We good or not? Are your boys gonna fuck with me or what?"

"As long as your ass stays retired, and you don't fuck with my money, yeah, we straight. You can relax and pull your skirt down. You got my word. No one around here is gonna fuck with you and yours. Now, begone, pussy."

I swallowed my pride and walked away at the sound of everyone laughing at me.

"Yo, you got the connect, let's keep this shit going," Shyne said. He and Daunte stopped by my house because work was drying up on the streets, and they needed to re-up soon.

"Nah, I'm out."

"I was hoping you'd reconsider. I'm not feeling working for Draper, but if he got that work, I gotta do what I gotta do to make this bread," Shyne said.

"I feel you, but you don't gotta be under his thumb for long. I put in a good word for all y'all with the connect."

"Yo, good looking out!" Daunte said.

I looked at Shyne. "Let me get your phone."

He tossed me his cell, and I put Wilfredo's number in it.

"Come correct when you call him. Stack your money up, and whenever y'all are ready, call him," I said.

"No doubt. Thanks, but what are you gonna do now?" Shyne asked.

"I don't know yet, but I gotta think of something."

I didn't know how long or when Draper would change his mind and renege on his word, so I needed a plan. The first part of it was to get my GED. I borrowed some practice books from the library on Forty-First Avenue and Twelfth Street. Lucky for me, when I reached out to Mr. Sealy, he didn't hesitate to help me study for it.

"I don't know what I was thinking. I'm never gonna pass this test," I said, throwing the practice book on the library floor.

Mr. Sealy picked it up and put the book back in front of me. "If you tell yourself that, then you won't. I know you can do it, but you have to put in the work," he said.

"I'm too far behind."

"Then use this time to catch up. I believe in you."

I needed to hear that. I needed someone to believe in me when I didn't believe in myself, and that positivity helped me pass the GED on my first try.

With that goal out of the way, Mr. Sealy also helped me assemble the second part of my plan, joining the Marines. Staying at home, I knew I'd either end up in prison or dead like Akeem. I had never put much thought into my future, but I knew I needed to do something fast to keep myself out of trouble and put decent, legal money in my pocket. I joined the Marine Corps. The service gave me the discipline I needed to turn my life around. It felt good knowing that my money was legit, and I didn't have to look over my shoulder every day wondering if the cops or some rival dealer were coming after me.

I spent six years doing active duty in the Marine Corps. I traveled the world and learned a lot, but there wasn't a day that went by that I didn't think about Queensbridge, Akeem, my pops, and my mom. I often spoke to my mom and Jerami to check on them and sent money back home, but I wasn't ready to go home yet, not until I grew up entirely.

It took some time for me to man up, but I finally found the strength after all these years to visit my dad's and Akeem's graves. I placed flowers on both of their headstones. I let them both know that I'd always miss them. I told Akeem his memory would always live with me, and I told my dad that I hoped I grew up to be the man he wanted me to become.

After visiting their graves, I felt strong enough to go home. I took the F train to the Twenty-First Street Queensbridge station. It amazed me that after all these years, Mom still lived here. She never admitted it, but I know she stayed to be close to Ms. O'Neil and Ms. Williams.

The neighborhood looked just like I had left it. I have so many mem- ories here, some good, some bad, but I felt at home. Some faces had changed, but Queensbridge was still Queensbridge. I nodded at some of the same dealers I knew when I was a kid that were on the same corners today, selling and hanging out.

As I walked to my mom's building, a tinted Chevy Tahoe cruised beside me and stopped. The people in the car were fidgety like they were gonna roll on me. The passenger window rolled down, and I braced myself when I heard a familiar voice say, "Yo, J! Is that you?"

I looked in the car and saw Shyne and Daunte.

"Oh shit! What's up?" I said.

They got out of the truck and gave me brotherly hugs.

"I ain't seen yo' ass in a minute," Shyne said. He took a step back to look at me. "You lookin' good, kid! You were diesel before, but now you're swole! Where you been, kid?" he asked.

"I did a stint in the marines for a bit. After that, I went to school on their dime, got a couple of degrees in education, and now I'm back to teach English in LIC High School."

"That's what's up. Somebody gotta try to teach these badass kids something. Yo, guess who's running shit now?" Daunte asked.

Shyne puffed up his chest and smiled confidently.

"Stop playin'. You're top dog now?"

"Yup! And Daunte's my right hand," Shyne said.

"How and when did this happen?" I asked.

"Soon after you left, Taevaughn took Draper out, and for a while, maybe like three years or so, he was running shit, but the cops caught up to him, and he had to do a bid for Draper's murder. With him out of the way, I've been running shit, and business has been good. Don't worry. While you were gone, I gave the word that you, Bill, and 'Keem's mommas were not to be fucked with. Now that you're back, I'll put the word out for you, too."

The streets were a vicious cycle, and history was constantly repeating itself. I knew it was only a matter of time before the streets got Shyne too, but for now, I thanked him and was grateful for what he did.

"I appreciate that, brother. Listen, I gotta get going. I'm surprising my brother and my mom—"

"Say no more. We're gonna link up. Take care of your fam," Shyne said.

I gave Shyne and Daunte dap and brotherly hugs again. They both got in the car, nodded, and pulled off.

I walked to my mom's old building and saw four boys with a radio sitting on the wooden benches in front of my old building, joking around and talking about basketball. They were blasting the Nas song "Memory Lane," and I thought that was fitting because they reminded me of Akeem, Bill, Draper, and me back in the day when we were still tight as friends and street life hadn't divided us yet. I missed those days and cherished those memories. Those times and this neighborhood made me the man I am today. Now, I'm old enough, strong enough, and wise enough to come back here and make a difference in my community.

CHAPTER 58

DEAR MAMA

Akeem's death had a rippling effect on all of us. Ebony decided to take action to change how minorities are policed and wanted to use her voice to influence how past and future police procedures and policies are handled. She attended John Jay College and majored in criminal justice, intending to join the NYPD, rise in the ranks, and become chief to rid the police department of cops like O'Sullivan. Six years have passed, and she has already joined the NYPD and passed the sergeant's exam.

Bill and Ebony were still going strong. Wanting to be close to her, Bill went to John Jay, too, and studied law. His reasoning was he saw first-hand how men like O'Sullivan picked on the poor and underprivileged, and he wanted to defend people legally who couldn't defend themselves. He worked his ass off as a public defender, but he was struggling to bring in money. I never forgot what Debbie did to help save Jerami, so I didn't hesitate to ask Bill for his resumé. I talked to the partners at my firm, and since they still owed me a big favor for convincing Mr. Harper to stick with them, I cashed in that favor to get Bill a job there. Every day, he greets me with a hug and a kiss to show his appreciation.

Seeing all the negative drama that came with being in the street caused my baby, Jerami, to get his act together and straighten up. He stayed in school and is now attending Johns Hopkins University to become an oncologist to help kids fight cancer.

For Jalen, Akeem's death was the catalyst to spark him to change. In no time, he quickly transitioned from hustler to soldier to scholar and became the man I always knew he could be, the man his father would've been proud to see.

Raising my boys wasn't easy, but I was grateful to have my support system of Tracy, Debbie, and even Carina. Carina still hasn't found the right man, but over the past six years, she stopped looking for a man to save her and saved herself. She's still going strong working at the hair salon, and she finally got her own place, so she wasn't sleeping in my living room on my couch anymore. I was proud of her for finally growing up.

Unfortunately for Debbie, her multiple sclerosis was causing her health to deteriorate fast. She was damn near bedridden, but to Tracy and me, she was our sister. We used our free time and worked around our schedules to care for her. Debbie was grateful and felt she didn't deserve all the help, but she helped save my youngest son's life. I'd do this and more to repay her for that debt.

With Jalen and Jerami turning their lives around, I finally made peace with God and thanked him for keeping my boys safe. I can't deny that, at times, I felt let down, forgotten, and abandoned by him, but things worked out. He helped me through it, and all the drama that I went through made me a stronger woman and a better mother.

www.ingramcontent.com/pod-product-compliance
Lightning Source LLC
Chambersburg PA
CBHW060513160726
47991CB00001B/20